THE COURTS OF THE MORNING

THE
COURTS OF THE
MORNING

JOHN BUCHAN

THREE RIVERS BOOKS

First published 1929 by Hodder & Stoughton Ltd.
This edition published 1982 by
Three Rivers Books Ltd.
Mill Green, Bampton, Oxfordshire

Copyright the Rt. Hon. Lord Tweedsmuir, CBE

ISBN 0-907951-01-5

Printed in Great Britain by
The Thetford Press Ltd., Thetford, Norfolk

CONTENTS

MAPS

PROLOGUE

I

THIS story begins, so far as I am concerned, in the August of 192—, when I had for the second time a lease of the forest of Machray. Mary and Peter John and the household had gone north at the end of July, but I was detained for ten days in London over the business of a Rhodesian land company, of which I had recently become chairman. I was putting up at my club, and one morning I was rung up by Ellery Willis of the American Embassy, who had been wiring about me all over the country. He seemed to be in a hurry to see me, so I asked him to luncheon.

I had known Willis in the War, when he had had a field battery with the American 2nd Corps. After that he had been on the Headquarters Staff at Washington, and was now a military attaché at the London Embassy. He seemed to have a good many duties besides the study of military affairs, and when I met him he was always discoursing about world-politics and the need of England and America getting close to each other. I agreed with him about that, but used to tell him that the best way was not to talk too much, but to send Englishmen and Americans fishing together. He was an ardent, rather solemn young man, but with a quick sense of humour, and Mary said he was the best dancer in London.

He cut at once into business.

"You are a friend of Mr Blenkiron's—John S. Blenkiron," he said. "I want to know if you have heard from him lately?"

"Not for months," I said. "Blenkiron was never a regular correspondent, and the fount has dried up since last December."

He looked grave. " That's bad," he said.

" There's nothing wrong? " I asked anxiously.

" Only that nobody knows what has become of him."

" But that was always the old ruffian's way. He likes to cover his tracks, like Providence, and turn up suddenly when he is not expected. There's a lot of the child in him."

Willis shook his head. " I expect there's more to it this time than that. I'll tell you what we know. He made a dive back into Wall Street last fall, and did some big things in electrolytic zinc. Then he went to Santa Catalina, and returned to New York in the second week of January. On the 27th day of that month he sailed for Panama in a fruit-steamer, having previously shut up his office and wound up his affairs as if he were thinking of his decease. From that day no one has clapped eyes on him. He has nothing in the way of family life, but I needn't tell you that he has plenty of friends, and they are beginning to get anxious. All that we can find out is that last March a little Jew man turned up in New York with an order from Mr Blenkiron for a quarter of a million dollars. It was all right, and the money was handed over, and the shape it took was a draft on Valparaiso to be paid after countersignature by our consul there. We got in touch with the consul, and heard that the money had been collected on Mr Blenkiron's instructions by some fellow with a Spanish name."

" That sounds queer," I said.

" It certainly does. But there's something queerer still. In June Mr Neston of the Treasury got a letter—he had been a business associate of Mr Blenkiron's at one time and they used to go bass-fishing in Minnesota. It didn't come by mail, but was handed in one evening at Mr Neston's private residence. It bore no name, but there could be no doubt it was from Mr Blenkiron. I have seen a copy of it with Mr Neston's commentary, and I can tell you it was great stuff. The writer warned his old friend that there might be trouble brewing in certain parts of the world which he did not specify, and he begged him, as he was a good American, to keep his eyes skinned. He also said that he, the writer, might have to ask some day soon for help, and that he counted on getting it. The funny thing was that the letter was in a kind of cypher. I understand that Mr Blenkiron used to write to his friends in a high-coloured version of our national slang, and that he had a good many private expressions that were Choctaw to those that did not know him. That letter might have been read as the perfectly natural expression of a light-headed American, who had been having too many cocktails and was writing drivel about his health and his habits and the fine weather. But, knowing how to construe it, it made Mr Neston sit up and take notice. . . . There was another thing. I have said that the letter had no name, but it was signed all the same. It seems that in any very important and intimate communication Mr Blenkiron used to make a hieroglyphic of his surname and stick J. S. after it in brackets. That was meant to be a kind of S.O.S. to his friends that the thing was mighty important. Well, this letter had the hieroglyphic in three places, scrawled in as if the writer had been playing absent-mindedly with his pen. Mr Neston's conclusion was that Mr Blenkiron had written it in some place where he was not allowed to communicate freely, and might be in considerable danger."

I admitted that it looked like it, and said that if Blenkiron had been captured by bandits and held up to ransom, I could vouch for it, from what I knew of him, that his captors had done the worst day's work of their lives. I asked what his Government was doing about it.

"Nothing official," said Willis, "for we are in this difficulty. We are afraid of spoiling Mr Blenkiron's game, whatever it may be. Washington has a very high respect for his talents, and we should hate to cross him by being officious. All the same, we are anxious, and that is why I have come to you."

He proceeded to give me one of his lectures on international affairs. America, by his way of it, was in a delicate position, in spite of being rich enough to buy up the globe. She was trying to set her house in order, and it was a large-sized job, owing to the melting-pot not properly melting but leaving chunks of undigested matter. That was the

real reason why she could not take a big hand in world-
affairs—the League of Nations and so forth; she had too
much to do at home, and wanted all her energies for it.
That was the reason, too, why she was so set on prohibition
of all kinds—drink, drugs, and aliens. But her hand might
be forced, if anything went wrong in the American continent
itself, because of her Monroe Doctrine. She didn't want
any foreign complications at the moment. They would be
very awkward for her, and possibly very dangerous, and
she would resolutely keep out of them, unless they occurred,
so to speak, opposite her front yard, in which case she would
be bound to intervene. Therefore, if anyone wanted to do
her the worst kind of turn, he would stir up trouble in some
place like South America. Willis believed that Blenkiron
had got on the track of something of the kind, and was trying
to warn her.

That sounded reasonable enough, but what was not reasonable was Willis's straight request that I should put on my
boots and go and look for him. "We can't do anything
officially," he repeated. "An American would be suspected
where an Englishman would get through. Besides, I
believe you are his closest friend."

Of course I at once disabused him of that notion. I knew
old Blenkiron too well to be nervous about him; he could no
more be badly lost than Ulysses. I saw Willis's point about
American politics, but they were no concern of mine. I told
him in so many words that my travelling days were over,
that I was a landowner and a married man and the father
of a son, with all sorts of prior duties. But he was so
downcast at my refusal, and so earnest that something
should be done, that I promised to put the matter before
Sandy Arbuthnot. I proposed in any case to go to Laverlaw
for a couple of days on my way to Machray.

II

LAVERLAW is a very good imitation of the end of the world.
You alight at a wayside station in a Border valley, and drive
for eight miles up a tributary glen between high green hills;

then, when the stream has grown small and you think that the glen must stop, it suddenly opens into an upland paradise —an amphitheatre of turf and woodland which is the park, and in the heart of it an old stone castle. The keep was once a peel-tower, famous in a hundred ballads, and the house which had grown round dated mostly from the sixteenth century. I had never been there before, for the old Lord Clanroyden had lived sick and solitary for years, and Sandy had only succeeded in the previous February. When I arrived in the early gloaming, with that green cup swimming in amber light and the bell-heather on the high ground smouldering in the sunset, I had to rub my eyes to make sure that the place was not a dream. I thought it the right kind of home for Sandy, a fairy-tale fortress lying secret in the hills, from which he could descend to colour the prose of the world.

Sandy met me at the gates and made me get out of the car and walk the rest of the way with him. In his shocking old tweeds, with his lithe figure, his girlish colouring, and his steady, glowing eyes, he fitted well into that fantastic landscape. You could see that he was glad to have me there, and he made me welcome with all his old warmth, but in the half-mile walk I felt a subtle change in him. His talk didn't bubble over as it used to, and I had a feeling that he was rather making conversation. I wondered if being a peer and a landowner and that sort of thing had sobered him, but I promptly dismissed the idea. I wasn't prepared to believe that external circumstances could have any effect on one who had about as much worldliness as a fakir with his begging-bowl.

All the same there was a change, and I was conscious of it during the evening. Archie Roylance and his young wife were staying there—like me, for the first time. I am prepared to rank Janet Roylance second only to Mary as the prettiest and most delightful thing in the world, and I knew that she and Sandy were close friends. In the daytime she was always, so to speak, booted and spurred, and seemed to have the alertness and vigour of an active boy; but in the evening she used to become the daintiest little porcelain lady; and those who saw Janet as a Dresden shepherdess in a drawing-room would scarcely believe that it was the same person who that morning had been scampering over the heather. She was in tremendous spirits, and Archie is a cheerful soul, but they found it heavy going with Sandy.

We dined in what had been the hall of the thirteenth-century keep—stone walls, a fireplace like a cave, and Jacobean rafters and panelling. Sandy wore the green coat of some Border club, and sat like a solemn sprite in the great chair at the head of his table, while Janet tried to keep the talk going from the other end. The ancient candelabra, which gave a dim religious light, and the long lines of mailed or periwigged Arbuthnots on the wall made the place too heavy a setting for one whom I had always known as a dweller in tents. I felt somehow as if the old Sandy were being shackled and stifled by this feudal magnificence.

The Roylances, having been married in the winter, had postponed their honeymoon, and Janet was full of plans for bringing it off that autumn. She rather fancied the East. Sandy was discouraging. The East, he said, was simply dusty bric-à-brac, for the spirit had gone out of it, and there were no mysteries left, only half-baked Occidentalism. " Go to Samarkand, and you will get the chatter of Bloomsbury intellectuals. I expect in Lhasa they are discussing Freud."

I suggested South Africa, or a trip up through the Lakes to the Nile. Janet vetoed this, because of Archie's stiff leg; she thought big-game hunting would be bad for him, and she considered with justice that if he were in the neighbourhood of wild beasts he would go after them.

Archie himself was inclined to South America. He said he had always had a romance about that part of the world, and he understood that it was the only place which still held some geographical secrets. Also it appeared that, though a poor linguist, he could talk a sort of Spanish, owing to having spent some time in the Madrid Embassy.

" I've never been there," said Sandy, " and I never want to go. It's too big and badly put together, like a child's mud castle. There's cannibal fish, and every kind of noxious insect, and it's the happy home of poisons, and the people are as ugly as sin. The land isn't built according to our human scale, and I have no taste for nightmares."

"All the same, it's tremendously important," Archie replied. "Charles Lamancha says that all the big problems of the future will be concerned with the New World. It might be rather useful to me in politics if I went and had a look round."

Sandy laughed. "Better go to the States. That's the power-house where you press the button."

This gave me the chance to talk about Blenkiron, and I told them what I had heard from Ellery Willis. Archie, who had only seen Blenkiron in the last year of the War, was rather excited; Sandy, who knew him intimately, was apathetic.

"He'll turn up all right. Trust John S. You can't mislay a battered warrior like that. You'd better tell Willis that he is doing a very poor service to Blenkiron by starting a hue-and-cry. The old man won't like it a bit."

"But, I assure you, Willis is very much in earnest. He wanted me to start out right away on a secret expedition, and to quiet him I promised to speak to you."

"Well, you've spoken," said Sandy, "and you can tell him I think it moonshine. Blenkiron will come back to his friends when his job is done, whatever it may be. . . . Unless Archie likes to take the thing on?"

He seemed to want to drop the subject, but Janet broke in:

"I always understood that Mr Blenkiron had no relations except the nephew who was killed in the War. But I met a girl last month who was a niece or a cousin of his. She told me she had been staying in the Borders and had been taken to see you at Laverlaw."

Sandy looked up, and I could have sworn that a shade of anxiety passed over his face.

"Her name was Dasent," Janet went on. "I can't remember her Christian name."

"Probably Irene—pronounced Ireen," said Sandy. "I remember her. She came over with the Manorwaters. She seemed to have got a little mixed about Scotland, for she

wanted to know why I wasn't wearing a kilt, and I told her
'because I was neither a Highlander nor a Cockney stock-
broker.'"

He spoke sharply, as if the visit had left an unpleasant
memory.

"I should like to meet a niece of Blenkiron's," I said.
"Tell me more about her."

In reply Sandy made a few comments on American young
women which were not flattering. I could see what had
happened—Sandy at a loose end and a little choked by his
new life, and a brisk and ignorant lady who wanted to
enthuse about it. They had met 'head on,' as Americans
say.

"You didn't like her?" I asked.

"I didn't think enough about her to dislike her. Ask
Janet."

"I only saw her for about an hour," said that lady. "She
came to stay with Junius and Agatha at Strathlarrig just
when I was leaving. I think I rather liked her. She was
from South Carolina, and had a nice, soft, slurring voice.
So far as I remember she talked very little. She looked
delicious, too—tallish and slim and rather dark, with deep
eyes that said all sorts of wonderful things. You must
be as blind as a bat, Sandy, if you didn't see that."

"I am. I don't boast of it—indeed I'm rather ashamed
of it—but I'm horribly unsusceptible. Once—long ago—
when I was at Oxford, I was staying in the West Highlands,
and in the evening we sat in a room which looked over the
sea into the sunset, and a girl sang old songs. I don't
remember whether she was pretty or not—I don't remember
her name—but I remember that her singing made me want
to fall in love. . . . Since I grew up I've had no time."

Janet was shocked. "But, Sandy dear, you must marry."

He shook his head. "Never! I should make a rotten
husband. Besides, Dick and Archie have carried off the
only two women I love."

After that he seemed to cheer up. I remember that he took
to telling stories of poisons—I suppose the mention of South
America set him off on that. He showed us a box with

three tiny pellets in it, things which looked like discoloured pearls, and which he said were the most mysterious narcotics in the world, and one of the deadliest poisons. They reminded me of pills I once got from an old Portugee prospector, which I carried about with me for years but never touched, pills to be used if you were lost in the bush, for one was said to put you into a forty-hours sleep and two gave a painless death. Sandy would explain nothing further about them, and locked them away.

What with one thing and another we had rather a jolly evening. But next morning, when the Roylances had gone, I had the same impression of some subtle change. This new Sandy was not the one I had known. We went for a long tramp on the hills, with sandwiches in our pockets, for neither of us seemed inclined to shoulder a gun. It was a crisp morning with a slight frost, and before midday it had become one of those blazing August days when there is not a breath of wind and the heather smells as hot as tamarisks. We climbed the Lammer Law and did about twenty miles of a circuit along the hill-tops. It was excellent training for Machray, and I would have enjoyed myself had it not been for Sandy.

He talked a great deal and it was all in one strain, and —for a marvel—all about himself. The gist of it was that he was as one born out of due season, and mighty discontented with his lot.

" I can't grow old decently," he said. " Here am I— over forty—and I haven't matured one bit since I left Oxford. I don't want to do the things befitting my age and position. I suppose I ought to be ambitious—make speeches in the House of Lords—become an expert on some rotten subject—take the chair at public dinners—row my weight in the silly old boat—and end by governing some distant Dominion."

" Why not? " I asked.

" Because I don't want to. I'd rather eat cold mutton in a cabman's shelter, as Lamancha once observed about political banquets. Good Lord, Dick, I can't begin to tell you how I loathe the little squirrel's cage of the careerists.

All that solemn twaddle about trifles! Oh, I daresay it's got to be done by somebody, but not by me. If I touched politics I'd join the Labour Party, not because I think them less futile than the others, but because as yet they haven't got such a larder of loaves and fishes."

"I want a job," he declared a little later. "I was meant by Providence to be in a service, and to do work under discipline—not for what it brought me, but because it had to be done. I'm a bad case of the inferiority complex. When I see one of my shepherds at work, or the hands coming out of a factory, I'm ashamed of myself. They all have their niche, and it is something that matters, whereas I am a cumberer of the ground. If I want to work I've got to make the job for myself, and the one motive is personal vanity. I tell you, I'm in very real danger of losing my self-respect."

It was no good arguing with Sandy in this mood, though there were a great many common-sense things I wanted to say. The danger with anyone so high-strung and imaginative as he is that every now and then come periods of self-disgust and despondency.

"You're like Ulysses," I told him. "The fellow in Tennyson's poem, you know. Well, there's a widish world before you, and a pretty unsettled one. Ships sail every day to some part of it."

He shook his head.

"That's the rub. As I've told you, I can't grow up. There's a couple of lines by some poet that describes me accurately: 'He is crazed by the spell of far Arabia, It has stolen his mind away.' Far Arabia—that's my trouble. But the Ulysses business won't do for an ageing child of forty. Besides, what about the mariners? Where are the 'free hearts, free foreheads?' We used to have a rather nice little Round Table, Dick, but it is all broken up now and the wood turned into cigar-boxes for wedding presents. Peter is dead, and you and Archie are married, and Leithen and Lamancha are happy parts of the machine."

"There's still Blenkiron."

"He doesn't count. He was a wandering star, that

joined us and revolved cheerfully with us for a little, and then shot back to where it belonged. . . . You can't alter it by talking, my dear chap. I'm the old buccaneer marooned on a rock, watching his ancient companions passing in ocean liners."

We had reached the top of the hill above Laverlaw and were looking down into the green cup filled with the afternoon sunlight, in which the house seemed as natural a thing as a stone from the hillside. I observed that it was a very pleasant rock to be marooned on. Sandy stared at the scene, and for a moment did not reply.

" I wish I had been born an Englishman," he said at last. " Then I could have lived for that place, and been quite content to grow old in it. But that has never been our way. Our homes were only a jumping-off ground. We loved them painfully and were always home-sick for them, but we were very little in them. That is the blight on us—we never had any sense of a continuing city, and our families survived only by accident. It's a miracle that I'm the sixteenth Clanroyden. . . . It's not likely that there will be a seventeenth."

III

I LEFT Laverlaw rather anxious about Sandy, and during our time at Machray I thought a good deal about my friend. He was in an odd, jumpy, unpredictable state of mind, and I didn't see what was to be the outcome of it. At Machray I had a piece of news which showed his restlessness. Martendale, the newspaper man, came to stay, and was talking about boats, for his chief hobby is yacht-racing.

" What's Arbuthnot up to now? " he asked. " I saw him at Cowes—at least I'm pretty sure it was he. In an odd get-up, even for him."

I said that I had been staying with Sandy in August and that he had never mentioned Cowes, so I thought he must be mistaken. But Martendale was positive. He had been on the Squadron lawn, looking down on the crowd passing below, and he had seen Sandy, and caught his eye. He knew him slightly, but apparently Sandy had not wanted to be recognised and had simply stared at him. Martendale noticed him later, lunching out of a paper bag with the other trippers on the front. He was dressed like a yacht's hand, rather a shabby yacht's hand, and Martendale said that he thought he had a glimpse of him later with some of the crew of the big Argentine steam yacht, the *Santa Barbara*, which had been at Cowes that year. " The dago does not make an ornamental sailor," said Martendale, " and if it was Arbuthnot, and I am pretty certain it was, he managed to assimilate himself very well to his background. I only picked him out of the bunch by his clean-cut face. Do you happen to know if he speaks Spanish? They were all jabbering that lingo."

" Probably," I said. " He's one of the best linguists alive. But, all the same, I think you were mistaken. I saw him a fortnight later, and, I can tell you, he isn't in the humour for escapades."

In November, when I ran up to London from Fosse for a few days, I got further news of Sandy which really disquieted me. It appeared that he had gone down to the grass countries to hunt—a fact which in itself surprised me, for, though a fine horseman, he had always professed to hate hunting society. But for some reason or other he kept a couple of horses at Birkham and spent a lot of time there. And he seemed to have got mixed up with a rather raffish lot, for since the War the company in the Shires has not been what you might call select. The story told to me was that at a dinner where much champagne was swallowed Sandy had had a drunken row with a young profiteering lout, which had just about come to blows. He seemed to have behaved rather badly at dinner and worse later, for after having made a scene he had bolted, shown the white feather, and refused to take responsibility for what he had done.

Of course I didn't believe a word of it. In the first place, Sandy was as abstemious as a Moslem; in the second place, he had the temper of a seraph and never quarrelled; and, in the third place, he didn't keep any white feathers in his collection. But the story was repeated everywhere and, I am sorry to say, was believed. You see, Sandy had a great reputation in a vague way, but he hadn't the kind of large devoted acquaintance which could be always trusted to give the lie to a slander. And I am bound to say that this story was abominably circumstantial. I had it from an eye-witness, quite a decent fellow whose word it was hard to disbelieve. He described a horrid scene—Sandy, rather drunk and deliberately insulting an ill-tempered oaf in the same condition, and then, when it almost came to fisticuffs, funking the consequences, and slipping off early next morning without a word of explanation.

I hotly denied the whole thing, but my denials did not carry very far. Sandy had disappeared again, and his absence gave gossip its chance. The ordinary story was that he had taken to drink or drugs—most people said drugs. Even those who believed in him began to talk of a bad break-down, and explained that the kind of life he had led was bound some day to exact its penalty. I tried to get hold of him, but my telegrams to Laverlaw brought the answer that his lordship had gone abroad and left no address for letters.

Three days after Christmas I got the shock of my life. I opened *The Times* and found on the foreign page a short telegram from New York which reported the death of Mr John Scantlebury Blenkiron on board his yacht at Honolulu. The message said that he had once been well known as a mining engineer, and that at various times he had made *coups* in Wall Street.

I took the first train to London and interviewed Ellery Willis at the Embassy. He confirmed the news, for he had had a wire from Washington to the same effect.

"What did he die of?" I demanded. "And what was he doing at Honolulu? And in a yacht? He loathed the sea. He used to say that he would as soon take to yachting for pleasure as make his meals off emetics."

"He must have been ill some time," Willis suggested.

" That would account for his disappearance. He wanted
to be by himself, like a sick animal."

I simply wouldn't credit it, and I asked Willis to wire
for details. But none came—only a recapitulation of the
bare fact. When a week later I got the American papers,
my scepticism was a little shaken. For there were obituaries
with photographs. The writers enlarged on his business
career, but said nothing about his incursions into politics,
nor did they give any further news of his illness. I was
almost convinced, but not quite. The obituaries were full,
but not full enough, for Blenkiron had been a big figure,
and one would have expected the press to go large on his
career and personality. But the notices all gave me the
impression of having been written to order and deliberately
keeping wide of the subject. There was nothing in the way
of personal reminiscences, no attempt to describe his
character or assess his work. The articles were uncommonly like the colourless recitals you find in a biographical
dictionary.

I wired about it to Sandy, and got a reply from his butler
that he was still abroad, address unknown. I wished that
I knew where to find the niece who had visited Laverlaw
in the summer, but Janet Roylance, to whom I applied,
could tell me nothing. She and Archie were setting out
almost at once on their delayed honeymoon, and had chosen
South America.

I have one other incident to record before I bring these
preliminaries to a close. Palliser-Yeates came to stay with
us for a week-end in January, and one night, after Mary
had gone to bed, we sat talking in the library. He had
never known Blenkiron, but he was a friend of Sandy, and
to him I unburdened my anxieties. I thought he listened
to me with an odd look on his face.

" You don't believe the stories? " he asked.

" Not one blessed word," I said. " But the poor old chap
has managed to get himself a pretty fly-blown reputation."

" Perhaps he wanted to," was the astounding answer.

I stared, and asked him what he meant.

" It's only a guess," he said. " But Sandy has for a long time had a unique reputation. Not with the world at large, but with the people who matter in two hemispheres. He was known to be one of the most formidable men in the world. Now, suppose that he was engaged, or about to be engaged, in some very delicate and dangerous business. He would be marked down from the start by certain people who feared him. So he might wish to be counted out, to be regarded as no longer formidable, and what better way than to have it generally believed that his nerve had gone and that he was all to pieces? If I wanted to create that impression, I would lay the foundation of it in the Shires, where they make a speciality of scandal. If that was his purpose, he has certainly succeeded. By this time the rumour has gone all over Europe in the circles where his name was known."

I was digesting this startling hypothesis, when Palliser-Yeates told me the following story:

He had been in Paris just before Christmas on some business connected with Argentine banking, and one of his South American colleagues had taken him to dine at a restaurant much in vogue among the *rastas*. I think it was on the Rive Gauche, not a specially reputable place, but with amazingly good food. The proprietor was from the Argentine, and all the staff were South Americans. Palliser-Yeates noticed one of the waiters, not at his own table but a little way off, and he recognised the man's face. The hair and skin were darkened, but he was positive that it was Sandy—Sandy in a greasy dress suit and a made-up black tie. When the room filled up and got rather noisy, he made an errand to speak to the conductor of the orchestra, and managed to get a word with this waiter. He cannoned against him in one of the doors and said, " Sorry, Sandy." The waiter knew him perfectly, and whispered from behind his pile of dishes, " Don't give me away, John. It's damnably serious. And never come here again." So Palliser-Yeates took himself off, and had scrupulously held his tongue except for telling me. He said that Sandy looked well enough, and seemed to have mastered his job, for you couldn't detect any difference between him and the rest of the outfit.

When I heard this, I decided to go to Paris myself and have a look at the restaurant, for anxiety about Sandy was coming between me and my sleep. There was something about Palliser-Yeates's story which took my memory back a dozen years to old Kuprasso's dancing-house in Constantinople and the man who had led the Company of the Rosy Hours. Sandy was on the war-path again, and I was bound to keep an eye on him.

But two days later I had a letter—from Blenkiron. It had a typed address and a Southampton postmark—which was no clue, for it had probably been brought over by a passenger in a ship and posted at the port of arrival. The handwriting was Blenkiron's unmistakable scrawl. It ran as follows:

" The papers will say I have gotten across the River. Don't let that worry you. But the Golden Shore at present is important and I may have to stay there quite a time. Therefore keep up the requiems and dirges until further notice."

Also at last I got a reply from Sandy, in answer to my string of letters. It was a telegram from London, so he had left Paris, and it merely contained Abraham Lincoln's words: " You stop still and saw wood."

After that I stopped still. Both Blenkiron and Sandy were up to some devilry, and I had an instinct that they were working together. I have set down here my slender personal knowledge of the beginning of the strange events now to be related. The rest comes from the actors themselves.

BOOK I

THE GRAN SECO

THE open windows, protected by wire blinds as fine-meshed as gauze, allowed the cool airs from the sea to slip in from the dusk. The big restaurant was in a pleasant gloom broken by patches of candlelight from the few occupied tables. The Hotel de la Constitución stands on a little promontory above the harbour of Olifa, so the noise of the streets comes to it only like the echo of waves from a breakwater. Archie Roylance, looking into the great square of velvet sky now beginning to be patterned by stars, felt as if he were still at sea.

The Vice-Consul interpreted his thoughts.

" You are surprised at the quiet," he said. " That is only because we dine early. In a little there will be many lights and a jigging band and young people dancing. Yet we have good taste in Olifa and are not garish. If you will be my guest on another occasion, I will take you to a club as well equipped as any in Pall Mall, or to a theatre where you will see better acting than in London, and I will give you a supper afterwards which Voisin's could not better. We have civilisation, you see—for what it is worth."

The Vice-Consul, whose name was Alejandro Gedd, was a small man with a neat, dark, clean-shaven face, and high cheek-bones from which his critics deduced Indian blood. As a matter of fact they came from another ancestry. His grandfather, Alexander Geddes, had come out in his youth from Dundee as a clerk in a merchant's house, had prospered, married a pretty Olifera, begotten a son, and founded a bank which rose in the silver boom to fortune. That son had married a lady of pure Castilian descent, whose beauty was not equal to her lineage, so the grandson of old Geddes had missed both the vigour of the Scot and the suave comeliness of the Olifera. Don Alejandro was an insignificant little man, and he was growing fat. The father had sold his interest in the bank at a high figure, and had thereafter dabbled in politics and horse-breeding; the son, at his death, had promptly got rid of the stud and left the government of his country to get on without him. He had been sent to an English school, and later to the Sorbonne, and had emerged from his education a dilettante and a cosmopolitan. He professed a stout Olifa patriotism, but his private sentiment was for England, and in confidential moments he would speak of his life as exile. Already he had asked Archie a dozen questions about common friends, and had dwelt like an epicure on the recollections of his last visit—the Park on a May morning, an English garden in midsummer, the Solent in August, the October colouring of Scottish hills. His dinner-jacket had been made in the vicinity of Hanover Square, and he hoped that his black stock and his black-ribboned eyeglass were, if not English, at any rate European.

Archie was looking at the windows. "Out there is the Pacific," he said, "nothing nearer you than China. What is it like the other way?"

"The coastal plain for a hundred miles. Then the foot-hills and the valleys where the wine is made. A very pretty light claret, I assure you. Then, for many hundreds of miles, the great mountains."

"Have you travelled there much?"

Don Alejandro shook his head. "I do not travel in this land. What is there to see? In the mountains there are nothing but Indians and wild animals and bleak forests and snow. I am content with this city, where, as I have said, there is civilisation."

"A man I met on the boat told me about a place called the Gran Seco. He said it was bound to be soon the greatest copper area in the world."

Don Alejandro laughed. "That ill-favoured spot becomes famous. Five years ago it was scarcely known. To-day many strangers ask me about it. The name is Indian-Spanish. You must understand that a hundred miles north of this city the coastal plain ends, and the Cordilleras swing round so that there is no room between them and the ocean. But at the curve the mountains, though high, are not the great peaks. These are far to the east, and you have for a big space a kind of tableland. That is what we call the Gran Seco—the Great Thirst—for it is mostly waterless and desert. But it is very rich in minerals. For long we have known that, and before the War there were many companies at work there. Now there is one great company, in which our Government has a share, and from which Olifa derives much of its wealth. The capital employed is mostly foreign—no, not American—European, but of what country I do not know. The labourers are the people of the hills, and the managers are Europeans of many nationalities. They pass through this city going and coming— through this hotel often—perhaps we may see some of them to-night. They are strange folk who do not mix freely with us of Olifa. I am told they are growing as wealthy as Rockefeller. There are no English among them, I think —Slavs mostly, with some Italians and now and then a German, so I do not come across them in the way of business, and it would appear that they have no time for pleasure. . . . May I ask, Sir Archibald, for what purpose especially you honour us with a visit? I want to know how best I can serve you."

Archie wrinkled his brow. " You are very kind, Don Alejandro. The fact is we're here mainly for the fun of it. This is a sort of belated honeymoon trip. Also, I'd like to know something about the politics of Olifa and South America generally. You see, I'm a Member of Parliament, and I've an idea that this part of the globe may soon become rather important. I have brought several introductions."

Don Alejandro waved his hand deprecatingly.

" That will be readily arranged. Your Minister is on leave, and the Embassy has left you in my hands. Without doubt you will be received by our President. I myself will take you to our Minister for External Affairs, who is my second cousin. Our Minister of Finance will expound to you our extravagant prosperity. But of politics in the old sense you will find little. We are too rich and too busy.

When we were poor we talked government all the day. And we had revolutions—dictatorships tempered by revolutions. My father more than once saved his neck by the good blood of his racing stable. But now we are very tame and virtuous. Our Government is rich enough to be enlightened, and our people, being also rich, do not trouble their heads about theories. Even the peons on the estancias and the vaqueros in the hills are content. Olifa is—how do you say?—a plutocratic democracy—a liberal plutocracy. Once it was a battered little packet-boat, now it is a great liner careless of weather and tides. It has no problems, this fortunate country."

"Jolly place for a holiday," said Archie. "Well, we mean to have a good look round. What do you advise?"

Don Alejandro became lyrical. "You can go south for eight hundred miles in an ever-widening plain. There you will see such orange groves as the world cannot match, and nearer the mountains the savannahs which are the richest pasture on earth. I will write to my cousin at Veiro, and he will entertain you at the stud farm which was once my father's. It will not be like an English Sunday afternoon in the country, where a fat stud groom with a bunch of carrots takes the guests round the stables. It is a wild place between the knees of the hills, but there is some pretty horseflesh there."

"Can I get up into the mountains?" Archie put in, but Don Alejandro was not to be interrupted.

"You must visit our great cities, for Olifa, though the capital, is not the largest. Cardanio has now four to five hundred thousand souls. That is the port from which our fruits and hides and frozen beef are shipped. And there is Alcorta in the hinterland, which is our little Birmingham. But madame will weary of these commercial glories. She will be happier, I think, among the horses at Veiro, or in some pretty hacienda. . . ."

Janet Roylance had paid little heed to the conversation, being engaged in studying the slowly increasing number of diners.

"I would like to go into the mountains," she said. "I

saw them from far out at sea, and they looked like the battle-ments of Paradise."

"A very savage Paradise you would find it, Lady Roy-lance. None of your green Swiss valleys with snow-peaks rising from meadows. It is all dusty and bare and cruel. Take my advice and be content with our sunny estancias——"

"Look at these chaps, Janet," said Archie suddenly. "There's a queer class of lad for you!"

Don Alejandro fixed his eyeglass and regarded four men who had taken their seats at a table a little way off. It was a curious quartet. There was a tall man with hair so pale that at first sight he looked like an albino; he had a bony face and skin like old parchment, but from his bearing it was clear that he was still young. Two were small and dark and Jewish, and the fourth was a short burly fellow, with the prognathous jaw of a negro but the luminous eyes of a Latin. All were dressed in well-cut evening clothes, and each wore in his buttonhole a yellow flower—to Archie it looked like a carnation. The notable things about them were their extreme pallor and their quiet. They sat almost motionless, speaking very little and showing that they were alive by only the tiniest gestures. A waiter brought them caviare, and poured champagne into their glasses, and as they moved their arms to eat and drink they had an odd suggestion of automata.

Don Alejandro dropped his eyeglass. "From the Gran Seco," he said. "That is the *type Gran Seco*. European, I think—the tall man might be a Swede—going from or returning to their place of work. No. I do not know any one of them. Olifa is full of these birds of passage, who linger only for a day. They do not mix with our society. They are civil and inoffensive, but they keep to themselves. Observe the *chic* of their clothes, and the yellow button-holes. That is the fashion of the copper magnates."

"They look to me like pretty sick men," said Archie.

"That, too, is their fashion. Those who go to that un-couth place speedily lose their complexions. It may be the copper fumes or some fever of the hills."

"I should rather like to go there," said Archie.

Don Alejandro laughed.

"Ah, you are intrigued. That is like an Englishman. He must be for ever hunting romance. No doubt a visit to the Gran Seco can be accomplished, but it must first be arranged. The railway beyond Santa Ana is not for the public. It is owned by the company, and their permission is necessary to travel on it. Also there must be a permit from the Gobernador of the province, who is also the Company's president, for the workers in the mines are a brutal race and the rule of the Gran Seco must be like the rule of a country in war-time. . . . If you wish, I will put the matter in train. But I do not think it is quite the place for a lady. Such cheeks as madame's are not for the withering airs of the hills."

"I will follow the Olifero custom," said Janet. "Your ladies, Don Alejandro, are very fond of pearl powder."

The restaurant was filling up. It appeared that many Oliferos were dining, for large lustrous women's eyes looked out of dead-white faces. At the far end of the room, close to the band, a noisy party took their seats at a table. They were all young, and, since they had not troubled to change, their clothes made a startling blotch of colour among the sober black and white of the other guests. All looked as if they had just left a golf-course, the men in knicker-bockers of white flannel and both sexes in outrageous jumpers.

"Behold our protectors!" said Don Alejandro with a touch of acid in his tone. "Behold the flower of Yanqui youth! No. I do not know them—for that you must ask my colleague, Señor Wilbur. But I know where they come from. They are from the big Yanqui yacht now in the harbour. It is called the *Corinna*."

"Good lord! That was Mike Burminster's boat. I didn't know he had sold it." Archie regarded the party with disfavour.

"I do not know who is the present owner, except that he is a Yanqui. The guests I should judge from their appearance to have sprung from Hollywood."

"They were lunching here to-day," said Janet. "I saw them when Archie was inquiring about his lost kit-bag. . . . There was a girl among them that I thought I must have seen before. . . . I don't see her here to-night. . . . I rather like the look of them, Don Alejandro. They are fresh, and jolly, and young."

"Believe me, they will not repay further acquaintance, Lady Roylance." Don Alejandro was unconsciously imitating his Castilian mother. "They come here in opulent yachts and behave as if Olifa were one of their vulgar joy-cities. That is what they call 'having a good time.' Yanqui youth, as I have observed it, is chronically alcoholic and amorous, and its manners are a brilliant copy of the parrot-house."

The three had their coffee in the spacious arcade which adjoined the restaurant. It was Don Alejandro's turn to ask questions, and he became for a little the English exile, seeking eagerly for news—who had married whom, what was thought in London of this and that—till Olifa dropped from him like a mantle and he felt himself once more a European. Presently their retreat was invaded by other diners, the band moved thither from the restaurant, and dancing began in a cleared space. The young Americans had not lingered over their meal, and had soon annexed the dancing-floor. Fragments of shrill badinage and endearments were heard in the pauses of the music.

Don Alejandro advised against liqueurs, and commended what he called the Olifa Tokay, which proved to be a light sweet wine of the colour of sloe-gin. Holding his glass to the corona of light in the centre of the patio, he passed from reminiscence to philosophy.

"You are unfortunate pilgrims," he said. "You come seeking romance and I can only offer the prosaic. No doubt, Sir Archibald, you have been led to believe that we Latin Americans are all desperadoes, and our countries a volcanic territory sputtering with little fires of revolution. You find instead the typical bourgeois republic, as bourgeois as the United States. We do not worry about liberty, for we have learned that wealth is a better and

less troublesome thing. In the old days we were always
quarrelling with our neighbours, and because we conscripted
our youth for our armies there was discontent and presently
revolution. Now we are secure, and do not give occasion
for discontent."

"Someone told me that you had a pretty effective army."

"We have a very effective police. As for our army, it
is good, no doubt, but it is small. For what should we use
our army? We have no ambition of conquest, and no
enemy against whom we need defence."

"Still, you can't count on perpetual peace, you know.
You are rich, and wealth means rivals."

"Have we not the League of Nations?" Don Alejandro
cried merrily. "Is not Olifa even now a member of the
Council? And is there not the Monroe Doctrine, invented
by the great-grandfathers of those depraved children who
are dancing yonder?"

"Oh, well, if you like to put it that way——"

"I do not like to put it that way. I do not believe in the
League of Nations, and I do not love the United States,
and I regard the Monroe Doctrine as an insult to my race.
But what would you have, my dear Sir Archibald? We
have chosen prosperity, and the price we pay for it is our
pride. Olifa is a well-nourished body without a soul.
Life and property are as safe here as in England, and what
more can the heart of man desire? We have a stable
Government because our people have lost interest in being
governed. Therefore I say, do not propose to study our
politics, for there is nothing to study. To you in England,
with a bankrupt Europe at your door and the poison of
Communism trickling into your poverty, politics are life
and death. To us, in our sheltered Hesperides, they are
only a bad dream of the past. There is no mystery left in
Olifa. . . ."

As Don Alejandro spoke, the four men from the Gran
Seco were moving through the arcade. They held themselves stiffly, but walked as lightly as cats, deftly steering
their way among the tables and at the same time keeping
close together. They looked neither to right nor left, but,

as they passed, Janet and Archie had a good view of their waxen faces. The eyes of all—the pale eyes of the tall man, the beady eyes of the Jews, and the fine eyes of the Latin—had the same look of unnatural composure, as if the exterior world did not exist for them and they were all the time looking inward in a profound absorption. They had something of the eery detachment of sleepwalkers.

Don Alejandro was talking again.

"Be content, my friends, with what we can offer—our beauty and our civilisation. Think of us as a little enclave of colour between the glooms of the great sea and the clouds of the great mountains. Here man has made a paradise for himself, where during his short day of life he can live happily without questioning."

Archie had been looking at Janet.

"I think we both want to go to the Gran Seco," he said.

II

ARCHIE left Janet writing letters and started out next morning to explore the city. The first taste of a foreign town was always to him an intoxication, and, in the hot aromatic sunshine of that month which for Olifa is the sweet of the year, the place seemed a riot of coloured and exultant life. He descended the broad terraced road which by easy gradients led from the hotel to the twisted streets of the old city. Some of the calles were only narrow ravines of shade, where between high windowless walls country mule-carts struggled towards the market-place. Others were unhappily provided with screeching electric tramways, so that the passer-by on foot or on a horse had to mount high on the ill-paved side-walk to avoid destruction. Presently he came into a hot market-place, where around an old Spanish fountain were massed stalls laden with glowing flowers and fruit, and strange unwholesome fishes, and coarse pottery, and garish fabrics, and country-woven straw hats. Through this medley Archie limped happily, testing his Spanish on the vendors, or trying with most inadequate knowledge to disentangle the racial mixture. The town Oliferos were a small race, in which he thought there must be considerable negro blood, but the countryfolk were well-made and up-standing, often with a classic and melancholy dignity in their faces. There were lean, wild-looking people, too, whose speech was not any kind of Spanish, with an odd angle to their foreheads and the shyness of an animal in their small anxious eyes, who squatted in their dark ponchos beside their mules and spoke only to each other. An Indian breed, thought Archie—perhaps from the foothills.

A maze of calles took him to the main Plaza, where a great baroque cathedral raised its sculptured front above a medley of beggars and vendors of holy medals. The square was shamefully paved, the façades of the old Spanish houses were often in disrepair, but the crumbling plaster and the blotched paint blended into something beautiful and haunt-ing. Here it was very quiet, as if the city hushed itself in the environs of the house of God. To Archie it seemed that he was looking upon that ancient Olifa, before the hustling modern world was born, Olifa as it had appeared to the eyes of Captain Cook's sailors when they landed, a city which kept the manners and faith of sixteenth-century Spain. He entered the church, and found a vast, cavernous darkness like the inside of a mountain, candles twinkling like distant glow-worms, echoes of muttered prayers and the heavy sweetness of incense. After it the Plaza seemed as bright as a mountain-top.

Another labyrinth brought him into a different world. The great Avenida de la Paz is a creation of the last twenty years, and runs straight as a ruler from the villas of the most fashionable suburb to the old harbour of the city. In its making it has swallowed up much ancient derelict architecture, and many nests of squalid huts, but, since it was built with a clear purpose by a good architect, it is in itself a splendid thing, in which Olifa takes a fitting pride. Where Archie struck it, it was still residential, the home of the rank and fashion of the city, with the white mass of the Government buildings and the copper dome of the Par-liament House rising beyond it. But as he walked westward it gradually changed. Soon it was all huge blocks of flats and shops, with here and there the arrogant palace of a bank or shipping company.

One of these caught Archie's attention. It was an immense square edifice built of the local marble, with a flight of steps running up to doors like those of the Baptistry in Florence. Two sentries with fixed bayonets were on guard, and at first he thought it a Government office. Then his eye caught a modest inscription above the entrance— *Administración de Gran Seco.* The name had stuck in his memory from last night's talk—linked with the sight of the four copper magnates and Don Alejandro's aloofness. The Gran Seco was a strange and comfortless place, and it was perched far up in the mountains. This gorgeous building was at variance with the atmosphere with which the name was invested for him, and he stared with lively curiosity at its magnificence.

Suddenly the great doors opened and a man came out, escorted by two bowing porters. The sentries saluted, a big limousine drew up, and he was borne away. Archie had a glimpse of a tall figure in dark grey clothes, and, what seemed out of keeping with the weather, a bowler hat. The face was middle-aged and bearded—a trim black beard like a naval officer's. As he passed, the man had glanced at him, and, even in that short second of time, there was something in those eyes which startled him. They seemed so furiously alive. There was nothing inquisitive in them, but they were searching, all-embracing. Archie felt that this was one who missed nothing and forgot nothing; he had had an impression of supreme competence which was as vivid as an electric shock. No wonder the Gran Seco was a success, he thought, if it had men of that quality in its management.

The broad pavements, the double line of trams, the shop-windows as soberly rich as those of the Rue de la Paix, the high white buildings narrowing in the distance to enfold a blue gleam of the sea, made an impressive picture of wealth and enlightenment. There was a curious absence of colour, for the people he passed seemed all to be wearing dark clothes; they were a quiet people, too, who spoke without the southern vehemence. Emancipation had come to the ladies of Olifa, for there were many abroad, walking delicately on the pavement, or showing their powdered prettiness in motor-cars. Here was none of the riotous life of the old quarter, and Archie had an impression of the city as elaborately civilised and of its richer inhabitants as decorous to the point of inanity. There were no peasants to be seen, nor a single beggar; the Avenida de la Paz seemed to be kept as a promenade for big business and cultivated leisure. Archie grinned when he remembered the picture he had formed of Olifa, as a decadent blend of ancient Spain and second-rate modern Europe, with a vast wild hinterland pressing in upon its streets. The reality was as polished and secure as Paris—a reticent Paris, with a dash of Wall Street.

One splash of colour caught his eye. It came from a big touring car, which had drawn up at the pavement's edge and had disgorged its occupants. The driver was a young man strangely clad in starched linen knickerbockers, a golf-jumper designed in a willow-plate pattern of blue and white, pale blue stockings, and a wide-brimmed straw hat. He sat negligently at the wheel, and as Archie stared at him he tilted his hat over his brow. Presently there emerged from the shop two girls and a second youth—the youth in snowy white flannels with a scarlet sash, and the girls in clothes the like of which Archie had never seen, but which in his own mind he classed as the kind of thing for a tropical garden-party. He noticed, since the extreme shortness of their skirts made their legs their most notable feature, that they had black patent-leather shoes with silver buckles, and wonderful shot-silver stockings.

" You all right, honey? " one of them addressed the driver.

" Fine. Got the candy you want? "

Then an argument arose between the two girls and the other youth, an argument conducted in a dialect unintelligible to Archie, and in voices which forcibly reminded him of the converse of a basket of kittens. The four in that discreet monochrome place were indecently conspicuous, but they were without modesty, and among the stares and whispers of the crowded pavement conducted their private dispute with the freedom of children. The driver at last grew bored.

" Aw, come on, Baby," he cried. " Get off the side-walk and come aboard. We got to hustle."

They obeyed him, and the car presently slid into the traffic, the driver's hat still tilted over his brows. Archie believed that he recognised one of the young women as a member of the party from the American yacht who had been dining in the hotel restaurant the night before. He rather resented their presence in Olifa. These half-witted children of pleasure were out of the picture which he had made for himself; they even conflicted with Olifa's conception of herself. " The United States," he told himself, " won't be too popular in Latin America if it unlooses on it much goods of that type."

At last the Avenida passed from shops and offices into a broad belt of garden, flanked on one side by the Customs House and on the other by the building which housed the Port authorities. Beyond them lay the green waters of the old harbour, and the very spot where the first Conquistadors had landed. The new harbour, where the copper from the Gran Seco was shipped, lay farther south, close to the railway-stations; the old one was now almost unused except for fishing-boats, and as a landing-place for the yachts which berthed in the outer basin behind the great breakwater. To the north was a little plaza which was all that remained of the first port of Olifa. It was a picturesque half-moon of crumbling stone, and seemed to be mainly composed of cafés and cinema houses.

Archie sniffed the salt breeze from the west, and limped cheerfully along the water-front, for he loved to be near the sea. In the outer basin he saw the funnels and top-gear of the yacht _Corinna_, on which he had aforetime enjoyed the Duke of Burminster's hospitality. It annoyed him that his friend should have sold or chartered it to the kind of people he had seen in the motor-car.

A launch from the yacht was even then approaching the landing-stage. Archie could read the name on a sailor's jersey. Two men were landed, one who looked like a steward, and the other a thick-set fellow in an engineer's overalls. They separated at once, and the second of the two walked in Archie's direction. Archie had a bad memory for faces, but there was something in this figure which woke recollection. As they came abreast and their eyes met, both came half unconsciously to a halt. The man seemed to stiffen and his right hand to rise in a salute which he promptly checked. He had a rugged face which might have been hewn out of mahogany, and honest, sullen, blue eyes.

"Hullo," said Archie, "I've seen you before. Now, where on earth . . . ? "

The man gave him no assistance, but stood regarding him in a sulky embarrassment. He sniffed, and in lieu of a handkerchief drew his hand across his nose, and the movement stirred some chord in Archie's memory.

"I've got it. You were with General Hannay. I remember you in that black time before Amiens. Hamilton's your name, isn't it? Corporal Hamilton? "

Like an automaton the figure stiffened. " Sirr, that's my name." Then it relaxed. It was as if Archie's words had recalled it for a moment to a military discipline which it hastened to repudiate.

"Do you remember me? "

"Ay. Ye're Captain Sir Erchibald Roylance." There was no " sirr " this time.

"Well, this is a queer place to foregather. I think the occasion demands a drink. Let's try one of these cafés."

The man seemed unwilling. " I'm a wee bit pressed for time."

" Nonsense, Hamilton, you can spare five minutes. I want to hear how you've been getting on and what landed you here. Hang it, you and I and the General went through some pretty stiff times together. We can't part on this foreign strand with a how-d'ye-do."

Archie led the way to a café in the crescent of old houses which looked a little cleaner than the rest.

" What'll you have, Hamilton? " he asked when they had found a table. " You probably don't fancy the native wine. Bottled beer? Or rum? Or can you face aguardiente, which is the local whisky? "

" I'm a teetotaller. I'll hae a glass o' syrup."

" Well, I'm dashed. . . . Certainly—I never drink myself in the morning. Now, about yourself? You're a Glasgow man, aren't you? Pretty warm place, Glasgow. Are you and the other soldier-lads keeping the Bolshies in order? "

Hamilton's mahogany face moved convulsively, and his blue eyes wandered embarrassedly to the door.

" My opinions has underwent a change. I'm thinkin' of anither kind of war nowadays. I'm for the prolytawriat."

" The devil you are!" Archie gasped. " So am I, but my opinions are still the same. What exactly do you mean? "

The man's embarrassment increased. " I'm for the proly —prolytawriat. Us worrkers maun stick thegither and brek our chains. I've been fechtin' for the rights o' man."

" Fighting with what? "

" Wi' the pollis. That's the reason I'm out here. I made Govan a wee thing ower het for me."

Archie regarded him with a mystified face, which slowly broke into a smile.

" I'm sorry to say that you're a liar, Hamilton."

" I'm tellin' ye God's truth," was the reply without heat. Embarrassment had gone, and the man seemed to be speaking a part which he had already rehearsed.

" No. You're lying. Very likely you had trouble with the police, but I bet it wasn't over politics. More likely a public-house scrap, or a girl. Why on earth you should want to make yourself out a Bolshie . . . ? "

" My opinions has underwent a change," the man chanted.

" Oh, drat your opinions! You got into some kind of row and cleared out. That's intelligible enough, though I'm sorry to hear it. What's your present job? Are you in the *Corinna*? "

" Ay, I cam out in her. I'm in the engine-room."

"But you know nothing about ships?"

"I ken something aboot ship's engines. Afore the war I wrocht at Clydebank. . . . And now, if ye'll excuse me, I maun be off, for I've a heap o' jobs ashore. Thank ye for your kindness."

"I call this a perfectly rotten affair," said Archie. "You won't stay, you won't drink, and you keep on talking like a parrot about the proletariat. What am I to say to General Hannay when I meet him? That you have become a blithering foreign communist?"

"Na, na. Ye maunna say that." The man's sullenness had gone, and there was humour in his eye. "Say that Geordie Hamilton is still obeyin' orders, and daein' his duty up to his lights."

"Whose orders?" Archie asked, but the corporal was already making for the door.

The young man walked back to the hotel in a reflective mood, and at luncheon gave Janet a summary of the events of the morning. He had been storing up his impressions of Olifa for her, and had meant to descant upon the old city and the market and the Cathedral Square, but he found these pictures obscured by his later experiences. "Most extraordinary thing. I ran up against a fellow who used to be Dick Hannay's batman—regular chunky Scots Fusilier and brave as a badger—Hamilton they call him. Well, he had the cheek to tell me that he had changed his views and become a Bolshie and had consequently had to clear out of Glasgow. I swear the chap was lying—could see it in his face—but I'm puzzled why he should want to lie to me. . . . He says he has some kind of engineer's job on the *Corinna*. . . . More by token, I saw a selection of the *Corinna* party in a motor-car in the Avenida. Dressed up like nothing on earth, and chattering like jays!"

"We had them here this morning," said Janet. "Pretty little savages with heads like mops. I've christened them the Moplahs."

"Was there a fellow in starched linen bags? He was the prize donkey."

Janet shook her head. "There was only one man with

them and he wore white flannels.   I can't quite make them
out.   They behave like demented trippers, and are always
pawing and ragging each other, but I came on the young
man suddenly when I went to the bureau to ask about
postage, and when the clerk couldn't tell me he answered
my question.   His whole voice and manner seemed to
change, and he became startlingly well-bred. . . .   I want
to explore the Moplahs.   And I would rather like to see
again the tall girl I had a glimpse of yesterday.   I can't
get it out of my head that I've seen her before."

III

On the following evening Janet and Archie dined as Don
Alejandro's guests at the Club de Residentes Extranjeros.
The club, situated in one of the squares to the north of
the Avenida, was a proof of Olifa's wealth and her cos-
mopolitanism.   In the broad cool patio a fountain tinkled,
and between it and the adjoining arcades tropical plants in
green tubs made the air fragrant.   The building was for the
most part a copy of an old Spanish town house, but the
billiard-room was panelled in oak with a Tudor ceiling, the
card-room was Flemish, and the big dining-room Italian
Renaissance.   The night was freshly warm, with light airs
stirring the oleanders, and, from the table which Don
Alejandro had selected, the patio was a velvet dusk shot
with gold and silver gleams like tiny searchlights.

The only other guest was the American Consul.   Mr
Roderick Wilbur was a heavy man, with the smooth pale
face of eupeptic but sedentary middle-age.   His years in
Olifa had not mellowed his dry, high-pitched New England
voice, or endowed him with a single Latin grace.   He
looked upon the other diners with the disapproving air of
a Scots elder of the kirk surveying a travelling theatrical
company, and the humour which now and then entered his
eye was like the frosty twinkle of a very distant star.

Don Alejandro was in a vivacious mood.   He was the
showman of his beloved city, but he was no less a repre-
sentative of his beloved Europe; he wished the strangers

to praise Olifa but to recognise him as a cosmopolitan.
Archie and Janet satisfied his patriotism, for, having hired
a car that afternoon and driven round the city, they over-
flowed in admiration.

"You were right," Janet told him. "There is no mystery
in Olifa. It is all as smooth and polished as a cabochon
emerald, and, like a cabochon, you can't see far inside it.
Your people have the satisfied look of London suburbanites
on a Sunday up the river."

"Your police are too good," said Archie. "One doesn't
see a single ragamuffin in the main streets. Janet and I
prefer the old quarter. Some day, Don Alejandro, we want
you to take us round it and tell us who the people are.
They look like samples of every South American brand since
the Aztecs."

"The Aztecs lived in Mexico," Janet corrected.

"Well, I mean the chaps that were downed by the
Conquistadors."

Don Alejandro laughed. "Our old quarter is only a
tourist spectacle, like the native city in Tangier. For the
true country life you must go to the estancias and the
savannahs. I have arranged by telegraph for your visit
to my cousin at Veiro."

"And the Gran Seco?"

"That also is in train. But it is more difficult and will
take time."

"I said there was no mystery in Olifa," Janet observed,
"but I rather think I was wrong. There is the Gran Seco.
It seems to be as difficult to get into it as into a munition
factory. Have you been there, Mr. Wilbur?"

The American Consul had been devoting serious attention
to his food, stopping now and then to regard Janet with
benevolent attention.

"Why, yes, Lady Roylance," he said. "I've been up to
the Gran Seco just the once since it blossomed out. I've
no great call to go there, for Americans don't frequent it
to any considerable extent."

"Wilbur hates the place," said Don Alejandro. "He
thinks that every commercial undertaking on the globe

should belong to his countrymen, and it vexes him that the Gran Seco capital should be European."

"Don't you pay any attention to Mr Gedd," said the big man placidly. "He's always picking on my poor little country. But I can't say I care for that salubrious plateau. I don't like being shepherded at every turn as if I was a crook, and I reckon the Montana sage-brush is more picturesque. Also they haven't much notion up there of laying out a township. They'd be the better of some honest-to-God Americans to look after the plumbing."

"See! He is all for standardising life. What a dull world the United States would make of it!"

"That's so. We prefer dullness to microbes. All the same, there's things about the Gran Seco which you can see with half an eye aren't right. I didn't like the look of the miners. You never in your days saw such a hang-dog, miserable bunch, just like some of our old Indian reservations, where big chief Wet Blanket and his wives used to drink themselves silly on cheap bourbon. And how in thunder does Castor get his labour? He's got a mighty graft somewhere, but when I first came here the Gran Seco Indians were a difficult folk to drive. I've heard that in old times the Olifa Government had trouble with them over the conscription."

"They were savages," said Don Alejandro, "and they are savages still. Castor has doubtless the art of dealing with them, for he himself is on the grand scale a savage."

Archie pricked up his ears.

"Castor? Who is he?"

"The Gobernador of the province. Also the President of the company."

"I saw a fellow coming out of the Gran Seco head office —a fellow with a black beard, who didn't look as if he missed much."

"That was Señor Castor. You are fortunate, Sir Archibald, for you, a new arrival, have already seen Olifa's great man, and that is a privilege but rarely granted to us Oliferos. He descends upon us and vanishes as suddenly as a river mist."

" Tell me about him," said Janet.   " Where does he come
from?   What is his nationality? "

Don Alejandro shook his head.   " I do not know.   Mr
Wilbur, who is a man of hasty judgments, will say that he
is a Jew.   He is certainly a European, but not a Spaniard,
though he speaks our tongue.   I can only say that he
emerged out of nothing five years ago, and became at once
a prince.   He rules the Gran Seco, and its officials are
altogether his creation.   And since he rules the Gran Seco
he rules Olifa.   He has, as Mr Wilbur would say, this
country of mine by the short hairs."

" He don't meddle with politics," said the American, and
Janet noticed that as he spoke he cast a quick glance around
him, as if he did not wish to be overheard.   Don Alejandro,
too, had lowered his voice.

" What nonsense! " said the latter.   " He is money, and
money is our politics to-day.   Once we Latins of America
were a great race.   We were Europeans, with minds enlarged and spirits braced by a new continent.   You are a
soldier, Sir Archibald, and will remember that the bloodiest
battles of last century were fought in La Plata and on the
Uruguay.   Our plains were the nursery of the liberties of
Italy.   But now we have but the one goddess.   We are
rich and nothing more.   Soon we shall be richer, and then,
my dear Wilbur, we shall be the devotees of your great
country, which is the high-priest of riches."

" I can't say that you're showing any special devotion
just at present," said the other dryly.   " My nationals—
thank God there aren't many—are about the most unpopular
in this State.   But quit talking about politics.   We're out
to give you a good time, Lady Roylance, and we want to
know just how you'd like us to set about it."

Janet was of a patient and philosophical temper, but
Archie liked to take his sensations in gulps.   So far Olifa,
he admitted to himself, had been a little boring.   The place,
for all its beauty, had a deadly commonplaceness—it was
the typical bourgeois State, as Don Alejandro had declared
the first night.   And yet he was conscious that this judgment

did not exhaust the matter. There were moments when he felt that Olifa was a strange woman in a mask of cheap silk, a volcano overspread with suburban gardens. Behind even the decorousness of the Avenida he savoured a mystery. Into the pleasant monotony of the days had come wafts of air from some other sphere—a peasant's face in the market, the bearded Gobernador, the pallid men in the hotel, even the preposterous figure of Dick Hannay's former batman. These things had stirred in him an irrational interest. . . . Perhaps if he went into the hinterland he would find the glamour of Olifa, of whose existence he was convinced, but which had hitherto contrived to evade him.

The club dining-room was full, and when they left it for coffee on the terrace beside the patio they had difficulty in finding chairs. It was apparently the practice to dine elsewhere and come to the club to dance, for a band was pounding out ragtime, and a dozen couples were on the floor.

" The Moplahs," Janet sighed happily.

It was beyond doubt the American party from the yacht, and in that place they were as exotic as a tuberose in a bed of wallflowers. They had conformed to convention in their dress, for the four men wore dinner-jackets, and the four girls bright, short-skirted, silk-taffeta gowns and long pearl necklaces. Among the powdered Olifero ladies and the sallow Olifero cavaliers their fresh skins made a startling contrast, and not less startling were their shrill, toneless voices. They chattered incessantly, crying badinage to each other and to the band, as they danced the half-savage dances with an abandon which now suggested wild children and now the lunatic waltzing of hares in an April moonlight. Janet laughed aloud, the picture was so crazily fantastic. A Spanish girl, in a frock with wide flounces and with blue-black hair dressed high and surmounted by a gold comb, was suddenly cannoned into by a fluffy-headed minx, who apologised in a voice like a vindictive kitten's, and was rewarded by a stony stare. Just so, Janet remembered, she had seen a greyhound repel the impudence of a Skye terrier.

" I don't see my tall girl," she said.

" The fellow with the starched linen knickerbockers isn't

here," said Archie. "I didn't see his face, but I think I would know him again. Who are they, Mr Wilbur?"

The American's eyes were hard with disapproval. "I can't tell you their names, but they're off the *Corinna*. They're in Burton Rawlinson's party. Mr Rawlinson isn't on board himself, and there can't be much of a restraining hand to shepherd the bunch. Some of them have been to my office, and I judge I'm going to hear of trouble with them before they quit these shores. They want this city to stop still and take notice of them."

Archie inquired concerning Mr Rawlinson.

"He's a fine man and a big man, one of the biggest on the Pacific coast. I've nothing against Burton. He's rich, and he's public-spirited, and he's gotten a mighty fine collection of pictures. I can't say I take to his offspring and their friends. There's more dollars than sense in that outfit."

"I like the Moplahs," said Janet. "I want to know them."

Archie, who was a connoisseur of dancing, observed that the men danced better than the women, a thing he had noticed before with Americans. "Did a fellow with starched linen bags ever come to your office?" he asked the Consul. "Slightly built fellow, a little shorter than me?"

Mr Wilbur shook his head. "Maybe, but I don't remember him. All their garments struck me as curious. Heaven knows what's going to become of our youth, Sir Archibald. They've quit behaving like ladies and gentlemen —running wild like bronchos, and their parents can't do the lassooing. They're hard cases at seventeen."

"There's an appalling innocence about them," said Janet and looked up smiling, for two of the dancers had left the floor and were approaching them.

The girl was small, and a little too plump, but very pretty, with a mop of golden curls like a mediæval page's. The young man was thin and beaky, and his longish hair was parted in the middle.

"Say, what about dancing?" he said. "Won't you cut

in?" He looked at Janet, while the girl smiled pleasantly on Archie.

"Most awfully sorry," said Archie. "I'd love to, but I've got a game leg."

"Pardon?"

"I mean I'm a bit lame."

Janet rose smiling and took the young man's arm.

"I don't know your name," said Mr Wilbur, who was a stickler for the conventions, "but I reckon you're with the *Corinna* party. This lady is Lady Roylance."

The youth regarded him solemnly. "You've said it, Grandpa," was his reply. "Come on, lady."

The girl was still partnerless, and Don Alejandro offered himself for the breach. He sprang to his feet and bowed deeply from the waist. "If I may have the honour," he said. Archie and the Consul were left alone to their cigars.

The dancing-place was soon crowded, and Janet and Don Alejandro seemed to have been completely absorbed into the whirl. Glimpses could be caught of Janet's porcelain elegance, and of an unwontedly energetic Don Alejandro in the grip of various corybantic maidens. The two men in the lounge-chairs presently ceased to be spectators and fell into talk.

Mr Wilbur, as if the absence of his colleague had unsealed his tongue, expanded and became almost confidential. He asked Archie for his impressions of Olifa, and when he was told "tidy and contented and opulent," nodded an acquiescent head.

"You're about right, sir. That's Olifa first and last—the Olifa of to-day. Better policed than New York, and just about as clean as Philadelphia. Manicured, you might say. But it wasn't always like that. When I first came here Olifa was the ordinary South American republic, always on the edge of bankruptcy and revolution, and this city had one of the worst names on the coast. The waterfront was a perfect rat-hole for every criminal in the Pacific—every brand of roughneck and dope-smuggler and crook—dagos with knives and niggers with razors and the scum of the U-nited States with guns. To-day you could take your wife along it in perfect safety any hour of the night. The Treasury was empty, for politics were simply who could get their hands first and deepest into it. There was bad trouble up-country, and there was always a war going on in the mountains, which the little under-fed and never-paid soldiers couldn't win. Now we've got a big balance in the budget and the peace of God over the land. It's a kind of miracle. It's almost against nature, Sir Archibald."

"Why, it's principally the Gran Seco," he continued, in response to Archie's request for an explanation. "That, as you know, is the richest copper proposition on the globe, and the Government has a big share in it. There's money to burn for everybody nowadays. But there's more than money. Olifa's gotten a first-class brain to help her along."

"The President?"

Wilbur laughed.

"The Excelentisimo is a worthy gentleman, and he has gotten some respectable folks to help him, but it isn't the President of this republic that has made the desert blossom like the rose. There's a bigger brain behind him."

"You mean the Gran Seco fellow—what's his name?"

"I mean Mr Castor. At least I reckon it must be Mr Castor, for there isn't anybody else. You see, I can size up the members of the Government, because I know them, so it must be the man I don't know."

"I see. Well, it's clear that I must get alongside of this Castor if I'm to learn much about Olifa. What's the best way to work it?"

"Through the President, I reckon. I'd like to help you, but I haven't much of a pull in Olifa just at the moment. You see, the U-nited States is going through one of its periodical fits of unpopularity. Olifa has waxed fat, like the man in the Bible, and she's kicking, and when a South American nation kicks it's generally against the U-nited States. Don Alejandro will fix an interview with the President for you, and he'll arrange your trip to the Gran Seco. He's a good little man, though he don't like my country."

Thereafter Mr Wilbur discoursed of his nation—its

strength and its weakness, its active intelligence, imperfect
manners, and great heart. He was a critic, but he was also
an enthusiast. To this man, grown old in foreign lands
in his country's service, America was still the America of
his youth. Her recent developments he knew only from
the newspapers, and he loyally strove to reconcile them with
his old ideal. America only needed to be understood to be
loved, but it was hard to get her true worth across the
footlights. " You English," he said, " have got a neat,
hard-shell national character, with a high gloss on it.
Foreigners may not like it, but they can't mistake it. It
hits them in the eye every time. But we're young and
growing and have a lot of loose edges, and it's mighty hard
to make people understand that often when we talk foolishness we mean wisdom, and that when we act high and
mighty and rile our neighbours it's because we're that busy
trying to get a deal through we haven't time to think of
susceptibilities. You've got to forget our untidy fringes."

" Like the crowd from the yacht," said Archie. " They
don't rile me a bit, I assure you. . . . Just look at the
way that lad dances. He might be David capering before
the Lord."

" That's because you've seen a lot of the world, Sir
Archibald. I reckon you've met enough Americans to know
the real thing."

" No, I've met very few. You see, I've never crossed the
Atlantic before. But I knew one American, and for his
sake I'm ready to back your country against all comers. He
was about the wisest and bravest and kindest old fellow
I ever came across."

Mr Wilbur asked his name.

" He's dead, poor chap. Died a few months ago. I
daresay you've heard of him. His name was Blenkiron—
John S. Blenkiron."

Archie had his eye on the Hebraic dancer or he might have
noticed a sudden change in his companion's face. When
Mr Wilbur spoke again—and that was after a considerable
pause—it was in a voice from which all feeling had gone,
the voice in which he conducted his consular duties.

"Yes. I've heard of Mr Blenkiron. Mighty fine man, they tell me. Just how well did you know him, Sir Archibald?"

"I only saw him for a week or two in the Amiens business of March '18. But they were pretty solemn weeks, and you get to know a man reasonably well if you're fighting for your life beside him. He was with a great pal of mine, General Hannay, and the two of them put up a famous show at Gavrelle. I can see old Blenkiron's face yet, getting cheerier the more things went to the devil, and fairly beaming when the ultimate hell was reached. I wouldn't ask for a better partner in a scrap. I'm most awfully sorry he died. I always hoped to see him again."

"Too bad," said Mr Wilbur, and he seemed to be absorbed in some calculation, for his brows were knitted.

A flushed Janet joined them, attended by two cavaliers who insisted on plundering the pot plants to give her flowers. Presently Don Alejandro also extricated himself from the dancers, with his black-corded eyeglass hanging over his left shoulder.

"These innocents are going to the Gran Seco," Janet announced. "They seem to think it is a sort of country club, but if your account is true, Mr Wilbur, they'll be like humming-birds in a dustbin."

"They surely will," said the Consul. "When do you expect your own permits, Lady Roylance?"

"They should be ready to-morrow," said Don Alejandro.

Archie and Janet left their caleche at the hotel gates, and walked up the steep avenue to enjoy the coolness of the night wind. At the esplanade on the top they halted to marvel at the view. Below them lay the old town with the cathedral towers white in the moonlight—a blur of shadows in which things like glow-worms twinkled at rare intervals, and from which came confused echoes of some secret nocturnal life. Beyond lay the shining belt of the Avenida, and the Ciudad Nueva mounting its little hills in concentric circles of light. On the other side the old harbour was starred with the riding lights of ships, and the lamps of the water-front made a double line, reflection and reality. To the south at the new harbour there was a glow of fires and the clamour of an industry which did not cease at sunset. To the west, beyond the great breakwater, sea and sky melted under the moon into a pale infinity.

Suddenly Archie's spirits awoke. He seemed to see Olifa as what he had hoped—not a decorous city of careerists, but a frontier post on the edge of mysteries. The unknown was there, crowding in upon the pert little pride of man. In the golden brume to the east were mountains—he could almost see them—running up to icefields and splintered pinnacles, and beyond them swamps and forests as little travelled as in the days of Cortes. Between the desert of the ocean and the desert of the hills lay this trivial slip of modernity, but a step would take him beyond it into an antique land. The whiff of a tropical blossom from the shrubberies and the faint odour of wood smoke unloosed a flood of memories—hot days in the African bush, long marches in scented Kashmir glens, shivering camps on Himalayan spurs. The War had overlaid that first youth of his, when he had gone east to see the world, but the rapture and magic were now returning. He felt curiously expectant and happy.

" I've a notion that we're going to have the time of our lives here," he told his wife.

But Janet did not reply. For three days she had been busy chasing a clue through her memory and now she had grasped it. She had suddenly remembered who was the tall girl she had seen with the party from the *Corinna* on the day of their arrival.

All night Archie dreamed of the Gran Seco. As he saw it, it was a desolate plateau culminating in a volcano. The volcano was erupting, and amid the smoke and fire a colossal human figure sat at its ease. Then the dream became a nightmare—for the figure revealed itself as having the face and beard of the man he had seen leaving the office in the Avenida, but the starched white linen knickerbockers of the preposterous young American.

IV

ARCHIE set out on his exploration of Olifa with his nose in the air, like a dog looking for game. The spell of a new country had fallen on him, as had happened fifteen years before when he left school. The burden of the War and all it had brought, the cares of politics, the preoccupations of home had slipped from his shoulders, and he felt himself again an adventurer, as when he had first studied maps and listened hungrily to travellers' tales. But now he had one supreme advantage—he had a companion; and Janet, who had never before been out of Europe, was as eager as he was to squeeze the last drop out of new experience.

He left over his more important letters for the moment and used those introductions which had been given him by the friends he had made during his time at the Madrid Embassy. The result was that the pair were taken to the heart of a pleasant, rigid little society—as remote from interest in the Government of Olifa as an unreconstructed Southern planter is from a Republican White House, or a Royalist Breton from the Elysée. Archie was made a member of the Polo Club and played with agreeable young men, who had their clothes and saddlery from London and their manners from the eighteenth century. A ball was given in their honour, where the most popular dance, to Janet's amazement, was a form of Lancers. They met composed maidens who were still in bondage to their duennas: and young married women, languishing and voluble, or discreet and domesticated, among whose emphatic complexions Janet's delicate colouring was like a wood-anemone among gardenias: and witty grandmothers running terribly to fat: and ancient hidalgos with beaks like birds of prey. It was a comfortable society, with the secure good manners of a tiny aristocracy, but it knew of no world beyond its pale, and was profoundly uninterested in its neighbours.

They went a little, too, into business circles, both Olifero and alien, the representatives of shipping and trading companies and the big foreign banks. This, too, was a pleasant world, good-tempered and prosperous. Here they heard much of politics, but it was business politics. The existing Government was spoken of with respect, but not with intimate knowledge; it functioned well, kept the country solvent, and left trade in peace. Politicians were a class by themselves, a dubious class, though it was believed that the present lot were honest. But they met none of the Copper people. These seemed to form an oligarchy apart, and were mentioned respectfully but distantly. When Archie asked about the Gran Seco he was only given statistics of output and an encomium on its efficiency. Of its President the commercial world of Olifa spoke as an ordinary automobile-manufacturer might speak of Henry Ford, as one who was a law to himself, an object to admire, but not to emulate.

"This is a queer place," Archie told Janet. "It seems to have two Governors—the Castor fellow and the President—and the ordinary man don't seem to know or care much about either. It's about time we started out for the Gran Seco."

But when Don Alejandro was approached on the matter he had to explain with many apologies that their permits had not arrived. There was some inconceivably foolish hitch, which he had not yet tracked down.

"But the American troupe got through straight away," Archie complained. "They left a week ago."

"I know. That is a way Americans have. Perhaps in your case the difficulty is Mr Wilbur. Officiously and quite unnecessarily he interested himself in getting your passes, so he said—and he may have exhausted his purchase in franking his countrymen through and raised a prejudice. As I have told you, his nation is not loved by our Government."

Don Alejandro went on to explain that the delay could only be a matter of days. "Meantime, why not visit my cousin at Veiro? There you must go some time, and this hiatus gives you the chance."

So to Veiro they went—fifty miles by train and twenty

by motor-car along a superb concrete highway, which suddenly gave out four miles from the house, so that the journey was completed by a sandy track over primeval prairie. They arrived just at sunset, when the place swam in a clear coppery gold. The house was low and white and seemed to cover acres, with its adobe outbuildings, its great corrals for the cattle, and its trim red-roofed stables built on the English model. The palms of the coast had been left behind, and at this elevation the tropics had faded from the landscape. The garden was ablaze with coverts of hibiscus and plots of scarlet zinnias among the rough lawns, and the wind-breaks which flanked it were of acacias and walnuts. A big irrigation dam to the right caught the last rays of the sun, and beyond it the tender green of the alfalfa fields seemed a continuation of its waters. Far to the east, above the lifting savannahs, was a saw-like edge of tenuous white mountains which seemed to hang in the central heavens. There was a succession of thin spires now picked out with gold and rose. Archie asked their name.

"Los Doce Apóstolas—the Twelve Apostles," said the driver, and rattled off a list of uncouth syllables.

Don Mario Sanfuentes, the cousin of Don Alejandro, was small, spare, and blue-jowled, with the figure of a groom and the profound solemnity of the man who lives with horses. His wife was dead and his ranch and stables were to him both family and profession. He greeted his visitors with the grave courtesy of manner which needs no words to emphasise it. Their rooms were wide chambers with scrubbed wooden floors and windows looking across a broad verandah to a hundred miles of space, as bare and fresh as a convent dormitory. They had their meals in a dining-room which contained the remnants of the Sanfuentes heirlooms—cabinets of lacquer and tortoiseshell, a Murillo which had been an altar-piece in one of the forgotten churches of the Conquistadors, fantastic tapestries now faded into a mellow confusion, an Italian triptych of carved ivory, and a great galleon of tarnished silver. But they sat mostly in Don Mario's own room, where in the evenings a wood fire was lit in the wide fireplace—a room where every table was littered with books and papers and cigar-boxes and quirts and crops and spurs, and from the walls looked down the delicate heads of those descendants of the Darley Arab, the Byerley Turk, and the Godolphin Barb whose fame has gone abroad wherever men love horses.

By day Archie and Janet rode with their host about his estate, examined his young stock, and tried out promising colts on the gallops, where by assiduous care a better turf had been got than in the ordinary savannah. At every meal the talk was of horses, but at night, when the fire was lit, Don Mario from the depths of his well-rubbed armchair would speak at large of the land. In modern Olifa he had little interest, but he told of the diversions of his youth—his pack of foxhounds which had to be so constantly re-newed from England that he gave up the game in despair, tiger hunting in the forest country, punitive expeditions against Indian horse-thieves from the hills. The time passed in a delicious calm: a combination, said Janet, of Newmarket and Scotland. And then on the last day of their stay came another visitor.

" I cannot tell you about this country," Don Mario said, " for I am an old horse-breeder who lives apart. But I have bidden young Luis de Marzaniga to sleep the night. His mother was cousin to the husband of my great-aunt's niece. Luis has travelled abroad and seen the world, but especially he has travelled in Olifa. No. He is no poli-tician, nor is he engaged in business. He is like me—what you call a country gentleman. But he has youth and in-quisitiveness, both of which I have long since lost."

So, when the Roylances, having bathed and changed after a long ride in the sun, came down to dinner, they found a strange young man awaiting them. Don Mario's evening garb had been a little like that of a deaf-mute at a funeral, but this young man wore the trimmest of dinner-jackets and the neatest of patent-leather shoes. His hair was as fair as Archie's; but some colouring in his skin had made him sunburn not to Archie's brick-red but to a rich golden-brown. His eyes were brown, and the large expanse of white in them was the only foreign thing in his appear-

ance. Otherwise he looked like a young English cavalry
subaltern, whose duties permitted him to hunt three days
a week.

Dinner that evening was a cheerful meal. Don Luis
chaffed his distant kinsman, with whom he was obviously
in high favour, and Don Mario expanded in silent laughter.
All spoke English—Don Mario very correct and stilted, Don
Luis nobly ungrammatical but notably idiomatic. To Janet's
questions he replied that his education had been chiefly in
Olifa, but that he had visited Europe seven times, and
during the last six months of the War had had a commis-
sion in the French Air Force. He had only just returned
from Paris.

The mention of flying woke up Archie, and for a little
the room hummed with technicalities. Archie inquired concerning the Olifa Air Force, and was told that it was efficient but small—not more than five squadrons. The Olifero
did not take readily to the air, and the pilots were mostly
foreigners—Germans who had found their career cut short
at home, and, Don Luis thought, one or two Russians. " It
is like all our army," he said, " a little force of expert
mercenaries. Olifa needs no army. In the future she will
fight her battles with gold."

Don Luis was very ready to talk. He answered Archie's
many questions on sport with enthusiasm, and drew sketch-
maps to illustrate the lie of the land. As to politics, he had
not Don Mario's apathy. He was ready with amusing
portraits of Olifa's statesmen and with cogent summaries of
policy. He was also a humorist, and had a repertoire of
tales. But he was a discreet young man, and ventured no
opinion of his own. He was neither reactionary nor progressive, only an interested spectator.

On the Gran Seco he was highly informing. He described the nature of the copper deposits, and the new
processes which had reduced costs and made it the Golconda
of Olifa. Castor he knew only by sight. " We of Olifa
do not meet him, but we worship him from afar. He is
the god who dwells in the sanctuary."

" The American Consul thought there might be trouble

some day. The mine-labourers are rather a savage lot, aren't they?"

Don Luis laughed.

" I think the wish may be—how you say?—mother to the thought. Señor Wilbur does not love the Gran Seco. No doubt it is a difficult place, but Señor Castor is beyond doubt a Napoleon and flourishes on difficulties. It will be all right."

" Why does he keep the place so tightly shut? We have been waiting a fortnight for a permit to enter."

" So! Then there must be some foolish mistake of clerks. Señor Castor is not likely to be uncivil—least of all to a charming lady and to a member of the English Parliament. He is a lover of Europe."

Don Luis had many questions to ask in turn, and it slowly dawned upon one of his hearers that this candid and friendly young man was taking in more than he gave out. Archie was drawn to speak of his own past—his eastern travels, his experiences in the War, even of his friends, who could mean nothing to a South American who had only once been in England. He found himself quoting Sandy Arbuthnot by name, as if he had been in his club at home.

" I beg your pardon," he said confusedly. " You can't be interested in my yarning about people you never heard of."

" But I am deeply interested. Your friend is a wise man. How do you call him—Arbuttnot? "

" He was Sandy Arbuthnot, but his father is dead and he is Lord Clanroyden now."

" A lord! Clan-roy-den. Por dios! That is a strange name."

" Scotch," said Archie.

" Ah yes—Scotch. That is your Highlands? Your Gran Seco? This Lord Clay-roy-den, he is in Scotland? "

" I'm blessed if I know where he is at the moment. He's never long off the road."

Janet, too, to her surprise found herself talking to this stranger as if she had known him from childhood. She described vivaciously her encounter with the Moplahs.

" They are common as lentils in Olifa at certain seasons,"

said Don Luis, " those noisy, emancipated American children. They have gone, you say, to the Gran Seco, where Americans are not loved. There may be work then for Señor Wilbur."

" They are really rather nice," said Janet. " I think I have met one of them before. . . . Archie, I didn't tell you, but I believe the tall girl who was with the Moplahs the first day and whom we never saw again was the Miss Dasent who came to Strathlarrig. She was some sort of relation of Mr Blenkiron."

" Not really? " exclaimed the interested Archie. " That's curious. Did you ever hear of Blenkiron, Don Luis? He died the other day—American, rather a great man—he was the chap I was telling you about in the Shark-Gladas affair."

The other shook his head. " I do not think so. But American names are so difficult that it is hard to remember. They are worse than Clan-roy-den."

Don Mario made it his habit to retire to rest at ten o'clock, and Janet, being very sleepy, followed soon after. Archie and Don Luis lit a final cigar, and in the smoking of it strolled into the moonlit verandah. On this side of the house the view was not broken by outbuildings, and beyond a string of paddocks the eye passed to an endless sweep of yellow savannah which faded in the distance into a golden haze. The air was fresh, and, though the night was still, cool wafts seemed to drift soundlessly down from the hidden mountains.

" My countrymen and yours fought each other for three hundred years," said Don Luis, " but a Spaniard and an Englishman, when they meet, usually understand each other. I presume, with your permission, on that old sympathy, and I ask you boldly what are you doing here? "

The young man's manner had changed from the debonair ease which had marked it at dinner. It had become at once confidential and authoritative.

" Fact is, I don't know," was Archie's reply. " Principally, Janet and I are on a postponed honeymoon. I had a notion to pick up something about South American politics, which might be useful to me in Parliament."

" And you find Olifa rather barren ground? "

" I did at first. . . . Now, I am not so sure."

" Will you let me advise you? We are both young men and have served in war. Stay a little in Olifa if you have not yet exhausted the charm of the capital, and then take your delightful lady on board the first ship and go straight home."

" Home? Why in the world? " Archie stared at the speaker.

" You can go to Valparaiso and Buenos Ayres if they amuse you. But get out of Olifa."

" But why? "

" I cannot tell you why. I am your friend, and a friend may venture to advise without reasons."

" But what's the trouble? Olifa is a great deal more peaceful than Europe. You don't mean to say that there's danger. . . ."

" Olifa is a mask—you have not seen her face. Look in front of you. You see nothing but flat pastures. But beyond you know that there are wild mountains. So I tell you that behind the flatness of Olifa there are wild things."

" Well, I'm blessed! D'you know, Don Luis, you are making Olifa rather attractive. You are giving me a very good reason why I should stay."

" But madame . . ."

" I don't know. For heaven's sake, don't tell her what you're telling me, for if she gets a notion that there's mystery abroad she won't stop till she is up to the neck in it. But of course I can't let her run any risks. . . ."

" I do not think that you will be able to help yourself—if you stay. You may be caught up in a tide which will carry you to things very different from your respectable English politics. . . . And these things will not be a honeymoon."

Archie stared at his companion's face. The moon was very bright and the face which it revealed was grave and set.

" You are talking in riddles," said Archie. " I wish you would be more explicit. You tell me to get out of the country, because if I stay I may have trouble. You can hardly leave it at that, you know. What kind of trouble? Perhaps it's the kind that Janet and I might rather fancy."

"That is why I warn you. You are a young man with a wife. It is easy to see that you are not the type which avoids danger. But a wife makes a difference—especially such a lady as yours. You would not wish to involve her, and yet you may unwittingly, if you do not leave Olifa."

"Supposing I were a bachelor, what would you say?"

Don Luis laughed. "Ah, then, I should speak otherwise. I should make of you a confidant—perhaps an ally. You wish to visit the Gran Seco, but your passports are unaccountably delayed. I might offer to take you to the Gran Seco, but not by Santa Ana and the Company's railway."

Archie pondered. "Everything in this country seems to turn on the Gran Seco," he said, "and we don't seem to be able to get there."

"It may be that that blunder of officialdom is doing you a service," said Don Luis solemnly.

"Well, I've no desire to go there and get tangled up in a local shindy, which I take it is what you are hinting at. I remember Mr Wilbur said that the miners seemed to be an ugly crowd. I'm very much obliged to you, Don Luis."

"You will not tell anyone that I have warned you."

"Certainly not. . . . I'm rather inclined to take your advice, and tell Gedd to drop the passport business. I didn't come here looking for trouble—and, besides, there's my wife."

But in this Archie was not wholly candid. He told himself that what he called a "dago revolution" had no charms for him, especially with Janet to take care of. But he realised that this phrase did not exhaust the mystery in Olifa, which had been slowly accumulating in his mind till the sense of it was like an atmosphere about him. Also he had taken a strong liking to Don Luis. The young man had a curious appeal in his alternate gaiety and gravity. There was that in him which seemed to beckon to wild and delightful things; he was such a companion as Archie a dozen years ago would have welcomed to ride with over the edge of the world. But Archie—*rangé,* married, lame of one leg—decided with a half-sigh that such visions and such comrades were no longer for him.

v

On their return to the city they were met by an incensed Don Alejandro. Not only had the permits for the Gran Seco not arrived, they had been definitely refused. It was not the work of the Government—this he had ascertained from his second cousin, the Minister for External Affairs. The refusal came from the Company itself, and Don Alejandro was positive that it was due to the interference of the American Consul. No doubt Wilbur had meant well, but apparently he had pressed the request so that the Company had assumed that he was its principal sponsor, and had naturally refused, since they thought they had done enough for his unpopular country by permitting the entrance of the party from the *Corinna.* There was no doubt about it. Don Alejandro had heard from a friend who was deep in the Company's affairs that Wilbur was the cause of the refusal.

To Janet's surprise Archie seemed rather relieved than otherwise. "Just as well, perhaps," he said. "We should probably have got fever or something, and we didn't come six thousand miles to look at a mining district. We have plenty of them at home."

He had not told Janet of Don Luis's warning, but he had brooded over it, and with his separation from the giver its good sense seemed to grow more convincing. Why on earth should Janet and he waste time in visiting a dusty plateau, even though it was the source of Olifa's prosperity and might have importance in Olifa's future politics? He would learn little in a hurried tour, and it wasn't his line to pick up gossip and go home and raise a racket in Parliament about Gran Seco atrocities. . . . They would go south to Cardanio and Alcorta, and might make a short trip into the mountains. The Twelve Apostles would bear inspection from closer quarters. . . . After that they would go home by Panama, and perhaps visit Jamaica. His mother's family had once owned big plantations there, established by an ancestor who had left the country hurriedly after Culloden.

So they fell back upon Olifa society, and Archie played polo daily at the club, and they gave a dinner at the hotel; and were just preparing to set out for Cardanio, when they were bidden to luncheon by no less a person than the President. A superb card of invitation, surmounted by the Olifa arms in gold, gave Archie the title of " Right Honourable," and designed Janet as the " Honourable Lady A. Roylance." Archie consulted Don Alejandro as to his garments, and was informed that the manners of Olifa were English and that they might both wear what they pleased. So Janet and he appeared at the President's mansion in their ordinary clothes, to find most of the men in evening dress with ribands and stars, and all the women in Paris hats and what looked like wedding gowns. Janet promptly had a fit of giggles, and it was a flushed and embarrassed pair who made their bow to the heavy, sallow, bull-necked Excelentisimo.

The day was hot, the place where they sat was as heavily upholstered as a Victorian dining-room, and the conversation had the languor of a ceremonial banquet. Janet, as the guest of honour, sat on the President's right hand, while Archie at the other end was sandwiched between a voluminous elderly woman who was the President's wife and a sleepy Frenchwoman whose husband was Don Alejandro's kinsman. His head had been confused by many introductions, but he had made out that kinsman, a Sanfuentes of the younger branch, and a tall man with a forked beard who was Aribia, the Minister of Finance. There was a vacant chair on Janet's right side.

The meal seemed interminable. The food was pretentiously good, and the guests seemed to have been starved for days, for they refused none of the dishes. Sweet champagne was served, and the Olifa Tokay, but when Archie, greatly daring, asked for a whisky-and-soda, it was brought him, and to his surprise was pre-War whisky. There seemed to be about twenty footmen, all in knee-breeches, mestizos who

in their gaudy liveries had an air of comic opera. Archie
tried his bad Spanish on his two ladies, and, having exhausted the beauties and greatness of Olifa, the distress of
Europe, their families, and his visit to Veiro, was hard
put to it for topics. Señora Sanfuentes received every
mention of Don Alejandro with a shrug and a giggle,
Madame la Présidente did not appear to have heard of him.

Suddenly there was a movement in the company. Someone had entered and taken the vacant chair by Janet's side.
The light in the room was very dim, and Archie saw only
a tall figure, to greet whom the President and the other
men rose and bowed. The man, whoever he was, was not
in evening dress. Later, he saw Janet's fair head inclined
towards him, and from the vivacity of her manner she
seemed to be finding interest in the new guest.

At last, with a marvellous course of fruits and sweet-
meats, the meal came to an end. The hostess rose
heavily and led the ladies from the room, and the men
moved up to a semi-circle round their host. Room was
made for Archie next to the President, and beyond that
impressive figure sat the late arrival. With a thrill he
recognised the man he had seen the first day leaving the
office in the Avenida, the great Señor Castor, the Gobernador of the province of the Gran Seco and the head of the
Company.

Huge cigars had been provided, but the Gobernador had
refused them, and, after asking his host's permission, had
lit a short briar pipe. It was some minutes before the
President formally introduced them, being himself engaged
in a whispered conversation, so Archie had the opportunity
to study the great man's features. Seen at close quarters
they were not less impressive than in the fleeting view
in the Avenida. The brow was broad and high, and had the
heavy frontal development above the eyebrows which
Archie had been told betokened mathematical genius.
The complexion was pale, but clear and healthy; the
nose short and finely formed, and springing from the
forehead like the prow of a ship. The mouth was hidden
by the beard, but it might be guessed that the lips were

full. The eyes were the compelling feature. They were large and grey and set rather wide apart, and, though narrow-lidded, gave their possessor an air of steady, competent watchfulness. There was thought in them, and masterfulness, but no hint of passion, only a calm, all-embracing intelligence. Among the beady opaque eyes around him, this man's were like pools of living light contrasted with scummed morasses. The face was grave and composed, but when Archie's name was spoken it broke into a curiously pleasant smile.

The Gobernador of the Gran Seco addressed him in flawless English. He inquired after his journey, spoke of the pleasure with which he had made Janet's acquaintance, and, on being informed by the President that Archie was a member of the British Legislature, asked one or two shrewd questions about current British politics. In five minutes' talk across the table he seemed to take soundings of Archie's mind, and elicited his special interests. He even detected his love of birds, and had something to say of the need for a sound ornithologist to investigate certain of the mountain areas. Archie had a feeling that this astonishing man, if he had been told that his hobby was marine zoology or Coptic antiquities, would have talked about it with the same intimate intelligence.

" You will visit us, I hope, in our little mountain kingdom. Perhaps you have heard of our Gran Seco? "

" I've heard about nothing else. But there's a hitch somewhere, and I've been told that we can't get passports for the present."

The Gobernador frowned.

" What incomprehensible folly! That is a matter which shall at once be set right. I cannot think how the mistake has arisen. Your hotel? The Constitución? Permits shall be sent round to you this afternoon, and you have only to fix the day of your journey and we shall make all arrangements. What must you think of us, Sir Archibald? Believe me, we are not accustomed to treat distinguished strangers with impoliteness."

The manner of the Gobernador was so open and

friendly that Archie's distaste for the Gran Seco and his memory of Don Luis's talk straightway vanished. The President observed that in old days the Gran Seco had been a closed country, and that, as Sir Archibald would realise, it could not be thrown open in a day.

"I am positive Sir Archibald will understand," said the Gobernador. "We have established, as it were, a Sheffield and a Birmingham in a rude hill-country, and we must limit our administrative problems. The sixteenth century and the twentieth can co-exist only if the latter is given in small doses. Slowly they will harmonise—but slowly. You have the same problem in your India. I understand that you do not permit tourists, however well accredited, even to enter some of the hill-states."

"That's true," said Archie. "When I was there, they wouldn't let me put a foot across the Nepaul border."

"Also we are a big business, with our secrets, and we cannot have agents of our rivals prowling about the place, which is, so to speak, all one workshop. But we welcome visitors who recognise our difficulties and submit to our modest rules."

"It is the Yanquis who give trouble," said the President darkly.

The Gobernador laughed. "Some Yanquis. I do not share his Excellency's distrust of the whole of that great nation. The bright special correspondent on the look-out for a 'scoop' is the most dangerous of created things. But we welcome the reasonable journalist. You may have read a series of articles on Olifa in the *Saturday Evening Post*. There you had the Gran Seco accurately portrayed with our full assent. Yet on the whole it is not the journalist who perplexes us most. It is the Yanqui tripper on a circular tour. We cannot have them making drunken fools of themselves in a place where the prestige of the white man is his only security."

"There was an American party at the hotel," said Archie. "Noisy young devils from a yacht. I think they went up to the Gran Seco a week ago."

The Gobernador shrugged his shoulders.

"We do not antagonise the great, we who are business men. But those young people will not be given the privileges which await you, Sir Archibald."

Archie felt as if he were being treated with especial frankness and friendliness, and his susceptible soul was in a pleasant glow. Then the conversation became general, and he had leisure to observe the company. The Gobernador said little, the Olifero statesmen much, but it seemed to Archie that they all talked under his eye and for his approbation. After an argument there came a hush, as if they deferred to him for the ultimate word. But he scarcely spoke. He sat silent, watchful, now and then smiling tolerantly. Once only he intervened. The Minister of Finance was discoursing on some aspect of the policy of the United States, and his comments were caustic. The Gobernador looked across at Archie and spoke in English.

"Yanquis are unpopular in England?" he asked.

"No. I shouldn't say that. Americans are popular with us, as they always have been. You see, we get the best of them. But the abstract thing, America, is unpopular. She always seems to have a rather left-handed Government."

A spark seemed to kindle in the other's eye.

"That is right. No section of humanity deserves blame. It is governments, not peoples, that offend."

Then the spark died out.

As Janet and Archie walked back to the hotel they spoke of the luncheon party. They had taken the road through the old town, and were in the market-place among the stalls.

"That man Castor doesn't belong here," said Archie. "He has nothing in common with those bland Oliferos. He's nearer to that lot," and he pointed to a group of Indians in shaggy ponchos squatted by the fountain.

"He is one of the most extraordinary people I ever met," said Janet. "Can you guess what he talked to me about? Ossian—Papa's *bête noire*, you know—Lord Balfour, and

Marcel Proust! And I believe he could have talked just as well about clothes and Paris models."

" I never in my life got so strong an impression of all-round competence. . . . I like him, too. I think he's a good fellow. Don't you? "

" I'm not so sure," said Janet. " I should like to see him clean-shaven. I've an idea that the mouth under that beard of his might be horribly cruel."

VI

THE Gran Seco has not often appeared in the world's literature. Francisco de Toledo first entered it in the sixteenth century, but after that there is no mention of it till Calamity Brown wandered thither from the coast in the late years of the eighteenth. That luckless and probably mendacious mariner has little good to say of it; it was the abode of devilish insects and devilish men, and, if we are to believe him, he barely escaped with his life. In the nineteenth century it was partially explored by the Spanish naturalist, Mendoza, and a Smithsonian expedition investigated its peculiar geology. Its later history is written in the reports of its copper companies, but Sylvester Perry visited it in his celebrated journey round the globe, and it has a short and comminatory chapter in his *Seeing Eyes*. Mr Perry did not like the place, and in his characteristic way has likened it to a half-healed abscess, sloughed over with unwholesome skin.

Mr Perry was partially right. The Gran Seco is not built to the scale of man and it has no care for his comforts. But it has its own magnificence. Its gate is the town of Santa Ana, in whose market-place stands the colossal figure of the crucified Christ, first erected by Pizarro, many times destroyed by earthquakes, and always replaced, since it is the defiance of the plains to the mountains. But the gate is far from the citadel, for the avenue is a hundred miles long. The Gran Seco railway, now a double line most skilfully engineered, and wholly controlled by the Company, runs first up a long valley where only in mid-winter a river flows. Then it passes over tiers of high desert, sinks into hollows where sometimes there are waters and forests, climbs again in tortuous gullies, till at length it emerges upon the great plateau; and always beside it can be traced the old highroad where once rode Toledo's men-at-arms, and only the other day the ore from the mines jolted down-country on mule-back. But there are still many miles to go before the city of Gran Seco is reached, sunk in a shallow trough among its barren and blistered hills.

At first sight Sylvester Perry's phrase seems to have a certain justice. Twenty years ago in the hollow there was only a wretched Indian puebla roosting among the ruins of an old city, for the copper from the distant mines was exported in its crude form. It was chiefly what is called virgin copper, with a certain amount of malachite and azurite ores. Ten years ago a new city began to rise, when the sulphuretted ores were first mined, and smelting was started. There was a furious rivalry among the companies till they were united in a great combine, and the whole mineral wealth gathered under a single direction. Process succeeded process, furnaces were multiplied till they covered many acres, wells were sunk and pumping-stations erected, great dams were built in the hills to catch the winter rains, and street after street rose in the dust. The Castor methods of calcination and electrolytic refining soon quadrupled its size. To one looking down from the surrounding ridges the place seems a hive of ugly activity: on one side a wilderness of furnaces and converters, with beyond them the compounds where the workmen are housed; on the other a modern city with high buildings and clanking electric trams. By day it is an inferno of noise and dust and vapours, with a dull metallic green the prevailing tint; by night a bivouac of devils warmed by angry fires. Mr Perry is right. The place has the look of a gangrening sore, with for the sur-rounding skin the pale shaley hills. And the climate is in itself a disease. In winter the hollow is scourged and frozen, and in summer the sun's heat, refracted from naked stone, strikes the face like a blow.

In the streets the first impression is of extreme orderliness. The traffic is methodically conducted by vigilant police in spruce uniforms—for the most part of the Indian or mestizo type, with European superintendents. They are a fine body of men; too good, the spectator decides, for such an environment. The main street, the Avenida Bolivar, is broad and paved with concrete, and along it rise structures which would not disgrace New York. The Regina Hotel is larger than the Ritz, and there are others; the offices of the Company's administration form a block scarcely smaller than Carlton House Terrace; there are clubs and many apartment houses, all built of the white local stone. But the shops are few and poor, and there are no villas in the environs, so that the impression grows that the Gran Seco is a camp, which its inhabitants regard as no continuing city. Hourly the sense of the bivouac expands in the traveller's mind. The place is one great caravanserai for pilgrims. These busy, preoccupied people are here for the day only and to-morrow will be gone.

Other things will soon strike him. There seem to be no peasants. No neighbouring countryside obtrudes itself into this monastic industry. Every man—there are few women— is regimented by the Company. If the traveller is escorted to the area of the smelting and refining plant (and his passports must be very high-powered to ensure this privilege), he will see the unskilled work done by Indians and mestizos—men with faces like mechanical automata—but the skilled foremen are all European. He will puzzle over these Europeans, for however wide his racial knowledge, he will find it hard to guess their nationality, since their occupation seems to have smoothed out all differences into one common type with a preoccupation so intense as to be almost furtive. In the streets, too, in the clubs and hotels, he will be struck by the waxwork look of some of the well-dressed employees. They are inhumanly pale, and so concentrated upon some single purpose that their faces are expressionless and their eyes unseeing.

He will be much shepherded and supervised, and, though his *permission de séjour* is for only a few days, he will be apt to find these days pass heavily.   If he is a mining expert, he will not be allowed to indulge his curiosity, for the Castor processes are jealously guarded.   If he is the ordinary tourist, he will find no sights to repay him, and for the only amusement an occasional concert of austerely classical music, given by the Administration staff.   He will probably leave the place with relief, glad to have seen the marvel, but thankful that his lines are cast among ordinary humanity. At the station, on his departure, he will be presented with a wonderful booklet, containing an eloquent speech of the Gobernador, and extracts (with illustrations) from the recent articles on the Gran Seco in the *Saturday Evening Post*.

The young party from the *Corinna* did not appear to find the time hang heavy on their hands.   There were ten of them, five of each sex, with no older person to look after them, though a very moderate chaperonage seemed to be exercised by a tall girl with fine eyes and a pleasant Southern voice.   That their purchase was considerable was shown by their entertainment, for they were shown everything and went everywhere; that they were unwelcome visitors, unwillingly privileged, was proved by their close oversight. Indeed they were uncomfortable guests, for they made a patch of garish colour in the drab of the Gran Seco and a discord in its orderly rhythm.   The mere sight of them in the streets was enough to send the ordinary policeman to the Commissary to ask for instructions.

They were patently harmless, but deplorably silly.   The Regina was turned by them into a cabaret.   They danced every night in the restaurant to the disquiet of the diners, and they chaffed mercilessly an unsmiling staff.   Bedroom riots seemed to be their speciality, and it was an unlucky official of the Company who had his quarters in their corridor.   When they were entertained to luncheon by the Administration they asked questions so sublimely idiotic that the Vice-President, a heavy sallow man, called Rosas, of Mexican extraction, actually coloured, thinking that he was being made a fool of; and their visit to the smelting plant was attended by the same exasperating buffoonery. Presently it appeared that their idiocy was congenital and not a pose. Their jazz chatter and jazz manners were the natural expression of jazz minds, and must be endured because of the prestige of Mr Burton Rawlinson. So " Baby " and " Bawby " and " Honey " and " Gerry " went their preposterous way, and the Gran Seco shrugged outraged shoulders and spat.

Nevertheless there were signs, had there been eyes to note them, that the yacht party was not quite what it seemed. In unguarded moments, as Janet had already observed, they could be betrayed into sanity and good breeding. At nights, too, when their ragging was over, there were odd discussions in the privacy of bedrooms. At least one of the young men would sit far into the dawn working at notes and plans.

Presently, as if they had had enough of the city, they extended their revels into the surrounding country. They procured two touring cars, and, after some trouble with the Commissary of Police, embarked on long excursions. The mines lie in three main groups—the San Tomé, the Alhuema, and the Universum—and they visited all three. There they seemed to find much to interest them, and the managers feverishly telephoned to headquarters for instructions. These children were imbeciles doubtless, they reported, but they were poking their noses into forbidden places. So on their return the troupe had to interview the Commissary of Police, who politely cautioned them against breaches of the regulations of the province.

Their next escapade was more serious. They packed luncheon-baskets and departed, as they said, for a visit to the caves of Marequito—a permitted excursion. Then for three days they disappeared, the police were furious and anxious, and a posse was sent out in motor-cars to discover their whereabouts. Six of the party—five girls and a man —and one of the cars were found two hundred miles off in a valley under the high peaks called the Spanish Ladies. They told a pitiful story; they had lost their road, exhausted their food, and had had to spend chilly nights on the ground. The other car had gone off the day before to find supplies, and had not returned.

The inspector of police wrung his hands. "Do you not know that in these parts the natives are dangerous? You have narrowly escaped throat-cutting." The party was sent back to the city in disgrace, but they did not seem to feel their position. They were inordinately cheerful, and scarcely looked as if they had suffered a three days' fast.

In spite of the police activity no word came of the other car, till two days later it returned brazenly of its own accord. The occupants told the same story—a lost road, a breakdown, semi-starvation, a lucky meeting in the end with an intelligent vaquero who put them on the way to the San Tomé mine. This party did indeed show some signs of privation, and one of the four men had his arm in a sling, the result, he said, of a fall from a rock when he was trying to get a prospect.

There was a stern inquiry at the office of the Commissary, and the four were closely cross-examined about their journey. But they proved to be bewildered and obtuse. Their accounts conflicted, and when maps were placed before them they were quite unable to point out their route. "Can't you realise that we were lost?" they repeated, "lost like a tick in a wood-pile? What d'you keep worrying about? It's no good quoting lists of your darned hills. We can't locate them."

After this episode the American party showed better behaviour. For the last days of their stay they confined themselves to the city, and got up a fancy-dress ball in the Regina, into which they dragged some of the unwilling residents. The young man with his arm in a sling did not appear at this function; indeed he did not leave his room, being a little fevered—so he told the hotel servants—by his accident, though he refused to see a doctor. This was perhaps natural, for in the small hours after his return there had been some rough surgery in his bedroom. One of his companions had cut out a pistol bullet from above his left elbow, and the tall girl, who had once nursed in a hospital, had done the bandaging.

Archie and Janet were very different visitors. It almost appeared as if they were welcome ones. A special coach was attached for them to the Santa Ana train, and this was shunted on to the Gran Seco line. It contained two compartments, in one of which they were given excellent meals, while the other was on the lines of an observation car, so filled with bridal flowers that Archie looked anxiously about for rice and slippers. They were also given a guide, a well-mannered young Olifero who unobtrusively offered information. He pointed out the objects of interest on the way to Santa Ana, and during the hour of waiting there conducted them over the cathedral, which has a famous altar-piece, and, under the great crucifix, told with pride the tale of the first Conquistadors. The long climb into the Gran Seco was enlivened by his anecdotes. He showed them the valley where Toledo's men had been ambushed by Indians, the corner where the copper convoy had once been destroyed by a landslide, the gully which had long defied the railway engineers. At the frontier station he had managed their passes for them, and as the train crawled on to the plateau had sketched for them vivaciously the history of the mining industry.

"We can't tip this fellow," Archie whispered to Janet. "He's a gentleman." And his wife had agreed.

He saw them to their hotel, where rooms had been secured for them by the Administration. On parting, Archie and Janet warmly thanked him, and asked him his name. The young man smiled pleasantly. "That is nice of you, for I think we shall meet again. They call me Carlos Rivero." He added, "I am a friend of Luis de Marzaniga," and it seemed to Archie that his eyes said something confidential which he could not fathom.

The Moplahs were in the hotel, but in a somewhat chastened mood. The tall girl, whom Janet believed she had recognised, did not appear, nor did the young man in the starched linen knickerbockers, though Archie looked for him longingly. But the corybants of the Club de Residentes

Extranjeros were there and greeted them with boisterous friendliness, though, somewhat to Janet's surprise, they did not invite them to join their party.

In any case that would have been impossible, for the newcomers found a complex programme provided for their entertainment. They had no occasion to hire a car: the Administration provided one, a neat Daimler limousine which at all hours waited on their convenience. They were shown every phase of the great industry, and the day after their arrival they lunched with the Administration. The Gobernador himself appeared at the meal, an honour which, it was hinted, was almost unexampled. He apologised for the absence of the Vice-President, the same who had been made to blush by the Moplahs. " My colleague," he said, " sends his profound apologies, but at the moment he is suffering from a slight attack of jaundice. He deeply regrets that he cannot be here to welcome you, for he has many friends in your country and in Europe. He is of Mexico, and a Mexican is like a Russian—his country is so remote from the life of the world that he must needs adopt all countries. He is the true international."

The meal was a Spartan one compared to the banquet at the President's mansion, but the food was perfectly cooked, and, for a place in the heart of wild hills, extraordinarily varied. The company were all grave, pallid, perfectly mannered, with expressionless eyes and no gestures—what Don Alejandro had called the *type Gran Seco*. There was nothing of the hustling liveliness which Archie associated with a luncheon of commercial magnates. Also all seemed to be in awe of their President, and hung on his lips. Castor talked indeed, brilliantly and continuously, but it was a monologue, and he went through a series of subjects, adorning each and then dropping it. There was none of the give-and-take of good conversation. Yet the time passed pleasantly, and when they rose from table Castor offered to show them his office.

It was on the first floor of the main building, lit by four large windows, into which travellers on the top of the tram-cars could look and see the great man at his work. Here there was no seclusion or mystery. The big bright chambers gave its occupant no more privacy than an aviary gives a bird, for not only could it be looked into from the street, but at one end was a glass partition separating it inadequately from a room full of busy secretaries. There were maps and plans of the Gran Seco on the walls, a complicated mechanism of desk telephones, a bookcase full of mining reports, an immense safe, a cigar cabinet—and that was all. It might have been the office of a real-estate agent in a provincial town in the United States or Canada. The contrast between Castor's personality and his modest habitation was so startling that Janet laughed.

The Gobernador seemed to understand her feelings. " I have other lairs," he said, smiling. " One, much grander, is in Olifa, and I have my rooms too in Paris and London. But this is my true workshop."

He opened a door, which revealed a tiny bedroom and bathroom.

" Compact, is it not? " he said. " I need no more. I am a simple man."

That night Archie and Janet dined in the hotel with the Financial Secretary, and afterwards went to hear Beethoven performed by a string quartet in the music-room of the Gran Seco Club. When they returned to their apartments, Archie was loud in his praises of his hosts.

" Odd, isn't it? to find Castilian manners in business grandees! We didn't find them at Veiro, for old Sanfuentes was just like the ordinary country gentleman at home. But these fellows here are all hidalgos. I feel noisy and rather vulgar among them. And, good Lord! what must they think of the Moplahs?

" Castor too! " he went on. " What rot it was Gedd and Wilbur making him out a mystery man! He's an extra-ordinarily clever fellow, but as open as the day. A mystery man couldn't live in a place like a cricket pavilion!"

" Did you ever read a poem called ' How it strikes a Contemporary'? Browning, you know."

" No," said Archie.

" Well, the poem is all about a tremendous mystery man —the Corregidor, Browning calls him—and he lived in just such a way as Mr Castor. How does it go?—

> *' Poor man, he lived another kind of life*
> *In that new stuccoed third house by the bridge,*
> *Fresh-painted, rather smart than otherwise!*
> *The whole street might o'erlook him as he sat*
> *Leg crossing leg—and——'*

I can't remember it all, but anyhow he played cribbage every night with his housekeeper and went to bed punctually at ten."

Their permit for the Gran Seco had specified no time-limit. For two days they explored the details of the industry, were conducted through vast laboratories, studied the latest type of furnace and converter, pored over blue prints in offices, and gave themselves vile headaches. Archie declared that the smelting works were like the Ypres Salient after a gas attack. He tried to be intelligent, but found himself gravely handicapped by his lack of all scientific knowledge. " I have had the meaning of a reverberatory furnace explained to me a dozen times," he complained, "but I'm hanged if I can keep it in my head. And what Bessemerising is remains for me one of Allah's secrets. It's no good, Janet, this isn't my pidgin. Thank God, we're going to the Mines to-morrow. I think that should be more in my line."

They were taken to the Mines through a sad grey country, a desert of shale and rock. "Calcined," Archie called it, having just acquired that word, and Janet said that she supposed it must be like the landscapes in the moon. Every stream-course was bone-dry, and the big dams they passed, with the green water very low in their beds, only accentuated the desiccation. Yet, where wells had been sunk, the soil was not without fertility, and the thin grasses seemed to give a living to considerable flocks of sheep and goats. They passed many ruins—not only old mine workings, but the remains of Indian villages, which suggested that at one time the Gran Seco had been a more habitable country.

At the Mines they were shown little, for there was little time. Managers were ready with sheafs of statistics, and at the Universum they lunched luxuriously. But of the miners at work they saw nothing. They returned invigorated by the keen air of the steppes, and Archie, who had caught from a ridge a glimpse of the snowy peaks of the Spanish Ladies, had had his appetite whetted for further travel. But the Administration was not encouraging. That was all Indian country—policed, it was true, for it was the chief recruiting-ground of labour, but not open to ordinary travel. " We could send you there," said an urbane secretary, " but you would have to take an escort, and you would have to submit to be treated like a schoolboy. You will understand, Sir Archibald, that this Gran Seco of ours is in parts a delicate machine, and the presence of ever so little extraneous matter might do harm."

That evening after dinner Janet and Archie were in their sitting-room. The Regina was full of the preparations for departure of the Moplahs, who were going down-country by the night train, and their shrill cries could be heard in the corridor, since their rooms were on the same floor.

" We're extraneous matter here," said Archie. " What about it, Janet? They've given us a very good show, but I'm disillusioned about the Gran Seco. Wilbur must have been pulling my leg. The place is as humdrum as the Potteries, and just about as ugly. I should have liked to have had a shot at the high mountains, but I can see their reason for not encouraging visitors in their labour reserve. I rather like the crowd—they behave well and they must be the last word in efficiency. . . . Confound those Moplahs! This is like living beside a hen-coop!"

Janet looked serious, and, as was her way in such a mood, she sat with her hands idle in her lap.

" Let's get away from this place," she said. " I hate it!"

" Why in the world . . . ? "

" I hate it. Those soft-spoken, solemn men have got on my nerves. I think there's something inhuman about them. Most of the faces of the people at the smelting works and at the Mines were like masks. . . . And at that awful

luncheon! . . . I believe that sometimes I saw the devil
grinning out from behind them. . . . And in the streets.
I saw one or two villainous ruffians, who should have been
in rags, but were as spruce as bagmen. I felt as if I
were in an orderly and well-policed Hell. . . . Why did
they shepherd us away from the Mines, for remember we
saw nothing there? Why won't they let us go into the
back country? I believe it is because they are concealing
something, something so bad that the world must never
know of it."

Archie stared.

" I must say you've got a lively imagination," he began,
but Janet was not listening.

" Let us go away—at once—to-morrow morning. I
should like to be going to-night. . . . Ring up the Administration and say we must get home in a hurry. . . . I think
there's something infernal about this big, noiseless machine.
I want to be back at Veiro, where there are human beings.
I want to be with the honest silly little Moplahs. I want
something more peaceful. . . ."

" I should have thought that the Gran Seco was more
peaceful than the Moplahs."

" No, it isn't, for there is death here and death is un-
settling."

" Well, we'll go off to-morrow, if you wish it. We're
not likely to want for peace in the next few weeks. The
thing is how to avoid boredom. . . . By the way, oughtn't
we to go downstairs and say good-bye to the Americans?
They're friendly souls."

But Janet was in a strange mood. " You go. I don't
think I'll come." She still sat with her hands in her lap,
looking straight before her.

But the Americans were already packed into the station
omnibus, and Archie could only shout to them from the
doorway, and receive in return blown kisses from the ladies
and hand-waves from the men. They seemed to be waiting
for a member of their party, and as Archie turned into the
hall he met the laggard charging through the crowd of
waiters and porters. It was the one who had not yet shown

himself, and Archie realised that it must be the driver of the car in the Avenida de la Paz, the youth in the linen knickerbockers.   What his present clothes were could not be guessed, since he wore a tweed ulster, but he had the same preposterous, broad-brimmed hat on his head.

To his surprise the young man, whom he had never met, made straight for him, and gave him his hand.   Something passed from it, and Archie's fist held a crumpled paper.

The next second he was gone, but not before Archie had had another shock.   For this was not the youth of the Avenida de la Paz.   It was Don Luis de Marzaniga, and in their moment of contact his eyes had looked into his and they had commanded silence.

Deeply mystified, Archie went upstairs with the paper pellet tight in his fingers.   When his door closed behind him, he opened it.   The scrap contained a scrawl in pencil in a large, irregular hand.   It read: *" Please be both in your sitting-room at eleven o'clock."*

He showed it to Janet.

" I said there was no mystery in the Gran Seco, but it seems I spoke too soon.   I'm hanged if I can make it out. It was Luis that gave me this paper, but it was Luis pretending to be that American lad in the linen knickerbockers. You remember he was the one of the Moplahs we never saw."

" We never saw the tall girl either.   I am positive that she was Miss Dasent."   Janet looked at her wrist-watch. " Eleven, the note said.   A quarter of an hour to wait."

That quarter of an hour was spent by Janet in the same contemplative immobility, while Archie tried to read, smoked two cigarettes feverishly, and occupied a few minutes in washing his hands.   The bedroom opened from the sitting-room, and beyond it was the bathroom which he used as a dressing-room.   He was just about to begin a third cigarette when he saw that the hands of the sham ormolu clock on the mantelpiece pointed to eleven.   After that he kept his eyes on the door which led to the corridor.

But that door did not open.   It was an exclamation from Janet that made him turn his head.

A waiter had appeared suddenly, entering from the bedroom. He carried a tray with three cups of maté, which he placed on the table at Janet's elbow.

"Look here, you've made a mistake," Archie said in his halting Spanish. "We gave no orders."

The man replied in English.

"Didn't you? All the same, you'd be the better for a cup. I'm going to have one myself. You might lock that door, Archie, and give me a cigarette."

While Archie stared thunderstruck, Janet laughed—a laugh which began as a low gurgle and ended in riotous merriment. She rose from her chair and stood before the waiter, her shoulders shaking, while she dabbed her small handkerchief on her eyes. Then, suddenly, she became grave. "You have been having a rough time, Sandy," she said, and she laid a hand on his shoulder. He winced, and drew back.

"So-so," he said. "That arm is still tender. . . . What malign fate brought the pair of you here?"

The waiter was to all appearance an ordinary mestizo, sallow-skinned, with shaggy dark hair, handsome after a fashion because of his pleasant eyes. He wore ill-fitting dress trousers, a shirt not too clean, a short alpaca jacket, and slippers rather down at heel. He smiled on Janet as he poured out the maté, and then from Archie's case he took a cigarette.

"Yes. I want to know just how you managed it," he continued. "Wilbur did his best to prevent you, and Luis told me he thought he had dissuaded you, and in spite of everything you bubble up. You're an incorrigible pair!"

"But why shouldn't we come here if we want?" Janet asked.

"Because it's deadly danger—for yourselves and for others. You go to lunch with the Administration, and the Vice-President hears of it just in time to have a touch of jaundice. You blunder into this hotel, and I can only save myself by making this assignation. You two innocents have been complicating my life."

Enlightenment broke in on Archie. "You were the bounder in the linen bags—the fellow that drove the car."

" I was. You were within an ace of recognising me, if I hadn't tilted my hat."

" Then what was Luis doing, got up in your rig? "

" He took my passport. This is a country of passports, you know, much more efficient than anything we had in the war zone in France. He came into the Gran Seco by a back door, and so didn't require one. But it was essential that mine should be used and that I should be believed to be out of the place. It was equally essential that I should remain here."

" How did you manage your present camouflage? "

The waiter looked down with pride at his spotty shirt. " Rather successful, isn't it? I have a bit of a graft in this line. My weeks in the Café de l'Enfer were not altogether wasted."

He finished his maté and lit a cigarette. He looked at the two before him, Janet with her girlish wind-blown grace, Archie with his puzzled honesty, and he suddenly ceased to be a waiter. His brows bent, and his voice from friendly banter became the voice of authority.

" You must clear out at once," he said. " To-morrow morning. Do you know that you are walking gaily on a road which is mined in every yard? "

" I knew it," said Janet. " I felt in my bones that this place was accursed."

" You don't know it. You cannot know just how accursed it is, and I have no time to explain. What I have to tell you is that you must go down to Olifa to-morrow morning. You will be encouraged to stay longer, but you must refuse."

" But look here, Sandy "—it was Archie who spoke— " they have nothing against us. Janet and I can't be in any danger."

" No, but you are a source of danger to others. Myself, for example, and the Vice-President, Señor Rosas."

" Rosas—I never heard of him."

" A very pleasant Mexican gentleman. You once knew him as Mr Blenkiron."

"Good Lord! But he's dead!"

"He is officially dead. That is why it won't do for him to meet old friends."

"Sandy dear," said Janet, "you mustn't treat us like this. We're not babies. We'll do what you tell us, but we deserve more confidence."

The waiter compared his Ingersoll watch with the sham ormolu clock.

"Indeed, you do, but the story would take hours, and I have only three minutes left. But I will tell you one thing. Do you remember my showing you at Laverlaw the passage in the chronicle about the Old Man of the Mountain, the King of the Assassins, who lived in the Lebanon, and doped his followers with hashish and sent them about the world to do his errands? Well, that story has a counterpart to-day."

"Mr Castor!" Janet exclaimed. "Archie liked him, but I felt that he might be a devil."

"A devil! Perhaps. He is also a kind of saint, and he is beyond doubt a genius. You will know more about him some day."

"But you are sending us away. . . . Sandy, I won't have it. We are too old friends to be bundled off like stray dogs from a racecourse. You are in some awful pickle and we must help."

"I am sending you away," said the waiter gravely, "because I want your help—when the time comes. There's another woman in this business, Janet, and I want you to be with her. I want you both. I pay you the compliment of saying that I can't do without you. You will go back to Olifa to the Hotel de la Constitución, and you will make friends with an American girl there. She is expecting you and she will give you your instructions."

"I know," said Janet. "She is Mr Blenkiron's niece—a Miss Dasent. What is her Christian name?"

The waiter looked puzzled. "I'm afraid I don't know. I never asked her."

VII

THE waiter at the Regina was an exemplary servant. He dispensed the morning meal of fruit and coffee with soft-footed alacrity. At the mid-day déjeuner, when it was the custom of the Company's officials, including some of the greatest, to patronise the hotel, he had the big round table in the north window, and in a day or two had earned the approval of his fastidious clients. Miguel was his name, and presently he was addressed by it as if he had been an old feature of the establishment. Those solemn gentlemen talked little, and at their meals they did not ransack the wine-list or summon the cook, but each had his little peculiarities of taste which Miguel made it his business to remember. He was always at their elbow, smiling gravely, to anticipate their wants. In the evening the restaurant was less full, only the guests living in the hotel and a few junior officials, for it was the custom of the magnates to dine at the club. In the evening Miguel was frequently off duty in the restaurant, engaged in other branches of hotel work, and twice a week he had his time after 7 p.m. to himself.

The waiter did not spend his leisure hours in his attic bedroom, which was like an oven after the sun had beat all day on the slatted roof. Once or twice he joined his fellow-employees in a visit to the cinema or to a shabby little gaming-room where one drank cheap aguardiente and played a languid kind of poker. But generally he seemed to have business of his own, and the negro porter at the back entrance grew familiar with his figure arriving punctually on the stroke of midnight, and chaffed him heavily about an imaginary girl. It was no one's business to keep a watch on this humble half-caste, whose blood showed so clearly in his shadowy finger-nails and dull yellow skin. But if he had been followed, curious things might have been noted. . . .

He generally made for a new block of flats on the edge of the dry hollow which separated the smelting works from the city, and he frequently varied his route thither. The place, with its concrete stairs and white-washed walls, was not unlike a penitentiary, but it housed many of the works engineers and foremen. He would stop at a door on the third landing, consult his watch as to the hour, wait a minute or two, and then knock, and he was instantly admitted. Thence he would emerge in half an hour, generally accompanied by someone, and always in a new guise. Sometimes he was a dapper Olifero clerk with a spruce collar and an attaché case; sometimes in rough clothes with big spectacles, so that his former half-caste air disappeared, and he might have been an engineer from Europe; sometimes a workman indistinguishable from an ordinary hand in the furnaces. He always returned to the same door about half past eleven, and issued from it once more the waiter at the Regina.

Between the hours of 7.30 and 11 p.m. the waiter seemed to have a surprising variety of duties. Occasionally he would pass the evening in one of the flats, or in a room in another block which adjoined the costing department. There he would meet silent people who slipped in one by one, and the conversation would be in low tones. Maps and papers would lie on the table, and there would be much talk of the names on certain lists, and notes would be pencilled alongside them. Sometimes there would be a colloquy of one or two, and then the waiter would do most of the talking—but not in Spanish. Sometimes the meeting would be at a café in a back street, which could only be entered by devious ways, and there, over glasses of indifferent beer, the waiter would make new acquaintances. His manners were odd, for he would regard these newcomers as a sergeant regards recruits, questioning them with an air of authority. There were strange ceremonies on these occasions, so that the spectator might have thought them meetings of some demented Masonic lodge. Sometimes, too, the waiter in one of the rooms of the big block of flats would meet a figure with the scorched face of a countryman and the dust of the hills on his clothes—often in the uniform of the Mines Police and once or twice dressed like a

mestizo farmer.   Then the talk would be hard to follow—
strings of uncouth names, torrents of excited description,
and a perpetual recourse to maps.

But the waiter's most curious visits—and they happened
only twice during his time at the Regina—were to a big
house behind the Administration Headquarters, which stood
in what for the Gran Seco was a respectable garden.   At
such times the waiter became the conventional clerk, very
dapper in a brown flannel suit, yellow boots, and a green
satin tie with a garnet pin. He was evidently expected, for,
on giving his name, he was admitted without question, and
taken to a little room on the first floor which looked like
the owner's study. " Señor Garcia from the Universum "—
thus he was ushered in, and the occupant greeted him
gruffly with " Come along, Garcia. Say, you're late. Have
you brought the figures I asked for? "—followed by the
injunction to the servant, " I can't be disturbed for the
next two hours, so I guess you'd better disconnect the telephone. If anyone calls, say I'm mighty busy."

Then the occupant of the room would lock the door and
pay some attention to the windows, after which he would
greet the waiter like a long-lost brother.   He was a big
man, with a sallow face but a clear healthy eye—a man who
looked as if he would have put on flesh but for some specially
arduous work which kept him thin.   He would catch the
so-called Garcia by the shoulder as if he would hug him,
then he would pat his back, and produce such refreshments
as are not usually offered to a junior clerk. Strangely
enough, there would be no mention of the awaited figures
from the Universum.

" How much longer can you stick it? " he asked on the
second occasion. " You're looking peaked."

" I've another week here. Then I break for the open.
I doubt if I could keep it up for more than a week, for
people are asking questions. Have you squared it with old
Josephs and notified the Universum people "

The big man nodded.   " But after that you're beyond my
jurisdiction. Peters in the Police is prepared for you, but
it's up to you to slip over to him without exciting comment.

The cook-boy at the Universum has got to perish. Can you manage that neatly?"

"I'll try. I'll have to do a lot of perishing in the next fortnight, before Luis picks me up. I'm terrified of going sick, you know. The Regina hasn't done me any good, and the Tierra Caliente isn't exactly a health-resort."

The other looked at him with affectionate anxiety.

"That's too bad. . . . I haven't an easy row to hoe, but yours is hell with the lid off, and the almighty vexation is that I can't do much to help you. Just at present the game's with you. For the love of Mike keep on your feet, sonnie. You don't mean to go far into the Poison Country?"

"Not a yard farther than I can help. But Luis says I must be at least a couple of days there. Don't worry. I'll take care of myself."

After that the conversation was conducted in low tones, as if even the locked door and the guarded window might have ears. But had that talk been overheard, one phrase would have puzzled the eavesdropper, a phrase which constantly recurred and was spoken by both with a certain hesitation, even in that secret room. It was "Los Patios de la Mañana," which, being translated, means "The Courts of the Morning." It might have been a mere password, or the name of some authority to which the speaker was subject, or a poetic description of a place. Most likely the last, for a map was produced—an amateur map neatly drawn and coloured, inscribed not with names but with letters. It showed steep gradients, so it must have referred to some mountain district.

At their parting the Roylances were mentioned. "They're back in Olifa," said the big man, "and Babs is looking after them good and sure. I'm mighty relieved that Babs has got a wise lady to keep her company. You're certain you can make use of Sir Archibald?"

"I can use him right enough," was the answer, "if he'll stay quiet on the ice till I want him."

A week later the waiter Miguel was seen no more at

the Regina. When the occupants of the big table in the north window inquired of M. Josephs, the proprietor, as to his absence, they were told that he had been lent to the mess at the Universum Mine.

Miguel was four days at the Universum. He had a variety of tasks, for not only did he wait at table in the big adobe mess-room, but he lent a hand in the kitchen, for he was the soul of friendliness. Indeed he carried his willingness too far, for he was found in the kitchens of the compounds, where the Indian miners were fed like pigs at troughs, and was peremptorily ordered back. He had little leisure these days, but he managed to do various things not quite within the sphere of his duties. For one thing, he became intimate with the engineering staff, which contained two Scots, one American, and three Italians, and he used to gossip with them at their table when the room emptied at the end of meals. Also he was found sometimes in their office among blue prints and specimens of ore, and on these occasions the door happened to be locked. If he was not permitted inside the compounds, he used to fossick about the mines themselves, when the shifts of sallow, hollow-eyed labourers were going up or down. Occasionally he talked to them when no overseer was at hand, and he seemed to know something of their *patois,* for they replied, furtively, and once or twice volubly, when no one was looking.

The cheerful inquisitiveness of the mess waiter was his undoing. For on the evening of the fourth day there was a sad accident. Through a mysterious blunder a small packet of lentonite was detonated, and a corner of the compound wall was blown down and a great crater made in the earth. For some inexplicable reason Miguel seemed to have been in the neighbourhood at the time and he was the only casualty. Fragments of his clothing were found, and a bit of a hat which he was known to be wearing, and it was assumed that his remains were dispersed among the two acres of debris. The fatality was duly reported to the Administration and to M. Josephs, and the agreeable half-caste waiter ceased to be on the register of the Gran Seco.

Next morning a certain Featherstone Peters, a captain of the Mines Police, whose station was ten miles or so from the Universum, introduced at breakfast to his troopers a new recruit, who had just arrived to report. Peters was a tough, grizzled fellow of fifty, who had fought for the Boers in the South African War, had been in the old Macedonian gendarmerie, and was believed by his friends to have done a good deal of gun-running in Morocco. The new recruit, whose name was Black, was a sallow youngish man, who looked as if he had fever in his blood. He spoke English fluently but ungrammatically, and gave out that his father had been in the Italian Consulate at Alexandria. He was good company, and entertained the men with yarns which enthralled even that collection of hard citizens.

For the next week Black was engaged on patrols far up into the Indian country. The map * shows that east of the city of Gran Seco lies the land of rolling desert hills where the copper is mined, but beyond that the traveller enters a region of deep-cut desiccated valleys—a plateau, but with the contours of highlands. It is the Indian territory, whence the Mines' labourers are drawn, a place of sparse tillage but much pasturage, a place, too, which in recent centuries has been drying up, since the wretched pueblas are often on the site of what, from the ruins, must once have been considerable cities. It is called the Tierra Caliente, for there is little shade from a merciless sun, and the stages are long from water to water. The midday heat falls like a suffocating curtain, and does not lift till night arrives with the speed of a wind from the far snows.

It was patrol not escort duty, but the new recruit saw many of his fellow-policemen engaged in the latter task. The processions of labourers had the melancholy of a funeral cortege, and Black, who was well-read for one in his position, was reminded of the pictures of the Zanzibar slave-caravans in old books of African travel. It was a sight which visitors to the Gran Seco were not allowed to see, for there were no permits for the Indian country. The gangs bound for the Mines were not shackled, but they

* See map on end-papers.

were closely shepherded by armed police escorts, and the faces of the men showed every degree of sullen and hopeless ferocity. But the gangs returning from the Mines to the villages were a spectacle to send a man to his prayers. "Returned empties," Peters called them. Young men crawled and tottered like dotards, all were terribly emaciated, their eyes had lost every human quality and had the blank impassiveness of beasts. Yet the Mines were a business concern, famed for feeding their workers well and for utilising the latest scientific conclusions on hygiene and industrial fatigue. Had not the intelligent press of America and Europe borne testimony to their progressiveness?

As Black and Peters watched one gang pass, the latter spat vigorously and observed: " I've never taken stock in all that meeting-house stuff about individual liberty and the rights of man. But I guess there may be something in it. That outfit kind of makes one think."

Black said nothing, but his bright feverish eyes seemed to miss little. He was obviously on good terms with his officer, for he was constantly going off on little journeys of his own, which could scarcely be interpreted as police duty. These journeys took him generally into the Indian pueblas, and on two occasions he did not return to the police bivouac till the following day. He was obviously a sick man, and when the patrol reached the limit of its journey, Peters was heard to complain loudly that the new recruit should be in hospital. By this time they were nearing the eastern edge of the Indian country, with the peaks of the Cordilleras within a day's march. The land was changing, for they had come to a watershed. The line of the great mountains was not the watershed, for, as in the case of the Nepaul Himalaya, they stood a little beyond it. It was a country of running waters, and the streams flowed east, cutting a path through the range in deep gorges on their way to the distant Orazon.

They arrived at a ruined village of mud where a couple of Indians had made their camp—hunters they seemed, tall active fellows of a different stamp from the broken men of the pueblas. Peters appeared to know them, for he called them by their names, and addressed them in pidgin Spanish which they understood. That night he told his troopers that the patrol was ended. He had been instructed to report on this eastern frontier of the Gran Seco, and next morning they would turn back. All to the east, he told them, was a God-forgotten country, which nature and man had combined to make unhealthy for Christians. He asked questions of the Indians and expounded their replies. There was fever there, and much poison, and very bad men, and valleys so deep that from the bottom one could see by day the stars and the moon. The troopers were impressed, and looked anxiously at the menacing mountain wall, with its coronal of snowfields now rosy in the after-glow.

But next morning Black was in no state to travel. Peters condemned the cussedness of things and declared that he could not afford to wait another hour. He was not unkind, and he did his best to ease the sufferer, but duty was duty and his called him back to headquarters. Black must be made as comfortable as possible, and the two Indians, whom he knew to be trustworthy, would look after him till the bout of fever had passed, and put him on his way home. After breakfast the patrol jingled off up the slope, and left Black wrapped in a foxskin kaross, drowsing in a corner of the ruins, while the Indians twenty yards off sat hunched and meditative beside their brushwood fire.

Black was really sick, but not with malaria. His vitality had run down like a clock, since too much had been demanded of it, and his trouble was partly a low nervous fever, and partly a deep fatigue. When the police had been gone an hour, the two Indians held a consultation on his case. Then they proceeded to strange remedies. They seemed to be friends of his, for he grinned when they bent over him and submitted readily to their ministrations. The country was volcanic, and close at hand, hidden in a crinkle of the hills, a hot sulphur spring bubbled from the rocks. They undressed him, and carried him, wrapped in the kaross, to the pool, where they plunged him into the most violent bath which he had ever encountered. Then they dried him roughly with a fine leather poncho, and rubbed the skin of his back and chest with an aromatic ointment. After that one of them massaged him for the space of an hour, a cunning massage which seemed to remould flaccid muscles and adjust disordered nerves and put him into a state of delicious stupor. Lastly, he was given a bitter brew to drink, and then permitted to sleep. This he proceeded to do for eighteen hours, and when he awoke in broad daylight the following morning his head was cool and his eye was clear, though he was still shaky on his feet. Peters had left enough provisions, and he ate the first enjoyable meal he had known for weeks.

There was another figure at breakfast, a fair young man with a golden-brown skin, who, judging by the dust on his boots and breeches, had ridden far that morning.

" My felicitations, Señor," the newcomer said.   " I do not think you have taken any hurt in the last weeks, and that is a miracle. But where we are now going we must go on our feet, and for that you are not yet able. I am in command for the moment, and my orders are that to-day you rest."

So Black slept again and awoke in the afternoon with a most healthy hunger.   The newcomer sat by him and rolled and smoked many cigarettes, but he would not permit the patient to talk. " Time enough, my friend. We do not part company for a little while. But I will show you this to cheer you."

He exhibited a small tinsel medal, such as humble pilgrims purchase at some famous shrine.   On one side it bore a face which was clearly that of the Gobernador of the Gran Seco.

Black puzzled over it, for he was still dazed, and asked whose was the head.

" It is that of our noble leader," the young man laughed. " Yours and mine—he who is to lead this unhappy people to freedom."

Black seemed to see the obscure joke, for he too laughed.

" Jesucristo! " said the young man, " but that is a chief to fight for! "

VIII

BLACK slept soundly all night, and next morning rose renewed in body and mind. The party set out down the glen of the stream, one of the Indians carrying food and blankets, while the other remained behind with the horses. Black had his pistol, but he had left his police carbine at the bivouac, while the newcomer had no weapon at all. "What do I want with a gun?" he had said lightly in reply to his companion's question. "We are going into the Poison Country —El País de Venenos—where lead and powder are trivial things. A gun is of as little use as a single lifebelt would be to a man proposing to cross the Atlantic in a skiff. We are now in the hands of the older gods."

It was a strange land which they entered, when the stream which they were descending plunged into the shadow of the high peaks. It was fed by many affluents, and presently became a considerable river, running in a broad grassy vale on which the dew lay like hoar-frost. Suddenly the hills closed in like a wall, and the stream leaped in a great spout into a profound ravine, where in pot-holes and cascades it poured its way from shelf to shelf of the mountain ribs. The sides of the glen were cloaked with bush, which in the lower levels became tall timber trees. In the woody recesses the freshness went out of the air, mosses and creepers muffled the tree-trunks, gaudy birds and butterflies flitted through the branches, and a hot, headachy languor seemed to well out of the sodden ground.

The party, guided by the Indian, kept high above the stream, following paths no wider than a fox's track. As they advanced they descended, the ravine opened, and from a promontory they looked into a great cup among the cliffs, brimming with forest, with above on the periphery the hard bright line of the snows. Black, who was apparently something of a scholar, quoted Latin. It was a sight which held the two men breathless for a moment. Then Luis shook his head. "It is beautiful, but devilish," he said. "The malevolence rises like a fog," and Black nodded assent.

They found themselves in an eery world, as if they were sunk deep in a hot sea. Moisture streamed from every twig and blade and tendril, and a sickening sweetness, like the decaying vegetation of a marsh, rose from whatever their feet crushed. Black remarked that it was like some infernal chemist's shop. Under the Indian's direction they took curious precautions. Each man drew on leather gauntlets which strapped tight on the wrist. Each shrouded his face and neck with what looked like a fine-meshed mosquito-curtain. Also they advanced with extreme caution. The Indian would scout ahead, while the other two waited in the sweltering vapour-bath. Then he would return and lead them by minute tracks, now climbing, now descending, and they followed blindly, for in that steaming maze there was neither prospect nor landmark.

That there was need for caution was shown by one incident. The Indian hurriedly drew them off the trail into the cover of what looked like a monstrous cactus, and from their hiding-place they watched four men pass with the softness of deer. Three were Indians, not of the pueblas in the Tierra Caliente, for they were tall and lean as the Shilluks of the Upper Nile. The fourth was a white man in shirt and breeches, gauntleted and hooded, and his breeches were the type worn by the Mines Police. But he was not an ordinary policeman, for, as seen under the veil, his face had the pallor and his eyes the unseeing concentration of the magnates of the Gran Seco.

Black looked inquiringly at Luis, who grinned behind his mosquito-mask. "One of the Conquistadors," he whispered, and the other seemed to understand.

In that long, torrid day the party neither ate nor drank. Just before nightfall they descended almost to the floor of the cup, where they were within hearing of the noise of the river. Here they moved with redoubled caution. Once they came out on the stream bank, and Black thought that he had never seen stranger waters. They were clear, but with purple glooms in them, and the foam in the eddies was not the spume of beaten water, but more like the bubbling of molten lead. Then they struck inland, climbed a tortuous gully, and came into a clearing where they had a glimpse of a cone of snow flaming like a lamp in the sunset.

The place was cunningly hidden, being a little mantel-piece between two precipitous ravines—on the eyebrow of a cliff, so that from below it was not suspected—and protected above by a screen of jungle. An empty hut stood there, and the Indian proceeded to make camp. A fire was lit in a corner, and water from the nearest rivulet put on to boil. It might have been a Jewish feast, for all three went through elaborate purification ceremonies. Food had been brought with them, but no morsel of it was touched till the hands of each had been washed with a chemical solution. The food-box was then sealed up again as carefully as if it were to be cached for months. The hut floor was swept, and before the bedding was laid down it was sprayed with a disinfectant. There was no window, and the door was kept tightly shut, all but a grating in it over which Luis fastened a square of thick gauze netting. The place would have been abominably stuffy but for the fact that with nightfall a chill like death had crept over the land, as if with the darkness the high snows had asserted their dominion.

Later in the night men came to the hut, silently as ghosts, brought by the Indian, who, though not of their tribe, seemed to know them and speak their tongue. They were of the same race as the three whom the travellers had encountered in the forest that afternoon and had stepped aside to avoid. Strange figures they were, lean and tall, and in the lantern light their cheek-bones stood out so sharp that their faces looked like skulls. Their eyes were not dull, like those of the Gran Seco magnates, but unnaturally bright, and their voices had so low a pitch that their slow, soft speech sounded like the purring of cats. Luis spoke to them in their own language and translated for Black's benefit. When they had gone, he turned to his companion.

"You have seen the people of the País de Venenos. An interesting case of adaptation to environment? What would the scientists of Europe not give to investigate this curiosity? These men during long generations have become immune to the rankest poison in the world."

" They terrify me," said Black. " I have seen men very near to the brutes, but these fellows are uncannier than any beast. They are not inhuman, they are unnatural. How on earth did you get a graft here? "

" They have their virtues," said Luis, " and one of them is faithfulness. My graft is ancestral. Centuries ago one of my family came here and did them a service, and the memory is handed down so that only a Marzaniga can go among them. Indeed, I think that my blood has something of their immunity. I take precautions, as you see, but I do not know if in my case they are so needful."

Black asked about the poison.

" They are many," he was told. " There is poison here in earth and water, in a hundred plants, in a thousand insects, in the very air we breathe. But the chief is what they call *astura*—the drug of our friends the Conquistadors. Once this country was guarded like a leper-settlement, so that nothing came out of it. Now, as you know, its chief product is being exploited. The Gran Seco has brought it within its beneficent civilisation."

The Indian was already asleep, and, as the two white men adjusted their blankets, Black commented on the utter stillness. " We might be buried deep under the ground," he said.

" There is no animal life in the forest," was the answer, " except insects. There are no birds or deer or even reptiles. The poison is too strong. But there is one exception. Listen! "

He held up his hand, and from somewhere in the thickets came a harsh bark, which in the silence had a horrid savagery.

" Jackal? " Black asked.

" No. That is one of our foxes. They are immune, like the men, and they hunt on the uplands above the forest where there is plenty of animal life. I think they are the chief horror of the place. Picture your English fox, with his sharp muzzle and prick ears, but picture him as big as a wolf, and a cannibal, who will rend and eat his own kind."

As Black fell asleep, he heard again the snarling bark and

he shivered. It was as if the devilishness of the Poison Country had found its appropriate voice.

They stayed there for four days, and in all that time they did not move from the little mantelpiece. Every night ghosts which were men slipped out of the jungle and talked with them in the hut. Black fell ill again, with his old fever, and Luis looked grave and took the Indian aside. The result was that on the third night, when the men came and Black lay tossing on his couch, there was a consultation, and one of the visitors rolled in his hands a small pellet. It began by being a greyish paste, but when rolled it became translucent like a flawed pearl. Black was made to swallow it, and presently fell into a torpor so deep that all the night Luis anxiously felt his heart-beats. But in the morning the sickness had gone. Black woke with a clear eye and a clean tongue, and announced that he felt years younger, and in the best of spirits.

" You have tasted *astura*," said Luis, " and that is more than I have ever done, for I am afraid. You will have no more, my friend. It cures fever, but it makes too soon its own diseases."

The four days were cloudless and very warm. The forest reeked in the sunshine, and wafts of odours drifted up to the mantelpiece, odours such as Black had never before known in nature. The place seemed a crucible in some infernal laboratory, where through the ages Natura Maligna had been distilling her dreadful potions. His dreams were bad, and they were often broken by the yelp of the cannibal foxes. Horror of this abyss came on him, and even Luis, who had been there before and had grown up with the knowledge of it, became uneasy as the hours passed. These days were not idle. Information was collected, and presently they had a fairly complete knowledge of the methods by which those whom they called the Conquistadors worked. Then on the last night came a deluge of rain, and Luis looked grave. " If this continues," he said, " we may be trapped; and if we are trapped here, we shall die. Then it will be farewell to the Courts of the Morning, my friend."

But in the night the rain stopped, and at dawn they hooded and gauntleted themselves and started back. It was a nightmare journey, for the track had become slime, and the queer smells had increased to a miasma. Their feet slipped, and they made shrinking contact with fœtid mud and obscene plants whose pallid leaves seemed like limbs of the dead. The heat was intense, and the place was loud with the noise of swollen rivulets and the buzz of maleficent insects. Black grew very weary, but Luis would permit of no halt, and even the Indian seemed eager to get the journey over.

They did not reach their old camp till the darkness had long fallen, but the last hour was for Black like an awakening from a bad dream. For he smelt clean earth and herbage and pure water again, and he could have buried his face in the cool grass.

The next day they left the Indians behind and rode over the mountains by intricate passes farther to the south, which brought them to a long valley inclining to the south-west. Three nights later they slept in an upland meadow, and by the following evening had crossed a further pass and reached a grassy vale which looked westward to the plains. Luis pointed out a blue scarp to the north.

" That is the Gran Seco frontier," he said. " It is guarded by patrols and blockhouses, but we have outflanked them. I have brought you by a way which the Gobernador does not know—only those of my family and perhaps two others. We may relax now, for our immediate troubles are over."

They slept at a camp of vaqueros, and in the morning Black had several surprises. The first was an ancient Ford car which stood under a tarpaulin in the corner of one of the cattle-pens. The second was the change in his garb upon which Luis insisted. The uniform of the Mines Police was carefully packed in the car, and in its place he was given the cotton trousers and dark-blue shirt of an ordinary peon on the estancias. Luis drove the Ford all day through rolling savannah, with beside him a lean mestizo servant, to

whom he talked earnestly, except when they halted for food
at an inn or met other travellers. In the evening they came
to a big hacienda, low and white, with wide corrals
for cattle, and red-roofed stables which suggested Newmarket.

Half a mile from the place a girl, who had seen them
approaching, cantered up to them on a young Arab mare.
The car slowed down, and driver and peon took off their
hats.

" You are a day behind time," she said.

" Well, what about it, Miss Dasent? " It was the peon
who spoke, and there was anxiety in his tone.

" Only that you have missed his Excellency the Gobernador," said the girl in her pleasant Southern voice. " He
paid us a visit of ceremony yesterday, to talk about horses.
Curious that he should have chosen the day you were
expected. Don Mario thinks that Lord Clanroyden had
better not sleep in the house. If he will get out at the gate
of the cattle-yard, I will show him the way to the overseer's quarters."

IX

WHEN Archie and Janet came down to dinner that evening
at Veiro they found Don Luis de Marzaniga, a little thinner
and browner than before, but spruce and composed as if he
were about to dine at his Olifa club. He kissed Janet's
hand, and asked Archie if he had enjoyed the weeks since
his return from the Gran Seco.

" I've been obeying orders," was the answer. " There's
my commander-in-chief. She'll tell you how docile I've
been, and how I've never bothered her with questions, though
Janet and I are sick with curiosity."

The tall girl, whose name was Barbara Dasent, smiled.
" I'll testify that he has been a good boy."

She was very slim, and at first sight the delicate lines of
her neck and her small head gave her an air of fragility
—an impression presently corrected by the vigour and grace
of her movements. Her face was a classic oval, but without

the classic sculptural heaviness, her dark hair clustered about her head in childish curls, her clear skin had a healthy pallor which intensified the colouring of lips and eyes. These eyes were a miracle—deep and dark, at once brooding and kindling, as full of changes as a pool in the sunlight, and yet holding, like a pool, some elemental profundity. The lashes were long and the eyebrows a slender crescent. Janet had crossed the room and stood beside her, and each was to the other a perfect foil. Yet, though they had no feature in common, there was an odd kinship, due perhaps to the young freedom of each, their candid *regard* and a certain boyish gallantry of bearing.

At dinner, under the Sanfuentes Murillo, Luis cross-examined Archie about his recent doings. It appeared that, on Miss Dasent's instructions, he had been travelling widely in the coastal flats of Olifa. He had been given introductions from the Minister of Defence, and had been the guest of several regiments, attended an infantry camp of instruction, and taken part in cavalry manœuvres. Also he had visited various flying-stations, and had made several flights. The result was unqualified admiration.

" I can't claim to be a military pundit," he said, " but I know a first-class thing when I meet it. All I have to say is that Olifa has got the most completely professional outfit I have ever seen. There isn't one lesson of the Great War she hasn't learned. Her infantry tactics are the sort of thing we were feeling our way to before the Armistice. Her tanks are the latest pattern, better than anything I've seen in England, and, by Jove, she knows how to use them. Her army is mechanised to the full, but not too far, for she has the sense to see that cavalry rightly handled will never be out of date. And she has an amazing good staff, picked from up and down the earth, all as keen as mustard—like what we used to imagine the German staff to be, but less hidebound. Of course I don't know what strength she has in the way of reserves, and I can't speak of the fighting spirit, but there's no doubt she has a most efficient standing army for a nucleus. What puzzles me is why she should want anything so good when she's so secure."

Luis asked about the Air Force.

"That was the only thing with which I was a little disappointed," Archie replied. "It's extraordinarily good in the scientific way—the last word in machines and engines and all that sort of thing—but just a little lacking in life. Those chaps don't spend enough hours in the air. They've got all the theory and expert knowledge they can carry, but they haven't got as much devil as we have. Too serious, I should say. Keener about the theory than the game."

Luis had been listening closely. "You are very near the truth, Señor Roylance," he said. "We in Olifa have all that science and money can give us, but we have not enough soul. What is your English word—*guts?* "

"Oh, I didn't say that."

"But *I* will say it. And it is perhaps fortunate. I do not blame my nation, for our army is not national, since its leaders are mercenaries."

"I'm still puzzled. What do you want it for? I never got any figures of man-power and reserves, but if you've an adequate shaft behind this spear-head, you've a superb fighting-machine. What do you mean to use it against?"

Luis laughed. "It is the conventional insurance premium which our rich Olifa pays. Pays carelessly and without conviction. That is why, as you truly say, our army is made up chiefly of mercenaries. We have collected the best soldiers of Europe who were out of a job. It is a police, if you choose. If a little political war came with a neighbour, Olifa would use her pretty toy and ask only that she got her money's worth. . . . Unless, of course, it was a war which touched her heart, and then she would fight in the old way—with her people."

They sat late at table, Archie answering Luis's questions and illustrating his views by diagrams on the backs of envelopes. Presently Miss Dasent left the room, and on her return said something to Don Mario. He rose and led the way to his sitting-room, where, according to custom, a wood fire crackled on the wide hearth. The curtains, usually left untouched to reveal the luminous night, were now closely drawn. A man in a flannel suit stood with his back to the fireplace.

Janet blinked at him for a moment, and then ran up to him with both hands outstretched.

" Oh, Sandy dear, I have been miserable about you. Thank God, you're safely back. You're desperately thin. You're not ill? "

" I'm perfectly well, thank you. But I've been pushed up to the limit of my strength. It's all right. I've done it often before, you know. I only want to lie fallow for a bit. It's good to see you and Archie. . . . I feel as if I had come home."

" Are you safe here? " Janet asked anxiously.

Luis answered. " Perfectly—at present. The Gobernador must suspect something or he would not have been here yesterday. But he can know nothing. We have pickets out, and at the worst we shall get ample warning. To-night, at any rate, we can sleep sound."

" We have asked no questions," said Janet. " For the past week Archie has been behaving like the intelligent tourist, and I have been sketching in water-colours. We want to be enlightened, Sandy dear."

The man addressed—he looked very young in the dim light, for his hair had grown long and was tousled like a boy's over his forehead—flung himself into an armchair and stretched his lean shanks to the blaze. He slowly filled an old pipe and looked round at the audience—Don Mario erect and prim, Luis sprawling on a couch, Archie swinging his long legs from a corner of the table, Miss Dasent very quiet in the shadow, Janet standing on the tiger-skin rug, an incarnate note of interrogation. He looked round and laughed.

" You ask a good deal. Luis knows everything, and Miss Dasent. Don Mario knows as much as he wants to. But you two are newcomers, so I must begin from the beginning. Sit down on that stool, Janet, and, Archie, get off the table. I'm going to make a second-reading speech, as they say in your little Parliament. After that the House can go into committee. . . .

" First of all, I need hardly tell you that the world to-day is stuffed with megalomania. Megalomania in politics, megalomania in business, megalomania in art—there are a dozen kinds. You have the man who wants to be a dictator in his own country, you have the man who wants to corner a dozen great businesses and control the finance of half the world, you have the man who wants to break down the historic rules of art and be a law to himself. The motive is the same in every case—rootlessness, an unbalanced consciousness of ability, and an overweening pride. They want to rule the world, but they do not see that by their methods they must first deprive the world of its soul, and that what would be left for their dictatorship would be an inanimate corpse. You see, for all their splendid gifts they have no humour."

" What is Mr Castor's nationality? " Janet asked irrelevantly.

" He has none. He was born in Austria, and I think he has a Spanish strain in him. Blenkiron has a notion that he has English blood, too, but he cannot prove it. The man is like Melchizedek, without apparent origin. He's what you call a *weltkind,* the true international."

" *He* has no humour," said Janet with emphasis.

" I agree. But he has most other things, and one is a clear and searching mind. His strength, and also his weakness, is that he has no illusions. For one thing, he does not possess the illusion which ordinary people call a creed. He does not want to re-make the world on some new fantastic pattern, like the Communists. He has none of Mussolini's arbitrary patriotism. He wants to root out various things, but I doubt if he has a preference for what should take their place. I don't profess to understand more than bits of him. He is an egotist, but in the colossal sense, for he has no vanity. He considers that he has been called on to do certain things, and that he is the only man living who can. The world, as he sees it, is suffocating from the debris of democracy, and he wants to clear it away. He does not hate it, he despises it. He is the scientist and philosopher, who would introduce the reign of reason and the rule of law, but first some decaying refuse called popular liberties must be destroyed. Therefore he is against Britain, but only half-heartedly, for he thinks that with us democracy is tempered by more rational instincts, and that in any case our number is up. But for America he has the unfaltering contempt which a trained athlete might have for a great, overgrown, noisy, slobbering, untrained hobbledehoy. With America it is war to the death."

" I've known other people take that view," Archie put in.

" With him it is not a view, it is a crusading passion. In Castor you have the normally passionless, scientific mind kindled to a white heat. The mischief is that he is inhuman—not cruel, but inhuman. He will use the ordinary stuff of humanity to further his ends as ruthlessly as a furnace swallows coke. He will do any evil in order that what he considers good may come."

" That is the definition of a devil," said Janet.

" Not quite. Castor is just as near being a saint. If he had a different religion he might deserve to be beatified, for he is scrupulously loyal to what he believes to be the right. He's not evil—he just happens to have missed the human touch. He knows nothing of friendship—nor, of course, of any kind of love. His world is a narrow cell with the big dynamo of his brain purring in it. He is cruel, simply because he cannot conceive the feelings of anybody but himself, and is not interested in them. He is a master over *things,* and over men so long as he can treat them as things. If he were Emperor of the world I have no doubt he would be a just ruler. As it is—well, I have been seeing too much of his methods these last days to be in love with him."

He paused for a second to shake out the ashes from his pipe.

" Well, I've given you what Blenkiron would call the 'general Castor proposition.' Now, how would a man, obsessed by this idea, set about realising it? First of all, he would want money, money on a gigantic scale. He has got it in the Gran Seco. Remember, he is a very great practical engineer and chemist—Blenkiron, who should know, says the greatest in the world—and he is a first-class man of business. Second, he would want a base, and a well-camouflaged base. He has got that in the republic of Olifa. You have seen for yourselves how completely Olifa is in his power. He has changed in a few years the whole character of her governing class. He has made her Government rich and supine, and got it under his thumb. The thing is a miracle of tact and diplomacy. The Olifa ministers do not share in his secrets, they know very little of his schemes, but he has organised them as he wanted, and they do his bidding without a question. Up in the Gran Seco he has his laboratory and factory, and in the State of Olifa he has his outer barrage, the decorous, bourgeois republic which keeps watch at his door.

"Thirdly, he had to have his staff and his army to operate for him throughout the globe. He has got that, too—slaves who mechanically obey him. You have seen some of them in your Olifa hotel and in the Gran Seco. You have lunched with them, and Janet says that they made her flesh creep."

"The *type Gran Seco*," said Archie.

"The *type Gran Seco*. Have you any notion who they are? They look like robots, with their pallid faces and soft voices and small, precise gestures. All their individuality seems to have been smoothed away, so that they conform to one pattern. Nevertheless, they were once men of brains and character. Their brains they have kept, but their characters have been stereotyped, and they have surrendered their wills into the hand of their master. They have been most carefully selected from every nation. One or two you have known before, Archie."

"I swear I haven't."

"But you have. The Gran Seco is the port for missing ships. Men who have foundered somehow in life—respectable careerists who suddenly crash on some private vice—fellows who show the white feather—soldiers without regiments, financiers without credit—they are all there. Do you remember Lariarty, Archie? He was about your time at Eton. There was a bad scandal about him in 1915."

"Good God! Of course I do. I heard he was dead."

"He sat opposite you a few weeks ago when you lunched with the Administration. You couldn't recognise him. Everything that once was Lariarty has gone out of him, except his brain. You remember he was a clever fellow. And Romanes—the man who was in the 23rd—people said he was with the Touaregs in the Sahara. He is one of them, but I believe at the moment he is in Europe. And Freddy Larbert, who was once a rising man in the Diplomatic Service. He did not hang himself at Bucharest, as they said he did, for to-day he is in the Gran Seco. I could mention others, and they come from every country—Russian aristocrats who were beggared and Russian revolutionists who were too clever, broken soldiers and blown-on politicians and speculators who missed their market. The Gran Seco is the true Foreign Legion, and it needs no discipline. Castor asks only for two things, brains and submission to his will, and once a man enters his service he can never leave it."

"Why?" Archie asked.

"Because he does not want to. Because the Gran Seco is his only home and away from it he is lost. I told you that Castor was like the Old Man of the Mountain in the chronicle I showed you at Laverlaw. There is nothing new under the sun. Castor rules his initiates as the old ruffian in the Lebanon ruled his Assassins. You remember he gave them hashish, so that their one desire was to get their job in the outer world finished and return to the Lebanon to dream. Castor has the same secret. As I have told you, he is a mighty chemist, and this continent is the home of drugs. One in particular is called *astura* and is found in what they call the País de Venenos, the Poison Country in the eastern mountains. The secret of it was lost for ages till he revived it, and, except as a legend in the Marzaniga family, it was unknown in Olifa. This *astura* is deadly poison, but it can be used in two ways as a drug. In one preparation it takes the heart out of a man, but gives him increased physical strength, till suddenly he cracks and becomes doddering. That preparation Castor uses to turn out docile labourers for the mines. He gets marvellous results in output, and the reports say that it is due to his scientific management and his study of industrial fatigue, but we know better. The other preparation does not apparently weaken the bodily strength, though it alters the colour of the skin and the look in the eyes. But it is a most potent mental stimulant, and its addicts tend to live for the next dose. It kills in the end, but only after a considerable period, and during that period it gives increased intellectual vitality and an almost insane power of absorption, varied by languors like the opium-eater's. Those who once take to it can never free themselves, and they are the slaves of him who can supply it. Willing slaves, competent slaves, even happy slaves, but only the shadows of what once were men. Lariarty and Romanes and Larbert and others are among the initiates. They go about the world on Gran Seco business and they do Castor's will as little wheels obey a master-wheel. They have a name for their brotherhood. They call themselves the new Conquistadors—conquerors, you see, over all the old standards and decencies of human nature."

Archie inquired what precisely they did in their journeys about the world. He had rumpled his hair, and his eyes looked as if he were painfully adjusting a manifold of experience in the light of a new idea.

"First of all, they make money. They are the most efficient bagmen alive. For the rest, they break down things and loosen screws, and they have unlimited funds at their disposal, for Castor spends nearly as fast as he earns. . . . No, no. Not Bolshevism. The donkeys in Moscow have in a sense played Castor's game, but they were far too crude for him, and to-day I fancy he finds them rather a nuisance. By their folly they are creating a reaction in favour of that democracy which he hates. . . . Remember, I don't know him. I've seen him, but have never spoken to him. I can only speak at second-hand of his methods, but I'll give you Blenkiron's summary. Blenkiron says that half a century ago Abraham Lincoln fought a great war to prevent democracy making a fool of itself. He says that Castor's object is just the opposite—he wants to encourage democracy to

make a fool of itself, to inflate the bladder till it bursts.
. . . His instruments? The press, for one thing. He
has a mighty grip on that. The politicians, too, and every
kind of fool organisation for boost and uplift. You'd be
amazed to learn how many gushing societies, that look like
spontaneous ebullitions of popular folly, have his patient
direction behind them. He is the greatest *agent provocateur*
in history."

"But the thing is impossible," Archie exclaimed. "He
can't bring it to a head, and I take it that he knows he is
not immortal and wants some sort of result in his lifetime."

Sandy nodded. "He has a general ultimate purpose, but
he has also a very clear, practical, immediate purpose. He
wants to make trouble for America—before she can set her
house in order. The United States, Blenkiron says, have
reached the biggest crisis in their history. They have got
wealth and power, but they have lost the close national
integration they had when they were poorer. Their best
men are labouring like galley-slaves to discipline their
country. They have to give it an adequate law, and a
proper public service, and modernise its antediluvian con-
stitution. Castor wants to catch them at the moment of
transition, when they haven't found their balance. He
believes that bad foreign trouble, which they couldn't afford
to neglect, would split the unwieldy fabric. Democracy, of
which America is the incoherent champion, would become
a laughing-stock, and he and his kind would have the re-
ordering of the fragments."

"I think," said Janet, "that he has taken on too big a job.
Does he imagine that any alliance of Latin republics would
have any effect on America? I have heard you say yourself
that she couldn't be conquered."

"True." The speaker's eyes were on the other girl who
was sitting in the shadow outside the circle of firelight.
"No Power or alliance of Powers could conquer America.
But assume that she is compelled to quarrel with a group of
Olifas, and that with her genius for misrepresenting herself
she appears to have a bad cause. Has she many friends on
the globe except Britain? Most countries will flatter her

and kowtow to her and borrow money of her, but they hate her like hell. Trust them not to help matters by interpreting her case sympathetically. Inside her borders she has half a dozen nations instead of one, and that is where Castor comes in. A situation like that, when she was forced to act and yet didn't want to and didn't know how to, might, if properly manipulated, split her from top to bottom. Look what happened in the Civil War, and she was an integrated nation then compared to what she is now. Twenty years ago the danger would not have been there; ten years hence, if all goes well, it may be past; but to-day, Blenkiron says, there is precisely as big a risk of a blow-up as there was in Europe in June 1914. The men who count in America know it, even without Blenkiron telling them."

"Mr Blenkiron discovered Castor?" Janet asked.

"Yes. He came on the track of some of Castor's agents, and in his slow, patient way worked backwards to the source. Then he succeeded in laying himself alongside of Castor. How he managed it, I can't tell. You see, he's a big engineering swell, and I daresay he made himself useful over the actual copper business. Not as John Scantlebury Blenkiron, of course—as Señor Rosas, the agreeable denationalised Mexican, who has lived long enough in the States to have a healthy hatred for them. He must have had a pretty delicate time, and I don't suppose he was ever free from anxiety till he managed to arrange for his opportune decease. He was never in Castor's full confidence, for he didn't belong to the Conquistadors and never touched *astura*—gave out that he had to be careful in his habits because of his duodenum. His graft was that he understood the mining business like nobody else except Castor. But he had to be very cautious and had to stick like a limpet to his rock. Till he got in touch with Luis, he was next door to a prisoner."

Janet asked how that had been contrived, and Luis replied.

"Through Wilbur. I am afraid you underrated that drawling New England Consul! Wilbur is a great man. He was a friend of mine, and enlisted me, and then we enlisted others.   After a time—after a long time—we got in touch with Lord Clanroyden."

Archie drew a deep breath. " I think I see the layout," he said. " That is to say, I see what Castor is driving at. But I can't for the life of me see what we can do to stop him. . . .   Unless we got America to chip in first."

" That was Blenkiron's original plan," said Sandy. " But it was too difficult—might have precipitated what we wanted to avoid.   So we decided to do the job ourselves."

Archie stared at the speaker, and then whistled long and low.   " You haven't lost your nerve, old man," he said at last.   " I'm on for anything you propose—likewise Janet— but what precisely are the odds?   About a million to one? "

Sandy laughed and hoisted himself out of the chair. " Not quite so bad! Stiffish, I agree, but not farcical. You see, we hold certain cards."

" I should like to know about them," said Archie. " You seem to me to have taken on one of the toughest proposi- tions in history.   A species of Napoleon—unlimited cash —a big, docile, and highly competent staff—a graft every- where—and at his back the republic of Olifa with the latest thing in armies.   I assure you, it won't do to underrate the Olifa field force.   And to set against all that you've Blen- kiron, more or less a prisoner—yourself—Miss Dasent and her friends—with Janet and me as camp-followers.   It's a sporting proposition."

" Nevertheless, we hold certain cards.   There's a fair amount of explosive stuff in the Gran Seco and we have been organising it."

" The Indians? "

" The Indians. Castor has bled them white with his accursed forced labour, but there's still a reserve of manhood to be used—very desperate and vindictive manhood.   Also, there is an element among the white employees.   You have the Conquistadors at the top and the Indians at the bottom, and between them the foremen and the engineers.   They are the weak point of Castor's scheme, for they are not under his spell and know nothing of *astura*. He had to have skilled men and men whose interest lay in asking no questions, but he could never count upon their loyalty. He recruited every kind of scallywag and paid them lavishly, for he wanted people whose interest lay in sticking to the Gran Seco. But he has always had his troubles with them, and he and his Conquistadors in self-protection had to have their bodyguard. What sort of bodyguard? Oh, the usual bad-man type, the killer, the gunman. . . . You must have noticed them in the Gran Seco, quiet, steady-eyed, frozen-faced fellows—the Town Police is full of them, and so was the Mines Police till Blenkiron began to weed them out. . . . Well, Blenkiron has had a lot to do for the past year with recruiting both the foremen and engineers and the Mines Police, and we have managed to get them pretty well staffed with our own men. Hard cases, most of them, but a different kind of hard case. Blackguards often, but a more wholesome brand of blackguard. The Gran Seco at this moment is a sort of chess-board of black and white, and we know pretty exactly which are the white squares. If a row begins, we calculate that we have rather the balance of strength on that cheerful plateau. But I hope there will be no row. I don't like that crude way of doing things."

Archie passed a hand over his forehead.

" I don't know what you're talking about," he said plaintively. " There must be a row, a most unholy row. You want to raise the Indians, assisted by your friends in the Police and in the Mines, against the Administration. The Gobernador, if he is what you say he is, will resist like a tiger, and he has his gunmen behind him, and Olifa at the back of all. You will have to fight Castor. . . ."

Sandy smiled. " Oh, no. We will not fight Castor. We mean to fight *for* him. Castor will be our leader. The Indians in the back-country are wearing medals with his face on them, and look to him as their deliverer. That's the advantage of being a mystery man. No one knows him, except the Conquistadors, who don't count. He is going to be the Bolivar of the Gran Seco, the pioneer of liberty."

" Good God! Do you mean to say you are working in with him?"

" No. I won't go as far as that. But we hope to make him work for us. He won't like it, but it's the obvious move in the game. It will not be a rising of the oppressed against the Administration, but a revolt of the whole Gran Seco, oppressed and oppressors, against the tyrannical government of Olifa. And in the forefront of the battle will be Castor, like a new Uriah the Hittite."

Janet, who had been listening with a strained face, suddenly broke into one of her fits of helpless laughter. " That was your idea, Sandy. Mr Blenkiron never thought of anything so wild."

" It is not wild. It is common sense. It's ju-jitsu, where you use the strength of your opponent to defeat him."

" It is not common sense," Archie declared vehemently. " It is insanity. If Dick Hannay were here, he'd say the same thing. Supposing you unite the Gran Seco, with Castor at your head, what better off are you? You're up against Olifa with an army that will crumple you as easy as winking. You are cut off from the sea. You have no base and no communications. Where are you to get your munitions? Olifa will smash you in a week—or, better still, starve you out in a month."

" May be," said Sandy calmly. " That's the risk we run. But it isn't quite as bad as you think. We have a base, and presently you'll hear all about it. Also, I rather think it will be a new kind of war. I always had a notion of a new kind of war—an economical war—and I'm going to have a shot at it, even though we take a good many chances. You've been doing useful work, old man, in sticking your nose into Olifa's army system, and you naturally have a high regard for it. So have I. But it's an old-fashioned system."

" You're wrong. It's the most up-to-date thing on the globe."

" It has learned all the lessons òf our little scrap in France and Flanders, and I daresay it would make a very good showing in that sort of business. But it won't be allowed to, for it's going to be a different kind of business. We're the challengers, and will decide the form of the combat. The

Olifa army is as rigid in its up-to-dateness as the old British army was rigid in its antiquarianism. Castor is going to puzzle it."

Archie called fervently upon his Maker.

" You're as mad as a hatter," he cried, " but it's a madness I've got to have a hand in. You promised to let me in, Sandy. I'll do anything I'm told. . . ."

" I gave you a promise. But now you know what we propose, do you still hold me to it? What do you say, Janet? I can't put the odds better than three to one. We may all be blotted out. Worse still, we may end in a fiasco with our reputation gone for good. This is not your quarrel. I've no business to implicate you, and if you both slip down to Olifa and take the next steamer home, I admit I'll be happier in my mind."

" You want us to go home? " Janet asked. Her slight figure in the firelight had stiffened like a soldier on parade.

" I should be easier if you went."

Miss Dasent rose and came out of the shadows.

" You say it is not Sir Archibald's quarrel," she said. The clear sweet pallor of her skin was coloured by the glow from the hearth, and her dark eyes had the depth of a tragic muse. " But is it *your* quarrel, Lord Clanroyden? Why are you doing this? Only out of friendship for my uncle? If you say that, I cannot believe you. I could understand you taking any risk to get my uncle out of the Gran Seco—that would be your loyalty—but this is more than that. It cannot be for America's sake, for I have heard you say harsh things about my country. What is your reason? You can't expect Lady Roylance to answer till she has heard it."

Sandy flushed under the gaze of the dark eyes.

" I don't know. I never analyse my motives. But I think —I think I would go on with this affair, even if your uncle were out of it. You see, down at the bottom of my heart I hate the things that Castor stands for. I hate cruelty. I hate using human beings as pawns in a game of egotism. I hate all rotten, machine-made, scientific creeds. I loathe and detest all that super-man cant, which is worse nonsense than the stuff it tries to replace. I really believe in liberty, though it's out of fashion. . . . And because America in her queer way is on the same side, I'm for America."

"Thank you," the girl said quietly.

Janet held out her hand.

"*We* shan't stay out, Sandy. I wouldn't let Archie go home if he wanted to. We're both too young to miss this party. It's what I used to dream about as a child at Glenraden. . . . Is there anything to drink? We ought to have a toast."

"I said I would be happier if you went home," said Sandy, "but I lied."

Luis jumped to his feet. A whistle had blown faintly out-of-doors, and a second later there was another low whistle in the corridor.

"Quick," he said to Sandy. "That is José. The outer pickets have seen something, and passed the word back."

The two men slipped through the curtained window into the darkness. Don Mario rang a bell and bade a servant bring maté and other drinks, and no more than five glasses. Earlier in the evening the company had numbered six. Then Luis re-entered by the window, drew the curtains, and dropped into an armchair with a cigarette.

Presently there was the sound of a motor-car on the hard earth of the courtyard, and the bustle of arrival in the hall. The door of Don Mario's room was thrown open, and the butler ushered in three men in the uniform of the Olifa police. Two were junior officers, but the third was no less than Colonel Lindburg, the commissioner of the province in which Veiro lay.

The Colonel was a tall Swede, with a quick blue eye, close-cropped hair, and a small jaw like a terrier's. He greeted Don Mario heartily, announcing that he was on his way to Bonaventura, and had called to beg an additional tin of petrol. Luis he already knew, and he was introduced to the others—Sir Archie who limped about to get him a chair, Janet who was turning over an American picture paper,

Miss Dasent who was busy with a small piece of needle-work. The group made a pleasant picture of a family party, just about to retire to bed. The Colonel noted the five glasses, and when the servants brought mint juleps the three officers toasted Don Mario and the ladies. The newcomers talked of horses, of the visit of the Gobernador on the previous day, of the cool air of Veiro as compared with the Olifa heats. "You were not here yesterday, Señor de Marzaniga," the Colonel said, and Luis explained that he had only arrived from his ranch that afternoon.

They stayed for twenty minutes, finished their juleps, and, at a nod from the Colonel, rose to go. Don Mario and Luis accompanied them to the door. One of the peons made himself useful in filling the tank of the car, and was rewarded with a twenty-peseta piece.

When the sound of the car had died away, the two men returned to the ladies. Luis was laughing. "They are clumsy fellows, the police. There were four of them, not three. The fourth was young Azar. He asked permission to wash his hands, and, since he knows the house, for he has been to see the yearlings, he took the opportunity of inspecting all the bedrooms. Pedro heard him tramping about upstairs. Also that story of too little petrol was stupidly contrived. They had four full tins."

The curtains opened and the peon entered, he who had been so useful with the car. He held up the twenty-peseta piece.

"I have got my stake," he said. "Janet, you shall keep it. This little coin against Castor's millions."

With his rough clothes and dark skin he seemed to have shrunken to the leanest of lean scarecrows. He swayed a little, and caught Janet's shoulder.

"Sandy, you are worn out," she cried in alarm.

"I'm rather done up. Luis, you must put me in a place where I can sleep for a round of the clock. I must say good-bye, for it won't do for us to be together. . . . Luis will look after you."

He took the whisky-and-soda which Don Mario brought

him, and, in the toast he gave, Janet heard for the first time a name which was to haunt her dreams.

" I drink," he said, " to our meeting in the Courts of the Morning."

x

MR SYLVESTER PERRY in his *Seeing Eyes* asked a question which has often been asked by travellers, why the Gran Seco had no other route to the sea except by the three-hundred-mile journey south to the port of Olifa. Its city is not more than a hundred miles as the crow flies from the Pacific. The answer which Mr Perry gives is that which he had from one of the transient managers of the struggling copper companies, that on the western side of the plateau the mountains simply cascade into the sea. Archie, who had asked himself the question, reached the same conclusion from a study of a map prepared long ago by the British Admiralty. The close lines of the hatching, though they must have been largely a matter of guesswork, showed that the sailors who had surveyed the coast had no doubt about its precipitous character, and up in the northern apex, where the great peak of Choharua overhung the ocean, the contours made the drop as sheer as the side of a house.

Oddly enough, about this time the same question occurred to the Gobernador. That northern angle had been left alone in his careful organisation of his province, for up there was neither wealth to be got nor men to get it. He called for the reports of those who had penetrated its recesses and all spoke with the same voice. The plateau rose in sharp tiers to meet the curve of the mountains, and these tiers were waterless desert. Higher up there were forests, which might some day be used for mine timber, and it might be possible to divert the streams from the snows, which now flowed seaward in sheer ravines, to the Gran Seco watershed. These things, however, were for the future. The Gobernador closed the reports and rolled up the maps, with a mental note that some day soon he must undertake a complete scientific survey of his province.

It had become necessary for him to pay one of his hurried visits to Europe. The Gobernador led a life as arduous as Napoleon's during the early years of his Consulate. Like Napoleon, he had made himself the master of every detail in every department, and, like Napoleon, he had instituted a zealous inquest for capacity, and, having found it, used it to the full. But, unlike the First Consul, he did not need to keep a close eye on his subordinates; they had become automata, minor replicas of himself, whose minds worked in accurate conformity with his. Of this loyalty there could be no doubt; they had lost the capacity for treason, since treason implies initiative.

But on certain matters he kept his own counsel. There were letters from Europe and the United States, specially marked, which he opened himself, and which were never answered or filed by his most efficient secretaries. There were visits to various South American cities of which no report existed in the Gran Seco offices, though at the other end, in various secret Government bureaus, there may have been some record. In recent months these curious activities had increased. Messages in the Gobernador's most private cypher had been more frequent. He had begun to take a minute interest in the policing of his province, in the matter of passports, in the safeguarding of every mile of the frontier. Distant police officials had been badgered with questions, and the special bodyguard of the Administration had been increased. Also the Sanfuentes of the younger branch, who was Olifa's Minister for External Affairs, had twice journeyed to the Gran Seco—an unheard-of affair—and had been closeted for hours with the Gobernador, and on the second visit he had been accompanied by Señor Aribia, the Minister of Finance. New business, it appeared, was on the carpet, and for a fortnight the Gobernador did not appear at the Administration luncheons.

There was an air of tension, too, in the province, which, like an electric current, made itself felt in more distant quarters. It affected Olifa, where there was an unwonted bustle in various departments, and high officials went about with laden brows and preoccupied eyes. It affected the foreign consulates and embassies of various South American States. It was felt in certain rooms in Washington, London, Paris, Berlin, and Rome, large rooms decorated and furnished in the deplorable style of Government offices, where behind locked doors anxious men talked far into the night. There was even a little extra stir in the dovecotes of Moscow, where a pale young man, who spoke bad French, had an interview with five others whose power was so great that even the governing caste knew them only by numbers, and thereafter a dozen insignificant-looking people crossed the Russian frontier with passports for various remote lands. It especially affected Mr Roderick Wilbur, the American Consul in Olifa. That heavy man spent two energetic days, and a still more energetic night, which was largely occupied in burning papers. Then, leaving his office in the charge of his assistant and under the general care of Don Alejandro Gedd, he announced that he was about to take a holiday, and departed for the capital of an adjacent republic. There his holiday consisted in sitting in the office of the British Consul, and, being permitted to use his cypher, in sending, by way of the British Embassy in Washington, a series of messages which brought two of his Ministers out of bed at one in the morning.

Yet in the midst of this activity the Gobernador must go journeying. His mission was, he said, to Europe, and in two months he would return. To Señor Rosas, the Vice-President of the Company, he committed the temporary charge. As the two sat in the big bright room on the first floor of the great Administration Headquarters, into which travellers on the top of the tramcars could stare, while the clack of typewriters around them was like the noise of frogs in a pond at night, they made an interesting contrast. Both were big men, but while the Gobernador was hard and trim and spare, the Mexican looked sallow and flabby, as if he had been meant for a fat man but was kept lean by overwork and anxiety. Nevertheless his eye was clear and healthy. There was no intimacy between the two, but there was obviously respect. For Señor Rosas had under his special charge the most difficult element in the community, the white foremen and engineers, who did not belong to the close brotherhood of the Conquistadors or the Bodyguard, and were not subject to the harsh discipline of the mine labourers. They were the nearest approach in the Gran Seco to a free society, and needed careful handling.

Instructions were given, minute instructions, reports were referred to, diagrams consulted, calculations made, and the Mexican took many notes. Then the Gobernador pushed the papers aside, and his penetrating eyes dwelt on the other's face. There was no cordiality between these two, only the confidence of a business partnership. They addressed each other formally, as was the custom in the Gran Seco.

" I am not satisfied with the Police, Señor," he said. " I have information that there is a leakage somewhere. It is certain that in recent months unlicensed persons have been inside our border. They may still be here. If they have gone, what have they gone to do? I have given instructions to make the mesh closer. That is not your province, I know, but as my substitute I look to you to see that the work is done."

The Mexican met the steady gaze of the other with an almost childlike candour. The hard lines of the jaw and cheek-bones made his large ruminant eyes at once innocent and unfathomable. English was being talked, and he replied in the drawl which he had learned in the States.

" I reckon you can trust me, Excellency, to hand over this territory to you a little bit more healthy than when you left it. I'm to expect you back in two months' time? "

The other smiled. " That is my official leave. I may return earlier. . . . I have much to do, but it may take less time than I expect. Perhaps in a month . . . or less . . ."

" Then you've got to fly to Europe."

" Europe is for the public, Señor. My business may be done nearer home. As yet I cannot tell."

" Say, you're taking precautions? You're not going alone? You're a lot too valuable a commodity to be touring about like an ordinary citizen. There's heaps of folk that are keeping something for us. You got to take precautions."

The Gobernador frowned. " It has never been my custom, as you know, Señor. A man who goes in fear of his life is a fool—he had better be dead."

" That's sound as a general principle. But I guess this is a special emergency, and I can't have you running risks. You got to take the three men you had when you last went north. You know the bunch—Carreras, and Dan Judson, and Biretti. I'll have them washed and tidied up so as to do you credit. They won't obtrude themselves, and they'll do as they're bid, but they'll be at hand in case of dirty work. If there's any shooting, I'll say they shoot first. You aren't justified in taking risks, Excellency. There's a darned lot too much depends on you. I reckon you're too big a man and too brave a man to be afraid of having some fool say you take mighty good care of your skin."

The frown relaxed. " I suppose that is common sense. I will take the men with me."

In Olifa the Gobernador did not go to a hotel. He had his rooms in the great Gran Seco building in the Avenida de la Paz. He did not leave the building much—at any rate by day; but he was a magnet to draw the eminent thither. Señor Vicente Sanfuentes and Señor Aribia visited him there, and on two occasions the President himself, modestly on foot, and not accompanied by the tossing plumes and bright harness of the Presidential Guard. Also General Bianca, the Minister of War, who had been in a dozen of the old wars of Olifa, came to pay his respects, and with him came the departmental heads, the Chief of Staff, the Director-General of Transport, the officer commanding the Olifa district, all youngish men, who had found in Olifa a market for professional talents which were no longer valued in Europe.

Among the callers was Colonel Lindburg, the commissioner of police of one of the provinces. He had a report to make. "Acting upon your instructions, Excellency, we have inquired into the doings of our friend Don Luis de Marzaniga. He spends his time between the country house, where he lives alone with his widowed mother, and his cattle-ranch in the Vulpas valley. In an ancient car he is at all times bumping over the roads between the two. Also he is often at Veiro, for he advises the old Don Mario about his young stock. I am satisfied that every movement of Don Luis for the past month can be amply explained."

"And Veiro?"

"You yourself have seen, Excellency. Don Mario has entertained the young English baronet and his wife, and the American girl, Señorita Dasent. They were sent to him by his foolish cousin, Don Alejandro Gedd. I have had the place watched, and, except for Don Luis, no one else has visited there."

The Gobernador appeared to be satisfied, and, after compliments, Colonel Lindburg withdrew. But when the policeman had gone the great man opened a dispatch-box and took from it a small memoranda book. He re-read in it a message which he had received from Paris a month earlier, warning him that there was reason to believe that one X—— (the name was obviously in code) had left Europe and was probably in Olifa. At the same time he turned up certain reports handed to him by the most trusted member of the Administration's special police. These recorded various odd actions on the part of several members of the Mines engineering staff, on whom the Administration had chosen to keep a special eye. There seemed, said one report, to be a good deal of private meeting and talking among them, as if some agent had arrived to stir them up. A mysterious visitor had been seen, but the trail of him had been lost before he could be identified; his physical appearance had suggested Señor de Marzaniga, with whom, as a member of an ancient and intransigent Olifa family, the secret service was well acquainted. The

Gobernador brooded over these notes. There was nothing of special importance in them; weekly, daily, he was in the habit of receiving similar communications; but some instinct had led him to single these out, and he had diverted the Olifa police to what had proved to be a wild-goose chase. . . . He was not satisfied, but he dismissed the thing from his mind. He had too many hard certainties before him to waste time on speculations.

It was surprising during these days how much time the great man gave to the study of the press. Not the Olifa press, but that of every other South American country, and of the United States. His sitting-room was often like the reading-room in a public library, for he seemed to have an insatiable appetite for the journalism of the New World. Often he studied it in conjunction with the Olifa Ministers, and the study appeared to give them pleasure. There was at the moment an awkward situation in Mexico, and a more awkward one in connection with the little republic of Costemala, where Washington was upholding with several warships and a considerable force of marines an administration which apparently was not desired by the Costemalans. There was also trouble in the Canal Zone, where a certain State, hitherto most amenable to America's persuasion, had displayed a sudden recalcitrancy. The American people seemed to be in a bad temper over these pin-pricks, an influential Senator had made a truculent speech, various patriotic societies had held monster demonstrations, and the press was inclined to be flamboyant. There was a great deal of talk about America's manifest destiny; responsible newspapers discoursed upon the difficulty of a high civilisation co-existing side by side with a lower, and of the duty of the imperfect democracies of the South to accept the guidance of the mature democracy of the North. The popular press waved the flag vigorously, published half-tone pictures of stalwart American marines among the debased citizens of Costemala, and graphs showing how trivial was the wealth and how trumpery the armed forces of Latin America as compared with their own. The rest of the New World, it said, had got to learn to be democratic or take its medicine.

These heroics did not go unchallenged, for on the Gobernador's table were clippings from high-toned American weeklies, and addresses by University professors, and speeches of cross-bench public men, who, also in the name of democracy, denounced what they called a policy of imperial brigandage. The Gobernador read both sides with an approving eye. " This thing has been well managed," he told Señor Sanfuentes. " Holloway has not disappointed me."

The press of the Latin South had a quieter tone, but it was notable for its curious unanimity, which extended even to the phrasing. The United States, it announced, was forsaking democracy for imperialism, the white robes of liberty for the purple of the tyrant. Very carefully and learnedly and urbanely, with many references to past history, it stated the case for the sacrosanctity of nationalities. It did not refer to the League of Nations, but professed to base its arguments on America's past professions, and the great republican cause to which the continent was dedicated. There was an admirable good temper in its tone, and a modest but complete defiance. It could not believe that the great hearts and the wise heads of Washington would be betrayed into this dictatorial folly. The sounder elements in the United States would prevent it. It appealed from Philip drunk to Philip sober.

The Gobernador studied the journalism of the Latin republics with special attention, and his visitors shared his satisfaction. " There is not a word wrong or a word too much," observed Señor Aribia, who was himself a newspaper-owner. " This will make havoc among the mugwumps."

" What a fortunate chance," exclaimed the Minister for External Affairs, " that the trouble with Costemala and Panama has arisen just at this moment! " His prominent eyes twinkled.

" It is indeed a fortunate chance," said the Gobernador gravely.

XI

On the third day of the Gobernador's stay visitors of a different type came to the building in the Avenida. Archie, in a new suit of flannels, limped up the steps, and had his card sent up to the great man. While he waited, Janet appeared, in a summer costume of pale blue linen, with a cornflower-blue hat which brought out delightfully the colour of her eyes and hair. They were admitted at once, for they had evidently come by appointment. The tall porter who conducted them to the lift looked approvingly at the lady, and the three men who were lounging in the corridor outside the Gobernador's private room made audible and appreciative comments. The three were dressed like the ordinary Olifero clerk, but they bulged a little at the hips; their names were Carreras, a Spaniard, Biretti, an Italian, and Daniel Judson, who passed as an Australian.

The Gobernador seemed to welcome the Roylances' intrusion. He had many questions to ask—about their impressions of the Gran Seco, about Veiro and Don Mario, what class of polo Olifa afforded in Archie's view, the date of their return home. His manner towards them was paternal, as to two attractive children who had strayed into a dusty office.

"The heats are beginning," he said, "and Olifa loses its pleasant visitors. The Americans have fled, I understand—the noisy young people, I mean, who were in the Gran Seco when you were there."

"All but one," said Janet. "Barbara Dasent, whom you met at Veiro, is still here. The *Corinna* is back in the Old Harbour, and she will give us a lift to Panama. . . . Excellency, I am going to be very bold. We want you to come and dine with us one night before we go."

The Gobernador looked at the girl, flushed, laughing, like a child who is in doubt as to how its audacity will be taken; he looked at Archie, very cool and sunburnt; and then he looked at Janet again. He was a student of human nature, but he had never in his varied experience met such

a type before. Here was beauty without egotism, one who
seemed to him to look out upon life in a mood of mingled
innocence, mirth, and adventure, a woman without those
feminine arts which had always wearied him, but with a
charm the stronger for its unconsciousness. The Gobernador
did not allow himself holidays, but, like all mortals, he
needed change, and Janet seemed to offer a new atmosphere.

"I thank you, but, alas! I do not go into society," he
said. "There are difficulties, you see. You are at the
Hotel de la Constitución? Well, if I dined with you at
the hotel, there would be something of a scene. That is not
vanity on my part, Lady Roylance, but there are so many
people who wish me to do things for them or to ask me
questions that I cannot safely go into public places."

His face showed that he wished to accept, and Janet was
emboldened.

"We quite see that. Besides, the hotel is a noisy place.
What we propose is that you come and dine with us on
the *Corinna*. It will be deliciously cool on the water, and
only Barbara Dasent will be there. Then we can have a
proper talk, and Archie and I will sit at your feet."

The Gobernador smiled. "Your invitation is very
seductive. I think I can arrange to-morrow night. I will
be on the quay at the Old Harbour at half past seven—
the *Corinna,* I think, lies in the outer basin. . . . By the
way, I have to take certain precautions—the Government
insist on it. There are three men who always attend
me . . ."

"That's all right," said Archie. "We'll send the big
launch. I say, this is topping. I only wish you were coming
on with us to Panama!"

The three men, Carreras, Biretti, and Judson, took their
duties seriously. As soon as they heard that the Gobernador
was to dine on board the American yacht, they set about
preparing for emergencies. They were supreme ruffians,
each with a string of murders to his credit, but they were
loyal to their immediate paymaster. They arranged with
the Port authorities—for the Gobernador's bodyguard had
considerable purchase in Olifa and often acted without

consulting their master—that a harbour patrol boat should be lying adjacent to the *Corinna* between the hours of seven and eleven on the following night. In response to an agreed signal it should close the yacht. They also took counsel with one of the *Corinna's* engineers, for in their profession they left nothing to chance. This was a rough, sulky-looking fellow who spoke with a strong Glasgow accent. He must have had a past uncommon among the hands of a well-appointed yacht, for on his arrival in Olifa he had been welcomed into a life of which the authorities of that respectable capital knew little. He seemed to have ample leisure, and spent it for the most part in shadowy back streets. In small wine-shops, in rooms remote from the public eye, he drank and gambled and talked with queer customers. They were not the ordinary riff-raff of the port, but some of them men of good presence and manners, with pale faces and absorbed eyes and a great gift of silence. It was a furtive company, which dispersed always one by one, and did not talk till it was certain of secrecy.

Carreras, Biretti, and Judson had joined this group on their arrival, and the Scotsman had become their special intimate. To the others he was Señor Jorge, but Judson, who seemed to have known him before, called him Red Geordie. The massive set of his jaw and his sullen blue eyes seemed to have earned him respect, for, when he spoke, he was always listened to. There was some bond between him and the Gobernador's three, for they told him of the approaching visit to the *Corinna* and the precautions they had taken. The consequence was that on the following morning he, too, became active. He put on his engineer's uniform and visited the Port authorities, where he interviewed a variety of polite officials. After that he descended into the harbourside quarters, and had speech with others who were not polite. It is probable that he returned from his round of interviews a little poorer than when he started.

The early tropic dusk had fallen when the Gobernador's car deposited him at the quay of the Old Harbour, and from a taxi in his wake descended his three attendants.

Archie Roylance was waiting on the steps, and conducted his guest to the trim launch, manned by two of the yacht's hands and the sulky Scottish engineer. The three trusties bestowed themselves forward, and a look of intelligence passed between them and the engineer. Archie fussed about to make the Gobernador comfortable in the stern, and wrapped a rug round his knees to avert the evening chill from the water.

The launch threaded its way through the shipping of the Old Harbour and came into the outer basin where the *Corinna* lay alone, except for a patrol boat a quarter of a mile off. In the dusk the water-front was a half-moon of twinkling lights, while beyond them the Avenida de la Paz ran in a great double belt of radiance to the starry cone of the Ciudad Nueva. Against the mulberry sky a thin fluff of smoke stood out from the *Corinna's* funnels.

" Getting up steam, sir," Archie observed. " We've said good-bye to Olifa and we start in the small hours. A place always looks its jolliest when you are leaving it."

The dining-room of the yacht was already cool with the land breeze drifting through its open port-holes. The little table, bright with linen and glass and silver, was only large enough for the party of four. The Gobernador, sitting between Janet and Barbara Dasent, was in good spirits, and looked appreciatively at the soft harmony of colours. Some sunset gleam had caught the water and the reflection of it brought a delicate glow into the room. Even Barbara's paleness was rosy.

They talked of many things—of Europe, of politics, of books, of the future of mankind (these were some chaotic speculations of Archie, who seemed to be nervous and had the air of a lower boy breakfasting with the headmaster), of England a little, and much of America. The Gobernador was the soul of courtesy, and was accustomed to respect the prejudices of others. But Barbara was in a mood of candour about her countrymen and she occasionally forced him into a polite agreement. Something had happened to Barbara, for she talked fast and brilliantly, and her eyes had an unaccustomed vivacity.

" We are overrun with silly women," she said. " The United States is a woman's country, Excellency, and we let them paint the picture which we show to the world. I do not think it is an attractive picture—a mixture of shallow *schwärmerei* and comfortless luxury—a life of plumbing, and dentistry, and bi-focal glasses, and facial and mental uplift, and snobbery about mushroom families, and a hard, brittle sweetness stuck on with pins. No wonder you do not like us! "

" I did not say that, Miss Dasent. I am not sure that I assent to any of your complaints, except the *schwärmerei*; and that I think is not confined to your ladies."

" I was making a catalogue of the details of the picture we present to the world. It is an ugly picture, and I know you hate it. So do I. . . . All the same it is a false picture, for we are the worst publicity agents on earth. The trouble is that we have had no second Columbus. Nobody from outside has ever discovered the true America."

The Gobernador dissented.

" You are hard on yourselves. If I want acrid criticism of the United States, I pick up an American novel. Or I take the saying of one of your own Presidents that the modern American millionaire has usually a daughter who is a foreign princess and a son who is in a lunatic asylum. I do not take that sort of thing at its face value. You are a great people which has not yet found itself."

" You do not like us."

" As a student of humanity I am deeply interested in you."

" You are tolerant, because you do not like America. I am intolerant because I love it."

The Gobernador raised his glass and bowed. " A very honourable confession of faith. If all her daughters were like you, Miss Dasent, it would be right that America should remain a woman's country."

The talk drifted to lighter matters—to music which Barbara and the Gobernador discussed with a technical profundity appalling to Archie; to a German novel which had set the world talking; to European personalities in art and politics.   Presently they left the dining-room, and ascended to a shelter on the upper deck from which the harbour was seen like a gulf of blackness rimmed by fiery particles. The Gobernador, who noticed everything, observed that the patrol boat was no longer there and that the *Corinna* swam alone in an inky solitude.   He saw no signs of his bodyguard; no doubt, he decided, they were ensconced in the shadows beyond, where the lifeboats swung from their davits.

But the three trusties were not there.   They had spent a turbulent evening, and were now in a less comfortable state than their master.   They had insisted on having their meal in close proximity to the dining-room, and the surly Scotch engineer had shared it with them.   Between them these convivial souls had consumed a good deal of liquor, which appeared to go rapidly to the heads of the visitors. The engineer had then proposed an adjournment to his own quarters for further refreshment, and had shepherded them down a narrow alley-way, he himself going last.   There was a heavy iron door, and as each of the three passed through it, on the other side he was caught round the middle by powerful arms which prevented him getting at his hip-pocket.   Other hands swiftly gagged him, and still others removed his gun.   The thing was done in almost complete silence.   Only one of the three managed to put up a fight, and he was promptly laid low by a terrific upper-cut from a seaman who had once been known as Battling Hubby, the pride of Jersey City.   In something under three minutes the three heroes were gagged and trussed, and reposing, in a somewhat unreposeful state of mind, on a pile of awnings.

"That's a tidy bit of work, Geordie," the pugilistic seaman observed to the morose engineer, and the answer was, "I've seen waur."

Then the engineer did a curious thing.   He went aft, and with a lantern signalled to the patrol boat which lay a quarter of a mile off.   The signal was observed, and presently the boat moved quietly away, leaving the *Corinna* solitary in the outer basin.

Coffee was served to the party on the upper deck, and the guest filled his ancient briar. The steward, as he left, gave a message to Archie: " Hamilton's compliments, sir, and the men has finished the job forward "—at which Archie nodded. He was sitting in an alcove, with a small electric bell behind his arm. The Gobernador sat in a wicker chair, with a lamp on his left side, so that, by the configuration of the deck, his splendid head was silhouetted against the opaque velvet of the harbour waters. Janet and Barbara on lower chairs were sitting literally at his feet.

The guest seemed to have fallen under the spell of the night which was drawing round them as close as a mantle. The shore lights did not speak of human habitation; rather they seemed as remote as a star, an extension of the infinite stellar system which faintly patterned the darkness. The stillness, the brooding canopy of the night, silenced the others, but with the Gobernador it acted as a stimulus to talk. He seemed to sit above them like an impersonal mind, his profile growing clearer as the light went out of the background of the sea.

" You are a soldier? " he asked Archie.

" I was. Keen, but undistinguished. The Air Force wasn't a place for high strategy. But I've always lived among soldiers and heard their chat."

" It has been a great profession, but it is closed now, Sir Archibald. Science has reduced war to an everlasting stalemate. It was always on the edge of stalemate. Consider how few moves any general had to his hand. He could break a line or he could outflank it, and he could do either only by superior force or by surprise. But science has now created a norm of weapon and munitionment, which is substantially the same for all armies. It has eliminated the human factor of superiority both in general and troops. It has established, too, a norm of intelligence which makes surprise impossible. Therefore there is no room to-day for a military Napoleon. The Napoleon of the future must win by other methods than war. Do you agree? "

" No," said Archie; " I respectfully disagree. I can't argue properly, but I know what I think. First, I don't believe you can ever get rid of the human factor. Science has to be applied by mortal men, and the efficiency of its application will depend upon those who use it. You can never create what you call a norm either of character or of brains. Second, I agree that the old rules of war are a back number. A modern army can conquer savages, but in the old style of warfare it can't conquer another modern army. But I believe that one modern nation can still conquer another. You need a wider definition of war, sir. It's far more than marching and counter-marching, and frontal and flank attacks, and number of men and weight of guns and speed of transport. It's the effort of one people to smash the *moral* of another, and there are a thousand ways of doing that."

" I assent. But not in the field."

" Yes, in the field. We've been frozen into convention for two thousand years. The autumn of 1918 saw the end of that regime. Now mankind is going to discover new ways of exercising superiority—in the field, but not by the old field tactics. Conquest is always a spiritual conquest, and means will be found for making spirit act directly on spirit."

" You are quoting. Whom?" The voice from above had a sudden interest.

" A friend of mine who thinks a lot about these things. You wouldn't know him."

" I differ from him absolutely. You are still clinging to the old notion of something incalculable and mystic which can defeat reason. You are wrong, for reason is the only power. Every day we are rationalising life, and what we cannot rationalise we can isolate and nullify. You young people are relics of the Middle Ages."

" But so is human nature." It was Barbara who spoke.

" Do not misunderstand me. We allow for the spasmodic impulses of human nature. But we analyse them and evaluate them, and by understanding them we can use them. Liberty, for example. That ancient instinct can be worked out to four places of decimals, and can consequently be used by reason. Is the human intelligence to submit docilely to be governed and thwarted by blind reactions which mankind shares with the brutes?"

"You are very clever, Excellency, but I think that there is always an unknown *x* which will defeat you. You are too clever, for you would make science and reason rule over a dimension to which they don't apply. Humility may be more scientific than arrogance."

The guest laughed pleasantly. "I think you also are quoting. Whom, may I ask?"

"A friend. Sir Archie's friend."

Had anyone been observing Archie closely, he would have noticed that he had looked at his watch, and then made a movement towards the electric button behind his elbow. The act seemed to afford him some satisfaction, for he gave a sigh of relief and lit a cigarette.

The Gobernador had turned to catch Barbara's reply.

"I should like to meet your friend," he said, and then suddenly he flung his head back and listened. The throb of the propeller was felt through the vessel, and the ear caught the swish of moving water.

"You will soon have that pleasure," said Barbara, "for we are taking you to him."

In an instant the guest was on his feet. "What nonsense is this?" he asked sharply. His tall figure towered menacingly above the others, who remained seated in their chairs.

"It is all right, sir," said Archie. A change had come over the young man, for the diffidence, the lower-boy shyness, which had been noticeable all the evening, had gone. Now he seemed to be at his ease and to be enjoying himself. "I know it is a bit of a liberty, and we apologise and all that sort of thing, but it had to be done. You see, we greatly admire you and we want you to be our leader. . . . It is no use shouting for your bodyguard. I'm afraid we had to handle them a little roughly, and at this moment they are trussed up and adrift in a boat. The tide's all right and they'll be picked up to-morrow morning in the harbour. . . . Please don't do anything rash, sir. Our men are all about, and they carry guns. You see, we really mean business."

The Gobernador had his face averted so the other three could not see his change of mood. But a change there was, for he flung himself down in his chair and refilled his pipe.

"I'm a busy man," he said, "and you are doing more harm than you can realise. Also I am afraid you are making serious trouble for yourselves. But I suppose I must submit to this prank. I was right when I said you were still in the Middle Ages. You are a set of melodramatic children. . . . I hope you don't mean it to last long. By the way, where are you taking me?"

Janet clapped her hands. "I have won my bet. I knew you would take it well. I told you when we asked you to dinner that we were going to sit at your feet. That is true, you know. We want you to lead us."

"We are going to help you to discover America," said Barbara. "You will be our new Columbus."

"You will meet the friend," said Archie, "whom Miss Dasent and I have been quoting."

"Perhaps you will now tell me his name," said the Gobernador.

"We call him Sandy," Archie said casually. "His name used to be Arbuthnot. Now it's Clanroyden."

The recovered urbanity of the Gobernador was suddenly broken. A cry escaped him, and he turned his face away to the racing seas, but not before Janet had seen his brows knit in a mood so dark that she unconsciously reached for Archie's hand.

XII

WHEN the *Corinna* was beginning to move out of the dusky harbour of Olifa, a wireless message was sent from it to an address in the Gran Seco. That message consisted of two words: *Francis First*. There had been various schemes agreed upon for the handling of the Gobernador, and the numeral was intended to signify the one which had been adopted. By a happy chance, the first and simplest had succeeded.

The receipt of this brief message was like a spark to

powder. The events of the next few days in the Gran Seco cannot be told in orderly history. They had the speed and apparent inconsequence of moving pictures, and can only be set forth as flashes of light in a fog of confusion.

At the Universum Mine the manager woke as usual, breakfasted on his veranda, read his mail, and was a little surprised that certain telephone calls, which he had expected, had not come through from Headquarters. He was about to ring for his secretary and bid him call up the Gran Seco city, when the chief engineer, a Texan named Varnay, appeared on the scene and accepted a cup of coffee and a cigar. The manager was a newcomer who had been specially chosen by the Gobernador, a highly efficient machine whose pragmatic soul dwelt mainly in graphs and statistics. The Texan was a lean, lanky, hollow-eyed man, whose ordinary costume was dirty duck trousers and shirt-sleeves. To-day he wore breeches and boots and a drill jacket, and in his belt was an ostentatious revolver. The manager opened his eyes at this magnificence and waited for Varnay to speak. He was itching to get at his secretary and start the day's routine.

The Texan was in no hurry. He poured himself out a cup of coffee with extreme deliberation, lit his cigar, and blew smoke-rings.

" The new draft will be in by midday," said the manager. It was the day in the month when a batch of fresh labour arrived, and what Peters had called the " returned empties " began their melancholy journey to the pueblas.

" Yep," said the Texan. " The outgoing batch went last night, and the new outfit arrived an hour ago."

The manager jumped to his feet. " Who altered the schedule? " he cried angrily. " Who the hell has been monkeying with my plans? I've had the schedule fixed this last month, and the Universum Mine has got to be run according to it. I'll flay the man that stuck his clumsy hoof into it."

He was about to cross the veranda to the bell which would have brought his secretary when the quiet drawl of the other detained him. The Texan had stuck out his long legs, and was regarding with abstracted eyes a butterfly which had perched on his coffee-cup.

" Sit down, mister," he said. " Things have been happening this morning in this outfit, and I got to put you wise about them. The Universum is closed down till further notice."

" By whose order ? " the manager barked.

" By the Gobernador's."

The manager cursed with vehemence and point. He was the boss, and any instructions from Headquarters came through him. What misbegotten son of a yellow dog had dared to usurp his authority? If this was a hold-up——

" Say, this love-talk don't cut no ice," said the Texan without heat. " You haven't been let in on this scheme, because you're a newcomer and wouldn't have got the hang of it. Say, listen. Things have been going crooked in this little old country, and his Excellency is going to straighten them out. Those dagos in Olifa are giving us a dirty deal, and we reckon it's time a white man took charge. It ain't sense. We're using up these poor goldarned Indians and chucking them aside like old boots. That's bad business, mister, and the pueblas won't stand for it."

" You fool! What can the Indians do? "

" You'd be surprised," said Varnay gently. " But it ain't the Indians only. There's the Police, and there's all of us white men who think the time has come for a clean-up."

" Man, that's rebellion," the manager cried, his orderly soul shocked to its roots.

" Why, yes. I guess it's rebellion. But you've no cause to get scared, for we're not rebelling against the boss. It's our boss rebelling against Olifa."

" You're a liar. Headquarters would never be such God-forgotten idiots. They're business men and know where their profit lies."

" I don't say there mayn't be some pikers at Headquarters and a bit of trouble, but I reckon that his Excellency Señor Castor is a mighty clever man, and it's him we follow.

Why, the vaqueros are all wearing medals with his face on them, and they look up to him as a God Almighty."

The shaken manager at last turned to the telephone. But there was no answer from Headquarters and the bell failed to bring his secretary.

"The lines were cut last night," said Varnay, "after our orders came through. . . . But see here, mister. We want to treat you on the square. You've not been let in on this deal, and you've no cause to mix yourself up in it if you don't want to. We're going to town presently, but there's no reason why you shouldn't get on ahead and judge things for yourself. There's an automobile at your disposal whenever you like to start."

The manager took the hint, and departed with a box full of confidential papers and the balances left in the pay-chest. He was loyal to his employers, but it remained for him to find out who these employers were.

At the Alhuema Mine things went with equal smoothness, for the manager there was in the plot. But at the San Tomé there was some unpleasantness and for an hour or two a difficult situation. The San Tomé manager had only just come, having been before in the Administration at Headquarters. He was a young American from Montana, who had had experience of copper-mining in half a dozen quarters of the globe, and had earned a reputation as a go-getter and a firm handler of coloured human material. He was set on making good, for there was a girl waiting for him at home, and he had the contempt of the youth of his country, scientifically trained and furiously ambitious, for all things which cannot be set out in graphs and figures. Also, having just come from the city and having heard for months the intimate talk of Headquarters, he was not easy to bluff.

The situation was complicated by the fact that the white technical staff of the mine were not unanimous. Three of the engineers had refused to join in the plot, and had only refrained from prematurely exposing it on being assured that the thing had failed and had been abandoned. More-over, when the ringleader, a Scotsman called Melville, received the message which was to fire the train, it was found impossible to cut the telephone line to Headquarters. The outgoing draft of labour was too slow in starting, and the incoming draft, which was to give the rebels their armed force, was unaccountably delayed. The night was spent anxiously by Melville and his colleagues in a vain attempt to get into touch with Peters and the police. But Peters had his own troubles, for his squadron also had its doubtful elements. Headquarters had taken alarm and had just drafted into it some of the more desperate characters in the Mines guard. The consequence was that there was shooting, and at daybreak, when Peters had his force ready for the road, two dead men and three trussed-up prisoners were left behind.

Early in the morning, when Melville played his hand, the young manager was beforehand with him. The manifesto of the malcontents infuriated him, and their use of Castor's name did not convince, for he rang up Headquarters and thereby precipitated trouble in the city two hours before it was due. Believing that he had to deal with a piece of common brigandage, and having been promised immediate reinforcements, he resolved to hold the fort. He had the three malcontent engineers, his staff of Olifero clerks, his half-caste servants, and his own stout heart. He put his house into a state of defence, and he had one conspicuous asset, for in the same building was the magazine of explosives, and, with such perilous stuff about, his assailants must go circumspectly.

About 10 a.m. Peters arrived with his police. The manager took them for his reinforcements, and Peters might have entered his house and taken peaceful possession, but for the fact that his greeting by Melville was observed from an upper window. A parley was attempted, and Peters and the manager sat opposite each other in chairs on the veranda, each with a revolver on his knee. The policeman was no diplomatist. His temper had been soured by his difficulties in the night watches, and he talked to the manager like a sergeant to a recruit, and was met by a stiff defiance. Did he imagine that a rising of Indians and a few mutinous police would worry the Gran Seco, much less the republic of Olifa with its potent army? The thing was moonshine. That the Gobernador was a party to it was an impudent lie. The manager knew the mind of the Administration better than any bush policeman. He would hold the place till succour arrived, and if there was any attempt to rush his defences, they would all go to glory—and he nodded towards the magazine. Peters retired discomfited, for he read in the stiff chin and the frosty eyes that this man would be as good as his word.

The *impasse* continued till noon, while Peters and Melville consulted anxiously, for this delay was dislocating the whole programme. Then at long last the incoming Indian draft arrived, and with it a young man, the Olifero called Carlos Rivero, who had chaperoned Janet and Archie on their journey to the Gran Seco. When he heard of the trouble he proposed to interview the manager a second time, and under a flag of truce the two sat again on the veranda. But Rivero had no revolver on his knee.

What he said can only be guessed. But as an Olifero of an ancient stock he must have spoken with an authority denied to Peters. It is probable that he told the manager quite frankly certain things of which Peters had no knowledge. At any rate, he seems to have impressed him, and to have shaken his obstinacy. But the faithful servant demanded proof. If he were to act without superior instruction, he must be convinced that he yielded to the strongest of all arguments.

"Right," said Rivero. "You shall have your proof, Señor. You are familiar with the sight of an incoming draft—sullen, wolfish men herded by the police? Come and see what I have brought you. You have my word of honour that, if you are not convinced, you can return to this place to continue your defiance. More, Señor Melville shall be brought here and remain as a hostage."

The manager accompanied Rivero to the compound behind the Mines buildings which was reserved for the Indian labourers. And this is what he saw. A compact body of five hundred men, mounted on small wiry horses and each carrying a rifle at his saddle-bow. These lithe figures were

very unlike the weary, hopeless automata that had been
accustomed to stumble into the compound. They held themselves erect, and, if their faces were sullen, it was the sullenness of a grim purpose. There were white officers and
sergeants among them in the uniform of the Police, but the
impressiveness of the spectacle was not in them, but in the
solid, disciplined ranks of fighting men sprung out of an
older age.

"These," said Rivero, "are the labourers whom the
Gobernador is now calling to his side."

The manager stared, rubbed his eyes, and laughed.

"I reckon the game's with you," he said at last. "I climb
down. This is sure a business proposition."

The daily meeting of the heads of departments was held
as usual in the Administration Headquarters at ten o'clock,
with the Vice-President, the Mexican Rosas, in the chair.
The members met in a large room on the same floor as
the Gobernador's private office, but at the side of the building
away from the main street. The Vice-President said a word
to his private secretary, who sat in a little office behind the
chair, and when the meeting began the doors were quietly
locked, so that the only entrance lay through the secretary's
room. There was a vast amount of detail on the agenda that
morning, to which the meeting duly bent its mind.

During the night there had been odd happenings at the
railway-station. The daily freight train, which should have
left at 9 p.m., did not start; instead the freight train of the
day before, which on its up-journey should have passed the
other at the frontier station of Gabones, was ordered by telegraph to proceed without delay to the Gran Seco. Also the
up-coming passenger train, which was not due to leave Santa
Ana till noon, had been expedited, so that it arrived almost
empty about daybreak, and intending travellers that day
found themselves stranded at Santa Ana without a
connection. The down-going train was due to leave at
10 a.m., but it did not start. Those who meant to travel by
it found the station closed and under guard, and the yards
full of rolling stock. By 10 a.m. on that morning the whole

of the rolling stock of the Gran Seco line, with the exception of a few trucks delayed at Santa Ana, was concentrated at the Gran Seco terminus.

If the doings at the railway-station were curious, still more remarkable was what took place elsewhere in the city. In the area of the smelting and refining works there had been since the early morning a great peace. Walkers in the Avenida Bolivar suddenly awoke to the fact that the hum of industry, which day and night sounded like breakers on a beach, had ceased. The previous night had been a busy time for a certain section of the white employers, perhaps three-fourths of the total. They had begun by isolating the works area from the city and guarding the approaches. Then they had set about the compulsory conversion of the remaining fourth, a rapid business, and not unattended by violence. Three men attempted to break away, and were shot before they crossed the barrier. After that came the dealing with the Indian and mestizo labourers. Some were sent back to their pueblas under escort of a file of Mines Police, a few picked men were added to the white strength, but most remained in their compounds, which were put under guard. The furnaces were damped down, and by 6 a.m. the whole of the great works area was shuddering into quiet. The white employees, armed and disciplined, were waiting on the next stage.

An hour later mutiny broke out in the barracks of the Town Police. It had been skilfully prepared, for many of the chief officers were implicated, and at first it moved swiftly and surely. The armoury was captured, those known to be recalcitrant were made prisoners in their beds, and in less than half an hour the mutineers held the barracks and had at any rate immobilised the opposition. But a certain part of the police was on duty in the city, and beside these was that special force, the Mines Bodyguard, which was responsible not to the Commissary of Police but directly to the Administration, and which was not concentrated in one place but scattered in many quarters.

It was now that the ill-effect was felt of the failure to cut the line at the San Tomé Mine. For the manager of the

San Tomé had rung up the Administration secretariat about eight o'clock, and, since he babbled of rebellion, had been put through to the officer in charge of the Bodyguard. This man, Kubek by name, had long been uneasy and alert—indeed he had been the cause of the Gobernador's suspicions. The appeal from San Tomé put him on his mettle, and he at once mobilised his force. He could rely on the fifty members of the Bodyguard who had not been tampered with, and, as soon as he found out what was happening at the barracks, he turned his attention to the members of the Town Police on outside duty. He informed the Administration of what was happening, a message received but not circulated by Señor Rosas's private secretary.

The consequence was that by 10 a.m. the situation was as follows: The works area was held by a force of foremen and engineers, who had cut it off from the city and were waiting for the arrival of the Mines Police. The Town Police were in the main on the side of the rebels and waited in barracks, but some of their members were with Kubek, who had about two hundred men under him and was holding what he regarded as the key positions—a house at the corner of the Avenida Bolivar and the Calle of the Virgin, the Regina Hotel, and the house in the garden behind the Administration building which was the residence of the Vice-President. He believed that he had to deal only with the mutinous Town Police and with trouble at the Mines, and had no notion that the Mines Police were in the rising. The city as a whole knew nothing of what was happening. Promenaders in the Avenida Bolivar noted only the curious quiet and the absence of policemen on point duty.

Meantime the meeting presided over by Señor Rosas pursued its decorous way. There were marketing reports from Europe which had to be discussed, and certain difficulties which had arisen with the shipping companies. Mr. Lariarty presented a report on the latter subject which required close consideration.

At 11 a.m. the first contingent of the Mines Police under Peters arrived. They went straight to the works, where they found everything satisfactory, and gave directions to the forces assembled there. The latter had sent out scouts, who reported what had happened at the barracks of the Town Police. Peters was a cautious man, and, before effecting a junction, sent out patrols to discover if all was quiet in the city. His intention was to round up the Bodyguard man by man, for he knew all their lairs; but his patrols brought the disquieting news that the Bodyguard were forewarned and mobilised, and that they held the Regina Hotel and the corner house in the Calle of the Virgin. The third concentration, at the Vice-President's residence, they had not discovered. Their news meant that the approaches to the Administration Building were blocked and must be cleared. Peters accordingly got in touch with the Town Police and made his plans.

Just after noon, when the Board meeting had reached the question of a contract with Guggenheims, the noise of dropping fire began to be heard. A confused murmur penetrated too into the back chamber from the Avenida Bolivar. The Vice-President, who was frequently interrupted by the advent of his secretary with messages from the inner office, pushed his spectacles up on his brow and smiled benignly. "There's a little trouble, gentlemen," he observed. "Some foreign matter has gotten into our machine, and the police are digging it out."

Before 1 p.m. there was fighting at three points in the city, for the garrison in the Vice-President's house had revealed itself by sniping one of Peters's contingents. The Bodyguard were all desperadoes, and very quick with their guns, but they were hopelessly outnumbered, and, for the matter of that, outgeneralled. The Regina fell about 2.30, for it had not been difficult to force a way in from the back and take the defence in the rear. Nine of the defenders were killed, and the Police had seven dead and fifteen wounded. The house in the Calle of the Virgin resisted longer, for, being a corner house with fronts on two streets, it was less open to attack from behind. Yet that nest was smoked out before 4 p.m. and Peters could concentrate all his forces on the Vice-President's residence.

The Board meeting after three o'clock sat to a con-

tinuous accompaniment of rifle fire. But Señor Rosas with
a Roman fortitude held the attention of his colleagues to the
business of the agenda. The members seemed sunk in bewilderment, and it is difficult to believe that their minds
worked competently on their business. The Vice-President
did most of the talking. " It is all right, gentlemen," he
would say, on receiving a message from his secretary : " the
Police are managing this little affair very well."

At half past five the last defences of the Bodyguard fell.
It was a bloody business, for Kubek, who had learned the
art of street-fighting in Eastern Europe, put up a stout resistance till he got a bullet in his windpipe. Peters ruefully
calculated that that day the Police had over sixty men dead
and nearly a hundred wounded, but he consoled himself with
the reflection that the Bodyguard could not have a dozen
survivors. He himself was bleeding from two wounds, but
they must go untended, for he had still much to do. He
hastened to confer with a slight youngish man, who wore
civilian clothes—an old tweed jacket and riding breeches of
the English cut—and who had joined him at the smelting
works on his arrival that morning.

About 6 p.m. the Vice-President at last brought the Board
meeting to an end. His secretary had just handed him a
written message which seemed to give him satisfaction.

" Gentlemen," he said, " our labours are over for the day.
I thank you for the attention you have given to the Company's business under somewhat trying conditions. And
now, I judge, we are all going to have a bit of a holiday.
I ought to tell you that important events have just taken
place in this city, and our activities have got to close down
for a spell. There has been a revolution, gentlemen. The
workers of the Gran Seco have risen against the Government of Olifa, and they are counting on our President being
their leader. I have no authority to speak for his Excellency, but I guess it's more than likely that he will consent.
What I have got to say is that you gentlemen are free to
do what you please. You can't oppose the revolution in this
township, for it has already succeeded, but there's no call
for you to take a part in it unless you like. You can stay

on here, and "—here there was a significant pause—" I will make it my business to see that your comforts are attended to."

The members, hypnotised by the long tension of the afternoon, stared blankly at the speaker. Then slowly life seemed to waken in their opaque eyes. The man called Lariarty became their spokesman. He rose and bowed to the chair.

" I think we will go down to Olifa," he said.

At that moment there came the sound of explosions one after another in a chain, which set the windows rattling.

The Vice-President shook his head.

" I reckon that's impossible, gentlemen. What you hear is the blowing up of the rolling stock at the railway-station. There will be no facilities for travel to Olifa, till Olifa makes them afresh."

XIII

ABOUT 8 p.m., when the dark had fallen, two men groped their way into a room in the oldest quarter of the city, just above the dusty hollow which separated it from the works area. It was a hut in a yard, reached by a circuitous passage among sheds and the back premises of low-class taverns. The place was very quiet, for the inhabitants were out in the main streets, eager to catch what they could in the troubled waters. It was also very dark, till one of the men struck a light and revealed a dirty little cubby-hole which had once been an Indian cabin. Then he put his back to the door and listened, as if he were expecting others to join him.

The man at the door bore the marks of hard usage. He was dirty and dishevelled, there was a long shallow cut on his left cheek, and he limped as if from a wound in the leg. His face was white, his air was weary and dejected, but his eyes were as quick and ugly as a mad hound's. The other, who had seated himself on a barrel, was of a different type. He was neatly dressed in a dark suit, with a blue linen collar, a black tie, and a pearl pin. His face likewise was white, but it was with the pallor of settled habit and not of strain, and his eyes, opaque and expressionless, gave him an air of calm and self-possession.

" How many's left? " said the man at the door, as if in answer to a question. " God knows, and He won't tell. Mollison got away from the last bloody show, and Snell was on the Regina roof and presumably escaped the round-up. Bechstein was never in the scrap at all, for he was in bed this morning with a touch of fever. Radin got off, I hear, and no one saw Molinoff after midday. Let's put our salvage at half a dozen. Enough to do the job, say I, if there's any luck left to us."

The man on the barrel said something in a low voice, and the other laughed angrily.

" That blasted Mexican was at the bottom of it. Of course I know that, but how in hell can we touch him? He has gotten five thousand men to protect his fat carcase. Poor old Kubek! He never spotted that Rosas was in the game or there would have been one dago less in the world. It's the other we're laying for, the man that Kubek got on the trail of but couldn't get up with. I don't know his name, curse him, but I know the cut of his jib. If I can put it across him, I'll die happy. He's been up here off and on for months, slipping about in the dark like a skunk, and leaving no trace but a stink."

" He will not come here," said the man on the barrel.

" I say he will. Mollison knew where to find him, for they used to drink together. Pete is the stricken penitent now, anxious to stand well with the new authorities, and that God-darned mystery man is the brain of the business. He wants to round up the remnant of us, and Pete's going to help him. He's coming here at half past eight to be put wise by Pete about certain little things that concern the public peace. I reckon he'll find the peace of God."

There were steps in the alley, and the doorkeeper, looking through a chink in the boarding, was satisfied. He opened, and a man entered. It was a squat fellow with a muffler round his throat and the bright eyes of fever. " Snell's dead," he gasped as he dropped wearily on a heap of straw.

A moment later there came the sound of double footsteps,

and two men were admitted, one a tall man with high cheek-bones and the other a handsome youth with a neat fair moustache. Both wore bandages, one on his left arm and one across the forehead. But they seemed less weary than the others, and they remained standing, each with a hand in a side-pocket and their eyes fixed on the doorway.

Once again came double footsteps and the little party fell as silent as the grave. A hat was put over the lantern. The man at the door held up a warning hand and did not open it, but stood back a pace. There was a sound of fumbling with the latch, and the door opened slowly. Two men entered, one a bearded giant whose coat had been rent so that the left side flapped over his shoulder and whose lips were bleeding, the other a slim, youngish man in an old tweed jacket and breeches of an English cut.

No sooner were they inside than the covering was removed from the lamp. The doorkeeper had his back to the door, the man on the straw got to his feet, and the giant caught his companion from behind and held his arms. Four pistol barrels glimmered in the scanty light.

"Hullo," said the newcomer. "There are more friends here than I expected. You have done me proud, Mollison."

It was a strange and macabre scene. The man with the dark suit and the pearl pin sat unmoved on the barrel, his opaque eyes stolidly regarding him who seemed to be a prisoner. Bechstein, the man with the fever, had his revolver laid over one arm, as if he were uncertain of his shaking limbs. The doorkeeper lolled against the door-post grinning, Radin and Molinoff stood on each side like executioners, and the giant Mollison spat blood from his mouth, while his great face hung like a monstrous gargoyle over the slim figure of his captive.

That captive seemed very little perturbed.

"I owe you a good turn for this, Mollison," he said pleasantly. "Hullo, Bechstein! I heard you were ill in bed. I'm afraid you are taking liberties with your health. . . . I can't see very well, but can it be Radin, and, by Jove, Molinoff, too? The Devil has looked after his own to-day."

"He hasn't looked after *you*, my friend," said Mollison.

" Your number's up all right.   You're going to be a quiet
little corpse within sixty seconds, as soon as we have
tossed for who is to have the pleasure of sending you to
hell."

" Well, let go my arm and let me draw my last breath in
comfort.   I haven't a gun."

The giant ran one hand down the prisoner's figure.
" True enough," he said, and relaxed his grip.   " But don't
move, or you won't have sixty seconds."

" It's my right to kill the swine," said the doorkeeper.
" I was Kubek's second-in-command and I owe him one
for the chief."

The plea seemed to meet with general acceptance, and
the prisoner saw his time of probation shortened by this
unanimity.   For a moment he seemed at a loss, and then he
laughed with a fair pretence of merriment.

" By the way, you haven't told me what you have against
me.   Isn't it right that I should hear the charge? "

" Damn you, there's no time to waste," said the doorkeeper.   " You have been the mainspring of this tomfool
revolution, which has already done in our best pals and
will make life a bloody hell for the rest of us.   We
are going to give ourselves the satisfaction of shooting you
like a dog before we scatter."

" You don't even know my name."

" We know your game and that's enough for us."

The prisoner seemed to be anxious to continue the talk.
He spoke slowly, and in a pleasant, soft voice.   It might
have been noticed that he held his head in the attitude
of a man listening intently, as if he expected to hear more
steps on the cobbles of the yard.

" There's one here who knows me," he said.   " Tim—
Tim Lariarty," and he addressed the sphinx-like figure on
the barrel.   " You remember Arbuthnot.   I was at Brodie's
when you were at Ridgeway's.   We got our twenty-two
together, and we were elected to Pop the same day.   You
were a bit of a sap and got into the Sixth, while I never
got beyond the First Hundred.   You remember Sandy
Arbuthnot? "

The face of the man on the barrel did not change perceptibly, but there was a trifle more life in his voice when he spoke. "You are Arbuthnot? Of course you would be Arbuthnot. I might have guessed it."

"Then for God's sake, Timmy, tell that blighter behind me to put down his gun. I'll take my medicine when it comes, but I'd like to tell *you* something. You're a clever chap with a future, and I've got something to say to you about the Gran Seco which you ought to hear. Give me five minutes."

There was a protest, but the sphinx nodded. "Give him five minutes," he said and took out his watch.

The prisoner began to talk in his compelling way, and unconsciously the interest of his executioners awakened. Being on the edge of death, he had no reticences. He divulged the whole tale of the revolution, and he made a good story of it. He told of Blenkiron's coming to the Gran Seco, of the slow sapping of the loyalty of the Mines Police, of the successful propaganda among the technical staff, of the organising of the Indian pueblas, in which he claimed a modest share. The others dropped their pistol-hands and poked forward their heads to listen. The five minutes lengthened to six, to eight, to ten, and he still held his audience. He addressed himself to the man on the barrel, and sometimes he lowered his voice till the door-keeper took a step nearer.

Then he became more confidential, and his voice dropped further. "How do you think it was managed? A miracle? No, a very simple secret which none of you clever folk discovered. We had a base and you never knew it. Go into the pueblas and the old men will speak of a place which they call Uasini Maconoa. That means the Courts of the Morning—Los Patios de la Mañana. Where do you think it is? Listen, and I will tell you."

They listened, but only for his words, while the speaker was listening for another sound which he seemed at last to have detected. He suddenly caught two of the heads bent forward, those of Radin and Molinoff, and brought them crashing together. The doorkeeper could not shoot, because Mollison was in his way, and in an instant the chance was gone, for a blow on the head felled him to the ground. Mollison with a shout swung the dazed Radin and Molinoff aside and had his pistol in the air, when a report rang out and he toppled like a great tree, shot through the brain. The hut had filled with men, and the two whose heads had crashed and the fever-stricken Bechstein were throttled from behind and promptly pinioned.

Then the prisoner showed what the strain had been by fainting at the feet of the man on the barrel.

He came to himself, and found Peters holding a brandy-flask to his mouth. Peters had a whitish face.

"My God, sir," he stammered, "you will never be nearer death."

The young man seemed to have recovered, for he had strength enough to laugh.

"I cut it pretty fine, but there was no other way. I had to make myself ground-bait if we were to catch these pike. We've got them all now. . . . I think I could have held them for another five minutes, but I chose to precipitate things. You see, I saw by the flicker of the lantern that the door was opening, and that meant you. If I hadn't thought of that head-crashing dodge, I think I might have stopped a bullet."

The man on the barrel had risen and was looking sombrely on. The policeman jerked his head towards him. "What about that fellow?" he asked.

"Oh, let him alone," was the answer. "He is free to go where he likes. He was at school with me, and I owe him a good turn for this evening."

BOOK II

THE COURTS OF THE MORNING

JUST about the hour of sunrise a girl sat perched on a rock from which the ground fell westward into an abyss of blue vapour. East of her, after a mile of park-like land, the steep woods rose black as coal, and above them soared into the central heavens a great mountain of rock and shale, which, so sheer was the face, showed even to a viewpoint so near its summit cone of snow. The face and the plateau were still dipped in shadow, but beyond the mountain the sun was up, and its first beams, flooding through a cleft on the north shoulder, made a pool of gold far out on the western sea. The peak was the great Choharua, which means, in the speech of the old races, the Mountain of the Two Winds, for it was held to be wind-shed as well as water-shed.

The tropic dawn broadened fast, though the sun did not show himself. Presently all the plateau to the east was washed in a pure, pale light. The place seemed to sparkle with a kind of hoarfrost, though the air was mild, and its undulations, and the shallow glen of the stream which descended from Choharua, were sharp-rimmed black shadows in that silver field. Then greenness broke through the monotint, like the flush of spring in an English wood, and what had been like a lunar landscape sprang suddenly into clean, thin colours. The far cone of snow became rosy-red and crystalline, so that for one moment it hung like a translucent jewel in the sky. Then it solidified; the details of the shaly face sprang into hard reality; what had been unfeatured shadow showed now as sheer crag and intricate couloirs, specked with snowdrifts which were leaping waters. At last came the orb of the sun, first a crescent of red gold, and then by quick gradations a great burning archway in which the mountain seemed to be engulfed. The air changed to a glow of essential light, and in a moment it seemed that the faint scents of night became the warm spicy odours of day.

The girl was looking to the sea. The line of light, which a minute before had been on the horizon, ran shoreward, as if a tide of sheer gold was flowing in from the west. But the ocean was some thousands of feet below, and the shore waters remained in dusk long after the morning had conquered the plateau. Below her the chasm of blue mist slowly became luminous, and features detached themselves, tall trees near at hand clinging to scarps, outjutting headlands of green far down. The noise of the falling stream grew louder, as if it had been asleep during the darkness and had only begun to talk with the morning. The immediate foreground cleared, and curious things were revealed. There were buildings on the edge of the chasm from which wire ropeways ran down into the brume, the kind of thing by which in Norway the saeter hay is moved to the valley, and by which in the War in the eyries of the Dolomites the Italian army provisioned its look-out posts and gun-stations. Also there were revealed the beginnings of a path which descended the ravine in spirals, and something else—a framework of trestles and iron which decanted itself into the abyss like a gigantic chute. A stranger could now have made out the main features of the landscape—a steep glen down which the torrent from Choharua made its way to the sea, a glen, not a cliff, a place by which it was possible to have access from the shore to the plateau. But that shore would not reveal itself. It lay far below in a broad ribbon of mist, flecked like a bird's wing, which separated the molten gold of the sea from the gold-washed, re-created world of the morning hills.

The girl rose from her perch and drew long breaths of the diamond air. The waxing light revealed her companion, a tall man muffled in a blanket coat, who had been standing beneath her. She turned to him. " It is well called the Courts of the Morning, Excellency," she said. " Aren't you glad I made you come with me? "

He was busy lighting his pipe. When he raised his face

to her, there was a flicker of a smile around the corners of his deep-set eyes.

"I blame myself for not appreciating long ago the charms of this corner of my province. It is a place to intoxicate youth."

"And you?"

"I am no longer young. To me it is a picturesque mantelpiece between the sierras and the sea. I observe"—he nodded towards the ropeways and the trestles—"I observe your communications. Ingenious!"

"You may examine them at your leisure. We have no secrets from our leader."

"Your leader *malgré lui*. You foolish children are consistent in your folly. Tell me one thing, Miss Dasent. I am apparently at liberty. A charming young lady takes me out to admire the sunrise. Supposing I desire to leave—desire it very badly. I am a busy man and my business will suffer from my absence. . . . Say that I am resolved to end this folly and at this moment. What would hinder me?"

"Need you ask?" she said.

"I ask," he replied. Something minatory and grim had come into his face.

"I should hinder you," was her answer.

He took a step towards her, while she watched him keenly. As his foot was raised for a second step, she blew a small whistle, and he halted. Out of the rocks and bushes men had appeared by magic, lean Indian faces with their eyes fixed on the girl. She looked at her companion, and he smiled. Then she waved her hand and the faces disappeared.

"I thought as much," he said. "As I said, you are consistent in your folly." The momentary animation had gone out of his face, and left it placid, set, and inscrutable. He did not move when out of the chasm two figures emerged, so quietly that even the girl, who had been expecting them, started as their steps rang on the stony platform. They were young men, apparently much of an age, but very different in build. One was tall and burly, with an untidy head of tow-coloured hair and a face so rugged that the features might have been rough-hewn with an axe out of some pale wood. It would have made an excellent figurehead for an old China clipper. He wore a khaki shirt, khaki shorts, and football stockings, but there was something about him that smacked of the sea. His companion, who wore similar clothes, was slight and beaky, with a mop of longish dark hair. They were about to cry some greeting to the girl when they caught sight of her companion, and both stiffened, like men who had been trained, in the presence of a superior.

"Excellency, may I present to you two members of your staff?" she said. "This"—indicating the tall man—"is Lieutenant Roger Grayne, a naval officer. . . . This is Captain Bobby Latimer. You are not interested in these things, I know, Excellency, but Captain Latimer has quite a reputation in our Air Force."

The bare-headed young men saluted. "Pardon our rig, sir," said Grayne, "but we've been up all night. We're rather in want of a bath and breakfast. We've just been saying good-bye to the *Corinna*."

"Ah! Your line of communications?"

"One of them," said the girl, smiling.

"I venture to remind you," said the older man, "that the republic of Olifa possesses a navy."

The sailor laughed. "Not a very good one, sir. A trifle short in small craft and a whole lot short in practice. Olifa has never had much coast-patrol work to do, and she is mighty ignorant of this northern shore. I'd like to take you down below there and show you the landing. It's as cunningly tucked away as the ports the old-time buccaneers used to have among the Florida keys. It would take pretty bright men some months to hit it off."

"But supposing they were fortunate? What then?"

"Why then, sir, they could make it difficult for the *Corinna* and certain other craft, but they couldn't put any considerable spoke in our business."

"What would prevent them fighting their way up and cornering you like rats on this shelf?"

"Ye-es," was the answer. "They might—with Heaven's

own luck and plenty of time and no sort of regard for casualties. That four thousand feet of gully is a mighty difficult ladder to climb, and every rung has its nasty catch. I'm not worrying about our little backdoor to the sea. Come here, sir, and have a look down. The mist will be gone by now."

The Gobernador allowed himself to be led to a little platform of rock which projected above the gulf. On his arrival he had made the ascent in a thick fog, and had had no chance of noting the details. Now he saw that the path dropped at once into thick bush, while the trestles zigzagged till they were lost behind a spur of rock. Only the wireways ran straight in a dizzy angle till far below they seemed to terminate in a dull blur on the water's edge. But what he chiefly observed was that the shore made a little bay, which ran south and was sheltered from the ocean by a green conical spur. To a ship at sea that bay was securely hidden, and the ravine must appear as one of a hundred others on the scarred and wooded mountain face. There would be some intricate prospecting before it was discovered.

He turned to the others with a shrug of his shoulders. " I think I have had enough of the picturesque. What about breakfast? "

A path led them into the shallow trough of the plateau, where the stream from Choharua wound among lawns and thickets in shining links like a salmon-river. They crossed it by a rough bridge of planks, and then the land lifted gently under the shadow of the mountain, while the shelf broadened as it turned the southern skirts. Presently it flattened out to a miniature plain, and they came suddenly into an area of crowded life. It looked like a cantonment. Round a block of wooden huts lay a ring of tents, from which rose the smoke of morning fires. On the left there were horse-lines, and beyond them the tall masts of a wireless station. On the right were what looked like aeroplane hangars. A busy hum came from the place, and that mingled smell of wood-smoke, horses, and cooking food which since the beginning of time has been a mark of human concourse.

The western ocean was hidden by the lift of the shore scarp, but since the coast recessed at this point there was a gleam of water from the south. To the south-east lay the great wall of the sierras, but as it bent inland the land in front seemed to sink in craggy and forested foot-hills, giving the eyes a great prospect towards what seemed a second and lower plateau. The air was filled with an exquisite morning freshness, half of the sea and half of the hills, and the place seemed part eyrie, part sanctuary—an observation point over the kingdoms of the world, and also a tiny sheltered kingdom, brooded over by virgin peaks and guarded by untravelled seas.

The four stopped before one of the larger tents. A little way off a small party of Indians were off-saddling weary horses. The girl pointed to them.

" See, Excellency," she said. " Another of our lines of communication."

An hour later a small company assembled for breakfast in the staff mess hut. Janet Roylance was dispensing coffee to half a dozen young men in breeches and linen jackets, one of whom was her husband, while Barbara Dasent at the other end of the table was slicing a cold ham. The men rose as the Gobernador entered, and Janet pointed to a vacant chair beside her.

" Where is Sandy? " she asked. " Archie saw him an hour ago, and he said he was hungry enough to eat an ox."

" He is getting clean," said Archie. " He looks as if he had been having a dusty time. He likes tea, Janet."

" I know. I've got it for him. And Sobranye cigarettes in a china box. I remembered his tastes."

To a stranger there would have appeared to be no formality or restraint about the little party. It might have been a company of friends breakfasting at some country farm. The Gobernador made a hearty meal, and his watchful eyes seemed almost benevolent when they rested on Janet or Barbara. There was no reference to the hive of strange activities around them. The young Americans were recondite travellers and talked at large of odd places and odd friends. One of them, Eborall by name, whom the others called Jim, had been with Roosevelt on his Amazon expedition and had something to say of the uneasy life of the Brazilian forests. "We never struck a health-resort like this," he said. "They don't keep them on the east side of the Andes." Grayne, who was something of a naturalist, had a discussion with Archie Roylance about a type of short-winged buzzard that he had seen that morning. The young men spoke deferentially, with an eye on the Gobernador, like subalterns breakfasting with their commanding officer. Janet chattered eagerly in her rôle of the untravelled, to whom every new thing was a marvel. Only Barbara was a little silent. Her eyes were always turning to the door.

Presently it opened and a man entered. At first glance he seemed about the same age as the others, for a fine-drawn face often acquires an absurd youthfulness when, after some days of indoor life, it is first exposed to the weather. The tiny wrinkles around his eyes did not show under the flush of sunburn. He entered like a guest who, having arrived late at a country-house, makes his first appearance at breakfast and knows that he will find friends.

"Sandy, at last!" Janet cried. All rose, and the young Americans turned curious eyes on the newcomer, as on someone who had been eagerly awaited.

"There's a chair next to Barbara," Janet said. "Excellency, I don't think you have met Lord Clanroyden."

The two men bowed, but the newcomer did not offer to shake hands. They smiled on each other with conventional politeness, but the eyes of the elder man dwelt longer on the newcomer's face.

"What's the news?" Janet asked with a casualness that was obviously assumed.

"None at present, except that everything goes well. I must feed first, for my last bite was fifteen hours ago. After that I'm going to turn in and sleep a round of the clock. . . . How jolly it is to be up on this shelf again! I feel a new man already."

Sandy fell heartily on his food. "China tea," he murmured. "Janet, you saint! I haven't tasted it for weeks."

But the pleasant informality had deserted the company. Archie looked heavy with unspoken questions. The young Americans fell silent and kept their eyes furtively on Sandy, as if they were trying to harmonise a preconceived figure of their imagination with this ravenous reality. Janet rose. "I don't see why we should behave as if we were at the Zoo, and watching the animals feed. Your cigarettes are over there, Sandy. We'll leave you to finish your breakfast in peace."

But the Gobernador did not leave the room with the others. He filled his pipe and pushed the Sobranye cigarettes towards Sandy's plate. The latter, having finished the marmalade stage, began to peel an apple. "Please smoke," he said. "I'll join you in a second."

Presently he swung himself round to face the other, and lit a cigarette. His face had lost the careless youthfulness which it had borne when he first arrived. It was the face of an older and a different man, hard, fine, and alert, and his eyes were as wary as the Gobernador's. They seemed to be inviting a challenge.

The latter spoke first.

"I think you owe me an explanation, Lord Clanroyden," he said. The tones of his voice were perfectly quiet and assured. The question seemed to spring not from anxiety but from a polite curiosity.

"I owe you many, but they will have to come bit by bit. Meanwhile I can give you news. The night before last we occupied without serious trouble the city of the Gran Seco. At this moment I think I can fairly say that the whole province is in our hands."

"We! Our! What precisely do you mean?" There was an edge in the voice which proved that its possessor had been startled.

"It is a long story. But the name which the newspaper-readers of the world are associating with the revolt against the Olifa Government is your own, Excellency. You were the creator of the Gran Seco, and you are going to be its liberator."

" Liberator? From what? Am I to destroy my own creation? "

" The copper industry will not suffer. The Vice-President of the Company will see to that. There will only be a suspension of business—how long will depend upon the Olifa Government."

" Rosas? He is in this fool conspiracy? "

" Undoubtedly. You may call him the prime mover. You know him as Rosas the Mexican, but to his friends he is John Scantlebury Blenkiron—a patriotic citizen of the United States——"

The other cried out. " Blenkiron! But he is dead! "

" Only officially. He is an ancient friend of mine, and it is our good fortune, Excellency, that your paths never crossed till he joined you eighteen months ago. You need not blame your Intelligence service. Blenkiron has puzzled before this the most efficient Intelligence services. He had been watching your doings for some time, and when he put his remarkable talents at your service it was with a purpose. The first part of that purpose has now been accomplished."

Sandy paused.

" Go on," said the other. " I am deeply interested."

Sandy laughed. " We have no secrets from our commander-in-chief. But why should I waste time telling you what you know already? "

" I am not sure that I do know. This purpose? You do not want to cripple a great industry? You have no special grievance, I take it, against the republic of Olifa? You are not fanatics about forms of government? Am I to take it that your efforts are directed principally against me? "

" You may put it that way if you like. But we have no personal animus against your Excellency. Blenkiron, who has worked with you for nearly two years, rather likes you. We are all prepared to give you devoted allegiance."

" Provided I do what you want? "

" Provided you do what we want. We are anxious to prevent you making a fool of yourself."

It was the elder man's turn to laugh. " I suppose I

should be grateful, and I am certainly flattered. But I should like to know just what you consider my capacities in the way of folly."

" I hate to repeat platitudes," said Sandy, " but, since you insist, you shall have them. You have created a great industry, but you are following what seems to us an unbusinesslike line. You are using up your human material too rapidly. I put aside the moral question, and ask you simply if that is good business. Of course it isn't, and since you do not do things without a purpose we had to discover that purpose. Well, we know perfectly well what it is. You are trying to make bad trouble in a world which has already too much trouble. We do you the justice to admit that this is not blind malevolence. You have an ideal behind you, a philosophy, a very serious philosophy. Well, to be frank, we don't like your methods, and we don't like your purpose, and we hate your philosophy like hell. Do we understand each other? "

The Gobernador shook out the ashes from his pipe. His eyes, under his level brows, looked steadily on his companion. There was now no smile on his face, and in his gaze there was a serious perplexity.

" Lord Clanroyden," he said, " I have known about you for some years—under your old name. I have even made it my business to keep in touch with you through my informants. I have always regarded you as a person of quite exceptional intelligence. There have been times when I considered you one of the two or three most intelligent people in the world. . . . I confess that I am grievously disappointed."

" No wonder," said Sandy. " I have always been a bit of an ass."

" I don't complain that our aims differ. Your reputation was never that of a thinker. But you were reported to me as a practical man, uncommonly audacious, resourceful, and far-sighted. Now I find that you are audacious—but with the audacity of a crude boy. You have organised a childish little piece of banditry. You think you have fathomed my methods. Why, man, you have not learned

the alphabet of them. I have my lines down deep in every
country on the globe. The Gran Seco has purchase with
every Government. As soon as the news of your doings
has gone abroad, you will have the most potent forces set
at work to defeat you. The prosperity of the Gran Seco
is of vital importance to millions up and down the world.
The credit of Governments, the interests of a thousand
financial groups are involved. The very people who might
otherwise sympathise with you will be forced to combine
to break you."

"True," said Sandy. "But you realise that your name
as our leader will cramp the style of your supporters."

"Only for a moment. It will not be believed . . ."

"I am not so sure. Remember, you are a mystery man,
Excellency, whom the world has heard of, but does not
know. You have been playing a pretty game with the press,
but we too have made our plans. The newspapers by this
time will be full of character-studies of the Gobernador
of the Gran Seco, arranged for by us. In spite of yourself,
you are going to get the reputation of a high-souled humani-
tarian, a cross between Bolivar and Abraham Lincoln. I
think we shall get in first with our picture, and—well, you
know what the public is. It will be difficult to efface first
impressions, and that, I say, will cramp the style of your
people and give us time."

"But what earthly good will time do you? That is my
second charge against your intelligence. You have chosen
to fight me with weapons so infantile that they will break
in a week. . . . What were you and Blenkiron thinking of
to put your eggs in this preposterous basket? I have many
vulnerable points. *I* know that, if you do not. You and
your friends might have slowly organised the collective
stupidity of the world against me. You had your fulcrum
in America, and for lever you had all the crude sentimentality
of mankind. I have always feared such a crusade. Why
did you not attempt it?"

"I will tell you why," was the answer. "It was because
we respected you too sincerely. We knew that we couldn't
beat you at that game. To fight you in parliaments, and

cabinet councils, and on the stock exchanges and in the press would have been to fight you on your own chosen ground. We preferred to fight you on *our* ground. We decided to transfer the whole contest to a sphere in which your genius was not at home. You are the last word in civilisation, Excellency, and you can only be beaten by getting you into the ancient and elementary world where civilisation does not apply."

The other did not answer for a moment. Something in the words seemed to have started a new train of thought, and his eyes took on a profound abstraction. Then he leaned forward.

" There is method in that," he said. " I do not quarrel with your policy. But, in the name of all that is rational, where are your weapons? A handful of children, a disloyal colleague who has no doubt worked upon the turbulent element among our white employees, my kidnapping, and the fact that my administration was a somewhat personal matter—these may give you control of the Gran Seco for a day or two. But what then? There are the wealth and the army of Olifa to crush you like a nut on an anvil."

" Not quite so bad. You underestimate Blenkiron, I think. Remember he has been in the Gran Seco for some time, and he has not been idle. We have the Mines Police, and most of the Mines foremen and engineers. When I left yesterday, the place was as docile as a girls' school, and there was a very stout heart in our troops."

" Troops! " the other said. " You may have got your non-commissioned officers, but where can you get the rank-and-file for an army? "

" Where you got your labour, Excellency. Among the old masters of the country. You must have heard of the trouble that the Gran Seco Indians used to give to Olifa. They were never properly conquered till you came along. You policed them and dragooned them, but the dragoons are now on their side. A couple of years more and you would have drained the manhood from them and left them mere shells of men. But at present they are still a people, and a fighting people, and they are going to fight for liberty and vengeance. Not against you—they regard you as their saviour, and are wearing your medals round their necks —but against the oppressors of Olifa. . . . I think you lived too much of a sedentary life, Excellency. You took the word of your subordinates too much on trust. If you had lived as I have among the pueblas, you would have been a little afraid of what you found there. . . . Perhaps a little shocked, too. . . . Those rags and tatters of men, used up in the mines and flung on the dustheap! The remnant of manhood left in them is not a gentle thing."

"But against the army of Olifa! I have made it my business to see that that army is the most efficient for its size in the world. What can your savages and your gunmen do against the last word of science from the laboratory and the factory?"

"Nothing if we fight them in their own way. A good deal, I think, if we fight them in ours. We refuse to meet you on your own ground, Excellency, and you may be certain that we don't mean to meet the Olifa army on theirs."

"I cannot follow your riddles."

"Of course you can't. This is a very academic discussion we're having. If you'll allow me, I'll explain to you later the general layout. You're entitled to have everything shown you. It will interest you, as a thinker, for, though you'll scarcely believe it, we too have our philosophy of life. You are a very wise man, with a large experience of the world, but I believe we can show you something which you know nothing about."

The other was listening intently. "This wonderful revelation?" he asked. "What is it?"

"The meaning of youth," was the answer. "You have lived all your life in an elderly world, Excellency. Everything worked by rule, and even your lawlessness was nicely calculated. And all the old stagnant things were your puppets which you could move as you pleased. But there's another side of which you know nothing at all. You have your science; well, it will be matched against hope and faith and the simplicity that takes chances. We may go down, but we'll go down cheerfully, and, if we win, by God, we'll make you a new man."

A strange look came into the other's face. He regarded Sandy with a bewilderment in his stern eyes which seemed not altogether unfriendly.

" I cannot quite understand," he said, as he rose, " why you and your friends did not take the simple course. Since your quarrel is principally with me, a bullet in my head strikes me as the most satisfactory solution."

Sandy stood before him, a head shorter, a stone or two lighter, looking at the moment half his age. There was a dancing light in his eyes which answered the flickering spark in the other's. He laid a hand on the Gobernador's sleeve, as if the great man were a coeval.

" Nonsense! " he said. " We leave murder to your Conquistadors. We think so highly of you that we're going to have a try at saving your soul."

I I

THE wireless station on the plateau received its punctual bulletins of news from the outer world, copies of which were posted up in the mess-hut. From them it appeared that the republic of Olifa was already in the throes of a campaign. War had begun when on the 14th day of June the city of the Gran Seco had been seized by the rebels, and the whole province was in revolt. The whereabouts of Castor were not known; his lieutenants held the city, but he was reputed to be with the main force of the revolt, somewhere in the hinterland. Olifa had replied to the challenge. Her army was mobilised, and a Gran Seco Expeditionary Force was in being. The aged General Bianca, the Minister of War, did not take command; for that post the President had selected a younger man, General Lossberg, who had been military governor of the city of Olifa, and had come there after the European War with a high reputation from the Eastern Front, where he had been one of Mackensen's corps commanders. The Expeditionary Force was said to contain four divisions of infantry, a cavalry brigade, and four of the new machine-gun battalions.

The comments of the world's press on the outbreak were curiously restrained. Some influence must have been at work, for the current story represented the revolt as that of the leaders of the copper industry against an oppressive Government, which confiscated their profits and by inhuman laws was ruining their reservoir of native labour. Thus stated, humanity and sound business seemed to be on the side of the rebels. Strange tales were printed of the barbarities of conscripted labour, of men worn to husks and sent back to their villages to die. The picture presented was of enlightened magnates forced unwillingly into harshness by the greed of Olifa, until finally decency and common sense forced them to make a stand. A spontaneous labour revolt had been sponsored by the masters themselves, and at the head stood Castor, the Gobernador. It seemed a clear issue, on which the conscience of the world could not be divided. There were papers in England, France, and America which hailed Castor as a second Lincoln.

Yet the more responsible section of the press walked warily, which seemed to point to conflicting versions of the facts among those likely to know best. Such papers were guarded in their comments on the merits of the dispute, and treated it as a domestic Olifa question on which exact information was lacking. Patently the Gran Seco agents throughout the world were puzzled and were holding their hand. Their chief was playing a game on which they had not been instructed. The news columns of such papers were filled with sensational accounts of Gran Seco wealth and luxury and of Indian pueblas full of the broken and diseased, but the leading articles steered a discreet course. Castor was no doubt a great man, possibly a man of destiny, but the end was not yet—and Olifa had been of late a particularly docile and well-conducted republic. The world seemed to agree to make a ring round the combatants. Only the scallywags and the restless youth of all nations were prepared to take sides, and consulates and passport-offices were plagued by those who wished to reach the seat of war. There were perpetual queues at the door of the Gran Seco offices in London, New York, and Paris.

One body of men alone had decided views—the military critics. Among these there was a remarkable unanimity. The revolt, in their opinion, could not sustain itself for more than a few weeks. The details of the Olifa army were well known. It was officered by able professional soldiers, it had been a pioneer in mechanisation, and *The Times* had published from a contributor some striking articles on its efficiency; it had behind it a wealthy Government, and, should the need arise, a big population to conscript; above all, it had an open door to the sea. The rebels must be at the best a rabble of Indian labourers and European miners, with a sprinkling, no doubt, of soldiers of fortune. They might be armed after a fashion, but they could not compete with the armoury of Olifa. They had no communications open with the outer world. Assuming that they had laid in a store of ammunition, they could not supply wastage. The Gran Seco, which was largely a desert, could not feed itself, and the rebels would be starved out long before they were defeated. It was like a fugitive who had climbed a tree: the pursuit had only to wait below till he was forced by hunger to come down. General Weyland in the London *Times,* and Mr Winter Spokes in the New York *Herald-Tribune* reached the same conclusion.

The campaign had begun; according to the wireless Olifa was an armed camp, and everything was in train for an advance on the Gran Seco; but in the Courts of the Morning there was peace. There was activity enough. Daily aeroplanes left the shelf for long flights beyond the foot-hills, and over the arid steppes of the Gran Seco to the savannahs and forests of Olifa, now sweltering under the first deluges of the rainy season. Strings of convoys ascended by the rough paths and departed with their stores. Horsemen arrived hourly with messages, and every yard of the settlement was busy. Yet it seemed a peaceful busyness. The workers met at meals and in the evenings with the cheerfulness of weary but equable folk. There was no tension in the atmosphere. Castor for the most part had his meals in his own room, but he invariably appeared at dinner, and he seemed to be in good health and spirits. Though under constant surveillance, he had the illusion of liberty, and could walk abroad with Janet and Barbara as if he were a guest in a country-house. There was nothing about him of the feverish prisoner, and this disquieted Sandy.

"I haven't begun to understand him," he told Janet. "You see, all I know about him I know at second-hand from Blenkiron, and by deduction from his public career. I met him for the first time a week ago. Our only talk was just an exchange of polite challenges. We might have been shouting at each other from adjacent mountain-tops. . . . I don't like that calm of his. Here you have a man whose brain has never stopped working, and who has the ambition of a fallen angel. He sees us trying to play havoc with his life's work, and he makes no sign of impatience. What has his mind got to bite on? It can't be idle."

"He writes a great deal," said Janet. "He has told me about it. I don't think I quite understood, but isn't there an Italian called Croce? Well, he thinks Croce all wrong about something, and is trying to explain how."

"O Lord!" Sandy groaned. "The fellow is bigger than we thought. I didn't reckon on this superhuman detachment. He must be very sure he is going to win."

"Yes," said Janet thoughtfully. "But not for the reasons that the wireless gives. He told me that he thought that those military experts talked nonsense. I think he knows that he will win because he is bigger than we are. He has been studying us all most carefully. You especially, Sandy. Do you notice how he looks at you? I believe he was afraid of you before he met you."

"But not now?"

"No. I'm sorry, but I don't think he is so afraid of you now. I fancy he is always a little uneasy about anything he does not understand. But he thinks he is getting to the bottom of you."

"I daresay he is. But I'm nowhere near the bottom of him. None of the formulas fit him. It's no good saying that he is pure intellect. He's that, but he's a great deal more. On his record I ought to hate him. He stands for everything I most detest, and he has been responsible for the bloodiest cruelties. On the bare facts of the case Nero was respectable compared to him. . . . And yet I can't hate him—simply because I can't hold him responsible. He has no notion what he has done, for, with all his cleverness, there's an odd, idiotic innocence about him. I nourished a most healthy disgust till I met him. But now, confound it, I rather like him."

"So do I," said the girl emphatically. "Barbara doesn't, but I do. And I believe he rather likes us—even you, Sandy. You see, we are something that he has never quite met before, and we interest him desperately. He is busy summing us up, and that gives his mind something to work on. Now that I know him, I could no more hate him than I could hate a cyclone or an erupting volcano."

"You mean he is a sort of impersonal natural force?"

"No, I don't. He is a person, but very limited—as limited as a cyclone. His energies and his interests have been constricted into a narrow channel. I think he lacks imagination."

Sandy whistled.

"Good for you, Janet. I should have said that his imagination was the most deadly and colossal thing about him."

"Yes—yes. But it is only one kind of imagination. Milton could imagine the scenery of Hell and Heaven, but he hadn't enough imagination to understand his wife. He is still a little puzzled by us, and that makes him puzzled about himself. Up till now he had been mathematically certain about everything. If we make him uncertain, we may win. . . . Now, I'm going to take him for a walk and continue his education."

Presently, into the orderly routine of the plateau came something of the stir of war. Messengers from the lowlands became more frequent, and Sandy had to take his sleep when he could, for he might be called upon at any hour. The wireless operators were kept busy, and at night there was much activity in the ravine which dropped seaward, for unlighted ships groped their way into the secret gulf. The aeroplanes, which were still used only for intelligence purposes, and not for combat, brought back more authentic news than the war correspondents cabled to the press of the world, and that they gained it at some risk was proved by more than one that returned with damaged planes and bullets in its fuselage.

The Gobernador had shown little interest in the wireless messages from the world's capitals. He had left Olifa with no more than a suit of dress-clothes, and had been fitted out from the wardrobe of Archie, who was much the same height and figure. One morning Sandy came in to breakfast with a new light in his eye.

" Things are beginning to move, sir," he told Castor. " The time has come to get into campaigning kit. We shan't be a dressy staff, but we can't go about like earth-stoppers any more."

Thereafter everyone appeared in simple khaki tunics and breeches. Castor submitted good-humouredly to the change.

" You look like General Smuts, sir," Archie told him, " only a little darker and less benevolent."

Castor smiled. " That would seem to be in keeping. Like Smuts, I am an intellectual compelled by fate to be a leader of guerrillas. Is it not so ? "

That night Sandy and young Latimer pinned up on the wall of the mess-hut a big map mounted on calico, and proceeded to ornament it with little flags.

" There is your province, sir," he said, " a better map than anything the Surveyor-General has in Olifa. The colour-washes represent altitudes. The red flags are our posts, and the green are the Olifa army. I am going to give a staff lecture, for the bell has rung and the curtain gone up."

The map showed only the northern half of the republic, from Olifa city to the apex where the great mountains crowded down upon the sea. From the Courts of the Morning the land fell in tiers—first the wooded shelves, then the barrens of the Seco Boreal, and then the broad shallow cup where the Mines and the city lay. From the

Gran Seco city the country ran westward for a hundred miles till it ended in the rocky sierras of the coast. Eastward it rose into the savannahs of the Indian reserve and the Tierra Caliente, till it met the main chain of the Cordilleras. The map did not embrace this latter feature, and there was no sign on it of the pass into the Poison Country. The south boundary of the Gran Seco was a ridge of dolomite cliffs, broken apparently only at one place—by the long winding valley up which the railway ran from Santa Ana. From the contours it looked to be otherwise unapproachable from that side, save by one or two tortuous and difficult footpaths, at the head of which under Castor's administration there had been block-houses and patrols. There was no breach at either end, for on the west this southern ridge ran out in the coast sierras, and on the east became a buttress of the main Cordilleras *massif*. There were red flags in the city and at the Universum, clusters at two points in the Indian Reserve, one of them very close to the mountains, and a chain running up towards the Courts of the Morning. In the plain of Olifa there was a big green concentration at Santa Ana, and a green blob half-way up the railway.

"Lossberg has got his rolling stock at last," Sandy explained. "He has his pioneers and one of his machine-gun battalions at the frontier, and his cavalry patrols were last night within five miles of the Gran Seco city."

Castor donned a pair of horn spectacles and examined the map closely. He studied especially the Seco Boreal and the eastern frontier. He ran his finger along the southern rim.

"That was always a troublesome place," he said. "Practicable for a mountaineer or an Indian, but scarcely more. At least, so our reports said. But we had to watch it. Rosas"—he smiled—"was always very strong about keeping posts there."

He took a step backward and surveyed the map.

"It appears that the military gentlemen who write to the papers are right," he said. "I seem to be in a very bad strategical position. Olifa can force a passage—it may take a little time and she may have losses, but she can fight her

way up the railway to the Gran Seco. After that we are
at her mercy, at least so far as the city and the Mines are
concerned, for I do not suppose we can hope to win a field
action against her."

"Not a chance," said Sandy cheerfully.

"Then nothing remains but a guerrilla war on our
savannahs. I think she will beat us there, for ours is a
hard dry soil and tanks and armoured cars can go anywhere.
I speak as a civilian, but am I not right, Lord Clanroyden?"

"Perfectly."

"Our troops are mounted?"

"All of them."

"Where on earth did you get the horses? The Indian
ponies are a miserable breed."

"Not so bad as you think," Sandy smiled. "But we had
other sources of supply. Olifa is a famous horse-breeding
country."

"But how did you draw on Olifa? How did you get
the horses up?"

"Some day I will tell you—but not now."

The Gobernador looked puzzled.

"I take it we have a certain amount of food and munitions?"

"Enough to go on with."

"But not indefinitely. . . . Then it looks as if before
long our present dwelling-place would become a point of
some importance. It is now our *poste de commandement,*
and presently it may be our last refuge. We have access
to the sea. If we can find ships, we shall have to make a
moonlight flitting, as your people did at Gallipoli."

"I shouldn't wonder."

Castor took off his spectacles. "I speak with all modesty,
but was it not a blunder to let Olifa strike first? I should
have thought that our best chance would have been to
obstruct the railway—like—like my Dutch prototype in
your South African war. Can an inferior safely surrender
the offensive?" And he smiled pleasantly.

Sandy shook his head.

"It wouldn't have done. We should have given old Lossberg a lot of trouble, but he would have smashed us in the long run."

"Won't he smash us anyhow in the long run?"

Castor moved closer and again studied the map.

"God has been unkind to us in planting that wall of rock and snow in the east. It is most unfortunate that the southern wall of the Gran Seco runs clean up to the mountains without a convenient pass for honest guerrilleros to descend upon Olifa."

"Most unfortunate," said Sandy, but there was no melancholy in his tone. . . . "Well, that's the layout. Now I will expound the meaning of our flags."

He enumerated in detail the strength and composition of the various detachments, and then explained the composition and marching order of the Olifero forces. Castor listened attentively and asked questions. "We are holding the city lightly, but the Mines strongly. Ah, I see. We have a big detachment on the railway. Who, by the way, commands in the city? Rosas? We have given my friend the post of honour—and danger."

Day by day the green flags crept northward till they were spilled in clusters beyond the Gran Seco frontier. Every evening Sandy gave his staff lecture. It was noticeable, now that the campaign had begun, that his spirits rose, and though he had scarcely time to feed or sleep he showed no trace of weariness. Yet there was tension in the air. The faces of the men would suddenly go blank as some problem swept them into preoccupation. Even the Gobernador was not exempt from these sudden silences. He alone had no routine work, but Janet, who had become his chief companion abroad, reported that he was becoming temperamental.

"I think it is this place," she told Sandy. "I don't believe he has ever been much out-of-doors in his life before. He has always lived in cities and railway-carriages, and Nature is rather a surprise to him and puts him off his balance. He told me to-day that this living with sunsets and sunrises made him giddy. . . . His education is progressing.

I wish I knew what he was thinking when he has that blindish look in his eyes."

"He seems to be interested in the campaign," said Sandy. "As an intellectual problem, I suppose. Something for his mind to work upon."

The girl hesitated.

"Perhaps," she said. "But I think there is something more in it than that. He has been adopted for the first time in his life into a community. We others are busy at a game. He is like a child. He can't help hankering a little to play too."

Presently events began to crowd on each other. The green flags made a forest between the Gran Seco frontier and the city, and spread out till their right wing was very close to the Universum Mine.

"That's the cavalry," Sandy explained. "They're finding it a tougher job than they reckoned. Yesterday they tried a sort of Jeb Stuart ride round the city and came in for some rough handling from Peters. They've first-rate cavalry, but indifferent M.I."

Then came a halt and the green flags did not advance for a day or two.

"We put up quite a good little show," was Sandy's comment. "You remember the fifth mile-post down the line where it runs through a horse-shoe valley. That's our position, and it is pretty much like that of the Boers at Magersfontein. They can't find our trenches to shell us out of them. Lossberg is getting nervous about a frontal attack and is considering an enveloping movement. See! He has two of his machine-gun battalions moving east of the Universum. He's bringing up another infantry division, too. That makes three, besides oddments. A pretty good muster against our modest territorials!"

Two days later the red flags had fallen back two miles along the railway.

Sandy, with his eye on a smaller chart, elucidated the position on the big map.

"Our forward zone has gone, and now we're in our

battle zone, though we don't intend to have much of a battle. But we've got to stick it there for a couple of days. . . . You see this bunch of red flags east of the Mines? That's our counter-movement beginning."

"It looks as if we were shaping for a big field action," said one of the young Americans.

"Not a bit. We aren't looking for any barren victories. This is all directed to Lossberg's address. We know a good deal about him, and he's a cautious warrior. He's taking no risks, for he has the strength and he means to use it. . . . I hope to Heaven Peters doesn't dip in too deep."

To Janet and Barbara these days were as thrilling as the last act of a good play. Up in that quiet place, they seemed to watch the struggle like gods from the empyrean. The very map became like a crystal in which their fancy could see the hot mustard-coloured hills, the puffs of shrapnel on the ridges, the ant-like movements of little mortals. Even the Gobernador lost something of his calm, and the eyes under his level brows kindled. In these days the aircraft were never idle. Every hour of the day and night heard the drone of their going or returning.

On the evening of July 17th Sandy had much to tell.

"You will be glad to hear that Lossberg has got his reinforcements. This morning the last division of his Expeditionary Force crossed the frontier."

"You seem pleased?" asked the puzzled Janet.

"I am. I don't want unnecessary bloodshed, and these small holding battles take their toll. It's only a matter of hours now till we acknowledge defeat and fling up the sponge. It hasn't been a bad show, except that Peters went further than I intended. He pushed his counter-attack at the Universum a little too deep, and suffered accordingly. That's the worst of the enthusiastic amateur. . . . There will be a great Olifa triumph presently. It will be fun to see what the papers make of it."

Next day Sandy's good-humour had increased. He appeared at luncheon silent but beaming, and when an excited company gathered in the mess-hut before dinner he arrived like a breathless boy.

" I want a drink, for I've had a dusty afternoon. . . .
Thanks, Bobby, a whisky-and-soda. . . . We needn't wait.
I can give you the news now. Early this morning we fell
back from our last positions and all our troops have been
withdrawn from the city. Lossberg's cavalry patrols must
be in it now. . . . Also the Universum is in his hands,
and the Alhuema and the San Tomé whenever he likes to
have 'em. He will meet with no opposition. The first bout
is past and we've been knocked over the ropes. It's Lossberg's round. . . . You needn't look anxious, Excellency.
There hasn't been ten pounds' worth of damage done to the
Company's property."

" I wasn't thinking of the Company," said Castor, and
his face had become very grave. " Has all this happened
according to your plan? "

" More or less . . . except for Peters's venture. I didn't
want our casualties to go beyond two hundred, and they're
actually three hundred and seventeen. Still, your army has
not suffered badly."

" For God's sake don't call it mine. I'm your prisoner
and your enemy. What's the next step? When is this
infernal folly to cease? "

Sandy grinned benignly. " Properly speaking, the
infernal folly has just begun. The sparring is over and
the real business is about to commence."

The other considered. " Your plan, I take it, was to put
up just enough resistance to compel Olifa to send the whole
of her Expeditionary Force inside the Gran Seco. You
know, of course, that she has reserves? "

Sandy nodded. " But they will take some time to
assemble, and they will have to make their way up."

" Why should they not? "

" It may be difficult, for soon there will be a most imperfect railway."

" And Lossberg."

" Our first business was to get him in. Our business now
is to see that he does not get out."

Castor laughed, but there was no mirth in the sound.

"An ingenious plan! I have been obtuse. I might have guessed it."

Dinner that evening was a strange meal and a short one. There was little talk, since for the first time the unpredictable future brooded over all of them like a cloud. In the cloud there was no depression, but a certain awe. Sandy and Castor were the last to rise. The elder man had recovered his balance, and as they left the hut his eyes met the other's.

"We are declared enemies, Lord Clanroyden," he said, "and the gloves are off. I make you my compliments on your boldness. I take it you are about to leave me and assume the direct command of the revolutionaries?"

"As your lieutenant. I shall report to you regularly."

"Let that fooling stop. I am at present your victim, but some day soon the parts will be reversed. I have only one thing to say to you. You have succeeded for the moment in putting me out of action. But I am something more than a single man marooned up on this shelf of mountain. I have my bodyguard—everywhere in the world, and also in Olifa, and in the Gran Seco. You cannot destroy that bodyguard, though no doubt you have tried, for most of it is subterranean and secret. That force will be fighting for me. Its methods are what you would call criminal, for it does not accept conventional standards of honour. But it is resourceful and subtle and it will stick at nothing. What chance have you against it? You will be compelled to take risks, and that force I speak of will make those risks a certainty of death."

"I wonder why you tell me that. Is it meant as a friendly warning?"

"I am not your friend. It is a warning. I do not wish you to deceive yourself. I want you to know what is against you."

For a moment Sandy stared at Castor's face as if he sought something buried deep in the man. Then he laughed.

"Thank you, Excellency. . . . I hope they'll make you comfortable while I'm away. . . . If we meet again, we may be able to shake hands."

III

THE details of Lossberg's advance up the railway, when, with overwhelming superiority of numbers and artillery, and after various checks, he drove in the screen of the defence, and on July 19th entered the Gran Seco city, do not belong to this story. They will be found set out at length in the dispatches of the correspondents who accompanied the Olifa army. Those veracious writers gave ample information about the Olifa command, for censorship was thought unnecessary in such a case, but they were very much in the dark as to the *personnel* of the enemy. Castor was assumed to be commander-in-chief, and Rosas, described as a Mexican adventurer who had been once on the staff of Porfirio Diaz, was credited with such military talent as the rebels possessed. The correspondents had followed the military critics in assuming that the result was a foregone conclusion. But presently a new name appeared in their dispatches—Obro, an Indian word which was interpreted in Spanish as " el lobo gris "—" the grey wolf." El Obro was believed to be the name of a guerrilla leader much reverenced by the Indians, who was assumed to be lurking in the hinterland. As the weeks passed this name was to appear more often, till presently Castor and Rosas were almost forgotten and it had the headlines to itself.

On the day before the defence broke, Blenkiron was sitting on an empty shell-case in what had once been the garden of his house behind the Administration Buildings. An algarroba tree gave him a little shade from the pitiless sun, and, since he was grey from head to foot with dust and had a broad battered panama hat pulled down over his head like a burnous, he had something of the air of a cadi under a palm. Around him stood a small group in rough field-service kit, all of them dusty and a little hollow-eyed, their shoulders limp and rounded like those of men who have not lain flat in bed for several nights. The place was very quiet to be in the heart of a city. There was no sound except that of an occasional car driven at top-speed in the adjoining

street, though an alert ear might have caught at intervals
a curious pattering noise coming from the south, a noise
which at times grew into something like the beating of
muffled drums.

A man was speaking, a man with a drawl and a sleepy
voice. This was Escrick, the sub-manager of the Alhuema
Mine, who had once commanded a brigade of Australian
infantry in France. He had been in charge of the position
astride the railway, and had sited the trenches so skilfully
that Lossberg's guns had bombarded dummies and Lossberg's advance had been time and again held up by concealed
machine guns. He had now the task of drawing off his
men by night, a task which, having been at the evacuation
of Helles, he had no doubt as to his ability to perform.

Blenkiron, as the plan was unfolded, glanced at the paper
in his hands, and at Escrick's further elucidation with the
point of a riding-switch in the thick dust. Then he turned
to another man, a heavy red-faced fellow who was perpetually mopping his face with a blue-spotted handkerchief.
At his look of inquiry the man nodded.

"The last of the supply waggons leave this afternoon,
sir," he said. "Three of the centres are already stocked
up, and the fourth will be completed by midnight. The
men should be well on their way before daybreak to-morrow,
and all arrangements have been made for mining and
blowing-up the roads behind them."

"You're not leaving much behind?"

"Not an ounce of flour or a pound of bacon," was the
answer.

"I reckon that's fair. It's up to Lossberg to feed the
population of the city he captures. What's it they call them,
Luis? The *bouches inutiles*?"

Luis de Marzaniga smiled. "There won't be too many
of these useless mouths, Señor."

"Lordy, it's hot!" Blenkiron sighed. "Let's get inside
the shack and moisten our lips with lime-juice. The maps
are there, and I'll like to have a once-over before we get
back to our jobs."

A hut in the garden had been transformed into an office,

and on one wall hung a big plan made of a dozen sheets pinned together. It had none of the finish of the products of a Government Map Department, being the work of the Mines surveyors. Each of the men had a small replica, which he compared with the original.

There followed an hour of detailed instruction as to routes and ultimate concentrations. Four points were marked on the big map with red circles. One, lettered Pacheco, lay in the extreme south-west angle of the Gran Seco. Magdalena, the second, was a hundred miles farther north, under the shadow of the peaks called the Spanish Ladies. The third was near the centre of the northern part of the province, the Seco Boreal, and had the surprising name of Fort Castor: while the fourth, Loa, was at the opening of the neck of land which led to the Courts of the Morning.* The commandos under Escrick were to make for the two latter points, while Peters and his forces, which had been fighting in the Mines sector, had the two former for their objectives.

There was also to be a change in the command. Blenkiron, once the city had been surrendered, laid down his duties. The field force in the future would be divided between Escrick and Peters; and, under Castor as generalissimo, the operations as a whole would be directed by him whom the Indians called El Obro.

"I guess we'll keep to that pet name," Blenkiron said. "It sounds good, and kind of solemn. We haven't any use for effete territorial titles in this democratic army, and 'Sandy' is too familiar."

Then he made the men repeat their instructions till each was clear not only about his own task but about the tasks of the others—a vital thing in a far-flung force. After that he lectured them. . . . So far luck had been on their side. Their losses had been small; under estimate in the railway sector, and not thirty per cent. beyond it even after Peters's rash counter-attack. No officer had fallen, and only six had been wounded. One aeroplane, unfortunately, had been brought down, and the pilot and observer, both young

* See map on end-papers.

Mines engineers, killed. That was their most serious casualty. " A very nice little exhibition of the new bloodless conduct of war," said Blenkiron. But this was only the overture; the serious business was now about to begin, when they had to make the country fight Lossberg, as Washington made the geography of America fight Burgoyne and Cornwallis. " It's going to be a mighty tough proposition, but I reckon if we pay strict attention to business we'll put it through."

" Say, though," said Escrick, " what is going to be the upshot?"

" Peace, sonny. We've got to make the Excelentisimo at Olifa so dead-sick of the business that he'll want to deal. Same game as Robert E. Lee played before Gettysburg. We can't beat them, but we may make them want to deal. And in that deal Mr Castor is going to state the terms. And those terms are going to fix things more comfortably in this province, but principally they are going to fix Mr Castor. . . . You've got the schedule for to-night clear? Then we'd better dissolve this conference. I join you, General Escrick, at twenty minutes after midnight."

The men entered their dusty cars and departed, while Blenkiron went into his house, accompanied by Luis de Marzaniga, who seemed to be acting as his chief staff-officer. As they lunched frugally off sardines and biscuits, Blenkiron was in a cheerful mood, but a shadow seemed to hover about the face of the younger man.

" What's worrying you, Luis?" Blenkiron asked. " Things have panned out pretty well according to plan. There's snags good and plenty to come, but we needn't think about them just yet."

" I think, Señor, that there is one snag which we have forgotten."

" Meaning?"

" The *bouches inutiles* whom we are leaving to the care of General Lossberg."

" Why, man, we can't do anything else. The civilians in a captured city are not our concern. They're *his* funeral. He's bound to treat them well for . . ."

" It is scarcely a question of humanity. But some of these *bouches* may be mischievous."

" The Bodyguard? "

The young man took a paper from his pocket.

" Here," he said, " I have a list of the more dangerous of the Bodyguard and of those gentry whom we call the Conquistadors. I have made notes on each. . . . Kubek —he was happily killed in this very house. We found his body over there by the window. . . . Ramiro and Mollison, they were shot by Peters at the round-up. . . . Bechstein—dead of spotted fever. . . . Snell—died of wounds two hours after Kubek. . . . But Radin and Molinoff are at large—you remember that they broke away in the confusion, when the house in the Calle of the Virgin fell as Peters was taking them to the lock-up. . . . There are others, too. We know nothing of what became of Martel and Carvilho and Magee and Trompetter . . . and Laschallas, whom we used to think as dangerous as Kubek. Do you know that he, or somebody very like him, was seen last night in a drinking-den near St Martin's Port? "

" That only means that there are a handful of bad men loose. You can't corral all the scamps. Besides, a gunman's not too dangerous in a war where everybody has a gun."

" I wonder. Remember that these are a very special type of gunman. The Gobernador chose them for their brains out of the rascality of the globe. . . . Then there are the three ruffians you sent with him to Olifa. What were their names? "

" Carreras, Judson, and Biretti."

" Yes. Well, you may be sure they will come back, if indeed they are not back already. . . . I do not like it, Señor. They are dangerous grit to get into our wheels. I should be happier if I knew that they were in their graves."

" So should I. But I don't let that outfit worry me. I reckon they're part of the legitimate risk of war. Anything more? "

" The Conquistadors."

Blenkiron laughed aloud.

" That pie-faced bunch! Say, Luis, you're getting fanciful. What harm can those doped owls do us? They'll be waiting for Lossberg and making a fuss about their comforts. It's him they'll bite, not us."

"I wonder again. Lariarty was in the round-up which Lord Clanroyden organised. He was consorting with the Bodyguard. Is there not something there to make us think?"

" Why, Luis, you're barking up the wrong tree. Except for Castor, I reckon I know the Conquistadors better than any other man, and I've sized them up long ago. They're the most dangerous stuff on earth, so long as Castor has the handling of them, but without him they're no more good than dud shells. They've powder enough, but, lacking Castor, they haven't the current to fire the charge. Let 'em alone, and they'll just moon about and rot."

" And yet Lariarty was at the meeting which was nearly the end of Lord Clanroyden. He sat in the judge's chair. It is right to assume that he had some part in the plot. . . . I think you are wrong, Señor. I think the Conquistadors are like sick wolves—dying, if you like, but with enough strength to turn and bite. And, remember, their bite will be deadly, because it is poisoned."

Blenkiron looked perturbed. " I can't bring myself to think that. What could they do? They won't fit in with Lossberg."

" No, indeed. General Lossberg, if I understand him, will make nothing of them. He is a conventional soldier, and will fight his battles in the old professional way. . . . But what if the Conquistadors keep the same company that we found Lariarty keeping? They have no scruples. What if a dull anger and a craving for their drug—for presently they will get no more of it—what if that kindles their wits and screws up their nerves sufficiently for one desperate throw? The remnants of the Bodyguard, if they can find them, will be their executants. They will think chiefly of getting to Castor, and, failing that, of revenge."

" It will be hard to reach the Courts of the Morning."

" Maybe. But it may be less hard to reach you—or Lord

Clanroyden. Our army is not a machine, but a personal following. A well-aimed bullet might make it a rabble."

Blenkiron sat brooding for a moment. " I think you put the risk too high," he said at last, " but we can't neglect any risk. Have you put Intelligence on to the job? "

" Señor Musgrave and his young men have been too busy fighting battles. I have done a little myself."

" You have told me what gunmen survive, but you haven't located them. How about the Conquistadors? "

Luis took up another paper.

" Lariarty, whom Peters wanted to lock up, was set free by Lord Clanroyden. He has been living quietly in his rooms, playing much music on his piano. There are five others in the Gran Seco, and they profess to be waiting till the Mines are started again, whether by Lossberg or ourselves. They shrug their shoulders, and behave as if there were no war. The dandyism of their clothes has not changed, and they feed solemnly together at the Club or the Regina. What they do beyond that I cannot tell."

" Who's here beside Lariarty? "

Luis read from his paper.

" Señores Frederick Larbert, Peter Suvorin, Maximilian Calvo, Jacques D'Ingraville, Luigi Pasquali."

Blenkiron considered. " After Lariarty I should say that D'Ingraville was the danger. He's not so deeply dipped, and he's the youngest. Funny to think that he was once a French flying ace."

" I have something more to tell you. Romanes is returning. I had information this morning that two days ago he landed in Olifa and that he is now with Lossberg."

" H'm! I don't like that. Europe has a bad effect on those lads—breaks their temper and quickens their brains. And he won't get the dope to quiet him—not unless he goes into the Poison Country, and Peters will have a word to say to that. . . . Darn you, Luis, you've given me a thorn to lie on, just when I was feeling comfortable and meaning to hog it on my bed till sundown. What are you going to do? "

" I would beg leave of absence till eight o'clock. You

have no need, I think, for my services, and there are one or two inquiries I wish to make before we leave the city."

So, while Blenkiron, who had slept less than six hours in the past three days, did his best that afternoon to make up arrears, Luis de Marzaniga set out on his own errands. He visited the Club, and saw in a corner of the deserted dining-room three men lunching. They were just beginning, and in the dislocation of the service their meal was bound to be a slow one. Satisfied with his survey, he joined a young man, who was waiting for him in the street, and the two made a round of domiciliary visits. This young man knew his business, and the outer doors of three flats were neatly opened without damage to the locks. Two of the flats—those of Larbert and D'Ingraville—were in normal order, full of books and bibelots and queer scents, but the third, that of Peter Suvorin, was in a state of supreme untidiness. Its owner had been burning papers in the stove, his bedroom was littered with clothes, while a half-packed valise stood on the bed. "It seems," said Luis to his companion, "that Señor Suvorin is about to make a journey."

His next visit was alone, and to the Regina Hotel. There it was plain that he had a friend, for a word to the head-waiter in the almost empty restaurant got him an immediate interview with a servant in a little room behind the office.

"Señor Pasquali's apartments?" he asked. "You have watched them as I directed?"

"With assiduity. The Señor is going away soon. Where, I do not know, but he has had his baggage prepared as if for a rough journey. Also he has received every night at the hour of ten a visitor."

The visitor was described: a tall man, with a long dark face and high cheek-bones, like an Indian's. No, not an Indian—certainly a white man. There was a white scar on his forehead above his right eye. He spoke with Señor Pasquali in French.

Luis whistled. "That is our friend Radin," he said to himself. "Radin beyond doubt. What has that ugly rogue from the gutter to do with the superfine Pasquali, who plays Scriabin so ravishingly? They may be going travelling together—perhaps also with Suvorin. Luis, my dear, these things must be looked into."

Luis went out into the glare of the afternoon with a preoccupied face. He walked for a little down the Avenida Bolivar, and then struck through a nest of calles in the direction of the smelting works. His preoccupation did not prevent him keeping a sharp look-out, and presently in a jostle of market-women at a corner he saw a face which made him walk quietly back a little, slip up a side-street, and then run his hardest to cut it off. He failed, for the man had disappeared. After a moment's reflection Luis returned to the Administration Buildings and sought out the room given up to the headquarters of the Air Force. The true air base was the Courts of the Morning, but there was an aerodrome and a single squadron behind the city. There he cross-examined the officer in charge as to whether any Olifa planes had recently crossed their lines. He was told that four had been brought down, but that to the best of Head-quarters' knowledge no voluntary landing had been made. " But we cannot tell," said the officer. " We are not holding a continuous line—only two sectors."

" Then an Olifa plane might land someone in a place from which he could make his way here? "

" It is possible," was the answer. " Not very likely, but possible."

In the narrow lane Luis had seen Dan Judson, one of Castor's three trusties. Where Judson was one might look to find also Carreras and Biretti, and the probability was that all three had been landed from an enemy plane and were now in the city. Suvorin and Pasquali were making a journey, and Radin was privy to it. Luis's next business was to go to tea with Lariarty, whom he knew a little.

He found that gentleman quite openly preparing for the road. Lariarty's face was whiter than ever and his eyes looked tortured; but they also looked most furiously alive, and his whole body seemed to have woken into an hysterical life.

" Ho, Señor," Luis exclaimed. " Do you follow us into

exile? I thought you would await the conqueror here—seeing that you have no politics—and advise him wisely about Gran Seco business. That was also Señor Rosas's belief."

Lariarty looked at him with a composure which seemed to be the result of a strong effort, for the man was obviously ill at ease.

"Some of us remain," he said. "But not I. I wish to be at the Gobernador's side, for his interests are my interests. I have to-day been at Headquarters, and it is arranged that I go with General Escrick."

"What makes you so certain you will find the Gobernador with Escrick?"

"I am not certain. But if I am with the field army, it stands to reason that I must sooner or later come across the commander-in-chief."

"Who are staying behind?"

"All the others."

"Suvorin?"

"Yes."

"And Pasquali?"

"Certainly. Why do you ask?"

"No reason at all. . . . I congratulate you, Señor, on your courage, for we of Escrick's command must ride fast and far. You are perhaps out of training for the savannahs and the mountains?"

"I am not in good form. But there was a time when I was never off a horse."

Luis abounded in friendly advice, as from an old campaigner, and finally took his leave. "We shall meet in the darkness," he said, and was told that Lariarty had orders to report himself at midnight.

It was now within an hour of nightfall and Luis repaired to Blenkiron's house for a bath. As he splashed in the tepid water, he reflected. "I am certain that they are all going with Escrick," he told himself. "Lariarty alone will go openly, but the others will be there somehow—Suvorin and Pasquali and Calvo—likewise that trinity of cherubs, Judson, Carreras, and Biretti. Larbert and D'Ingraville will

wait here till Romanes comes, and then join them. . . .
There's going to be a gathering of the vultures somewhere
in the North. . . . They're after the Gobernador, and if
they fail to get him they may do some miscellaneous
shooting."

After his bath Luis made a careful toilet from a store of
clothes which he carried in an old saddlebag. A yellow shirt
with a fancy collar, flapping trousers of dirty grey, skin
brogues, a dark poncho, and a high-crowned, broad-brimmed
hat transformed him into a mestizo peasant, at least three-
quarters Indian. He rolled some cigarettes of leaf tobacco
and placed them behind his ear, and then sauntered across
the Avenida, down through the narrows of the Market, to the
cluster of yards and huts above the dry ravine which separated the city from the smelting works. His disguise was
perfect, for he stopped now and then to engage in a street-
corner argument, and mixed as naturally with the disputants
as if he were one of the vegetable-sellers whose mules lined
the causeway.

He found the place he sought, an alley close to the sunken
street called St. Martin's Port, where had stood centuries
ago a tiny monkish settlement. All had gone except a tooth
of ancient brick masonry, which had once been part of an
arched gateway. The street was a warren, full of bolt-
holes that looked like cul-de-sacs and cul-de-sacs that looked
like bolt-holes, but Luis seemed to know his way about it.
At the head of a court, the paving of which may have been
contemporary with Pizarro, there was a green gate in an
adobe wall. He pushed through it and said something to
a slatternly half-caste woman, who sat dozing in a chair
outside a second door. He opened this and stumbled into
what was obviously the back-room of a café, the front of
which was in another street. Stumbled, for he seemed suddenly to have become rather drunk.

There were few in the place, three or four peasants
drinking small glasses of aguardiente, and one man in the
shadows who had before him a tankard of beer.

Luis joined the group of peasants and gave his order.
An albino negro, a weird sight in that ill-lit place, brought

him his drink, and he commanded another glass for the man opposite him.   This was a gipsy-looking fellow with long earrings, who had been discoursing to the company on cock-fighting.   A dispute presently arose in which Luis's hic-cuping voice was predominant.   It was about the merit of Gomez's red cock which had won the championship at Maddalo on St. Rosalia's feast-day.

The dispute grumbled, died down, flared up, for all had the air of having drunk too well.   Then the talk became con-fidential between Luis and his *vis-à-vis*, and they shuffled a little apart from the others.   More drinks were brought. There was a sudden gust of quarrel, and Luis in dudgeon removed himself across the room.   But his new friend fol-lowed, and there seemed to be a reconciliation, for once again the two heads were close together and the talk was all of cocks and challenges.

In his new position Luis was scarcely a yard from the dark corner where the man with the tankard of beer was sitting.   There were now three of them there.   They looked viciously at the argumentative peasants, but there was no other part of the room which promised greater peace, and they remained sitting.   Luis was by way of now being very drunk, and he made his confidences at close quarters into the garlic-smelling ear of his companion.   But this position left his eyes free to wander, without the other noticing it, and he had a good view of the men in the shadows.

One had the face which he had seen three hours before in the crowded calle—a small man, very thickly made, with rabbit teeth, an underhung jaw, and a broken nose.   This was the famous Daniel Judson.   Beside him sat a taller man with a long, sallow, clean-shaven face and thick, dark eye-brows which made a straight band almost from ear to ear. This Luis knew for Laschallas, who, as he had told Blenk-iron, was the most dangerous of the survivors of the Body-guard.   But it was the man opposite the two who surprised him.   He wore a thin dark overcoat with the collar turned up, but the face above the collar had the unmistakable waxy pallor of Lariarty.

In the intervals of his drunken wrangling Luis tried to

catch their conversation. But not a word could he overhear. They spoke in low tones, and when he sidled nearer them, still in the embrace of his cock-fighting colleague, Judson arose and cursed them. The other was scared into sobriety, for Mr Judson in his wrath was not a pretty sight, and Luis had perforce to follow him and put as much distance as possible between the three and themselves. Presently he gave up the attempt to eavesdrop, extricated himself with some difficulty from his companion, and staggered out of the café by the road he had come. He had learned several things—that the trusties, or at least one of them, were in Olifa, that Laschallas was alive, and that Lariarty was not leading an idle life.

He went home, got into proper clothes and hunted up one of Escrick's staff-officers. There was a good deal of sound coming from the south, where the retreat from the trenches was being covered by machine-gun activity, and some of the troops already withdrawn were filing through the streets. What had been infantry was now being transformed into light cavalry at the horse-lines north of the city. Luis found the staff-officer he sought, and learned from him that the only civilian accompanying Escrick was Lariarty— Blenkiron himself had sanctioned it—for whom a seat had been provided in one of the staff cars. He left the office with injunctions that no civilian passes were to be given without further reference, and that the occupants of every car were to be jealously scrutinised.

Then he supped with Blenkiron, and told him what he had discovered. Blenkiron, still sleepy as an owl, was slow to take it in. " They can't do anything," he reflected. " They're bottled up in this city, whether it's me or Lossberg that's in charge. They're town rats, Luis; they won't thrive out in the wilds. Where are you going? "

" I thought I'd look up Lariarty and see if he's ready. I propose to keep an eye on that gentleman."

But when Luis was admitted by Lariarty's servant to Lariarty's flat he found no sign of impending departure. Lariarty, washed and perfumed, was wearing a smoking-suit of silk, and in the buttonhole of his jacket was a yellow picotee, such as Archie had remarked in the Gran Seco visitors the first night in the Olifa hotel. He was improvising on his piano. The nervousness of the afternoon had gone, and he seemed to be at ease with the world.

" Hullo, Señor," Luis cried. " You'll be late. We start in twenty minutes."

Lariarty smiled and went on playing.

" I am not coming. Not at present. I have been reconsidering the matter, and I think that it is my business to remain here. Here or at Olifa. My duty is to the Mines, and my knowledge may be needed."

Something had happened that evening, some news had reached the Conquistadors, which had caused them to change their plans. It would be as well, Luis thought, if they all remained in the city; he had not approved of Blenkiron's consent to Lariarty's departure, which seemed to have been the unthinking decision of an overpressed man. . . . But did this mean that all would stay behind? Was there no chance of a blunder in this midnight retirement? The last four days had been too feverish to allow of strict attention to the ritual of surveillance which had looked on paper so perfect. The thought made Luis hurry to the northern barrier.

The outlets from the city were few, and all were carefully barricaded. It was now midnight, and the troops were by this time safely out of the trench lines, where now a rearguard was conducting a noisy camouflage. The place was as bright as day with the great arc lights on their tall standards, and in their glare a mounted army was assembling, as shaggy a force as ever followed Timour or Genghiz. They had for the most part come straight from the line, and there was no sleep for them till they had put many thirsty miles between themselves and the Olifa van. Yet they were a cheerful crowd, and drank black coffee out of bottles and smoked their little acrid cigarettes before they jogged off, each squadron to its appointed place.

The officer in charge of the business, a young analytical chemist, saluted him.

"All goes smoothly, sir," he said. "The staff leaves in a quarter of an hour. The road is being kept clear for cars. Your advance party got off half an hour ago."

"Advance party!" Luis stammered.

"Yes, sir. They presented your instructions and I countersigned them, as your telephone message directed."

"Yes, yes, of course. Were their passes all right? I was afraid they might be slow in reaching them."

"They were all in order, with the Chief's signature."

"One car, you say?"

"They packed into one car. Rather a tight fit for six of them."

"Who was driving?"

"Mr Suvorin. He was the only one I recognised."

"A good car?"

"One of the new Administration Packards. There's nothing wrong, sir?"

"Nothing. I was just wondering when we would overtake them."

IV

In the Courts of the Morning there was still peace. The brooding heats, the dust-storms, the steaming deluges of the lowlands were unknown. The air was that of a tonic and gracious autumn slowly moving to the renewal of spring. The mornings were chilly, with a sea-fog crawling over the rim of the plateau; the days were bright and dry as old wine, the nights blue and starlit. There was peace in that diamond ether, but it was not the peace of lethargy but of ordered action. The place was as busy as ever, but it had no longer the air of a headquarters. It was now a base, a depot, and the *poste de commandement* was somewhere far below in the broken levels which spread dizzily towards the southern sky-line.

The Gobernador had been given his choice. "I can take you with me," Sandy had said. "It won't be a comfortable life, but you don't mind that. Or you can stay here in the watch-tower and follow our doings on the map."

"I am free to decide?" Castor had asked, and was told "Perfectly." He had considered for a little and had finally chosen to remain. "I am your enemy," he said, "and we should be at too close quarters for comfort. I shall stay here till something happens."

Sandy laughed. "I know what you mean. Well, I hope it won't, but if my luck gives out don't imagine that the show is over. You're the only one in your class, but I've heaps of alternatives in mine. Archie will keep you posted and I'll look in every now and then."

But Sandy did not come back. . . . The crowded days' work went on; horse and mule convoys came daily up the mountain paths and departed with their burdens; the receivers ticked busily in the wireless station; aeroplanes—fewer than before, for the fighting machines were mostly at advanced headquarters—departed at dawn and returned often after nightfall, while flares like forest fires burned to guide them to their landing-places. There was a special activity in the glen which led to the sea; it seemed as if its defenders had reached the conclusion that that port to the outer world would soon be discovered and closed, for almost every night some kind of tramp put in and unloaded and stole out before the following daylight. Busiest of all were the two girls. Barbara was in charge of the hospital stores, and it seemed that these were now urgently needed, for in the plains below men were suffering. With her staff of peons she worked early and late, with Janet as an unskilled assistant.

The latter had another duty laid upon her, and that was to provide company for the Gobernador. With Sandy's departure he had become the prey of moods. His former equability had gone, and he appeared to swing between a profound abstraction, when he seemed unconscious of his surroundings, and a feverish interest in them.

For example, he visited constantly the top of the ravine and would spend an hour gazing into the green depths which ended in a sapphire patch of sea. Once, when Janet accompanied him, he turned to her sharply.

"This place could be forced," he said. "Olifa has a

navy. . . . It would take a week—ten days perhaps—and she would lose a thousand men, but it could be done. Then this sanctuary of yours would fall. How would you escape?"

"I suppose by the hill roads to the south," Janet answered.

"But they will be blocked. It might be hard to force a way up here from that side, but Olifa could block the exits. What then?"

"I'm sure I don't know. I don't believe both disasters could happen at once."

"Why not?"

"Simply because things don't work out that way."

He laughed angrily. "You are all children. You trust childishly to fortune. That's well enough for Clanroyden and the others. They are soldiers and take chances. But what is to become of *you*?"

"Barbara and I went into this with our eyes open."

"You were a fool, then. And your husband was a fool to let you."

There were many similar occasions when his face looked sharp and anxious and there was a hard edge to his voice. But there were others, when the mountain spaces seemed to work on him as an opiate and he fell into a mood of reflection. From these fits he would emerge with cheerfulness almost, certainly with philosophy. At such times he seemed to enjoy Janet's company and would detain her in talk from her many duties. He would ask her questions about herself, her home, her views on life, with an engaging ingenuousness, as if he had discovered a new type of mortal and was labouring to understand it. He had a natural good-breeding which robbed his questions of all impertinence, and in this novel sphere Janet felt that she could regard him as an equal.

"This hill-top is bad for me," he once told her. "I have no facts to work upon and I begin to make pictures. Wasn't it Napoleon who said that we should never think in pictures, but always look at things as if through a telescope—bring reality close to one, but always reality?"

"Isn't that begging the question?" the girl replied. "Reality for us is what we make of things. We may make them conform to our picture. It is what we all do. It is what you have been doing all your life, Excellency."

"But your pictures and mine have been very different. I am a scientist and you are a romantic."

"You are the romantic. You have tried to force the world inside a theory, and it is too big for that. We humble people never attempt the impossible. You are a self-deceiver, you know."

"Why?" he asked.

"Because of your intellectual pride. It is only humility that sees clearly and knows its limitations."

"Lord Clanroyden, for example, is humble?" There was a not unpleasant irony in his voice.

"Profoundly."

"Yet he has challenged me. With his handful of amateurs he has challenged the might of Olifa. Was your Jack the Giant-killer humble?"

Janet laughed. "I think he was. Jack saw that the giants were far bigger than himself, but that, being overgrown, unnatural things, they were bound to be stupid and weak."

"You think that a colossus is always weak?"

"He must be if he is outside the human scale. If he has no other flaw, he will have the weakness of pride."

"You and your friends are very proud."

"Oh, I hope not. If we are, we shall be punished for it. Sandy—Lord Clanroyden—is daring, but that is not because he thinks too much of himself, but because he believes that he has great allies."

"Such as?"

The girl quoted:

> "*Exultations, agonies,*
> *And love, and man's unconquerable mind.*"

Castor laughed.

"That is Wordsworth, isn't it? It is a good answer, Lady Roylance, from your point of view. I am prepared to admit that Lord Clanroyden has allies—at any rate, he has friends. He need not be lonely."

"You are lonely?" she asked with kind eyes.

"I have always been rather lonely. . . . Perhaps . . . if I had met someone like you . . . long ago . . . I should not be so lonely to-day."

It was Archie who brought the first big news. One evening he appeared at dinner with his left arm in a sling. "Not a wound," he explained. "It was my own dashed silliness in getting too near the business end of a mule. I've been having a giddy time and I'm badly short of sleep. How are things going? *Pas si bête*, as they say—except for Sandy. Old Sandy has gone stark mad. At present it's a useful kind of madness, but the question is how long it will be till he goes clean off his rocker. He's been doing pretty desperate things."

Later he explained.

"Lossberg is making war according to the books. Sandy sits down and thinks out very carefully what the books direct and then does the exact opposite. He is trying to draw the enemy deep into the country, and for that purpose he is making a feature of Fort Castor. We've a pretty useful Intelligence service, and the best part of it is that section which we put at Lossberg's disposal. You see, having the country on our side, we have a lot of enthusiastic volunteers. Lossberg picks up some Indian or half-starved mestizo who is easily frightened into telling what he knows. The poor devil is obviously speaking the truth, for he is too scared and stupid to lie. Only what he says has been carefully pumped into him by our little lot. The result is that Lossberg has got it into his head that Fort Castor is our big base, and is stretching his claws round it as carefully as a cat stalking a mouse. He has moved up the better part of a division. But there's nothing in Fort Castor except mounted patrols. We put up a beautiful camouflage and let Lossberg's flying men have a discreet look at it once

in a while. But when he takes the place after some trouble
he won't find a tin of bully beef in it."

Somebody asked where Sandy was.

" He was in Magdalena yesterday. We are organised in
two armies. Escrick, with the Army of the North, is now
divided between Loa and Magdalena, and he has a covered
line of communications between them through the hills
behind, just like what Stonewall Jackson had in the Shenan-
doah valley. The enemy has spotted neither. Peters, with
the Army of the South, is playing the same game. Lossberg
thinks he is based on the Indian pueblas in the Tierra
Caliente from which he can threaten the Mines, and consequently he has a division strung out from the San Tomé
to the Universum and is building a sort of Great Wall of
China in the shape of blockhouses. Peters just does enough
to keep the Mines lively, but he isn't worrying about them.
All he wants is to get Lossberg rattled."

Archie pointed to the south-east corner of the big map.

" There's a spot there called Pacheco, just under the hills.
That's Peter's real base. He's got some nice country west of
that for his scallywags to operate in. There should be news
from that quarter pretty soon."

" Base? " he said in reply to a question of Castor's.
" Why, we haven't any proper base, and we haven't any communications to cut. We're the most lightly equipped force in
the world, for we don't go in for high living. A bit of
charqui and a bag of meal will last one of our fellows for a
week. Also we know all the wells and water-holes, and
Lossberg doesn't. Water is going to give him a lot of
trouble."

" Has he no one who knows the country? " Janet asked.

" Not as we do. He'll pick up somebody later, for we're
bound to have a traitor or two in our camp. Also there are
your gunmen, Excellency. One or two of them have been a
bit around. But he hasn't got anybody yet, and has gone
poking about, trusting to bad maps, and the lies we manage
to feed him."

" What about his Air Force? "

Bobby Latimer answered.

"So far we've managed to keep it in order. We've nothing on them in the way of flying, for they're nicely trained, but they can't just fight in our way. And they haven't any machines as good as our new Gladas. If this were a regular war, they'd be mighty good at contact work and bombing expeditions. You never saw prettier squadron flying. But we've no communications to bomb, and at present they're wasting their efforts every night on Fort Castor."

"But do none of their planes get abroad and discover your real whereabouts? Magdalena, for example—or Loa?"

"So far we haven't let them. We can beat anything they've got in pace and we seem to have more appetite for a scrap. There's been one or two very pretty dog-fights. Besides, it don't signify if they spot Magdalena or Loa or even Pacheco. We could shift somewhere else in a couple of hours."

"But you have a base." It was Castor who spoke. "Where we are sitting now is your base. If they take this, you are lost. If they even bomb it, you are deeply embarrassed."

"I think that's right," said Latimer. "Therefore it's up to us to let no enemy planes north of Loa. So far they haven't shown any inclination in this direction. They're too much occupied with General Peters."

"Yet at any moment they may discover it?"

"There's no reason in the nature of things why they shouldn't," said Archie. "But it's one thing for a chance plane to spot us and another thing for Lossberg to exploit his knowledge."

Three days later Archie returned in high spirits. He had two pieces of news.

The first was that Bobby Latimer had brought down an enemy plane north of Loa. The pilot and observer were alive, and the plane was not too badly damaged, so they had added one to their stock of aircraft—a Seaforth monoplane, on the mechanism of which he discoursed at length. Happily they had the spares for it. He welcomed this new sign of enterprise on the part of Olifa as likely to relieve the tedium of his job. When Janet observed that, if one enemy could get as far as Loa, a second might get farther, Archie was reassuring.

" The way I look at it is this. They've spotted Loa— they were bound to hear of it from spies and such-like. But they're so darned unenterprising that only one of their planes gets through. If these things be done in the green tree, what shall be done in the dry? Loa is an easy mark, but this place from Lossberg's lines would be dashed difficult, even for a swell like Bobby."

The other news was startling. Peters's raiders had made the garrisons at the Mines nervous, and, since it was assumed that the guerrillas were based on the villages in the Indian reserve and drew their supplies thence, it was resolved to clear that country and bring the women and children into a huge concentration camp near the city.

Archie was triumphant. " It's what Sandy has been playing for, but he scarcely hoped to bring it off. . . . Lossberg thinks the Tierra Caliente is an asset to us. Good Lord! it's a millstone round our necks. Presently we should have had to feed these villages—a thing we had budgeted for —and this means that we shall now be a thousand per cent. better off for supplies. He's a humane man, your General Lossberg. The concentrados will be a long sight better off with him than on their own, and if they get pinched a little when he gets pinched, we had made our book for that. Soon we'll all have to draw in our belts. . . . Sandy has made Lossberg hold the baby for him, which is what you might call strategy."

A light of reminiscence woke in his eyes.

" That was always old Sandy's way. Once at Crask, I remember, he fairly did *me* in. We were out rough shooting together and it was a blistering hot day. When we turned at the march burn, we were both a little bored, for we had seen very little, so by way of putting a spice of interest into the game, we agreed that I should carry what he shot and he what I shot, and I backed myself for a fiver to give him the heavier load. Well, I soon presented him with a hill partridge and a snipe, while he hadn't let off his gun. Then I'm blessed if he didn't shoot a roebuck and I had to sling the infernal brute on my back. After that he couldn't miss, and I hadn't the proper use of my arms. I staggered into Crask just about dead with heat, and laden like Balaam's ass—roebuck on back, string of grouse and blackcock round my neck, rabbits in my pockets, and one and a half brace of snipe in my hat."

For a day or two the plateau drowsed in its bright aromatic heat, and no news arrived except what the Olifa wireless told—how Lossberg had begun to clear the Indian country, and the rebels, baseless and foodless, were for certain no more now than bands of refugees clinging to the mountains' skirts. Fort Castor, their chief centre, had been occupied without serious opposition. It was anticipated that soon there must be a general surrender. Olifa was marching to an easy victory, and the President, in a public speech, spoke contemptuously of the rabble of amateurs which had attempted to defy the disciplined forces of the republic. The comments of the foreign press were no longer guarded. The military critics congratulated themselves on their prescience, and wrote, almost with regret, of the mathematical certainties of modern warfare.

Their views did not disturb Janet's peace of mind, but she had her own anxieties. She had an apprehension of some calamity approaching, and studied the blue sky for that enemy plane which might break through their guard. The drone of a machine arriving sent her hurrying out-of-doors, and she would wake with a start in the night and listen for a beat in the air which would be different from the beat of their own planes. Castor seemed to share her excitement; his eyes also were always turning skyward.

Then came two days of storm, when the thunder rattled among the crags of Choharua, and the rain fell in torrents, and the outlook was limited to six yards of swirling vapour. After that came a wind which threatened to uproot the huts, and which brought the sound of a furious sea even up to that ledge of mountain. During these days the wireless was disordered by atmospherics, but from its broken messages one thing emerged. Something had happened, something of vital importance, something which had got on Olifa's nerves. It could not be a battle? Surely Sandy had never been betrayed into measuring his meagre strength in lists chosen by the enemy.

Then one afternoon Archie arrived, a weary Archie who could scarcely speak for drowsiness.

" Has there been a battle? " Janet demanded.

" Not likely. But we've begun the offensive."

" What losses? "

" None. Practically none on either side. But there's been the deuce of a lot of destruction of property. Sandy says it's cheaper than human life and just as effective."

" What have you done? Quick! Tell me."

" We've cut the enemy's communications. I'm dropping with sleep, Janet. In six hours you'll hear everything."

In six hours a washed, shaven, fed, and refreshed Archie told this story.

" Ever since Lossberg started pushing out from the Gran Seco city, our army has more or less disappeared. He felt us, but he didn't often see us, barring, of course, our planes. Yet he was being sniped and shelled and bombed a good deal and Peters kept him lively at the Mines. Two things accordingly happened. The first was that Lossberg, not being able to get us into the open, thought we were far stronger than we were and grew more cautious than ever. The second was that he thought we had all our men in two places—up in the hills north-east of Fort Castor and in the eastern end of the Tierra Caliente. In that he was right—more or less—but he didn't know the length of our range. The consequence was that he thought that the city and everything south and west of it were safe, but that the east and north-east were formidable and needed a big striking force. So he held the railway with only three garrisons between the city and the frontier—at San Luca, at Villa Bar, and at Gabones itself—and small posts of six men each every four miles." *

* See map on page 358.

Archie with pencil and paper drew a sketch of the railway.

"You remember the big dry valley twenty-five miles down the line. I believe there's occasionally a trickle in it in January, but just now it is like the Prophet's Valley of Dry Bones. There's a big viaduct crosses it—sixteen arches, the biggest and costliest piece of engineering on the whole line. It would have taken a cog-and-pinion arrangement or miles of circuitous gradients to get the railway across the valley. So the engineers very properly decided on a bridge.

"Blenkiron always had his eye on the San Luca bridge, and so had Lossberg, for he had a post at each end, twenty men with machine guns at San Luca station—that's the north end—and thirty-five at the south end, at a place called the Devil's Ear. It was the only part of the line about which he showed any nervousness. But his posts weren't very well placed, for they were at the abutments of the bridge, and the bridge has sixteen arches, and the valley is more than half a mile wide, so that if there was trouble about the middle of the viaduct it would be some little time before the ends heard of it and arrived to help.

"Blenkiron—the scheme was his principally—wanted to cut the line at a place where it would be hard to mend. San Luca was an obvious spot, especially as the bridge was unguarded in the middle, since it was calculated that wandering bandits could do no harm to the huge stone piers. Lossberg's engineers in the Gran Seco could do any ordinary repairs that were required, but something very big would want help from Olifa. So Blenkiron's second job was to make it pretty hard for Olifa to get to San Luca, and that meant a simultaneous bedevilment of the railway somewhere well to the south of the Devil's Ear."

Again Archie had recourse to pencil and paper.

"You see this point here, twelve miles north of Villa Bar and about twenty-three from San Luca. The railway runs in a deep cutting, the beginning of the long climb to the watershed. On the east side there's a considerable mountain with a shaly face, which is shored up to prevent it slipping on to the metals. There was a little post about a mile off at a place called Tombequi—half a dozen sleepy

Oliferos who spent their days playing spadillo and begging for drinks from the passing trains.

"Well, it was Peters's outfit that got the job, and it was decided to make it a long-range business. You see, not one of our fellows had so far been seen within fifty miles of the railway after the city was surrendered, so Lossberg assumed that all was well there and took no precautions. We didn't want to alarm him, so we took Pacheco for a base, the better part of one hundred and fifty miles off. It's an ugly bit of country from there to the railway—the south rim of the Gran Seco basin, and on the north face of the rim an abomination of desolation, all pitted and tortured red rocks like the Sinai desert. The crest, however, is flattish, with a good deal of scrub on it, and there's water in one or two places—the actual springs, I fancy, of streams that go down into the Vulpas valley. There used to be posts there, but Lossberg had no use for them, and on that bit of frontier all he has is a few mounted patrols which keep to the low ground on the north side under the rocks. Accordingly we fancied the high ground above the rocks, where there was nobody to spot us except vultures.

"We left Pacheco last Tuesday night with Sandy in command. He insisted upon taking charge—said he wanted a little fresh air and exercise—I flew him over from Magdalena that evening. I never saw a fellow in such spirits— filled with 'em, drunk with 'em. There were two parties— one under a chap called Jervoise, mounted on wiry little Indian ponies, with some queer kit on their saddles. That was the Tombequi outfit. The San Luca crowd were coming in cars and weren't due to start from Pacheco till twenty hours later. A place had been agreed on as a rendezvous.

"It was a mad ride, and Sandy was the maddest thing in it. It looked as if he had been getting charged with electricity till he could hold no more and had to give some of it off in sparks. He's fit again too, fitter than I've ever seen him before. . . . We climbed out of the levels up long glens of loess till we struck the stony corridor that runs between the ridges. There was a big white moon, and the shale looked like snowdrifts and ice couloirs. There wasn't a sound, for there are no beasts or birds up there—only the thud of hoofs, an occasional clash of buckles, and Sandy humming his crazy songs.

"We did fifty miles before dawn, and then lay up for most of the day on the top of the ridge, where there were water and scrub. We were off again at nightfall, and next morning came to the place they call Tulifa, where there is a bad foot-track up from the Vulpas valley. Here we had to go cannily, for we had to get off the hills, which had become a series of knife-edges, and take to the sandy valleys to the north of 'em. Yet they made pretty fair cover for men in open order, and we had goodish guides, and by nightfall we weren't twenty miles from the railway. The staff-work had been top-hole, for we got to the appointed rendezvous just fifteen and a half minutes late. The cars had come through without a hitch and had been hiding all day in a ravine. There were three of 'em—Rolls-Royce chassis and bodies that looked like a travelling circus.

"At the rendezvous we separated. Sandy transferred himself to the cars, for San Luca was the main objective, and I went with him. Jervoise trotted off with his bandits according to plan. They had to work exactly to schedule, for there was a big freight train due to pass Tombequi at forty-three minutes past nine. The plan was to let it pass and blow up the line behind it, while we blew up the San Luca bridge in front, and so bottled it up. Our motto was 'Anything to give pain'! . . .

"I wasn't an eye-witness of Jervoise's show, but it ran like a clock. The roads were difficult and the party had to split up, but the sections arrived to a tick, and the only chaps who could complain were the poor devils of horse-holders, and the Olifa post, who were surprised at supper and put in the bag. No—there were no casualties, and we don't take prisoners. Jervoise annexed their trousers, and turned them loose. He don't like the raggedness of his outfit, and consequently has the eye of an old-clothes man for pantaloons. His lot made a fearsome mess, blew up the track in twenty places over a three-miles stretch, and tumbled down half the mountain-side on it. Sandy reckons it will take a fortnight's hard work to clear it.

" I was in the San Luca push myself. There was a dust-storm blowing up from the east and the moon was covered, and as we had no lights and the road was naked prairie I'm bound to say I felt a bit rattled. If you're loaded up with gun-cotton and blasting gelatine it isn't much fun to be ricocheting from boulder to boulder. We couldn't go slow and feel our way, for we had to keep to schedule time. But the weather was a godsend, for the wind drowned the noise of our wheels, and when we got to the bridge, the lights were burning clearly at each end and everything as peaceful as Clapham Junction.

" We didn't take long about the job, for the whole thing had been arranged to the last detail, with the help of a plan of the bridge provided by one of our fellows who had been in the railway shops. We laid the charges, lit the fuses, and, if you believe me, when we started off on the return journey we weren't two minutes out in our reckoning.

" It was all too easy, and that made me nervous. But we didn't miss fire. In the War I saw a good many mines go up, but never anything like this. The empty valley became suddenly like Tophet, spouting sheets of greeny-yellow flame, while a mushroom of black smoke wavered above it. Then the wind blew the mushroom aside, and we saw that two of the arches had gone and that the viaduct was like a man's mouth with the front teeth drawn. . . . After that there is nothing to tell. The posts on each side of the bridge started shooting into vacancy, and just as we left there came an agonised whistle from the south. It was the freight train slowing down to discover what the devil had happened."

Thus Archie to Janet. Before dinner he repeated the tale in its main features to Castor, who heard it with drawn brows.

" I make you my compliments," the latter said. " You have certainly instituted a new kind of war. Can Lord Clanroyden repeat the performance?"

" Whenever he pleases. You see, we have the real

mobility, and we have also knowledge of the country on our side. Lossberg already finds it hard to know what to do. He can't police the whole Gran Seco, and as soon as he gets away from his bases we give him beans. We're not too well off for stores, but we can always replenish at his shop. . . . No, we don't mean to make the railway unworkable. We can't afford that, for we want Lossberg to supply himself—that he may supply us. He's our Q. side. But we shall make it so difficult that the job will take up a lot of his time. He's vulnerable, you see, and we're not. We're not in the same elements. It's like a fight between a wolf and a shark."

"Then how can you hope for a decision?"

"We don't want any dramatic *coup*. We want to tire him out so that he'll see it's hopeless, and Olifa will make peace. On our terms, of course. . . . On your terms, that is to say," Archie added.

Castor smiled at the correction.

"You are convinced that you are invulnerable?" he asked. "What about the air? Olifa has twice your number of machines."

"She can't use 'em properly. That's our almighty luck. They're good average flying men, but they've no genius for the thing, and we've got the pick of the American fliers. Blenkiron saw from the first the necessity of that."

"If you had a genius against you it might be uncomfortable?"

"To be sure. In the air you don't reckon by quantity. One airman like Lensch—you remember?—the Boche who was killed in April '18—would put a different complexion on the business."

It was Janet who first saw the stranger. She had gone for a before-dinner scamper on the downs, and had turned for home, when her eye caught sight of a small monoplane coming in from the sea. That was not a route taken by their own planes, and the girl halted and had a look at it through her glasses. It was a strange make, one she had never seen before, and suddenly she realised what it meant.

Lossberg had at last broken the cordon, and the Courts of the Morning were discovered.

As she galloped furiously towards the huts, she saw that the alarm had become general. The visitor had dropped low and was cruising scarcely two hundred feet up, getting a full view of the details of the place. There were no anti-aircraft guns, and the rifle shots from the sentries left him unharmed. . . . Then one of their own planes rose, and the girl checked her horse to watch. The stranger let it approach, and then—contemptuously, it seemed—flew towards it. There was a burst of fire, the two planes seemed about to collide, and then by a curious manœuvre the stranger slipped out and turned his head for the sea. She thought she saw a hand wave in farewell. It was indeed farewell, for the pursuing plane was utterly outclassed in speed. Almost in a minute, it seemed to her, the stranger was a speck in the pearly haze which marked the meeting of sea and sky.

She found Archie and Castor outside the mess-hut.

" Do you still maintain your invulnerability? " the Gobernador asked, but Archie did not hear. He was engaged in a passionate soliloquy.

" There's only one fellow in the world who could do that trick," he exclaimed. " I've seen him do it a dozen times. . . . Who? A Frenchman called D'Ingraville. He used to go gunning for Lensch, and would have got him too, if Peter Pienaar hadn't chipped in first. But D'Ingraville died long ago."

" I think you are mistaken," said Castor quietly. " Captain Jacques D'Ingraville has been for several years a member of my staff."

V

THE new Administration Packard, which a little before midnight on the 18th of July carried six men beyond the northern barricades of the Gran Seco city, did not continue more than a few miles on the road which ran to Fort Castor. Suvorin, who drove—he had in the early days of motoring

won the Grand Prix in the race from Paris to Marseilles
—did not know the country, but there were men with him
who did. Obedient to their instructions, he turned to the
right at the San Pedro calvary, and for three hours bumped
and skidded along sandy tracks and over stony barrens.
It was apparent to one who kept an eye on the stars that
he was bending south in a wide circuit, and presently the
party came to the main highway between the city and the
Mines. Since the defence was not holding a continuous line,
but only two sectors, the party were no longer in the battle
zone. They did not cross the road till it had been carefully
reconnoitred, and once beyond it the car was again in a
moraine of boulders and banks of shale. The moon had
long set, and the headlights were working feebly, so that
it was more by good fortune than by skill that it came at last
to the respectable road which ran from the Universum Mine
to the railway-sidings south of the city. Here it turned
west and made better speed, till the dancing pencils of the
searchlights revealed the proximity of General Lossberg's
army. The travellers were in fact very near the General's
advanced headquarters, and a rifle-shot over their heads
presently brought them to a halt. Among them they must
have had adequate passports, for an hour later they were
partaking of the General's hospitality. He was in a good
humour, for he had just had word of the evacuation of the
city, and believed that now he was pressing hard on the
heels of the fleeing and broken rebels.

Of the six occupants of the car only one accompanied
the General on his triumphant entry. This was the driver
of the car, Peter Suvorin, a tall man with a bony face and
skin like old parchment, and hair so pale that he seemed
almost an albino. The others prepared to go down country.
General Lossberg entertained him and Pasquali to breakfast, and had an interview thereafter with the others in the
extremest privacy. They formed a curious contrast to the
trim Olifa staff. The General was very neat in his field-
grey uniform, a well-set-up figure which did not look its
fifty-eight years, square, tanned face, brisk, grey moustache,
steady, competent grey eyes—the whole a little marred by a

stupid mouth and a heavy, rather brutal chin. The motor-car party compared to him seemed like a wandering theatrical troupe. Pasquali, he who played Scriabin, was indeed sprucely dressed and wore an expensive fur-coat, but his prognathous jaw was blue and unshaven, and his dark eyes so opaque with weariness that he looked like a sick negro. Radin was a tall fellow, whose high cheek-bones suggested Indian blood, and who carried a recent scar above his right eye. Daniel Judson, short, thick, with rabbit teeth and a broken nose, looked like a damaged prize-fighter, and thick black eyebrows above a sallow face gave Laschallas the air of a provincial actor imperfectly made up. Trompetter, a Javanese Dutchman with a touch of the tar brush, had a broad, wedge-shaped face as yellow as a guinea, and little sharp pig's eyes. All, except Pasquali and Suvorin, were dressed in oddments, and, having been in close hiding, looked as unwholesome as the blanched insects below an upturned flower-pot.

Another joined the conference, a man with a light-cavalry figure, wearing a suit of thin tweeds which had been made not a month before in London. He shook hands with Pasquali and Suvorin, bowed to the General, and nodded to the others. Lossberg spoke to him at length, and he appeared to assent.

"You, Señor Romanes," said Lossberg, "and also Señor Suvorin enter the city with me. I will have you attached to my Intelligence section. These other gentlemen return in half an hour to Olifa, in the charge of Señor Pasquali. They will report to General Bianca and put themselves under his instructions. I must bid you good-bye, gentlemen, for time presses." And the brisk general not unwillingly left the group to an aide-de-camp.

So the party of five travelled in comfort that day down country, and, after many delays owing to freight trains, reached the city of Olifa on the following morning. They duly reported to General Bianca, but they did not take his instructions. They seemed to be concerned with urgent business of their own, for they disappeared into the under-world of Olifa, meeting every evening at a certain café in a back street. Yet there was nothing clandestine about their activity, for not a day passed without one or more of the five being closeted with high officials of the Army, the Marine, or the Police.

VI

IT was on the evening of the 9th day of August that D'Ingraville paid his brief visit to the Courts of the Morning. Archie departed at once to report, and returned next day to order certain precautionary measures. Two of their best fighting scouts, with Roger Grayne in charge, were stationed there, and arrangements were made for early notice of any future visitors from the air. By this time the camp at Loa was known to Lossberg and his next advance would be in that direction. But it was from the sea that the immediate danger was feared. Provision was made for closing the sea-ravine by explosions which would hurl down a thousand tons of rock and strip part of the gully as bare as the face of a wall. Since their communications with the outer world would thus come to an end, such action was to be taken only in the last resort, and it was anticipated that any ordinary attempt at landing could be repelled by the garrison of the ravine. Only if Olifa made an assault in force would heroic measures become necessary. The thing had to be faced, for D'Ingraville must have given Lossberg the exact position of their base, and, since it was obvious that it must be replenished by sea, it would be easy to discover the point of access to the shore. Plans had long been settled for evacuating the Courts of the Morning in case of need, and it was essential that an assault from the sea should be obstructed long enough to enable the plans to be methodically carried out. The one thing to guard against was surprise. A post was stationed on the shore, two others respectively a third and a half of the way up, and a strong garrison at the summit to guard the precipitous final section. All were connected by telephone with main headquarters and with each other, and there were numerous small mines laid which could be used in the detailed defence of each part of the route.

The incident, however, had shattered the peace of the plateau. The place was no more a sanctuary, for its secret had been laid bare. Barbara, busy with her hospital stores, seemed to be unconscious of the change, but Janet fell a prey to a perpetual apprehension. She tried to laugh at herself, but the ghost would not be laid. The shelf of mountain, which had seemed so secure and homelike, was now but a narrow ledge on a great cliff, and she herself a climber sick with vertigo. . . . The enemy was down below in the woody shelves, slowly creeping nearer, and the army of defence was apparently at the other side of the Gran Seco. He was out on the broad seas, waiting for the dark of night to swoop in upon the coast. She would stare down into the green depths of the ravine, and imagine it peopled with fierce faces, and horrible with smoke and blood. In the coverts of wildwood on the plateau enemy spies might be lurking—even far up on the grim face of Choharua. She pictured the enemy—men with evil, pallid faces, such as she had caught a glimpse of in the streets in her visit with Archie to the Gran Seco, and at the picture she thrilled with horror.

Her fears were worst at night, when she would awake at the slightest sound and lie for a space listening, with every nerve tense. . . . In the daytime she forced herself to cheerfulness, and managed to fill up every minute with duties. The weather was changing, and the spring rains were beginning. The sky, which for weeks had been an arch of crystal by day and by night a velvet canopy ablaze with stars, was now perpetually clouded, and often the plateau would be shrouded in a fine mist. This obscurity did not help her spirits. It seemed to offer cover for infinite chances of surprise by land, water, and air.

One thing only gave her comfort. She had decided weeks before to make herself a good pistol shot, and now she assiduously practised, under Roger Grayne's tuition. Grayne, large, rugged, shaggy, and imperturbable, was a fortunate companion for a nervous girl. Janet had always been a

fine rifle shot, and now she became a very fair marksman
with a revolver, and learned to shoot in any position.

"That's fine!" Grayne would say. "I shouldn't like to
be up against you in a rough-house, Lady Roylance. Say,
you're not worrying about this little business? It's all as
right as rain." And when, moved by his friendliness, she
confided to him her doubts, he laughingly disposed of them.
. . . The weather was far worse for Lossberg than for
them. Supposing his planes arrived on a compass course,
they were morally certain to come to grief, for the plateau
was tricky in a dead calm, and certain death in foul weather
to anyone who did not know it. . . . An attack from Loa!
It would take weeks for the enemy to fight his way through
the most difficult country on God's earth, and there were
roads by which every ounce of supplies could be got off
before Lossberg was within thirty miles. . . . The sea!
He admitted that there was a risk there, but there could be
no surprise. There was just the one narrow avenue of
approach, and that could be held against the whole darned
Olifa navy long enough to give them ample time to move.
"You see," he concluded, "we're so fixed that we can't be
surprised. Olifa's got to come in force to take our sea
approach, and coming in force means early notice. We're
not worrying about stray guardacostas. It's not as if one
man could wriggle through and bomb us in our beds. That's
the kind of game I don't fancy, but it's about as likely here
as for an army corps to come over Choharua."

But if Grayne was a solid comfort to the girl, the
Gobernador was very much the reverse. He, like her,
seemed to be the victim of nerves ever since D'Ingraville's
plane had vanished seaward. He was no longer friendly
and forthcoming, a pleasant companion indoors and abroad.
He had become silent and preoccupied, and meals were
Trappist-like banquets. Nor did he, as at the beginning
of his sojourn on the plateau, spend much of his time in
his own room. He seemed to dislike to be alone, and to have
nothing on which he could fix his mind. From morning till
night he roamed about the settlement, constantly turning
his eyes to the sky, always intent and listening. There

were no restrictions on his movements, so he went many
times to the sea-ravine, and sat on the rocks at the top of
it staring downward and seaward.

Once Janet found him sitting huddled there in a waterproof coat, when a shower had passed and a watery sun was
trying to shine. The air was stuffily raw, oppressive to the
walker, but chilly when movement ceased. He was squatting
like a figure of Buddha, and his eyes seemed trying to pierce
the clouds which drooped low over the sea.

" You are looking for your deliverers, Excellency? " the
girl asked.

He shrugged his shoulders.

" I told you," he said, " that folly is always punished.
But its punishment may be also a foolish business. This
holiday camp seems to be coming to an end."

" Perhaps. Do you know, your voice sounds as if you
were rather sorry? "

He did not reply, but unbuttoned the collar of his waterproof as if the weather choked him.

" I have seen you shooting at a target," he said at last.
" You can use a pistol? "

" Pretty well. I'm improving every day."

" Then you have the ultimate safeguard. You need not
fear the worst."

" I hope for the best," she said with enforced gaiety.
" Perhaps I may shoot General Lossberg."

" Lossberg! " he repeated almost bitterly. " You need
not fear Lossberg. I was thinking of something very
different, and I am glad to know that in the last resort you
will be safe. . . . Most women are afraid of pistols, but
you are different from most women. After all, it is a
merciful death."

Janet shivered, for the eyes which the Gobernador turned
upon her had that in them which she had never seen before.
There was anxiety in them, and something which was almost
tenderness. She understood that if she feared the coming of
his deliverers, so also did he—and not for his own sake.

" I'm afraid we are giving you a miserable time," she

said, trying to speak lightly. "We have dragged you out of your comfortable groove into an anxious place."

"You have upset the work of my life," he said gravely. Then he added, as if by an afterthought, "and the foundations."

"The foundations?"

"Yes. I had a clear course marked out, like a chart. Now the chart is overboard, and the rudder is swinging loose."

"There may be other charts," she said gently.

Then she averted her face and began to talk nonsense rapidly, for she realised that she herself must be the chart-maker.

VII

ON the evening of August 19th the rain, which had fallen all day, ceased, and a thin fog oozed out of the ground. By six o'clock night had fallen and a small wind had risen, and, since the sky was heavily overcast, the darkness was soon like the bottom of a cellar. . . . The moon would not rise for an hour or two, and, unless the weather changed, it would give little light.

At the foot of the sea-ravine, in a log hut above the jetty, the coast garrison was preparing supper. Behind was a short space of flat ground, much of which had been cleared, but a grove of dead fan-palms remained, whose withered leaves rustled and creaked in the wind. It was a noisy spot, for the torrent after its breakneck descent drove through the boulders of the beach in a fury of loud white waters. In that sheltered bay the sea was calm, but the stream made a perpetual clamour as of beating surf.

The garrison consisted of six Indians of the hills, four of Luis's haciendados, whom he specially trusted, and two of Grayne's ex-marines. The whole was in charge of one of the Alhuema engineers, a gnarled Ulsterman called Corbett, who had come to the Gran Seco from Rhodesia, and whose experiences went back to the Matabele wars. There was a small stove in the hut, and, since supper had just been cooked, the air in that tropical spot on the sea-level was like an orchid-house. A lantern stood on the trestled table, but windows and door were closed so that from the sea no light could have been observed. Only the white men and the mestizos sat at the table; the Indians ate their meal of boiled millet and syrup in their own circle apart.

Corbett mopped his brow. He had begun to fill a pipe and had stopped as if in a sudden distaste.

" I can't smoke in this blasted conservatory," he said. " Shade the light, Bill. I'm for a little fresh air."

He unbarred one of the windows and let in a current of steamy wind which stirred but did not cool the thick atmosphere of the hut. Outside the night was hot, noisy, and impenetrably dark. He stuck head and shoulders out, and promptly drew them back.

" Bill," he whispered, " come here! First stick the lantern under the table. . . . Look straight ahead. D'you see a light?"

The man called Bill stared into the blackness and then shook his head.

" Nix," he said.

" Funny," said the other. " I could have sworn I caught a spark of something. It might have been on the water, or on the land across the channel. No, not at the seaward end—at the end under the big red rock. . . . Here, Jones, you have a look-see. You're like a cat and can see in the dark."

The Indian addressed as Jones had a long look. " I see no light," he said. " But I can hear something which is not the wind or the stream. Bid the others be quiet."

He remained motionless for several minutes, like a wild animal that has been alarmed. Then he too shook his head.

" It has gone," he said. " For a second I thought I heard a man's voice and the noise of a ship."

" But the whole damn place is full of noises," said Corbett.

" This was a different noise. The wind is from the west and the sea carries sound."

" Where might it have been?"

"I think near the rock beyond the water."

"Same place as I thought I saw the light." Corbett rubbed his bristly chin. "Can't say I like that. Jones and me may be dreaming, but it's the first time we've ever imagined anything like it. We'd better get the patrols out. Bill, you stay here, with Jones and his two mates. Keep your ears cocked and your eyes skinned. And you'd better call up Number One and tell 'em that we're a bit anxious. Kittredge will take the southern beat up to the head of the gulf—same three as last night—and I'll go north. It's the water's edge we've got to watch, so there's no call to go fossicking in the bush. . . . Remember the drill, you all, if you hear a shot. We meet here again at midnight, when Bill and his little lot turn out. No smoking for you boys. Keep your pipes in your pockets till you get back."

We are concerned only with the doings of Kittredge and his party of three, whose beat lay south along the shore of the little gulf to where the land swung round in a horn of cliff to form the breakwater which separated the inlet from the ocean. He had with him one Indian and two of Luis's mestizos. Beyond the jetty the trees descended almost to the water's edge, high timber trees festooned with lianas, but for a yard or two on the seaward side the western winds had thinned the covert a little, and the track zigzagged among bare boles. Beyond, the hill dropped almost sheer, so that the traveller was wet by the tides, but farther on there was a space of treeless ground, covered with light grass and thorn bushes, and at the water's edge, where another stream entered the sea, a reed-swamp, haunted by wildfowl.

Kittredge divided his patrol. To the Indian he relegated the patch of forest, since he was the best man for a tangled country. The place where the cliffs dropped sheer to the water he left to one of the mestizos, for it seemed the easiest to watch, since its rear was protected. He himself with the other mestizo took the patch of savannah which stretched to the head of the gulf. They did not keep very near the sea because of the swamps, but chose the higher ground among the grass and scrub. It was not a good place for observation, since the ears were filled with the rustling of dry sedge in the wind, and the eyes in the darkness could have made out nothing except a light.

Kittredge and his man saw no light, and they heard little but the wind in the grass and reeds and an occasional stirring of wild duck. They made their way to the head of the gulf and about eleven o'clock turned for home. They expected to pick up the other mestizo in the cliff section, but could not find him, so they assumed that, since they were a little behind time, he had gone back according to instructions to the rendezvous in the hut. The Indian in the forest belt was still awaiting them. He had seen and heard nothing.

But the man in the cliff area had not gone home. He had sat for half an hour on the shelf of rock straining his eyes into the gloom. Then, being alone, he had become the prey of fears, for he was superstitious. He had said his prayers, and moved a little north, so that he could have the sheer rock-wall at his back. A movement in the sea startled him, till he decided that it was a fish. But he had become restless and nervous and again shifted his post, this time to a boulder which overhung deep water. He was just about to squat himself on it, when a sound halted him, and in a moment of panic he felt for his pistol. It was his last earthly act, for at that instant a knife was neatly driven between his shoulder-blades, and almost in the same movement his pistol was taken from his hand and his body slid quietly into the sea.

At Post No. 1, two-thirds of the way up the ravine, the telephone message from the shore had been duly received. It was a small post, and the officer in charge, an old colleague of Corbett's, was not inclined to disregard his warning. But since the post was at a turning, where the cliff was sheer above and below the path, there seemed no need for special precautions. Anything which came up the path would be instantly observed. But it occurred to him that it might be just possible to avoid the path and make a way across the creeper-clad precipice and the steep glen up a tributary stream, so he sent a man up the road to the only corner where such a short-cut could debouch.

This man, an Indian of the Gran Seco, was not accustomed to forests, nor to the thick steamy darkness of that gash in the mountains. He started at every sound—the cry of a piripipi bird, the rustle of a dead branch, the rooting of a wild pig, for all were unfamiliar. Presently, being a philosopher, he decided that every noise was alike and innocuous, and relapsed into meditation. His philosophy was his undoing. About a quarter of an hour before midnight, as he sat sleepily perched on the end of one of the many wooden bridges, something struck him, something as sudden and secret and deadly as a serpent's fang. Quick hands thrust his dead body into the thicket. He was not missed by Post No. 1 till next morning at breakfast.

At Post No. 2, the half-way post, placed beside one of the main platforms of the chute, the night passed without incident. There the ravine was broad and densely wooded, and the angle of the slope was only some 30 degrees. Nothing that night appeared on or near the path.

The garrison at the summit were in tents strung out on both banks of the stream before it began its descent, and completely commanding the path and the off-take of the chute and the wire ropeways. The current of the stream had been used to develop electric power for haulage, and the engine-house stood close to the left bank. The post was admirably sited to command the path, but, owing to the obstruction of the buildings, it had no long field of view to left or to right. The uppermost part of the ravine was wider than the lower, and very steep, but ribbed with lateral spurs. It was possible for an active man to make the ascent by one of these spurs without the cognisance of the summit garrison.

Geordie Hamilton, late of the Royal Scots Fusiliers, was not only in charge of the garrison but also of the engine-house, since by profession he was a mechanic. He and his men, mostly Mines workmen, were stalwart bulldogs to guard a gate, but they were not greyhounds to range at large. They had received Corbett's warning from the shore, and till well after midnight were very alert to watch the only area from which they anticipated danger. . . . The wind was rising, and the glen was full of sound. They did not hear, and if they had heard they would not have regarded, the fall of a stone in a subsidiary gully a quarter of a mile to their left, the creak of a log, and the long screech of metal on stone which means that nailed boots have slipped. . . .

Janet had gone to bed in a happier frame of mind. The Gobernador had caught cold, and Barbara, fearing fever, had given him a sleeping-draught and packed him between blankets. Moreover, she had shifted him from his ordinary quarters to another hut, one with a fireplace, which Janet and Archie had hitherto occupied, Janet removing herself to his in exchange. His new hut was close to the mess-room in the very centre of the compound; his old one was on the northern outskirts, selected originally in order that it might be specially guarded by sentries without making the fact too obvious.

Janet slept till a little after midnight, and then for no apparent reason she found herself wideawake. This was constantly happening to her nowadays, and she lay for a little with her nerves on stretch, listening for she knew not what. There was no sound except the wind, making odd little noises in the thatch and among the unseasoned planks of the hut. There were sounds, too, coming from inside, so she snapped her bedside switch and stared into the corners. But it was only the wind stirring a pile of old picture-papers and flapping a waterproof on a peg. Janet turned off the light and tried to compose herself to sleep again. She thought of a procession of ducks on a common and sheep coming through a gate, but it was no use. Very soon she realised that she was hopelessly wideawake and would not get to sleep again that night. She realised something more —that her nervous unrest had come back with redoubled force. She felt her heart beating and her fingers twitching and a ridiculous, unreasoning fear at the back of her head.

Very much ashamed of herself, she decided that there was nothing for it but to get up and dress. It was a wild night, as she saw when she opened the door, but there was some sort of moon, and her first idea was to go for a ride on the downs. . . . She wished she had a dog; Archie had found a mongrel terrier with the army and had meant to bring it to her but had forgotten. . . , She thought of going to look for Barbara, but felt some scruples about breaking into the beauty-sleep of one who slept like a log and had apparently no tremors.

She dressed and again looked out into the night. It was windy and mild, the sky was thick with low clouds, and the moon gave only the faintest light. She could see the outline of the next hut, but very dimly, and she realised that her notion of saddling a horse and going for a ride was impracticable. She felt that a gallop would restore her balance, but in such obscurity she would certainly break her neck.

Then she tried to read. She had been taking a course of Wordsworth, as something to distract her mind, and she resolutely plunged into the *Prelude*. But she found that the words did not make sense. The discovery irritated her so much that it almost restored her poise. " You little fool," she told herself, " what kind of wife are you for a soldier? You should be back in the schoolroom. You have got the vapours, my dear. You who used to laugh at your sister when she was afraid to go to bed at Glenraden because of the ghost on the tower staircase! "

Janet's annoyance did her good. But she could not get rid of an intolerable sense of expectation. She looked at her watch and saw that it was after one o'clock. Five hours till daybreak! She lay down again on her bed, shut her eyes, and tried to remember all the jolliest things in her life. A certain picnic in her childhood to the Sea Skerries —days with hounds in Warwickshire—her first London ball —escapades with her sister Agatha—that memorable day in the rain beside the flooded Doran when she had first found herself in Archie's arms. Archie! She thought of him with such a glow of pride and affection that she forgot her fears. . . . She began to picture their return to Crask and what she would do with the old house on the hillside.

Her fancy was toying pleasantly with the future, when suddenly she sat bolt upright. She had heard a sound which could not be the wind.

It was the sound of steps close to the hut, stealthy steps but unmistakable, as even a small noise can be in the midst of louder noises in a different key. She switched on the light. She had locked the door on going to bed, but had unlocked it when she looked out at the weather. To her horror she saw it gently open.

A man came swiftly into the room—and then another. Both had white faces and their brows were damp with sweat. One was a tall man with a hatchet face and a scar above his right eyebrow, the other was squat and muscular with rabbit teeth and a broken nose. Their clothes were much torn, as if they had had a rough journey.

The eyes of both showed amazement and disappointment. They were looking for something other than a scared girl.

" The Gobernador? " the first one cried, and " Where in hell's the boss? " came from the other.

Then Janet understood. She had her pistol under her pillow, and in a second had snatched it and fired. But it was wild shooting, the shot struck a rafter, and before she could fire again the men were upon her. They were men of quick decision and skilful at the job. A scarf was wound suffocatingly over her mouth and she was seized in a grip which seemed to crush the breath from her. She felt herself in the open air, and heard with almost her last moment of clear consciousness a voice saying, " If the bitch squeals, wring her neck."

After that she remembered little. She felt the colder breath of the night, and then swift movement in a man's arms. There was a noise in the air—she thought it was shots and cries, and sudden flashes of light. She was aware of being rushed along, of being suddenly dropped in cover, and then again of violent speed. She struggled till her limbs cramped, but she was like a baby in the hands of her captors.

And very soon weariness and panic did their part, and a merciful numbness fell upon body and mind.

Janet's shot had awakened the camp. The pickets had fired in answer, the big arc lights had been turned on, and in three minutes the place was feverishly awake. But the sentries had been withdrawn from Janet's hut, since the Gobernador was no longer there, and on that side the scrub came nearest, so that it was easy for the raiders to find cover. Yet they could hardly have escaped but for an unlucky blunder. Geordie Hamilton, hearing the uproar, had assumed that the camp was attacked by its landward approaches. That was the side from which he had always anticipated danger. Therefore, contrary to orders, he led the garrison straight to the camp, and all but stumbled on Radin, Judson, and Laschallas as they made their way to the sea-ravine. This meant that the post on its summit was empty, and the most difficult part of the descent was left unguarded.

Janet awoke from her swoon to find herself in the midst of water. She had a bad headache, and felt rather sick; also her body seemed to be a mass of aches. She was no longer bound, and had been laid on a rough couch of dirty cushions and tarpaulins. The weather had changed; above her was a blue arch of sky, and around her a circle of blue water, except on one side where a distant wall of green and umber told of land.

Slowly recollection came back to her, and with it her powers of observation. She saw that she was in a petrol launch, some ten miles out in the Pacific. There were four men on board. Two were the rabbit-toothed man and the tall hatched-faced fellow she had seen in the hut. Another was sallow with thick black eyebrows, and the fourth was plump and yellow, with sharp little eyes. She lay very still, for all her tremors had gone. She knew the worst now. There had been treachery among the company in the Courts of the Morning. D'Ingraville had located their base, but some traitor must have gone out from among them and told the secret of the sea-ravine. These ruffians had come to rescue the Gobernador, and they had known exactly in which hut he slept. They had been foiled by his cold, which proved that he was not privy to the plot, and at this conclusion Janet felt an unreasoning gladness. Not finding him, they had carried her off—no doubt as a hostage. At the thought her heart began to flutter again, but she resolutely steadied herself. The time for foolishness was past. She was not anticipating danger now, but in the thick of it, and must brace herself to meet it. She choked down every thought and memory which might weaken her resolution. Her business was to keep her head and play the game for her side. . . . But at the sight of the men with their evil faces she could not repress a shiver.

They were not unkind to her. One of them brought her water and a towel and she was able to make a sort of toilet. Another fetched her a cup of strong coffee, a box with biscuits in it, and a couple of oranges. She could not eat, but the coffee did her good, and her headache began to mend.

Then, from the land side, at a great height an aeroplane came flying. It must have been an assignation, for the men had been on the look-out for it, and a flag was hoisted. On nearer view it was seen to be a sea-plane. It circled twice round the launch, and then slid gracefully down till it floated like a bird on the water. The launch steered towards it, and its occupant was revealed as a slight, youngish man, with a fair beard, an oddly-shaped head like a faun's, and grey eyes that were set somewhat too close together.

His face, as he caught sight of Janet, expressed surprise. The man called Laschallas spoke to him in rapid Spanish, and his brows darkened. He seemed to be cursing them, and the reply was an impassioned defence. Then he shrugged his shoulders and bowed to Janet.

" I expected another guest, madame," he said in French, "but we must rejoice at what fortune has given us. You will do me the honour to accompany me."

The transhipment was a delicate business, and was not accomplished without a great deal of angry speech. Janet kept a tight hold on her nerves and accepted the inevitable. The four men in the launch were brutes, but what was this smiling, faun-like creature, and whither was he taking her? She felt desperately solitary, cut off from all that was normal and dear.

The plane lifted from the water, and turned seaward to gain elevation. Then it circled round, and steered for the wall of mountain.

VIII

JANET's pistol-shot, and the answering shots from the sentries, awakened the camp effectually, but in the thick night, with a volleying wind, it was hard to locate the trouble. Grayne, who was in command, naturally assumed that the danger lay in the neighbourhood of the Gobernador's hut, but Castor was discovered sleeping the heavy sleep of one dosed with aspirin, and Barbara, who slept next door, had heard nothing. The big arc lamps showed everything normal, and, since the light had been promptly switched off in Janet's hut by the raiders, it was presently decided that it had been a false alarm. The arrival of Geordie Hamilton and his garrison from the head of the ravine complicated matters, and it was the better part of an hour before peace was restored. No one doubted that the whole thing had been a blunder of a nervous sentry who had taken a whimsy of the wind for a shot. Barbara went back to bed.

She woke about dawn with an uneasy feeling. Why had Janet not been awakened by the noise—Janet, the lightest sleeper of them all? It was a mild blue morning after the rain, so she slipped on a dressing-gown and ran across to Janet's hut. To her surprise the door stood open, unlatched. The bed had been slept in, but the occupant had clearly got up and dressed. There was a faint smell which puzzled her, till she realised that it was powder; a shot had been fired in the place during the night. Then she noticed that the floor around the doorway was muddied, and that some of the furniture looked as if it had been violently pushed aside. Lastly, on one of the rafters she observed a jagged splinter which could only have been done by a bullet.

With terror in her heart she hurried to find Roger Grayne, and in five minutes the camp was astir. The tracks of the raiders were clear on the road to the sea, except where they had been overlaid by those of Hamilton's men. The Indian trailers had no difficulty in pointing to the very place where they had taken cover, and in deciding that there had been three men in the business, three men who, in departing, had been encumbered with a burden. . . . The very spot was found where they had circumvented Hamilton's garrison on their way up. At Post No. 1 it was discovered that one of the scouts had not come back, and his body was presently found in the thicket at the turn of the road. Down on the shore Corbett reported the absence of one of the mestizos who had gone on patrol to the head of the gulf. The section where the cliffs dropped straight to the sea was searched, and blood was found on the reef by the water's edge. The Indians scattered among the shore thickets, and soon reported that they had discovered the tracks of the raiders, both those going and those returning, and across the gulf evidence was found that a petrol-driven vessel had landed recently. The story was plain in all its details. Their base had been raided, and Janet had been carried off.

" They did not come for her." Barbara with tragic eyes clutched Grayne's arm.

" I guess they didn't. They came for the Gobernador. Some swine has double-crossed us and given away his exact location, only he didn't know that his Excellency was sick. They were certainly fooled about that. . . . But, my God! Miss Babs, we can't sit down under this. It's maybe bad strategy, but I'd rather they'd taken twenty Gobernadors than that little lady. Say, what do they want with her? A hostage, I guess. Who'd have thought Lossberg would be so bright? "

" But where is she? " Barbara cried. All the colour had gone out of her cheeks, and her face was a waxen mask of misery.

"Olifa, maybe. Yes, I guess she's in Olifa. Don't worry, Miss Babs. She can't come to any hurt. We're not fighting with savages who torture their prisoners. I wonder what Lossberg's next move will be?"

Grayne went off to give orders for the strengthening of the guards at the sea-ravine, since there lay their Achilles-heel, and Barbara bathed her face and tidied herself to meet Castor. This awful thing must be faced with a stiff lip, at any rate in the presence of the enemy. She was possessed with a cold fury against him. The enemy—his side—had made war on women and stolen that woman whom she had come to love best in the world.

Some rumour had already reached him, for he was in the mess-hut, evidently dressed in a hurry, since he had a scarf round his neck instead of a collar. She did not know what she expected to find in him—triumph perhaps, or a cynical amusement. Instead she found a haggard man with bleared eyes—no doubt the consequence of his feverish chill.

He startled her by his peremptoriness.

"Have you found her?" he cried. "Lady Roylance? . . . What has happened? . . . Tell me quick, for God's sake."

To her amazement he appeared to be suffering.

"No news—except that Janet has gone. We found the track to the water's edge, and there must have been a launch. . . . They murdered two of the guards . . ."

She stopped, for something in his eyes took away her breath. It was suffering, almost torment. She had never known him as Janet knew him, and had regarded him as a creature of a strange and unintelligible world, though she had reluctantly admitted his power. Now the power remained, but the strangeness had gone. He had suddenly become human, terribly human. She had come to upbraid and accuse; instead she wanted to pity. She found one who shared to the full in her misery.

"Oh, Mr Castor," she cried, "where have they taken her?"

"How can I tell?" he asked fiercely. "Have you sent for her husband?"

She nodded. " Sir Archie is at Loa. He will be here before luncheon."

" And Lord Clanroyden? "

" He is at the other end of the Gran Seco. He is busy with a big movement. He will be told, but I do not think he can come."

" But he must. What does his imbecile war matter? . . . Oh, you miserable children! You have played with fire and you will be burned."

There was so much pain in his voice that Barbara tried to comfort.

" But surely in Olifa she can come to no harm? "

" Olifa! Why do you think she is there? "

" She was carried off by sea. Where else could General Lossberg . . . ? "

" Lossberg! What has he to do with it? Lossberg is not the man to waste time on such a business. He has no desire for my company."

" But who? "

" There are others besides Lossberg—a far more deadly foe than the Olifa army. I warned Lord Clanroyden. I warned him that the true danger was not in the field. . . . Lossberg is not the man for midnight escapades. He is too stiff. Regular soldiers do not climb ravines by night and stick knives between the shoulders. That is another kind of war. That is the way of the Conquistadors. Remember that D'Ingraville, who first found us out, is one of them."

Barbara's face had become as haggard as his own.

" Then where can they have taken her? "

" I do not know," he said, " but not to Olifa—no, not to Olifa."

Archie arrived a little after midday. He looked suddenly much older, and Barbara noticed that his limp had grown heavier. He was very quiet, so quiet that it seemed impossible for anyone to express sympathy. In a level, almost toneless voice he asked questions, and carefully went over all the ground between the camp and the ravine-foot. He had a talk alone with Castor, and announced that he was going back to the Gran Seco, and would return sometime on the morrow.

Luis de Marzaniga, it seemed, had one foot in the theatre of war and one in Olifa; it might be possible for him to discover whether Janet had been taken to Olifa city. Also Sandy must be seen. He had cut the railway again, and was now engaged in worrying that section of Lossberg's army which lay around the Mines. Ammunition, it appeared, was getting low, and it was important to replenish the store by captures. It was necessary that Sandy should be consulted, and his Intelligence department might be able to help.

He flew off in the evening, a calm, self-contained, stricken figure, the sight of whom made Barbara want to howl. Once again it was halcyon weather, and the sight of smoke rising in straight spires in the blue twilight against the flaming background of the west almost broke her heart. About this time Janet should have been coming in from her evening gallop, shouting for her bath. . . . There was no dinner in the mess-tent that night, for no one could face a formal meal. Castor had kept indoors all day, and was now occupied in striding round the central square in the way passengers take exercise on board ship. He stalked across to Barbara.

" Lord Clanroyden must come at once," he said.

" He can't," she said. " Sir Archie says that he is needed most desperately where he is. He is conducting a war."

" You know him well. You have influence over him. Cannot you bring him here? "

The girl for a moment coloured.

" I do not think I have any influence with him, and if I had I would not use it to take him away from his duty."

" Duty ! " he said bitterly. " What duty is there in such a fool concern? He has started a fire which he cannot control, and soon it will burn down his own house. His own house, I say. He was a friend of Lady Roylance."

" So were you, I think," said Barbara quickly. " Have you too not kindled a fire which you cannot control? The Conquistadors and the Bodyguard were your own creation."

For a moment there was anger in his face, and then it died out, leaving it curiously bleak and pale.

" I think that is a fair retort, Miss Dasent," he said, and resumed his sombre constitutional.

Archie returned very early next day, not in the small Shark-Gladas, which was his usual means of travelling, but in one of the big Seaforths which were meant for bombing and load-carrying.

" I want to see Castor," he told Barbara. " I think he liked Janet, and he can help a lot. I've told Hamilton to report here in an hour, for there isn't much time to lose."

The three sat in the mess-hut. The Gobernador had recovered his trimness of bearing, but the almost insolent detachment which had hitherto characterised him seemed to have gone. His air was restless, and his voice, when he spoke, had a sharper pitch. There was something angrily defensive in his manner, something uncertain in the eyes which searched the others' faces.

" I want your help, sir," Archie said in his new, quiet, toneless voice. " You and my wife were friends, and I don't think you want her to come to any harm."

" Help," Castor broke out. " You make me impotent and then ask my help! I did not start this business. I am the victim of your absurdities. You have plunged this land into a war directed against myself. I am your prisoner, though you call me your leader. You have brought me into a world which is utterly unfamiliar. I have no mastery in it. I am accustomed to organise and govern, but I cannot organise the confusion you call war. I am a reasonable man, and this is the domain of the wildest unreason. . . . Then the crash comes, and you ask my help. You fools! You have made me more powerless than the rudest vaquero."

" I know, I know," said Archie soothingly. " I have no business to ask you for favours, but I don't think you will refuse all the same. You see, it is your old organisation that we have to fear, not the Olifa army. I do not think you want Janet to suffer at their hands."

" You have evidence? "

" A little. Enough to act upon."

" But I cannot control them. I am cut off . . ."

" No. But you can give me the benefit of your knowledge. Listen, sir. Our Intelligence have their own sources of news, and they are positive that Janet is not in Olifa. How they know I cannot tell, but we have never found them wrong. Further, they say that there are none of the Conquistadors or the Bodyguard now in Olifa. We may take it that the raiders belonged to one or the other. That is your own view, I think. Now, what facts have we? She was carried off in a launch—that we know. If she was not taken to Olifa, she may be hidden somewhere along the coast. That is possible, but not very likely—for two reasons. The first is that our own people know the coast, and my information is that there is no place on the whole line of shore under the mountains where any permanent camp could be made. If they landed Janet, it could only be for a day or a night—it can't be her final destination. The same is true of the low coastland farther south between the hills and Olifa, where there are nothing but malarial swamps. Janet may be there, but it is not likely, because of my second reason. Whoever carried her off wanted her for a purpose. They came for you, and took her instead, and they can only have taken her as a hostage. To use her as such she must have been taken to some place in touch with the Olifa army, and that must mean either Olifa or the Gran Seco plateau."

" But how could she reach the Gran Seco except by Olifa?"

" It is only a guess, but yesterday afternoon Peters reported from Pacheco that a plane had been seen flying eastward. It was marked like our own planes, and was flying high. Enemy planes are not allowed in that quarter, and, seeing it bore our own markings, no further notice was taken of it. But it was observed that it was a sea-plane, and since up to yesterday our army had no sea-planes, and Peters knew that, he thought it worth while to mention the fact."

" Well?"

" We have no sea-planes. That plane was not ours, though it pretended to be. It may have been Lossberg's, in which case he has diddled us. But I am inclined to think it was somebody else's. Janet was carried off in a launch. Why should not her captors somewhere out at sea have arranged for a sea-plane to meet them?"

Castor rose and walked to the big wall map.

"Show me the exact spot where the sea-plane was seen," he said.

Archie pointed with his finger.

"It was flying east?"

"East with a point of south."

"It was undoubtedly D'Ingraville. I think you are right, Sir Archibald. D'Ingraville met the launch and he has taken your wife with him."

"Where? Can you help me to that?"

Castor looked at the map again.

"It is the direction of the País de Venenos. You have heard of it?"

Archie nodded. "That was my own guess. Tell me more, sir."

"I can tell you very little. I have been there, but once only, and long ago. My colleagues, whom you call the Conquistadors, know it well. D'Ingraville, especially, and Pasquali. And Romanes—above all Romanes, who should by now have returned from Europe. . . . There is a drug there which they depend upon." The Gobernador spoke hesitatingly, like a man loath to divulge something of which he is scarcely proud.

"I know about *astura*. I am told that without it they will die."

"No—not die—not at once. But they will be unhappy. I have always believed that the Conquistadors would make some violent effort to replenish their supply. They will attempt to open up communications with the País de Venenos."

"You think they have gone there—with Janet?"

"I do not think that. It is not a place where white men can dwell. The Conquistadors perhaps—they are immune—but not the Bodyguard. Besides, I do not think a plane could land there, for it is a desperate country of gorges and forests. Somewhere adjacent, perhaps—from which the País could be visited."

Archie was on his feet, striding about excitedly.

"Somewhere adjacent!" he cried, and his voice was harsh with pain. "But where? There are thousands of miles of unexplored country. Somewhere where a plane could land—the sea-plane may have an under-carriage. . . . That must be in the hills. But Peters has all the Pacheco country patrolled, and beyond that the mountains rise like a wall. . . . If only I could get Luis, but Luis has disappeared on some job of his own. . . . Things aren't going too well with us at the moment, you know. We're terribly short of supplies, and Lossberg is getting cautious and won't stick out his head to let us hit it. . . . You've told me all you can think of, Excellency? Well, I'm off. Hamilton should be here to report."

Outside the door stood Geordie Hamilton, the same stocky, impassive figure that had stumped heavily through four years of fighting in France, his blue eyes looking sullenly forth from a mahogany face.

"You're coming with me, Hamilton," said Archie. "Got your kit? Full marching order. We don't know when we will be back."

"Where are you going?" Castor asked.

"To look for Janet." The young man's face seemed to Barbara to have regained a kind of peace. He would not return alone. Moved by a sudden impulse, she kissed his cheek.

"Thank you, Babs dear," he said. Then he held out his hand to Castor. "Good-bye, I think you wish me well, sir."

It was the first time that any of the party had shaken hands with the Gobernador.

I X

THE Seaforth flew first to Loa, where Archie asked for news of Don Luis. He was believed to be on the southern front, somewhere in the Pacheco area, where there was a good deal of activity. Loa itself was at present stagnant, a mere blockhouse to guard the road to the Courts of the Morning, and a forwarding depot for Magdalena. Lossberg's advance party, which a week before had been within twenty miles, had now withdrawn.

Then, hugging the skirts of the hills, and having a good deal of trouble with the eddies of wind that blew down the gullies, Archie flew south-east to Magdalena, Escrick's headquarters, under the snowy peaks of the Spanish Ladies. There he had an interview with Escrick's chief Intelligence officer and was shown the dispositions of the enemy in the Tierra Caliente. The nearest enemy planes were based on the Mines, and were probably at that moment busily engaged, since Sandy was worrying the Universum sector. But there was no one at Magdalena who had any knowledge of the approaches to the Poison Country; it was out of their area, and belonged properly to Peters.

The right course would have been to seek Peters at Pacheco, and above all things to find Don Luis. But Archie was not in a mood to think calmly. During the flight from the Courts of the Morning his anxiety about Janet had been rising to fever heat. Barbara's kiss of farewell seemed to have let loose a flood of dreadful fancies. He tortured himself with pictures—Janet small and solitary in the hands of men such as he had seen in the Gran Seco streets, men with evil, furtive eyes and corpse-like faces. . . . Weeks before Sandy had drawn for him a rough map of the whereabouts of the País de Venenos, as a preliminary for certain exploratory flights which were contemplated in the south-east angle of the province. . . . At the back of his head he still intended to go to Pacheco, but he felt an uncontrollable impulse first to do another thing. The straight route to Pacheco was over the eastern downs of the Tierre Caliente; but it was still afternoon, the moon would rise early, and even in the dark Pacheco could be reached on a compass course. To allay his anxiety by action of some sort had become a necessity. He decided to follow the line of the mountains, and find, if possible, the gate of the Poison Country which Sandy had described to him.

After that he would get in touch with Luis, and discover from him where in that neighbourhood a sea-plane might have landed.

He took the Intelligence officer into his confidence and explained his purpose. "I expect to be at Pacheco to-morrow. If I don't turn up there, you can tell General Peters the road I meant to take, and get him to tell Señor de Marzaniga. They'll know where to look for me, if I have to descend." He borrowed an extra revolver and a supply of cartridges for Hamilton, who had also his rifle. Likewise he borrowed two thick overcoats, for the nights were cold and he might be late. Hamilton ate a large meal, but Archie had no appetite for anything but a couple of dried figs.

The Seaforth left Magdalena a few minutes after 4 p.m. It was a warm bright afternoon, with the visibility so good that every rock and crinkle were clear on the mountain wall. Archie kept along the watershed where the barrens of the Tierra Caliente changed to a greener country, and where were the springs of the streams that forced their way through the range. The Cordilleras at that point are a double chain, and the country between the two is in part a maze of deep glens leading ultimately to valleys which debouch on the Orazon, and partly a high desert of shale and sand. Below him was an even level of greenish-grey downs, shading into umber on the west—a land in which there was no sign of human life. He flew low, and saw the ruins of Indian pueblas, the inhabitants of which had been removed to Lossberg's concentration camp. Then these ceased, and he swung nearer the mountains, till he found himself in a long hollow, like a ditch under ramparts. He saw the gleam of water far below, and realised that there were many streams, and that all seemed to be affluents of a considerable river.

It was almost dark before the country began to change. The bald screes of the hills gave way to patches of wood, and at the same time the upper slopes grew more precipitous. Then the hollow seemed to draw to a funnel and the mountains fell back a little to receive it. Two peaks stood like

sentinels, and between them lay a great wedge of darkness.
The sun was now behind the downs to the west, and as
Archie dropped lower the hollow seemed to be already brimming with dusk.   Inside the great wedge it was already
dark, but beyond were the shadows of dim green mountains.

The journey had taken longer than he thought.   There
was now no hope of getting to Pacheco much before midnight.   Archie resolved to descend on one of the green
levels and bivouac for the night.   But there was still light
enough to look inside the great gorge, for he decided that
these were the gates he had been seeking.   It was a foolish
thing to do at such a time of day, but his anxious mind was
beyond prudence.   He turned to his left and flew towards
the cleft.

The funnel was less dark than he had thought.   He was
flying low, and could see quite clearly beneath him the sudden
abrupt descent of the stream and the mat of forest into
which it fell.   Soon he had passed the portals and the great
cup opened out, lying in a clear green gloom like an emerald.
In front of him, perhaps six miles away, a mountain rose
out of the deeps, and its crest was a cone of snow, now rosy
with the sunset.   The periphery of the cup was also snow-
rimmed, gold and crimson where the dying sun caught it,
and elsewhere a cold blue grey.

He dropped still lower.   The forest was dense as the
grass on a lawn.   Tall trees now and then broke it, and
sudden rocky spurs, but, though he was less than five hundred feet above it, he could make out no details, except
where the river broadened into a leaden pool.   The vegetation was as thick as an animal's pelt.   A strange odour
ascended to him—sweet and stupefying and rotten. . . .
Could Janet be in that jungle of death?   Could any human
being be there and hope for life?   The place seemed like
a charnel-house encrusted by foul mosses.

Janet was not there—of that he had a sudden, complete
conviction.   The horror of the place grew on him, but he
still held on.   It was fast growing dark, and out of the
forest a fog was rising like a wraith.   He saw it billowing
up towards him, and started to climb. . . .

Then his eye fell on the petrol gauge, and he had an ugly shock. What on earth had happened? He remembered now —he had forgotten to refill at Magdalena as he had intended. But still he had started that morning with enough for a twenty-four hours' flight. The tank must have sprung a leak, for there were only about twenty minutes of petrol left.

He turned and flew in what he thought was the direction of the entrance to the gorge. There was just a chance that he might reach it in time and find a landing-place beyond it, for there could be no landing in this jungle. But the fog had enveloped him and was now far above him, a horrible, thick, choking whiteness which smelt of violets. He turned to look at Hamilton. That worthy, with the collar of his coat turned up, had his usual sullen calm. " It's comin' on for a thick nicht," he observed.

Archie looked again and saw that the main tank had gone dry. There was only the reserve tank left, and that would last at the most a quarter of an hour. He climbed steeply, for he remembered that he had been descending since he passed through the gorge. Below him was now thick darkness, but the mist above him seemed to hold the late sunshine. It might be thinner higher up, so he climbed towards the light.

Something not unlike panic had now seized Archie. If the petrol failed before he reached a landing-place, then he must crash in this noisome forest. Horror of the place gripped him like a nightmare. He climbed up and up, struggling to get above the mist, only dimly aware of the direction of his course. . . . Could he hit off the gorge in this suffocating gloom? Was it worth trying? He had seen the zone of snow which encircled the cup. Up there there must be open ground, where a landing might be made. So he contented himself with climbing, bearing blindly to the left. His one aim was to get above the forest.

It was certainly less dark. He was coming out of the main shroud of the fog, and the white veil seemed to have patches in it. The altimeter registered nearly twelve thousand feet. . . . But the forest was climbing with him, and suddenly below him he saw in the brume the top of a tall tree, a thin etching of black in the dimness. He must be far up the containing slopes. Then he observed from the gauge that only a few minutes more of petrol remained.

He came to a decision.

"Hamilton," he cried, "we've got to go overboard. Get your chute ready."

There was no change in the man's stolidity. He had practised this drill in the Courts of the Morning, and now quietly made his preparations. Archie directed his spotlight downwards, and once again a fluff of tree tops came into view.

"Quick," he said. "I'll follow in a second."

"I doot I'll get a dunt," said Hamilton grimly as he went over the left side of the cockpit. Archie saw that the chute had opened and righted at once, and that he was descending steadily into the void.

His own task was more difficult. He cut out the switches and pulled the plane into a stall. He meant to go out on the right, when suddenly the right wing began to droop, which meant that it would strike the parachute. He therefore steadied the plane, and followed Hamilton over the left side. He started head foremost, but the risers pulled him upright and the parachute opened. The plane above him was lost in an instant, and Archie, oscillating violently and feeling very sick, plunged into a gulf of primeval darkness. Something hit his head; then he hung for a second upside-down before slipping into what seemed a gigantic bramble bush which scratched his face. Another bump, a plunge, and Archie found himself standing on tiptoe on solid earth, with the ruins of the parachute and his great-coat hanked in the lower boughs of a tree.

x

ARCHIE took a good quarter of an hour to disentangle himself from his Absalom-like posture, since, owing to the constriction of his garments, he could not get at his knife, and his hands were numb with cold. When at last he was free, he pitched forward stiffly into a huge tree-fern, which kept him from rolling down the slope. The actual forest was thin, but the undergrowth was dense and water-logged, and the declivity so steep that every step must be watched. The fog was still there, but it was not thick, and a faint light filtered through it, so that it was possible to see the ground beneath and the trees above in a dim monotint.

His first business must be to find Geordie Hamilton. He shouted, but it was like speaking with the mouth muffled by folds of blanket. He argued that Hamilton must have descended not more than two hundred yards below him, and that the plane when he left it had been directly ascending the mountain face, so he tried to shape a straight course downhill. But the going was appalling. There were thickets of cactus to be circumvented, an occasional tall tree choked with creepers, and strips of sheer red earth. He stopped every few yards to shout for his companion, but no answer came; it seemed impossible to pierce that deathly stillness. Presently he realised that at this rate he would soon be lost. He halted and mopped his brow, for he was sweating under the burden of his heavy flying-clothes. And then he heard, apparently from the bowels of the earth, what seemed to be a groan.

" Hamilton," he cried, and, shouting his name, he made his way a little to the left.

At last a reply came, a miserable, muffled voice.

" Is't you, Sir Erchibald? " it said, and it was as if its owner were speaking from under deep water.

The place was a shallow ravine, and as Archie groped his way something very hard and sharp caught him in the neck.

" Hamilton, where on earth are you? " he cried in pain.

" I'm catched in a buss," came an answering groan. " For God's sake get me out, for I've gotten some awfu' jags."

Then Archie remembered his spot-light. It revealed a great clump of the aloe called *caraguata,* with Hamilton most intricately wedged among the sword-like leaves. Above the spikes, like a dissolute umbrella, waved the parachute. Hamilton hung face downward, his great-coat suspended above him and his legs splayed like a clumsy diver's. He had ceased to struggle, for every movement sent the thorns deeper into his tenderest parts.

Archie stripped to shirt and breeches, and set himself slowly to cut the victim out, but it was the better part of an hour before the work was done, and Hamilton, still apoplectic about the face, was cautiously examining his wounds. He had plenty of them, but only scratches, though he declared that his legs were so stiff that it would be a month before he could walk.

"You'll have to start right away," Archie told him. "We can't stay in this blasted hot-house. We must be pretty near the edge of the tree-line, and once we get above the forest we can find a place to sleep. So step out, my lad, game leg or no. You and I are about equal now."

Slowly and with many stumbles they began the ascent, guiding themselves by the lift of the ground. It was desperately laborious, for sometimes the way was up sheer banks of earth, the remains of old landslides, and as slippery as oil; sometimes through acres of great ferns where the feet sank into deep hollows among the roots: sometimes through cactus scrub which reduced their coat-skirts to rags; often through horrible oozing moss which sent up a stink like a charnel-house. The fog was dying away, and the rising moon made their immediate environment clear, but the better they could see the more hopeless the toil became. Hamilton panted and sobbed, and Archie's weak leg gave him many falls. The air had none of the wholesome chill of night. A damp heat closed them in, and when now and then a faint waft came up from the valley beneath it seemed to have a sickening scent of violets.

Often they stopped for breath, but they did not lie down. Instinctively they both shrank from contact with that unhallowed soil. Once Hamilton drank from a pool in a stream, and was violently sick.

"We must be about the height of the Matterhorn," Archie said, "and yet it's as hot as hell. This is a cursed place."

"'Deed, it's no canny," said Hamilton, gulping with nausea.

Before long it was clear that Hamilton's strength was giving out. Thickset and burly as he was, this greenhouse-mountaineering was beyond him. He stumbled more often, and after each fall took longer to recover. At last he stopped.

"I doot I'm done, sir," he wheezed. "This bloody cemetery is ower much for me! You gang on."

"Nonsense," said Archie, taking his arm. He was dog-tired himself, but to his more sensitive nerves the hatred of the place was such that it goaded him forward like a spur. "See, we'll take hands. We can't be far from the tree-line."

But it seemed hours before they reached it. Fortunately the slope had become easier and less encumbered, but the two men staggered on drunkenly, speaking no word, their eyes scarcely seeing, so that their falls were frequent, everything blotted from their mind but the will to bodily endurance. So blind were they that they did not notice that the fog was almost gone, and they had come out of the forest before they realised it. Suddenly Archie was aware that he was no longer climbing steeply, and then he was looking across a shelf of bare land which rose to a rim of a pale silver. He was breathing free air, too. A cool light wind was on his forehead.

"Hamilton," he cried, "I . . . believe . . . we're clear."

The two dropped like logs, and the earth they sank on was not the reeking soil of the forest, but the gravel of an upland.

Both lay for a little, their limbs too weary to stretch. Then Archie crawled to his feet.

"Let's go on a bit. I want to feel really quit of that damned Poison Valley. We must find a hole to sleep in."

They staggered on for another half-mile, weakly, but no longer so miserably. The sand and shale underfoot gleamed white as salt in the moonlight, and were broken only by boulders and small scrubby thorns. Then they found a shelf of rock which overhung so as to form a shallow cave. It was now as cold as it had been hot in the covert, the sweat had dried upon them, and the scratches on hands and face smarted in the frost. Each had a small ration of food in his pocket, charqui—which is the biltong the Gran Seco Indians prepare—some biscuits and chocolate, and Archie had a packet of raisins. They supped lightly, for thirst and hunger seemed to have left them, and, cuddled against each other for warmth, both were soon asleep.

Archie woke in an hour's time. He had slept scarcely at all during the past three days, and even deep bodily fatigue could not drug his mind. Wild dreams had assailed him—of falling down precipices of red earth into a fœtid jungle threaded by oily streams. He woke to find that the moon had set and that it was very dark. Far off there was a call like a jackal barking. There were other things alive on this shelf beside themselves.

Then he heard a sound close at hand—the padding of soft feet on gravel. His spot-light was beside him, and he flashed it in the direction of the feet. About ten yards away stood an animal. At first he thought it was a wolf from its size, till he saw its sharp muzzle and prick ears, its reddish fur, and its thick tail. It was a fox, one of the cannibal foxes of the País de Venenos that he had heard of from Sandy. The animal blinked in the light, and its teeth were bared in a snarl. Archie reached for Hamilton's rifle, which lay loaded beside them, but he was too late. The great brute turned and trotted off, and passed out of sight among the boulders.

" Enough to put me off fox-hunting for evermore," thought Archie. After that he did not sleep, but lay watching the dark thin to shadows and the shadows lighten to dawn. The sun seemed to leap with a bound over the far Cordilleras, and a morning mist, as white and flat as a snowfield, filled the valleys. Archie's heartsickness returned to him like a fever. Somewhere within the horizon was Janet, but by what freak of fortune was he to get her—himself a mere lost atom at the edge of his endurance, and as ignorant as a babe of this immense, uncharted, unholy world?

Both men soon realised that the País de Venenos had exacted its penalty. Hamilton was clearly in a fever, which may have been due to his many cuts, and Archie felt some-

thing like a band of hot steel round his head. For breakfast
they nibbled a little chocolate and ate a few raisins. Then,
as far as their bodily discomfort permitted, they discussed
their plans.

"We're up against some solid facts, Hamilton," said
Archie. "We're looking for my wife, and I believe she's
somewhere within fifty miles, but we've got to admit that
we're lost ourselves. All I remember from Lord Clanroyden's map is that if we keep going up the south wall
of the Poison Country we'll come to the main range, and
south-west of that lies Pacheco. The people we're seeking
must be up on the range, but they may be north or south
of the Poison Country. We couldn't cross that infernal valley, so let's hope they are on the south. Another thing—
we mayn't be able to get up the range—we're neither of us
in much form for mountaineering. Also, we've got about
enough food to last us with care for two days. We shan't
want for water."

"I'll no need much meat," said Hamilton sombrely. "I
couldna swallow my breakfast, my throat's that sair."

"We're both dashed ill," Archie agreed. "I feel like a
worm, and you look like one. Maybe we'll be better if we
go higher."

Hamilton turned a feverish eye upwards. "I doot it's
higher we'll be goin'. Anither kind o' Flyin' Corps.
Angels."

"That's as it may be. It's too soon to chuck in our hand.
. . . You and I have been in as ugly places before this.
We're both going on looking for my wife till we drop. We'll
trust to the standing luck of the British Army. I've a sort
of notion we'll find something. . . ."

"We'll maybe find mair folk than we can manage."

"Undoubtedly. If we're lucky enough to get that far,
we'll have to go very warily. We needn't make plans till we
see what turns up. At the worst we can put up a fight."

Hamilton nodded, as if the thought comforted him. A
fight with men against odds was the one prospect which held
no terrors for him.

The two very slowly and painfully began their march over

the shelf and up to the snow-rimmed slopes which contained it. The País de Venenos behind them was still a solid floor of mist. Happily the going was good—flat reefs of rock with between them long stretches of gravelly sand. Archie decided that he must bear a little to his right, for there the containing wall seemed to be indented by a pass. They must find the easiest road, for they were in no condition to ascend steep rock or snow. The wind was from the east and wisps of cloud drifted towards them, bringing each a light flurry of snowflakes. They had awoken shivering, and now as they walked their teeth chattered, for both were too sore and stiff to go fast enough to warm their blood.

Suddenly they struck a path—a real path, not an animal's track, but a road used regularly by human feet. Indeed, it seemed at one time to have been almost a highway. At one place Archie could have sworn that the rock had been quarried to ease the gradient, and at another, where it flanked a stream, it looked as if it had been embanked. In that wild place it seemed a miracle. Archie thought that he must be light-headed, so he examined carefully the workmanship. There could be no doubt about it, for his fingers traced the outlines of squared stones. Once this had been a great highroad, as solid as Roman work. It seemed to come out of the mist of the Poison Valley, and to run straight towards the pass in the ridge.

He pointed it out to Hamilton.

"Aye, there's been folk here langsyne," was the answer.

Archie bent over a patch of snow. "Not so long ago. Here are the marks of feet, naked feet, and they were made within the past twenty-four hours."

Slowly they tramped up the glacis of the range towards the pass. Hamilton walked like a man in a dream, stumbling often, and talking to himself. He seemed to have a headache, for he stopped at the water-pools to bathe his head. The pain in Archie's forehead grew worse as they ascended, till it became almost unbearable. He kept his fingers on his eyes to ease the throbbing behind them. But his mind was clear, and he could reason with himself about his condition. It might be the poisoning of the forest—most likely that was true in Hamilton's case—or it might be mountain sickness. He had once had a slight bout in the Karakoram, and he had heard that it was common in the Cordilleras. . . . Just before the summit of the pass he looked back. The tablecloth was lifting from the País de Venenos, and the white floor was now cleft with olive-green gashes.

The summit of the pass was a hollow between snowdrifts. There both men stood and stared, for the sight before them was strange and beautiful. Archie had expected another tableland, or a valley of rocks shut in between peaks. Instead his eyes looked over a wide hollow, some three miles in diameter. High ridges flanked it on all sides, and on the west was a great mass of mountain, which he believed must project like a promontory towards the Tierra Caliente. The slopes beneath them were at first boulders and shingle, but presently they became the ordinary grassy savannah, with clumps of wood here and there which seemed to be more than scrub. And in the centre of the hollow lay a lake, shaped like a scimitar, of the profoundest turquoise blue.

He unslung his field-glasses and examined the place. There was no sign of life in it. At various points on the shore he could detect what looked like millet fields, but there was no mark of human habitation. Then he examined a dark blur near the western end, and found something that might have been the ruins of a Border keep.

" We've struck a queer place," he told his companion, but Hamilton turned a blank face. He had almost lost the power of sight; his whole mind was bent on forcing his sick body into movement.

As they began to descend, an oppression seemed to lift from Archie's soul. The horror of the place where he had landed left him, now that he had come into a clean bright country. Also the band of iron round his brow fretted him less. He found that he moved with greater ease, and he could lend a hand to his tottering companion. When they reached the first grass he felt hungry, and they sat down to complete their breakfast. But Hamilton could only manage a single raisin, though he drank thirstily from a stream.

The whole place was a riot of blue light, the heavens above and the lake beneath; even the rim of silver sand seemed to catch a turquoise reflection. The air, too, was no longer the dry, throat-catching thing of the high snows, but fresh and clement. The sun warmed them gratefully, and Archie's eye recovered its old keenness. He saw a bird at last and the ornithologist awoke in him.

"By Jove, a black snipe," he cried. "The first I've seen."

The road they had followed skirted the northern edge of the lake and led them straight to the ruins near the western end. At close quarters the strangeness of the latter was increased. This had been a castle, like any Scots peel tower, the guardian of this fair valley. It had long been deserted, but the keep still stood foursquare, of a masonry which time and storm could not crumble. Archie examined it curiously. No mortar had been used, and the stones fitted into each other with such mathematical exactness that a knife could not find a lodgment. There were no signs of windows. Whoever dwelt here must have dwelt in darkness unless he had some means of artificial light. . . . Archie remembered a story which Luis had told him of the old lords of the mountains, who controlled the Poison Country. They dwelt secure, he had said, for they made a belt of poison round them, and in their windowless dwellings they lived by candlelight. No, not candles, Luis had added, something stranger—natural gas, or perhaps electricity— for he believed that they were great men of science. . . . At the recollection this clod of masonry, solid as a single boulder, seemed to link him up again with the vale of horrors behind him. The sunshine had become less bright, the place less innocent.

Beyond the keep was a meadow where the stream from the lake issued. Here Archie saw something which had been hitherto hidden by the ruins, and which made him drop Hamilton's arm and hobble at his best pace towards it. It was an aeroplane—a sea-plane, drawn up just beyond the sand of the shore.

Archie recognised the make—a Wentworth B—of which

there were none in the Gran Seco. His next observation was that it was out of action. The floats had been damaged, and the propeller was bent. Had it crashed? . . . It was D'Ingraville's machine beyond doubt. Had Janet travelled in it? What had befallen her?

With a sinking heart he examined the thing, and presently he was reassured. The machine was damaged, but there had been no serious accident. It must have alighted in the lake, for it had been drawn by human hands up on the shore. He saw the grooves and ribs which it had made in the sandy beach. . . . He examined it carefully. There was still a good supply of petrol in the tank. Could he use it? A further inspection convinced him that he could not. Repairs were needed, and he had no means of repairing it.

His first impulse was to destroy it. He could easily set it on fire and reduce it to a ruin of bars and wires. . . . But what good would that do? If Janet had come in it and was now somewhere not far off, this might be a means of escape. How, he did not know, but there was no point in burning a possible boat.

Then a few yards off he saw something white on the grass. It was a tiny fragment of cambric, with a monogram in one corner. Janet was always dropping handkerchiefs; he spent his time retrieving them.

He stood with the thing in his hand, and a lump rose in his throat. He wanted to cry, the first tears since his childhood. Janet had sent him a message, Janet who had disappeared into the darkness. By some miracle he had found touch with her, the one chance in a million had succeeded. A great wave of longing and tenderness engulfed him. He stood blindly, as visions of Janet passed before his eyes, her dancing grace, her whimsical humour, her friendly courage. He had picked up her handkerchief, here at the ends of the earth, as he had so often done at far-away Crask. . . .

Then suddenly, for the first time since her loss, there came to him hope. An unreasoning hope, but as vivid as a revelation. She was somewhere near—two days ago, not more, she must have stood on this very spot. He would

find her. Nay, he would rescue her. The Providence which
had led him thus far so strangely would not fail him.

With this new confidence something returned to Archie.
He became his normal self again, and felt desperately sleepy.
He had not slept for days.

Hamilton sprawled limply near the ruined tower, his
burning head pillowed on his arm. Archie got a piece of
tarpaulin and some broken struts from the sea-plane, and
made him a shelter from the sun, which was now very warm
in that bare place. He stretched himself at his side, and
in an instant was sound asleep.

He woke to the sound of voices. The covering had been
lifted, and around them stood a group of men. Hamilton
was sitting up and looking at them with sick eyes.

The men were Indians, but of a type which Archie had
never seen before. They were not of the Gran Seco breed,
for those were bullet-headed and muscular, whereas these
were of a leanness which made them seem inhumanly tall,
and their heads were the heads of white men. Instead of the
dull beady eyes of the Gran Seco, the eyes of these men were
large and bright and lustrous, as if they lived in a perpetual
fever. Their faces were so emaciated as to be almost
skulls. Unlike the Indians of Olifa and the Gran Seco who
favoured black ponchos, the ponchos of these men were of
a dark red—the colour of the raw earth in the País de
Venenos.

Yet, to his surprise, Archie felt no shrinking from them.
They were armed—with blow-pipes and slender lances—but
they seemed to have no hostile purpose. They stood in a
circle looking down gravely at the awakened sleepers.

Archie scrambled to his feet, and held out his hand as the
best gesture of friendship which he could think of. But
there was no movement in response. Their hands hung
stiffly by their sides.

He tried them in Spanish. He told them that he had
flown thither from the Gran Seco, and pointed to the sea-
plane to illustrate his mode of travel. He asked them if
they had seen any white man in the neighbourhood—

especially if they had seen a white woman. Archie's Spanish was apt to be of a biblical simplicity, and he explained his meaning with an elaborate pantomime. He was like a man who has a desperate message to deliver, but who finds himself stricken with partial aphasia.

It appeared that they understood something of what he said, for they began to speak among themselves, in voices pitched so low that they sounded like the murmuring of insects. Then one, who seemed to be their leader, spoke. It was a kind of Spanish, oddly pronounced and very hard to follow, but Archie gathered that he was ordered to accompany them. The speaker pointed down the ravine towards which the stream from the lake flowed.

"Right, my lad," said Archie, "I'll go with you fast enough," and he nodded and grinned and waved his hand. Then one of them bent over Hamilton, who had lain back on the ground again with his hands pressed to his head. It looked as if these strange people knew something of medical science, for the man felt his pulse and the beating of his heart. He spoke to the others, and they moved apart. In a few minutes a little fire had been made of driftwood and thorn-scrub, while two of them took charge of Hamilton. They stripped off his great-coat and tunic, and bared him to the waist, and then they proceeded to knead and pinch certain muscles, while his head hung limply over their knees. Then they prepared a queer little greyish pill which they induced him to swallow.

Meantime an iron girdle had been put on the fire, and on it a number of little dried kernels roasted. Archie was given a share, and found them palatable: they tasted like crayfish, but may have been a kind of caterpillar. Then a rough litter was made, out of their lances and the tarpaulin, and Hamilton, now in a deep sleep, was hoisted thereon.

Archie made a last effort to get some news to allay his anxiety and nourish his hopes. "White woman," he repeated, pointing down the glen of the stream. But he got no answer. The leader, whom he addressed, faced him steadily with his bright, inscrutable eyes. But before they moved off they did the thing which Archie had decided

against. They spilled petrol over the wings of the sea-plane
and applied to them a flaming brand from the fire. As
Archie looked back, he saw beside the blue lake in the
serene sunshine the bonfire burning garishly, like a sacrifice
before the altar of the immemorial tower.

<h2 style="text-align:center">XI</h2>

THE third day after Archie's departure, the threat to the
Courts of the Morning became urgent. The first word
came from Escrick's Intelligence; there had been a succession of small fights in the Loa district, and Grayne was
warned to extra vigilance. His planes patrolled in a wide
radius, and Grayne himself was confident that no enemy
machine could reach them. " D'Ingraville might, if he
isn't otherwise engaged," he said, " but they've gotten
nobody else of his class." But definite news came by way
of Olifa that there would presently be an attack in force
from the sea, and that Lossberg had relinquished his Fabian
tactics and was now clearly pushing northward. Loa might
have to be abandoned any hour, and then would come the
advance up the shelves of the foothills. It might be made a
slow and a costly business, but in the end it must succeed,
for the defence could not indefinitely oppose his superior
numbers, his Schneider batteries, and his ample machine
guns. The time was drawing near when they must give
up their mountain base.

The strangest thing about the new situation was its effect
on the Gobernador. It might have been expected that the
approach of his friends would put him into a state of
extreme restlessness, that he would wait eagerly for news
of each stage and welcome the hope of escape. Instead he
seemed to resent it. He spoke of it with irritation, as if
impious hands were being laid on something sacred. He
was resentful, too, of Sandy's failure—for he was certain
that he had failed.

" Lossberg has got his skirts clear," he told Barbara.
" He feels himself strong and secure enough to take the

offensive. That means that Lord Clanroyden's scheme has miscarried. Lossberg, in spite of his pinpricks, is getting all the supplies he wants, and has leisure to make a bold attack on our base. He is neither rattled nor embarrassed, and he has no notion of making peace. Clanroyden's was an ingenious plan, but it was bluff, and the bluff has been called. Once it fails, we have no second string. It is our turn to be driven from post to pillar . . . and there is far more against us than Lossberg. We have no news of Lady Roylance?"

There was more than exasperation in his tone as he spoke, there was an aching anxiety. Barbara, who in these last days had become a tense, silent being, looked at him curiously.

"I think that we have succeeded in one thing, Excellency," she said.

"What?"

"We have made you an ally. This war was directed against you. Now you speak as if you were sorry that it was not going better."

"Nonsense," he said sharply. "I am anxious about Lady Roylance."

Next day there was disquieting information. Loa had been evacuated in the night owing to Lossberg's pressure, and that general was now beginning his movement northward on scientific lines. His mounted troops were clearing and guarding his flanks, his pioneers were pushed forward to improve the roads for his batteries, and two of his mechanised battalions were already in the foothills. Their progress could be delayed, but with Sandy and the bulk of his force engaged at the other side of the Gran Seco it could not be seriously opposed. Sandy had long ago decided that it was no part of his business to resist any movement of Lossberg's too long.

Grayne rapidly calculated.

"He will take four days at the earliest to get here. We could lengthen them out to six, but it isn't worth it. That gives us plenty time, for we've got all the details of the evacuation settled long ago. The stuff we're taking with us has already begun to leave for Magdalena. . . . No, Miss Babs, I guess Lossberg can't hit off that road. It's our covered Valley of Virginia, and he could no more stop our using it than General Banks could stop Stonewall Jackson. It's way out of the reach of his patrols. But we can't cut it too fine. Before his first troops get to the place they call Three Fountains, every soul here has to be on the road to Magdalena and this place one big bonfire."

Barbara asked about the sea-ravine.

" We'll get early news of that from the air," was the answer. " I'm not going to waste one solitary man on holding it. We've had it mined and monkeyed with, so as it will be a steep mountaineering proposition for the dago sailormen, but it's not going to be anything more. We'll retire shelf by shelf and watch the fireworks."

Two nights later it was reported by wireless that destroyers had left Olifa for the north, and the following morning they were sighted by Grayne's air scouts about twenty miles south of the Courts of the Morning. This news enabled Grayne to adjust his time-table. The destroyers entered the gulf at 11.30 a.m., but they seemed to find difficulty with that uncharted coast, and it was well into the afternoon before they attempted to land their men. Corbett and his garrison had been withdrawn from the shore, and the hut left apparently intact. But the first mariners who entered it had various unpleasing surprises, with the result that the occupation of the beach became a matter of careful reconnaissance, and darkness had fallen before the last of the landing-parties was on shore. Corbett, now at Post No. 1, waited grimly for the morning advance.

The last day in the sanctuary was for Barbara like some strange motion-picture seen from uneasy stalls. She had nothing to do except to wait and watch. The Courts had been dismantled till they looked like a disused builder's yard. The tall poles of the wireless installation had gone, the huts were empty, the great storehouse was bare except for the inflammable material which could be fired by a single fuse. One solitary aeroplane patrolled the sky. White mechanics, troopers, mestizos, Indians, all had gone except the guard which was to accompany herself and the Gobernador. It was a clear bright day and rather cold. From the sea-ravine could be heard an occasional rumble and sputter of fire, but the only garrison left there now was Corbett and two of his lieutenants. The Olifa advance was three-quarters of the way up the ravine, and Corbett had been ordered, after seeing to the last great explosion, to make his best speed to the huts. As Barbara looked round the deserted camp which for weeks had been her home, she wanted to cry. Departure seemed a farewell both to her hopes and her friends.

The Gobernador, muffled in a great blanket-coat, joined her. He too looked at the bare walls and the desolate compounds.

" That is the curse of war," he said. " It makes one destroy what one loves."

" I feel as if I were leaving home," said Barbara.

" I did not mean this place," was the answer. " I was thinking of Lady Roylance."

Presently there fell on their ears a dull roar from the direction of the sea-ravine. Grayne appeared with his watch in his hand.

" Time to start now, Miss Babs. Corbett will be here in five minutes. Lossberg is a mile short of Three Fountains."

They mounted their wiry little horses, while the guardian aeroplane flew very slowly to the south. It was almost dusk, and as they turned into the forest trail they stopped instinctively for one look backward. Suddenly the Courts were bright with tongues of fire, and Corbett and his assistants joined them. It was to the accompaniment of roaring flames behind, which made a rival glow to the sunset, that the party disappeared into the gloom of the trees. As they bent eastward under the skirts of the mountain the crackling and the glow died away, and presently, at a headland above a deep glen, Grayne halted. From far down in the muffled foothills to the south came the chatter of machine guns.

" That is the last word," he said. " Lossberg is at Three

Fountains and our defence is falling back to join us. I'm
sorry. I'd got to like the old place."

For hours they rode through the dark forest. There was
no moon, and the speed was poor, for they guided themselves
only by contact. The Indians who led the way had to
move slowly to keep pace with the groping, jostling cavalcade
behind. Barbara and Castor rode in the centre of the group,
and, full of their own thoughts, spoke scarcely a word to
each other, except of apology for a sudden jolt. The
Gobernador had accompanied them without protest. He
seemed to have no ear for the distant rat-tat of the machine
guns of his friends.

About ten o'clock they halted to bivouac for the night.
It was a hollow tucked between the knees of the mountain
spurs. Some summer thunderstorm had once set the forest
alight, and for acres beside the stream there was bare
ground carpeted with moss and studded with the scarred
stumps of trees. Half a dozen fires were soon burning, and
supper was eaten from the saddle-bags. Barbara had her
sleeping-tent, but she ate with Castor beside one of the
bivouacs. She noticed how clumsily he dismounted from
his horse, and how stiffly he moved. This was not the life
he knew, and he was no longer young.

It was a quiet night without a breath of wind, but
chilling towards frost. The sky was ablaze with stars,
which there in the open gave light enough to show the dim
silhouettes of the overhanging hills. As the two sat
side by side in the firelight, Castor smoking his pipe, his
figure hunched in that position peculiar to townsmen who
try to reproduce in the wilds the comfort of a chair, the girl
realised that something had happened. Hitherto she had
felt it a duty to entertain the Gobernador, making conversation as one does with a stranger. Now she found that
there was no such need. She could be silent without impoliteness. He had become her friend, as he had been
Janet's, a member of her world, whose thoughts she could
instinctively discern, and who could anticipate her own.

For the last days she had been slipping dangerously near

the edge of her self-control. Janet's danger seemed only a part of the general crumbling of life. She had the sensation of walking on quicksands, with a thin crust between her and unspeakable things. But the ride in the forest—movement, even if it were towards the unknown and the darkness —had put vigour again into her blood, and now in this great hollow hand of the mountains, under a blazing canopy of stars, she felt an irrational hope. She turned to her companion, who had let his head sink back against the flaps of his saddle and was staring upwards.

"I thought the Courts of the Morning was a refuge," she said, "but I think it must have been also a prison. I feel freer now. . . . I feel nearer Janet."

He did not answer. Then he asked:

"Where were you brought up, Miss Dasent? What kind of life have you had? You can't be more than twenty-one or twenty-two."

"I am twenty-four," she said. She began to tell him of her childhood, for it comforted her to talk. She spoke of a rambling country-house high up in the South Carolina piedmont, with the blue, forested hills behind; of a childhood among old coloured servants; of winter visits to the Florida shores; of barbecues each autumn for the mountain folk; of spring gallops among upland meadows or on the carpeted trails in the pinewoods; of days with a bobbery pack of hounds in difficult pockety country. She found herself speaking easily and naturally as if to an old friend. Her school days in Charleston, her first visits to Washington and New York, her first crossing of the Atlantic—she made a pleasant picture of it all as stages in a progressive happiness.

"Why do you want to hear this?" she asked at length. "It is so different a world from yours—so very humble."

"It is a different world—yes. I can judge one thing about you. You have never known fear. No man or woman or animal has ever made you afraid."

She laughed. "How preposterous! I have been often terribly afraid."

"No. You have never met a fear which you were not

ready to face. You are brave by instinct, but perhaps you have not been tested. When you meet a fear which draws the blood from your heart and brain and the vigour from your nerves and still keep your face to it—that is the test."

"Have you known such a fear?" she asked.

"I? How could I? You cannot fear what you despise. I have been too unhappily fortunate in life. I began with advantages. I was educated by my father, who was an embittered genius. I inherited very young a great fortune. . . . I was born in Austria, and therefore had no real country. Even before the war Austria was a conglomerate, not a people. . . . I was brought up to despise the world, but I did not learn the lesson fully, for I excepted myself. I found that I was cleverer than other people, and that my brains enabled me to use those others. How could I ever be afraid of what I could use? For twenty years I have watched a world which I despised as futile, and pulled the strings of its folly. Some of those years were occupied by war. I took no apparent part in the war, for I had no fatherland, but I caught fish in its troubled waters. I evolved a philosophy, but I have never lied to myself, and I knew that I cared for that creed only because it flattered my egotism. I understood humanity well enough to play on its foibles. I thought that it was all foibles, save for one or two people like myself in each generation. I wanted to adjust the world so that it would be in the hands of this select few. Oh, I was supremely confident. I believed in the intellect, and mine told me that I was right. I even cultivated a dislike of the things and the people that were opposed to my creed. But there was no passion in my dislike—there is no passion in contempt, just as there is no fear. I have never been afraid—how could I, when I saw mankind like little ants running about on my errands? Therefore my courage has never been tried. But there is this difference between us—I know that you are brave, and I do not think that I am."

"What nonsense!" Barbara exclaimed. "You have amazing fortitude. Look how you have behaved since we carried you off."

"That was not fortitude, it was bewilderment. I have been beginning to wonder, to puzzle. I have never before been puzzled in my life. I have lost my contempt."

"That is a good thing," and she smiled. "My father had me taught Latin and I remember what an old bishop of the Middle Ages said. He said that the advancing stages in human wisdom were 'spernere mundum, spernere sese, spernere nullum.'"

He lifted his head sharply.

"I have gone through the first stage," he said. "I have despised the world. I think I have reached the second —I am coming to despise myself . . . and I am afraid."

The ride next day was in a difficult country, for it became necessary, in order to avoid the deep-cut ravines of torrents, to climb high up on the mountain-side. The path was good, for it had been used incessantly for transport during the past months, but the weather was vile, for the south-west wind brought a storm of rain, and the party rode all day in an icy bath. The track ran with water like a millstream, the trees were too scattered to give protection against the slanting spears of rain, and in the thicker coverts a steady shower-bath descended from the canopy.

Till the late afternoon the downpour continued, and what with slipping and plunging horses, water at every ford swirling to the riders' boots, and the relentless soaking cataracts of rain, there was no bodily comfort that day. Barbara, herself lithe and active as a boy, saw that the Gobernador bore the labour ill, and was very near the edge of his strength. He managed his horse clumsily, and often in the steeper places she took his bridle. At one of the fords it was only by a vigorous haul that she saved him from a ducking.

Before evening the rain ceased, the sun came out, and in that high cold place there was no steamy mist, only a tonic smell of wet mountain soil and a jewelling of every leaf and herb. The encampment at dusk was in a stony trough, where a shelf of rock made a deep overhang, and tents could be set up under it as under a roof. Barbara assisted the Gobernador to dismount, and so weary was he that he almost fell into her arms. She attended herself to his comfort, stripped off his soaking boots and blanket-coat, ransacked his valise for dry clothes, compounded with the assistance of Roger Grayne a merciless cocktail, and made his bed in a dry nook of rock not too far from the warmth of the fire. She found him curiously helpless. He was too weary to protest, and had as little knowledge of how to look after himself as a recruit on his first day's service.

After supper he seemed to recover. A woman who has nursed a man feels a protective interest in him, and Barbara found a new ease in talking to him. How had she ever looked on one so helpless as a great criminal! She dropped the formal " Excellency " with which she had been in the habit of addressing him. She had made him get into his sleeping-bag at once, and eat his supper among a pile of coverings. Now he reclined like an ancient Roman at table, the great fire lighting up the rocky antrum and silhouetting against the darkness his noble head and brows and the nose like a ship's prow.

" Do you know," he said, " I have hardly ever in my life endured bodily discomfort or pain? I have never been ill. I know so little of what is in the world."

He seemed to have divined the girl's thoughts. He had used human beings as pawns, careless of their sufferings. She thought that Janet was right—that he had a short-range imagination. That was his defence. His cruelties had been blindness, rather than purposeful crime. She looked on him with a kindlier eye.

Then they spoke—a sure proof of intimacy—of their friends. Grayne sat with them for a little, and then went off on a tour of inspection. As he went, Castor's eyes followed him. " That's a good boy! You have many like him? "

" Plenty. America produces them in bulk."

" And Britain. A different type, but the same in essentials. But they are only company officers—at the best, perhaps, brigadiers. It is commanders-in-chief that we need."

" There is Lord Clanroyden," said the girl.

" Perhaps. I am not sure. He has most of the gifts, but has he ever faced fear—faced it, and gone through to the other side? His eye is that of a leader, but I do not see in it the depths of the man who has passed the ultimate test."

" You are an acute observer," she said.

" I am becoming one," and he smiled. " I have observed something else. . . . If it is a liberty, I ask forgiveness. . . . I have noted that when he was near you you moved away, as if you shrank from too near a contact. A little nervous shiver ran over you. That does not mean dislike. I think it means that you are in love with him, for even when you moved away your eyes were happy."

" I think you are very wise," she said quietly. " But Lord Clanroyden will never have a thought for any woman. . . . I am going to give you a hot drink, and then you must sleep. To-morrow will be a long day."

Next day they came out of the foothills on to a high shelf of ground, under the peaks called the Spanish Ladies. By midday they reached Magdalena, which, since Fort Castor and Loa had gone, was now Escrick's only base. They were here at a lower elevation, and in ordinary savannah, greening already and scented with the curious nut-like odour of a mountain spring. The cantonments, hidden in a fold of ground, could be recognised from afar by the wireless poles. Magdalena was still secure, and apparently unknown to the enemy, whose nearest post was a hundred miles distant. But the place was under strict discipline, and it was through two lines of sentries that they made their way into the dusty circle of huts and horse-lines.

Escrick himself was there, and he and Grayne had much to discuss, so Barbara and the Gobernador lunched alone in the General's hut. The latter had lost his air of fatigue and bewilderment. His eyes scanned sharply every detail of the place, as though it was an environment, still unfamiliar, with which it was his business to become acquainted.

"These people are losing," he told Barbara. "I feel it in the air. I felt it a week ago in the Courts of the Morning. Just at present things are going badly for us."

But there was neither disappointment nor elation in his tone. He spoke briskly, as if he had come to some decision. Later, when Escrick and Grayne joined them, it was he who directed the conversation.

"Speak to me frankly, General," he said. "I am your commander-in-chief in name. I want an exact statement of the situation as you see it."

Escrick had still his quiet, sleepy manner. His blue eyes were as placid as ever, and his voice had its soft drawl. But he looked an older man, and his brick-red face had been fined down and sharpened.

"Things aren't so bad, sir. I would say there were going on according to plan, if that phrase hadn't got so blown upon. The loss of Loa don't signify, and we always realised that sooner or later we'd be shoved out of the Courts of the Morning."

"It will be the turn of this place next."

"I think not. Lossberg hasn't got on to the track of Magdalena. It will be Pacheco's turn first. He must know about Pacheco."

"Well, Pacheco be it! If he takes Pacheco, what will you do?"

"Shift somewhere else. It's a big country, and we aren't tied down to any lines of communication."

"But that can't go on for ever. Where are you going to get your supplies—your munitions and your food?"

"From Lossberg. We've been pretty lucky so far."

"The railway? How is that working?"

"So-so. We worry it a bit, but he's got the best part of a division on it now, and he's building blockhouses. The Chief isn't finding it so easy to keep it crippled."

"And the Mines?"

"That's what you might call the main front. We have a scrap there every second day. And of course we're busy over the whole country. We don't give Lossberg time to sit down and think."

"General, answer me one question." The Gobernador's face and voice had a sudden authority which Barbara had never observed before. He seemed to be again the chairman presiding at a council of the Gran Seco administration. "Are you certain that Lossberg is not winning?"

Escrick looked his questioner full in the face. "He ain't winning. But, if you press me, our side ain't winning either."

"Then he *is* winning. He has only to maintain himself and he is bound to win in the end. And that end is not very far distant. I should like to see your returns of supplies. Remember, I am a business man, and this is my subject."

Papers were sent for, and the Gobernador pored over them, making calculations with a pencil. Then he asked for a map, and a big one was spread out for him on a table.

"You are losing," he said at last. "If I made a graph of the position your line would be going down and Lossberg's slowly rising. You know that without my telling you. In rations and ammunition you have begun these last weeks to give out more than you take in. That can only have one end."

Escrick nodded. "Seems so," he said dryly.

"It was bound to happen. Our only chance was to delay its happening till we had made Lossberg think it could never happen. We were striking at his nerves, and the nerves of Olifa. But we have failed. Lossberg isn't rattled one bit. He is really rather comfortable. He is planted at the Gran Seco city and at the Mines. He is getting up his stuff by the railway, and he is going to get it quite easily when his blockhouses are completed. He has sufficient reserve of vitality to take Loa and drive us out of the Courts of the Morning. Presently he will drive us out of Pacheco and Magdalena. He won't get tired of the game and call on the President of Olifa to make peace. He is quite cheerful. Shall I tell you what will happen next?"

He leaned forward, till his lean face was close to Escrick's. "He is going to get the Mines started. At half-power or quarter-power, no doubt, but still started. He will find labour among the concentrados or he will import it. Soon there will be freight-trains running to Olifa as before. And we shall be driven back bit by bit into the mountains, getting fewer every day."

"We've had mighty small losses so far," said Escrick.

"They will come—never fear. From starvation, if not from bullets. Make no mistake, they will come. Do you know what we are now, General Escrick? A rebellion on the defensive, and that is the feeblest thing known to history."

The Gobernador spoke with a passion that silenced his hearers. There was no exultation in his voice; rather it seemed to be bitter with reproach and disappointment.

Then Grayne spoke.

"We're keeping our end up in one branch," he said. "The air. Bobby Latimer got two enemy planes yesterday. We've got the whip hand of them there all right. We can fly anywhere we like in this darned country, and if we weren't short of bombs we could mess up things considerable for old Lossberg."

Then Barbara asked a question which had been on her lips since the moment she arrived. She did not expect an answer, for Sir Archie's objective had been Pacheco and Janet's kidnapping had naturally not been made public in the army.

"Have you heard anything of Sir Archibald Roylance?" she asked.

Escrick shook his head.

"He came here five days back. I wasn't here, but he saw Lowson, my Chief of Intelligence. He was going to General Peters and he left a message that he was flying close to the mountains. He never turned up at Pacheco, and our planes have been all over the ground and can't find any trace of him."

A small cry was wrung from Barbara's lips. The Gobernador got to his feet and walked to the door. The fatigue of yesterday had returned to him and was shown in his cramped movements, but there was no weariness in his voice and eyes.

" Where is Lord Clanroyden? " he asked.

" At Pacheco. General Peters is having the heavy end just at present. Yesterday he had quite a show at the Universum."

" Telegraph to him that I am coming. Can you send Miss Dasent and myself by air? "

" Sure. One of Captain Latimer's men is going there this afternoon, for we're concentrating for another try at the railway. . . . But hadn't you better stay here, sir? Pacheco soon won't be too safe for civilians."

The Gobernador smiled. " I suppose I am a civilian, but I'm not thinking about safety. I'm going to Lord Clanroyden to help him to make peace."

Escrick whistled softly.

" You won't succeed, sir. From what you have said, peace must mean surrender, and we're not likely to be in the mood for that. Lossberg may drive us up into the snowfields, but devil a man of us will cry ' Kamerad! ' "

The Gobernador's smile broadened till he looked almost cheerful.

" I know, I know," he said. " Nevertheless I hope to make peace."

In the late afternoon, in a world of soft airs and a warm stillness, Barbara and Castor flew over the barrens of the Tierra Caliente. Thirty miles off on their left the great mountains flamed in the setting sun, and in the twilight they saw before them the line of steep cliffs which ran at right angles to the main range and made the southern wall of the Gran Seco. A little short of it they swerved eastward into the secluded valley of Pacheco.

Sandy was sitting in his hut with his elbows on a deal table, studying by the light of two candles a paper which lay before him. An aide-de-camp brought him a message which made him rise to his feet and stare blinkingly at the door.

The Gobernador stood before him, bent a little like a

man whose every limb aches with stiffness. He did not hold out his hand.

"Lord Clanroyden," he said, "I have come to take over the command with which you honoured me some time ago."

XII

BARBARA interposed. She ran forward and seized Sandy's hand.

"Janet!" she cried. "Have you any news of Janet?"

Sandy stood holding her hands, his face a study in perplexity.

"I don't know," he said. "I have just had this letter from Luis. He has disappeared for the last eight days. . . . Sit down, please, all of you. I'm very glad to see you. Tommy, get seats, and get a lamp of some kind. . . . You'll want food. Tell them at the mess. . . . Here is Luis's letter, brought by an Indian half an hour ago. I'm hanged if I know what to make of it."

The letter was an oblong of rough paper, which had been rolled inside a hollow stem. It might have been torn from a sketching-block. The message had been written with an indelible pencil, and was a good deal blurred. It ran:

For C.-in-C. Most urgent. Do not worry about the lady. Patrol by air line N22a to P13c—also by mounted patrols—let no man pass west or north. Send troop without fail on receipt of this up Cabalpas valley to camp foot of third left-hand tributary counting from Maximoras. From camp they should patrol in arc NNE to E. Do not leave Pacheco but await me. L. de M.

Barbara almost snatched the paper from him.

"It is from Don Luis. He has found Janet. She must be safe, for he tells us not to worry. But what does the rest mean?"

The aide-de-camp had brought a big paraffin lamp which illumined the great map on the wall.

"One thing we can settle," Sandy said. "Luis is referring to our map squares." He held the lamp high. " The line from N22a to P13c—there it is," and he drew a blue pencil along it. " Look. It is the chord of an arc which covers all the south-east angle of the Gran Seco. See, Excellency, it stretches from north of the entry to the País de Venenos right down to the southern wall. Well, that's simple."

He rang a bell and gave certain orders. " We shall want most of our planes for the job, and the railway raid to-morrow must be countermanded. It's a longish stretch of country, so we will begin at dawn. The mounted patrols can start to-night. . . . Now for the rest of it." He scribbled two words on a piece of paper. " Take this to Jeffries and get him to ask his Indian scouts about them. Send me the man who knows where Cabalpas and Maximoras are."

When the aide-de-camp had gone he turned to the Gobernador.

" You are in command, sir. How do you read this message ? "

" Apparently Don Luis de Marzaniga has found Lady Roylance. I hope she is safe, but I do not know. Perhaps he only wants to dissuade us from looking for her because he has other things for us to do. There are people in the mountains whom he wants to keep there. We can assume, I think, that these are Lady Roylance's captors. They must be the Conquistadors and their followers. But why does he want to keep them bottled up ? Perhaps he has a plan for taking them all prisoners at once, and does not wish them to scatter."

Sandy rubbed his chin.

" I think there must be more in it than that," he said. " To rescue Janet is desperately important. And Archie ! Where in Heaven has poor old Archie got to ? He has flown out of creation somewhere between here and Magdalena. But it doesn't greatly matter what happens to the Conquistadors. To hang them all in a bunch won't bring us nearer winning this war. I wish Luis hadn't been so cryptic. Perhaps he was having a hustled time when he scribbled this letter. No, we could find out nothing from the messenger. He was a friendly Indian of the foothills, and could only tell us that it had been passed on to him from a friend with a word which he was bound to obey. It may have gone through twenty hands before it reached us."

"But Luis himself will soon be here to explain," said Barbara.

"But when? And there may be a good deal to do before that."

There was a knock at the door, and the aide-de-camp returned accompanied by a tall Indian, whose belt of tiger-cat skins proclaimed a hunter.

"Colonel Jeffries says that this is the best of his scouts, sir. He knows where the places are."

Sandy looked hard at the man. "I have seen you before," he said in Spanish. "You were with Don Luis de Marzaniga and myself when he visited the País de Venenos."

The Indian stood stiffly to attention. "I was with you," he said. "I have known the Señor Luis since he was a child. What do you seek of me, my lord?"

"Where is Maximoras?"

"It is the place which we in our tongue call Hatuelpec, where once long ago was a great city. In six hours' riding from Pacheco towards the sunrise, you will reach a river under the mountain called the Blue Wolf. Into that river enters another flowing from the sunrise, and up that river in three hours you will reach a little plain full of great stones. That place is Hatuelpec, which you call Maximoras."

Sandy traced the route on the map. It led him into country marked only by vague contours of mountains, as blank as the heart of Africa in maps of a century ago.

"And Cabalpas?"

The man corrected him. "The name is Catalpas—or as we say Arifua. It is the little river which flows by Hatuelpec." *

"Do you know the third tributary on the left hand above Maximoras?"

* See map on page 338.

The Indian considered, and then a strange look came into his face. "I know the stream. It is the way to——" He stopped. "It is the way to a place which we call Iliyabrutla, which means the Thrones of the King."

"You have been there?"

"No, my lord, nor any of my race. It is a place accursed and the abode of devils."

"You can guide a party to the Catalpas valley?"

"Beyond doubt. But the road is not easy, for it is among the broken places of the hills. It is a journey of twelve hours for good horses."

Sandy turned to the aide-de-camp. "My compliments to General Peters and ask him to have ready a patrol of fifty picked troopers to start in an hour's time. They will take rations for three days. This man will be their guide. I suggest that Captain Rivero is put in command." Then to the Indian: "Go, brother, and God be with you. You will show the way to Maximoras."

"El Obro commands." The man saluted and went.

An orderly announced dinner, and they crossed the square to the mess-hut.

"I have taken to dining alone," Sandy announced. "To-night there will only be we three. I can't offer you much in the way of food, for we're short of what we used to call hospital comforts. We're getting very near to the 'hog and hominy' of your ancestors, Miss Barbara."

He spoke lightly and cheerfully, but as Barbara looked at him across the rough table she noticed a profound change. Before, she had seen him worn to the last limits of his physical strength, but there had always remained a certain lift and effervescence of spirit. Now, though his face was less haggard than she had seen it, it was also less vital. His eye had dulled, and there were lines of strain on his forehead and a tightness of suffering about his mouth. He sat, too, listlessly in his chair, like a man oppressed with a great weariness. He looked up suddenly and caught her eye and seemed to brace himself.

"We have some hope at last—about Janet," she said.

"A shred. A week ago it would have given me a

new tack of life, but now I seem to have got beyond hoping. The thing has tortured me so much that the ache is dull."

The girl looked at him and saw an anxiety deeper even than her own. Instinctively she tried to comfort.

"But it wasn't your blame. It was ours—up in the Courts of the Morning. We kept too slack a watch."

"The whole blame was mine. This war was made by me—by your uncle partly, but mainly by me. I seem to be fated to wreck the things I care about."

"That is the fate of all of us." The Gobernador had hardly spoken up till now. "That is also my fate. I have made a great industry, and now I am destroying it. I have become a friend of Lady Roylance, and she is in danger from that which I have created. I have had dreams, and now I am trampling on them."

The words seemed to touch a spring in Sandy which released a new vigour. His figure lost its listlessness, he sat upright, and into his eye came something of the old fire.

"You mean that? By God, then we cannot be beaten. We have won the big stake."

"No. You are wrong. We have still to win it. Supposing I died to-night, in what way would you be better off? Lossberg will wear down your resistance—in time, and his methods will not be gentle. The republic of Olifa will not be merciful conquerors. The old Gran Seco will be restored—without its Gobernador—and the people of the Tierra Caliente will be slaves again. Olifa will faithfully copy my methods, but without—if I may say so—my intelligence. You may in the end get fair terms for most of your white officers, since they are valuable for the industry, but you will get no terms for the rank and file. Therefore I say that whatever may become of *me*, you have not yet begun to win. At present you are losing with terrible speed. Can you deny it?"

"We can never lose," said Sandy. "Assume the worst —assume that we are broken up like a covey of partridges and forced in bands into the mountains. We can still make the Gran Seco a hell for any Olifa administration. They may start the Mines, but they'll only limp along. They must come to terms with us . . ."

Castor broke in. " Forgive me, Lord Clanroyden, but you do not understand the mind of such a state as Olifa. She has been peaceful and prosperous for a time, but it is not long since she had Indian wars grumbling all along her borders. She is accustomed to a skin-deep civilisation. Lossberg will enjoy the task of policing this territory, and Olifa will run the Mines again and not grumble at the decline in her profits. Remember, she has solid reserves which I have given her. . . . We must be candid with each other, if I am to accept the command with which you have honoured me."

Sandy fixed his eyes on the other's face.

" You have changed your views, Excellency. I congratulate you profoundly. But I am curious to know just why."

Castor smiled. " For once in my life I can give no reason—no logical reason. Put it that I am a little weary of my old self. Say that I lived in a rather dismal world and see the door ajar which leads to a brighter one. Put it any way you like. . . . I am here to help you to win this war, because victory will benefit me—oh yes, enormously. . . . I have not lost my ambitions, but they have a slightly different orientation to-day. . . . Now let us talk business."

The door opened and a new figure entered—a big man in a most disreputable suit of khaki. He had a full, rather heavy face, which had been burned to something very like the colour of his clothes. There was dust in his hair, and dust rimmed his large placid eyes.

" Say, this is a nice party," he said in a voice cracked with thirst. " Why, Babs child, I heard you were here. . . . I'm mighty glad to see you so blooming. And Mr Castor, too. . . . But I can't talk till somebody gives me a drink, for my tongue is stuck to the roof of my mouth, and I've gotten a hunger like nothing on earth."

A mess-servant brought him a long drink of lime-juice and sparklets, and the big man took his place at the table between Sandy and Barbara. He raised his tumbler to the Gobernador.

" I suppose," said the latter, " that I must forget Señor Rosas the Mexican and make the acquaintance of Mr John S. Blenkiron the American."

" That's so. So good an American that he poisons himself with soft drinks ever since his country went dry."

" I have told Lord Clanroyden that I have come here to take the command which he offered me."

The big man looked steadily at him, and his quiet ruminant eyes seemed suddenly to become a search-light. They saw something which he approved, for he bounded to his feet.

" That's fine. I'm proud to be working again with my old chief. We'll shake on that," and he held out a mighty fist.

" You've come from the Mines? " Sandy asked. " How are things going there? "

" So-so. The enemy's getting cunning up that way. He's extending his radius of defence and making a very pretty corral, with as much barbed wire as the Hindenburg Line. Our boys are terrible short of rifle ammunition, and we're cleaned out of bombs. Looks like we'll have to let up for a day or two, and that will give him a cruel chance to pick up."

Sandy gave him a short account of Luis's message and the action he had taken upon it. Blenkiron received the news with a furious interest.

" He tells us not to worry about Lady Roylance? Well, I guess he means she's not going to come to any harm, for Luis thought the world of her. And he has got that bunch of buckaroos located and wants to keep them tight. He's right there, for this world won't ever be a healthy place again till that cesspool is drained. We've got to put that job through before we can attend to other business."

" And then? " Castor asked. " Mr Blenkiron, just before you arrived I was giving Lord Clanroyden my view of the situation. We cannot afford to deceive ourselves. This rebellion was a gamble, but at the start the odds were not too desperate. You had certain assets—a hidden base, a very mobile army, and a special knowledge of the country.

Very wisely you did not try to meet Lossberg with his own weapons. Your aim was to fight a war without bloodshed, or as nearly as possible without it, and to let him waste his highly scientific blows on empty air. That was your strategy, and it was intelligent. Your hope was that after a little he would grow weary of it, and that Olifa would grow weary, and that you could make peace pretty much on your own terms. That also was intelligent. You were aiming directly at the *moral* of Olifa, and it is of course by striking at the *moral* of the enemy that wars are won. Have I put your views correctly?"

Blenkiron nodded.

"Well, it is clear that you are going to fail. You have fought a nearly bloodless war, your army is pretty well intact, but your supplies are running low. You have lost your secret base. You have failed to make Lossberg uncomfortable. His spirits are rising, and he is beginning to strike out quite boldly. He is rather enjoying himself, and fancies himself a conqueror. What are you going to do? To do nothing means that within a month you will be scattered among the mountains—mere guerrilleros."

No one spoke, and he went on.

"That mustn't happen. *We* "—and he emphasised the change of pronouns—" we must still strike at the enemy's *moral*, but we must change our methods. It is the republic of Olifa that matters. Hitherto we have been trying to weaken her *moral* by weakening Lossberg's. That hasn't worked—so we must strike directly at the *moral* of Olifa."

"How?" Blenkiron drawled.

"By carrying the war into Olifa. In the idiom of your country's history, Miss Dasent, by crossing the Potomac."

Blenkiron flung himself back in his chair.

"I recognise the old touch," he said, beaming. "There speaks the Gobernador of the Gran Seco. It's horse-sense, I don't deny, but just how are we going to do it? We're treed up here, like a 'possum. There's no way to Olifa except by the railroad, and that Lossberg has gotten policed like Broadway."

"True. But we have still the mastery of the air. You cannot send an army to Olifa, but you can send me."

For an instant a shade of suspicion rested on Blenkiron's face, but it soon vanished.

"I get you," he said. "You always had that little Government in your side-pocket."

But there was no response in Sandy's puzzled eyes.

"I don't understand," he said. "Bobby Latimer can land you wherever you like in Olifa, but how would you be further forward?"

"I must be landed where I can get into touch at once with the Government. You see, Lord Clanroyden, that Government have for some years been my very obedient servants. They are not clever people, only cunning, and they are not very brave. I have what you call a moral ascendency over them. If I appear among them suddenly from the clouds I think I can impress them. I do not believe that they like the prospect of a long guerrilla war, and I can expound to them with some force the financial reasons for making peace. I will be literally truthful with them. I shall tell them that the revolt was not of my making, but a spontaneous eruption, in which I was entangled, but I shall tell them also that I am now a convinced partner."

Sandy's fingers drummed nervously on the table.

"I believe you are wrong. How much did the Olifa ministers like you, Excellency? They admired you, obeyed you, feared you, but they probably hated you. They are not clever men, as you justly observe—it would be better for us if they were—but they are vain as peacocks. And jealous, too, at the back of their heads. They are getting triumphant dispatches from Lossberg, and they are swelling with pride. They think they are winning on their own account, they believe that the Gran Seco will fall into their hands and that they will be able to confiscate the Mines. Then they will get, not the handsome share of the profits which you allowed them, but everything. Don't tell me that they have any fears of not being able to run them without your assistance. Those gentry always believe they are heaven-born geniuses waiting for their chance."

Castor's face did not change.

"It is possible—but I do not think so. I cannot believe that my personal ascendency over them is so brittle. Anyhow, I am prepared to try."

"You realise the result of failure?"

"Yes. Lossberg will be entrenched in his authority. The value which its association with my name gives to our revolution will be gone. There may be trouble with foreign capitals."

"And you yourself?"

"Oh, I shall be utterly discredited. I shall probably find myself in one of the Olifa prisons, which I understand have not shared in the general progressiveness of the country. There may even be a regrettable incident, for they will still fear me."

"You are a brave man," said Sandy.

"I don't know. I have not been tested." Castor looked towards Barbara, as if to remind her of their conversation. "But I see no other way. I should prefer to have an army behind me, but we cannot fly an army over a wall of mountains, and there is no pass."

"You are wrong," said Sandy. "There is a pass."

Everyone stared at him—Blenkiron with puzzled eyes, Castor with a strained attention, as if doubtful of the correctness of his hearing, Barbara with awakening hope.

"There is a pass—a chain of passes—a way from the Gran Seco to Olifa. Luis alone knows it, for it is an old secret of his family. That is how he came to the Gran Seco so often before the war. You"—turning to Blenkiron— "thought it was by an aeroplane with some hidden landing-place in the mountains. I knew the truth, but I was sworn to tell no one. I have travelled the road once with him. It ends at the head of the Vulpas valley. That is how we got up the horses to mount our troops. Luis has been doing a busy horse-trade for months."

"But this alters everything," Castor cried. "If we had thought of it before——"

"I thought about it—thought about it till my head ached. I always meant it to be my last card, and it would have been if things had gone better.   If Lossberg had been getting pinched and worried, I meant to use this as the last straw —to leave Escrick and Peters to watch him, and to lead a picked mounted force through the passes up to the gates of Olifa.   I calculated that that would do the trick.   But —but—now—I don't see how it is going to work."

He stopped and looked round the table.   In each face, as his eyes rested on it, even in Castor's, the excitement seemed to die down.

" Because," he went on, " if Olifa is confident and has reasons for confidence, such a hussar-ride would have no effect.   She has still a part of her regular army left behind, and she has an enormous capacity for calling up reserves. We should have the people against us, and they would rise up at our backs and cut us off.   We should achieve nothing, and even if we managed to hack our way out, where should we be?   Back in the Gran Seco, with the game going hard against us."

He turned to Castor.

" Do you see any answer to that? " he asked.

" I am considering. . . .   I will tell you presently."

" Do you? " he demanded of Blenkiron.

" Not just right away.   I'm rather of your way of think-ing.   It isn't much good crossing the Potomac unless you can reckon on help from Maryland or Pennsylvania."

Suddenly Barbara spoke—eagerly—stammeringly.

" I think I understand Don Luis's letter.   The Con-quistadors have found a sanctuary in the mountains.   Why does he want none of them to get out?   To keep them together and deal with them all at once?   Perhaps, but I think he has another reason.   He does not want any message carried to General Lossberg.   What kind of message?   Not a prayer for relief, for at present no one is troubling them. It must be a message of information, vital information. What could that be?   Only that they have found the road through the mountains from the Gran Seco to Olifa, and they want to warn him so that he may prevent our taking it."

"Good for you, Babs," said Blenkiron. "I guess she's right, gentlemen. But it gets us no further."

"Wait a moment," said Sandy. "There may be something in it. The message is from Luis, who alone knows the passes. He evidently thinks these passes are our trump card, or he wouldn't be so keen to keep them open for us. Luis knows Olifa better than any one of us here. He knows it up to date, which none of us do, for he has been living with one foot there and one in the Gran Seco. He's a mysterious beggar, for he asked not to be given any responsible job—said he had other very important things to attend to. It looks as if Luis believed that there was a chance of doing something by a flank movement on Olifa."

There was a knock at the door and it opened to admit a young staff-officer.

"I apologise for intruding, sir," he said, "but Colonel Jeffries thinks it important. The patrols have just brought in a prisoner. He was on horseback, accompanied by an Indian servant, and he seems pretty well dead to the world. Where he came from we haven't a notion, but he asked to see you at once—said it was very urgent. He is not armed and he's a funny little rag of a man. He talks English perfectly, and looks like a gentleman. Says his name is Alejandro Gedd."

Blenkiron shouted. "Why, it's the British vice-consul. A good little citizen and a great pal of Wilbur. Let's have him in at once and feed him. What in thunder has brought him here? You'd as soon expect to see a canary-bird in Labrador."

Five minutes later the staff-officer ushered in the remains of the best-appointed dweller in the city of Olifa. Gone were the trim garments, the ribboned eyeglass, the air of being always freshly barbered. Don Alejandro's breeches and jacket were stained and torn, spectacles had replaced his monocle, he had a week's beard on his chin, his eyes were hollow with fatigue, and his dark cheeks had been burned almost black. He walked painfully as if from saddle-stiffness, and he was clearly aching in every bone. But at the sight of the company he tried to straighten himself, and he made an effort to bow to Barbara.

Blenkiron almost swung him off his feet and settled him in a chair. " Bring food," he shouted to the mess-waiter. " Whatever you've got, and also any hard drinks you can raise. Sandy, have you any champagne? We're mighty glad to welcome you, Don Alejandro, but don't say a word till you've got something under your belt."

A cocktail restored the little man to speech. He looked curiously at Castor, and addressed Sandy.

" Where is Luis de Marzaniga? " he asked. " He told me to meet him here. I left Charcillo four days ago."

" How have you come? "

" Through the passes. I had one of Luis's guides, but it's a fatiguing journey and terribly cold. I apologise for my appearance, but I thought it best to report at once. I shall be glad of a meal, for I miscalculated and finished my food this morning at breakfast. But first I should like a word with Luis."

" He is not here, but he is coming soon. We have no secrets among ourselves, Don Alejandro. You see before you the Commander-in-Chief and his Chief of Staff. You can speak freely."

" I only came to report to Luis. It is rather a long story and I shall have to refer to maps and papers. I came to explain to him the exact position at the moment of our Olifa revolution."

There was a complete silence. Blenkiron poured out a half-tumblerful of champagne and handed it to the stranger. He gulped it down and it seemed to send new blood through his body.

" What about your Olifa revolution? " Blenkiron asked in a queer tone.

" It's going famously." Don Alejandro's voice had lost its flatness. " Going like a fire on the savannah. When Luis and I laid down our lines three years ago, we never thought to have a chance like this. We have all of what you call the gentry behind us, and the haciendados can turn out anything between eight and ten thousand mounted men.

Also we have a big movement among the workmen in Alcorta and Cardanio, and we have the train laid in Olifa itself and only waiting for the spark. But the thing's ripe now and we can't keep it waiting much longer. We don't want to show our hand by any premature explosion."

Don Alejandro was surprised at the reception of his words. He looked around the table and saw four faces in which delight still struggled vainly with stupefaction. Also there was complete silence.

Then Blenkiron broke it.

"Luis certainly knew what he was doing when he sent that message. We'll have an army back of us in our interview with the Excelentisimo. I guess we'll get some help from Maryland when we cross the Potomac."

XIII

JANET woke with a start from her uneasy sleep. Her nights had been troubled of late, and she was accustomed to waking with a start.

The darkness was very thick and close around her, but it was not the closeness of a narrow room. There was a free draught of air and a sense of space, which suggested that she was under the bare vault of heaven. And yet the faint odour was not of the natural world, but of man's handiwork—hewn stone, and the dust of hewn stone, the smell of a place roofed and enclosed.

She lit the candle beside her mattress. It scarcely flickered when she lit it, though there was a sound of wind high up in the dark above her. She told herself that here she was safe, safe at any rate till the morning. Every night she came here, and the narrow entrance was blocked by a pile of cut stones which fitted as closely as a door. When she was first introduced to these sleeping-quarters she had been in a terror of loneliness and anticipation. And then she had realised that this was a merciful provision, that she had at any rate the hours of night to herself, and that not till the sun rose again and the blocks were removed would she have to face the true burden of captivity. Here in this vast dark place, like the inside of a mountain, she was for the moment free.

She tried to compose herself to sleep again, for she knew that she needed all her physical and nervous strength for the strain of a new day. But she could not stop her mind from racing. She counted the days she had been a prisoner—seven days, an inconsiderable week, which would have passed too soon in her normal happy life. Now in the retrospect it seemed to lengthen into an eternity. It was only by an effort that she could recall the details of her first coming—the dizzy journey half in the clouds; the Gran Seco like a cup below her brimming with the morning sunlight; the serpentine course among the valleys of the high hills; the blue lake on which the sea-plane had alighted; the march with her pilot in the tangled glens through a long day of heat and misery, among strange birds and insects and creepers like the clutching fingers of ghosts; the meeting with a patrol of his allies—the exquisite Pasquali, a man named Molinoff, and four strange Indians with red ponchos; the coming at last into a valley full of stones built in a circle around a huge rotunda. The jungle had not penetrated one inch into this dead city, for the lush vegetation stopped as if edged by a gardener, and the silent avenues were floored with fine white dust, and the walls were so polished and impenetrable that there was no crevice for a blade of grass. Here she had found bivouac fires and evil faces, faces which to her tired eyes were like the demons of a nightmare. They had given her food, and had been civil enough. D'Ingraville's manners during that awful day had been punctilious, and the men who received her had shown a cold and level politeness. They meant no ill to her —at least for the moment; their careful provision for her safety was proof of it; and when after some fluttering hours in the darkness of the first night she understood this, she had a momentary access of courage.

The following day she had realised her position more fully. She was a hostage, to be protected as such, a card when the time arrived to be ruthlessly played. She was given an Indian servant, who brought her water and towels, and her meals when she chose to feed alone. Otherwise she was welcome to sit with her captors, at least with one section of them. For she soon discovered that there were two groups in the camp. One was composed of men of the D'Ingraville type, who in dress and speech and manners were gentlemen. These she realised were the Conquistadors, of whom she had heard so much, and even in her loneliness and fear she could not repress her interest in them. . . . Some of the names she had known before. There was Lariarty, who had been at school with Sandy, and Larbert, whom she believed she had danced with at a Perth ball, and who had once been engaged to a distant cousin. Romanes, too, Cyril Romanes—she had known his name as a noted figure in the hunting-field and a polo-player of world-wide fame. The other names were new to her, Calvo, and Suvorin, and Pasquali, and Seminov, and Laringetti, and Duclos-Mazarin, and Glorian. They were of every physical type—D'Ingraville slim and fair with a pointed beard and a faun-like head; Suvorin, tall, bony, with a skin like old parchment, and hair as light as an albino; Calvo, short and fat; Pasquali, dark, elegant, and hooknosed; Lariarty with full, well-cut features and a fine brow; Larbert built on the scale of an athlete; Romanes with his neat light-cavalry figure. But all had something in common —the pallor of their faces, their small, considered gestures, and the opaquenss of their eyes.

The other group was of different clay. They were of the type of the four who had carried her off, men whose character showed brazenly in their faces. They fed apart from the Conquistadors, and, though they took their general orders from them, lived very much their own life. They gambled and quarrelled and occasionally fought, but since they had no liquor they were reasonably well behaved. They went off in twos and threes to hunt and prospect, and they always reported on their return to Romanes, who seemed to be in charge of the camp. There was little comfort to be had from looking at their faces, on which life had written too plainly its tale. But at any rate they could laugh. Sometimes into the frozen urbanity of the Conquistadors' talk the distant sound of their guffaws came like an echo of life in a world of the dead.

She had to keep a tight hold on her nerves to prevent a breakdown, when she sat among her strange companions. Sandy had called the Gran Seco a "port of missing ships," and these ships seemed to be phantoms, green with the weeds of some unholy sea. They were mechanically polite, rising when she entered and bowing like automata, helping her first to the monotonous fare; but their words to her were like the commonplaces of a French conversation book. She made many efforts to talk—of music to Pasquali, of hunting to Romanes, of home and friends to Larbert and Lariarty, but she found a wall of opaque civility. Those pages were shut for them, and would not be reopened. She realised that the memories of these men were drugged and their emotions atrophied. But not their minds. Very soon she understood that their minds were furiously alive.

For, after the first day or two, while they did not talk to her they talked among themselves before her. There was no danger to be feared from her, for she was securely in their power. They spoke as sparingly as they ate, but bit by bit she gathered the import of their talk. They were desperately anxious about something, and presently it was clear to her that this something was Castor. He was the one anchor of these missing ships. Without him there was no safety in any port. . . . The girl, as she watched, grew amazed and awed at the extent of Castor's power. He had plucked these derelicts out of the storm, and bestowed on them a dreadful simulacrum of peace. His drug had blotted out the past and given them a keen intellectual life in the present. Without him they were lost again, and all the power of their minds was devoted to winning him back. . . . Soon, from small pieces of evidence, she realised that the same thing was true of the ruffians of the Bodyguard. They, too, were loyal to their salt. The Gobernador had cast his spell over them, and they were resolved to return to his service. Both parties knew what the world did not know, that the Gobernador had been carried off, and was an unwilling figure-head of the rebellion. For Olifa they cared nothing at all, but they were determined that Castor should be set free, and the Castor régime restored.

On his account she was a hostage. She saw that they realised that Lossberg might win in the field, but that, even if the rebels were broken up and driven in commandos to the mountains, Castor might be carried with them. To retrieve him she was their chief instrument, their asset to bargain with. If bargaining was impossible, she knew that she need expect no mercy, for pity did not dwell among Conquistadors or Bodyguard. . . . Castor must be recovered, but it was also necessary that Lossberg should win, for if the rebellion succeeded there would be no hope of the restoration of the old life of the Gran Seco, and it was to this that they clung.

Janet gathered that they were satisfied with Lossberg's progress. She had heard Magee, who had arrived the day before her, exulting over the news he brought. But she gathered also that the Conquistadors were anxious. On the day after her coming the four men who had carried her off, Dan Judson, Laschallas, Radin, and Trompetter, appeared in the camp. They had come by the sea-plane, and apparently damaged it, for D'Ingraville cursed them with a cold bitterness. But others were expected, with messages from Lossberg, messages which must be brought by air, seeing that Sandy's patrols lay between the two camps. . . . These messages did not come. No planes of any kind broke through the cordon and brought news. It was clear that the Conquistadors believed that the messengers had started, and had been shot down, and that their chief preoccupation was to establish communications again.

Suddenly their anxiety seemed to acquire a sharper edge. Molinoff, Carreras, and Carvilho were out daily, but not as hunters, and every night they returned, bone-weary men. Janet, who had already taken her bearings by the sun, had some rough idea of the position of the camp. She knew nothing about the direction of the País de Venenos, but she realised that she must be in the Cordilleras, in a loop of the main chain, where it split into lateral valleys, and that due west of her lay the Gran Seco and her friends. She noticed

that the three men in their daily excursions always went
south, as if they were looking for something. One night
they did not return, and the following afternoon they staggered in drunken with weariness. But they had discovered
something of importance, for Molinoff before he tasted food
or drink sought out Romanes.

What the discovery was Janet could not learn, but at
supper that evening her hosts seemed to be shaken out
of their frozen composure. They talked—for them—
rapidly, and in low tones. Occasionally one of them would
look towards her to see if she was listening, and once
Romanes seemed to be about to address her, but changed
his mind. She pretended absorption in her food, but her
ears were open and she caught one thing. They were
determined to send a message to someone. That someone
could only be Lossberg. They had learned that which might
be vital to his success.

For the first time Janet was diverted from anxiety about
herself and about Archie's peace of mind. She saw dimly
a chance for action. She could not escape, but could she
not find out their secret—hamper them in some way—do
something to relieve the dreadful tedium of her impotence?
She lay awake half the night making futile plans.

Next day she had awoke with a new purpose in life,
She observed one result of the previous evening's discussion. The Indians in the camp were summoned to a council.
There were Indians such as she had never seen before—tall
men, incredibly lean, with faces like skulls and luminous,
feverish eyes. One of them seemed to be chosen for a
mission, for he was given a letter by Romanes which he
secreted on his body, and the next Janet saw was his red
poncho disappearing into the forest. . . . He was not the
only messenger. Magee, a wiry little ruffian who
knew the Indian speech and acted as interpreter, was also
entrusted with a message. To him no letter was given, but
Romanes spoke to him long and carefully, drawing plans
till he nodded his comprehension. Just before midday
Magee also disappeared into the forest which clad the slopes
to the westward.

There was a change in the manner of the Conquistadors. The necessity for haste seemed to have stripped off some of their civilised veneer. Before they had treated her with complete apathy; now she saw in their eyes suspicion, it might be malevolence. Oddly enough, it made her less afraid. She took it as good news. They had learned something which meant advantage to her friends, or they would not be so eager to forewarn the other side. Janet grew almost at her ease. And then she saw that in D'Ingraville's face which sent a shiver down her spine. The success of her own side meant that she would become valueless as a hostage. But she would remain a prisoner—and a victim.

Next day she had felt the same atmosphere around her of cruelty, gloating cruelty. Before she had been lonely, anxious, oppressed, but now she knew the real chill of fear. Whither could she turn? The Indians? They were savages out of some other world, and she had not a word of their speech. There was no pity in their gaunt, glowing faces. . . . The Bodyguard? They at any rate were human, for they could laugh. One of them, too, had a dog, a mongrel terrier, with whom Janet, having an invincible attraction for all dogs, had endeavoured to make friends. She had partly succeeded, but success was easier with one kind of animal than with the other. The Bodyguard that day was dispersed, except the three, Molinoff, Carvilho, and Carreras, who were resting after their labours of the previous days. Carreras had been one of the three trusties who had been hardly treated by Geordie Hamilton that evening on board the *Corinna,* and, since he had seen her there, he seemed to regard her with special rancour. As she passed them, where they grumbled and spat over a game of cards, she felt that among these squalid ruffians there was no refuge from the cruelty of their masters.

With no books, and nothing to occupy her thoughts, she had watched the hot afternoon decline to evening. She saw homing birds returning, especially one great eagle which had been hunting out in the plains. She saw the sun go down behind the hills, and kindle far off a blue peak which reminded her of Stob Dearg as seen from her room at Glenraden. The old happy world she had lost flitted through her mind in a chain of pictures which she had not the strength to repel. She shut her eyes tight, and the smell of wood smoke from the cooking-fires brought back the hall at Glenraden in winter-time, with her sister Agatha making tea, and her father stamping the snow from his feet, and the dogs tangled on the hearthstone. . . . But it was the picture of Archie which broke her heart, the picture which she had so resolutely fought to shut from her; Archie with his boyish laugh and tousled hair and flushed face, so absurd and unexpected and gallant and gentle. . . .

Janet had her supper alone in the immense rotunda where she slept. The Indian who brought it looked steadily before him and had no language but a grave inclination of the head. She heard the blocks being piled together, and knew that for another night she was safe. She blew out her candle and tried to sleep, but now it was not fear that thrilled her, but homesickness. She had gone clean over the horizon, away from the kindly race of men. She believed that she could face horrors, death if necessary, if only a friendly eye or voice were near, if only Archie could hold her hand. . . . But if Archie were here it would mean death for him. The thought terrified her till she remembered how vain it was. Archie would be looking for her with a breaking heart, but by no conceivable chance could he find her hiding-place. It was like being buried deep in the earth. . . . Archie was safe. That was something. . . . As for herself, whether Sandy lost or won she would not live to see it. A sense of utter hopelessness had come over her, the shadow of a dark and certain destiny. But in this certainty there was a kind of miserable peace, and she fell asleep.

She awoke with a start, lit her candle and watched the monstrous shadows run into the uppermost gloom. Then, as we have seen, she tried to sleep again, and slowly drifted from memory to vagueness, from vagueness to unconsciousness.

She woke again, this time to complete awareness. She

had heard a sound different from the light rumble of the wind or the fall of minute particles of dust. There was a human presence somewhere in the emptiness.

Panic shook her. Her sanctuary was no sanctuary, and her enemies were here. With trembling fingers she struck a match and held it to her candle. It seemed ages before the wick caught fire, and then it flickered thinly. She was on her feet now, her eyes wildly searching the darkness.

Suddenly a voice spoke from behind her.

" Please do not be alarmed, Lady Roylance. I am sorry to have disturbed you."

It was a pleasant voice—a foreign voice, for it spoke English with unnatural precision, and made three syllables of her surname. There was something reassuring about that precision. It seemed familiar, too.

" Who is it? " she asked, her voice still quivering.

A figure came out of the gloom. She held up the candle and it revealed an Indian, bare-legged and bare-footed, wearing a long tunic of cats' skins and on his shoulder a red poncho. In her amazement she almost dropped the candle and all her terrors returned.

He seemed to understand her fright, for he spoke rapidly.

" Please do not fear. I am a friend whom you know. I am a friend of your husband and of Lord Clanroyden. . . . Will you please dress a little, for I would like you to take a walk with me. I will retire. We cannot speak in this place."

" But who are you? " This time her voice had hope.

" My name is Luis de Marzaniga."

" Oh, Don Luis, Don Luis! " . . . Her voice was a wail, for violent relief often takes the tone of tragedy. " Oh, my dear, my dear . . . I am so glad. . . . I can't speak. . . . In a second I will be ready."

Janet's toilet did not take long, for she had no clothes but those in which she had left the Courts of the Morning. She pulled on a jumper, and thrust her feet into a pair of much-stained grey suède shoes. At her call Luis again came out of the darkness.

" I know I'm a fright, Don Luis. My hair won't stay

tidy, for I have lost most of my hairpins. I swear I shall be shingled as soon as I get home. . . . Archie wanted me to, before we came out here. . . . Have you any word of Archie? . . . We can't get out of this place, you know." She babbled like a happy child.

"No," he said, "but we can get above it. You have a good head, I hope, Lady Roylance, for I am going to take you nearer to the stars."

He led her to the south-eastern corner, and there her candle, which he carried, revealed a low recess. He motioned her to follow him and she found herself in a tunnel where she had to crouch, almost to crawl. He felt carefully the left side and suddenly he stopped and reached for her hand. "Follow close," he whispered. "The tunnel is a trap, which ends presently in a pit."

They squeezed through a subsidiary opening, and almost at once found the roof rise. "There is a staircase," he whispered. "It is built inside the wall, but it is in good condition. You can stand upright now." He blew out the candle and took her hand.

The steps were smooth and unbroken and they rose steeply. Then they seemed to turn a corner, where the darkness was exchanged for a faint green light. With every step the light grew, and the smell of earth and powdered stone began to change to the freshness of the outer world. Suddenly wind blew in their faces, and they emerged on a kind of barbican, with the stone slats of a roof rising steeply behind them, and in front, beyond a low parapet, the valley white in the moonshine.

Janet caught her breath. The sight was not only of a torturing beauty, but it seemed to be an earnest of freedom. She peered over the edge and saw far below her the dusty avenues of the camp, white and quiet as if under a mantle of snow. One of the cooking-fires still smoked feebly, but otherwise there was no movement in the place. The subsidiary towers, which recalled in their shape pictures she had seen of the Rhodesian Zimbabwes, were like solid cones of pale ivory, and their shadows were deep emerald. The valley, she saw, was thickly forested on all sides, the

trees now milky in the moon, now of the blackest jet. But
beyond its containing walls she saw what was invisible to
one below, peaks which must be high mountains, but which
under this vault of elfin light seemed curiously near and
foreshortened. To the west and south-west, apart from the
barrier ridge, the horizon seemed empty, and she realised
that she was very near to the edge of the hills. Over there
must lie the Gran Seco and her friends.

The girl drew long breaths of an air which seemed to
blend the aromatic strangeness of forests with the coolness
of the high snows. She felt in command once again of
herself and her fate. Below were her captors, but now she
stood above them.

" What is this place? " she asked.

He spoke a name.

" The Thrones of the Kings," she repeated.

" Of the King," he corrected. " Los Tronos del Rey.
There was only one king, but he was very great. When he
died, his captains and councillors were made to die with
him. He was buried here, and they in those lesser towers.
Once each was also full of gold and silver images and
uncountable treasure, but they were rifled long ago by the
ancestors of our people—my own among them. The
spoilers would have destroyed the tombs also, but they could
not. No hand of man can touch this masonry. High
explosives only, and happily they did not have them."

" Does the world know about it? "

He shook his head. " Only the Indians of the País de
Venenos, and they do not talk. The other Indians of the
hills regard it as accursed and will not approach it."

" But who brought these people here—the Conquistadors
and the others? "

" The man called Romanes was in touch with the País
de Venenos—also, I think, Pasquali. They got their drugs
there, and it was necessary for them to find a camp near.
I sanctioned it, for I have much power among the people of
the Poison Valley. It was by my authority that these
Indians accompanied them, and I myself joined them. You
admire my disguise? Since their first coming here I also

have been present to observe. . . . But I did not expect you, Lady Roylance, and you have given me anxious thoughts. . . . Also there is another development. Romanes, he who is the commandante, is a good soldier, and his mind is quick. He has discovered that which I hoped to keep hidden."

"I know," said Janet excitedly. "I saw yesterday that they had found out something which they thought desperately important. I tried to discover what it was—but of course I had no chance. They have sent off messengers to General Lossberg."

"They have. But I do not think those messengers will get through. One was an Indian, and he is already back with me in the forest, not a mile away. The other was the man called Magee. I think that by this time he may have had an accident."

"What was the news?"

"No less than the secret way out of the Gran Seco, the way by which I am accustomed to travel. Olifa believes that there is no road but the railway, except for a stray cragsman. The Gobernador also believes this. But there is a way through difficult passes into the Vulpas valley. Once I showed it to Lord Clanroyden, and it is a road which a light army can travel."

"I see, I see," Janet cried. "Then Sandy might use it, unless Lossberg gets there before him."

"Lossberg will not get there before him. And Lord Clanroyden will beyond doubt use it, since it is the only path to victory."

Janet clasped her hands. All fear for herself had gone, and she joyfully felt herself already united with her friends, since she was again in the game. "I thought I was hidden hundreds of miles away from the rest," she said, "and I find that I am at the key-point."

Luis looked down upon the small figure whose hair was dull gold in the moonlight, and he smiled.

"But you cannot stay here," he said. "It is too dangerous. It is very necessary that you escape not later than to-morrow night—to-night, I mean, for it is now past midnight."

"I long to get away. . . . I admit I have been horribly frightened. . . . But is there nothing I could do if I stayed?"

"You are brave. But no, there is nothing you can do. You will understand that these people are now in a dangerous mood. You are their hostage, but any day they may think that you can be of no use as a hostage, and then . . . they will not be merciful. They are very complete rascals, and it is necessary to keep them here till Lord Clanroyden has made his great stroke. That I think I can undertake through my friends. But we cannot have one of our own people left in their hands. They will be helpless, like imprisoned starving dogs, but they have nasty fangs. . . . No, you must go to-morrow night—this night."

"Will you come with me?"

"No. I will follow you by another road. But I will see that you are accompanied. It is a journey which will need courage, Lady Roylance. Also to-morrow will need courage. Your warders will be in a difficult temper, and you must act a part. You must appear to be in deep sorrow, and I think you had better be a little ill. Yet you must go among them, for when they see you sad and helpless they will be encouraged and perhaps hopeful, and it is very necessary to keep their hope alive for another day. If they have hope they will not think yet of revenge. . . . You will sup in your big bedroom, as you did to-night, and an hour before moonrise I will come for you."

"But how can you get out of this place?"

"By the way which I shall use to-night. The old builders had many tunnels and passages, which I and my Indians have long known. That is simple. It will be harder to get out of the valley, but there is a road for bold hearts, and after a little your friends will meet you. That I have arranged. . . . And now you must go back to bed and sleep very well, for you have much to do to-morrow."

"I shall sleep," Janet cried. "I do not think that I have really slept since I came here, but now . . ." Her face glowed with happiness; she seized his hands and held them, like a child who finds in a gesture what it cannot find in words.

"You have not asked me who will be your escort," he said.

"I feel so strong," she laughed, "that if you gave me the right direction I think I could escape alone."

"Not so, my dear lady. It is too hard a task for one, even one so gallant. But you will be given full directions, and two trusty companions. One will be a Scotch soldier, whose name is Hamilton."

Janet dropped his hands and stared open-mouthed.

"Geordie Hamilton! Fusilier Geordie! How on earth did he get here? He was in the garrison in the Courts of the Morning."

"He is here. He arrived, having fallen sick on the way, but he is now cured. The other . . ." He paused.

"The other?" Janet repeated, with a sudden wild anticipation.

"The other is your husband."

XIV

JANET looked out next morning on a new world. Hitherto her eyes had been turning inward, busy with her own grief. Now she was in a mood of confidence, almost of exhilaration, and the outer scene made a sharper impact upon her senses. She saw the strange beauty of this glen of sepulchre, the uncanny shafts of ghostly stone, the avenues white and crackling in the heat, the cincture of green forest, the sentinel and enveloping mountains. The sight of a far blue peak seen through a gap seemed a promise of liberty. Her youth had returned to her and she was almost in a mood for singing. . . . Then she remembered the part she had to play, and composed herself to a decent bewilderment.

She soon found that she had no need to dissemble, for her new-gained cheerfulness evaporated during breakfast. Her hosts seemed overnight to have changed their attitude.

Their formal politeness had gone, and they treated her roughly, like an embarrassing chattel. Behind their iron composure a deep restlessness was patent. Their schemes were going awry, they could not get in touch with their allies, the place which they had thought a strategic vantage-ground was in danger of becoming their prison.

They talked freely before her, too, and, with what she had learned from Luis, she could follow the drift of it. They spoke of methods of access and egress. Now that the sea-plane was useless, and Lossberg's planes seemed unable to arrive, they discussed the land routes. Some had come by the País de Venenos, but that was a difficult road, and it would land them in that eastern part of the Tierra Caliente where the patrols of Peters and Escrick were too active for comfort. There was a way through the hills direct to the west, the way by which they had dispatched Magee, but that also was slow and difficult, and came out on to the plateau too near Pacheco. They spoke of a road to the south, the road their daily scouting parties had taken, and in that appeared to lie their chief hope. But it had clearly been no part of their plan to leave—rather they expected Lossberg to make contact with them, and Janet knew the reason. They commanded the secret outlet to Olifa; they were the forward observation-post for Lossberg; but unless Lossberg received and acted on their intelligence, they would be more in the nature of a forlorn hope.

They had other anxieties. Janet gathered that the Bodyguard was getting a little out of hand. It had been docile enough when it believed that it was being led back to Castor and its old life. But if it scented failure it would take its own road. She realised that the only tie between the two parties was a common interest; remove that, and there would remain only dislike and contempt. For the first time she heard a note of natural passion among these marionettes, when Lariarty spoke of a wrangle he had had with Judson. For the first time, too, she heard an oath on their discreet lips. Into the face of Romanes there had come a spark of human anger. "By God," he said, "I'll show these curs who is top dog."

Janet played well her game of an ailing and heartbroken prisoner, but she was unregarded. Presently she was to have a striking proof of her hosts' suspicions. The day before in her loneliness she had had thoughts of throwing herself on the mercy of the Bodyguard, and had tried to enter into conversation with them, but had been surlily rebuffed. The most she had succeeded in was a half-hearted friendship with the mongrel terrier that belonged to Carreras. She passed a group of them who were playing cards in the shade of one of the towers, squatted in the white dust. The dog ran to her and she stopped to fondle it.

Suddenly she felt her arms pinioned and looked into a grinning face.

"Come and join our little party, dearie," a voice said. "We're better men than the deadheads up the way. We're all of us free, white, twenty-one, and hairy chested, and we know how to be kind to a pretty girl."

She struggled to release her arms, but the man's grip remained, while the card-party laughed. Even in her terror she noticed how curiously low the ears were set on his head. "Let her alone, Jake," said one of them; "she ain't yours. We've got to toss for her, and act on the square."

The man released her. "I guess that's right. Run away, my beauty. We got a bond on you, and it's soon goin' to be cashed in." As she hurried off, not daring to look behind, she heard again the ill-omened laughter.

At the midday meal her fears were increased. She was curtly told by Romanes that she must prepare to change her quarters. That evening after sundown she would be sent with D'Ingraville to another place. He was perfectly frank. "It is for your own safety, madame," he said. "You are in danger here at the moment, for there are fools among us. It is not yet in our interest that you should come to any harm."

There was no need of acting now. With a face like a sheet she stammered that she was feeling too unwell to travel. "To-morrow, I will be better," she wailed. "But not to-day, please—not to-day."

They talked among themselves. "There is no hurry,"

said D'Ingraville. "If she is sick, I cannot carry her to Agua Secreta. It is the devil's own road."

Romanes demurred, but in the end was persuaded. "A word of advice to you, madame," he said at last. "Do not show yourself this afternoon. Keep in this vicinity, and above all do not go near the camp of those others. Do you understand me?"

Janet understood only too well, for the leering faces of the card-players that morning had chilled her with a new and terrible fear. . . . What refuge could she find between now and sundown? . . . Could she get hold of Luis and tell him of this fresh peril? He alone would be able to protect her, for if it came to a fight she did not believe that the Conquistadors could stand up against the Bodyguard. . . . She was in terror of both parties, but she wondered if it would not have been wise to go with D'Ingraville. The Indians—Luis—would follow her, and could rescue her. But she remembered Luis's strict injunction that she was to be in the great rotunda after nightfall and before moonrise. He had made his plans, and had told her that they were urgent. . . . If only she could find him! . . . She had seen two of the Indians at a distance that morning bringing in logs for the fires. But now there was not a sign of any Indian. She peered down the avenues, quiet in the blinding glare of the afternoon, and not a soul was to be seen. She felt very small and solitary and forlorn.

Then she remembered the roof to which Luis had taken her. There she could hide herself and be at peace till sunset. At the thought her courage returned. She ran across the patch of sun which separated her from the rotunda, and plunged into its deep shadows. . . . At the entrance lay the blocks which every night were used to make a door. She longed to wall herself up like a condemned nun, but each block required two men to lift. . . .

There was no light in the vast place except the shaft from the door, and a dimness far up which may have come from a crack in the roof. She groped in the far corner till she found the entrance to the tunnel. . . . She tried to remember what Luis had done. They had crawled in for some yards, and then he had found an opening on the left-hand side. She ran her hand along the wall, and found such an opening, but the next second her hand was in the void. It was a shaft, not a passage. . . . Very carefully she crawled a little farther along the main tunnel. Luis had said it was a trap, so she must not go too far. Again her hand found an opening in the left wall, and this time it touched solid floor and solid roof. She crept in, and to her joy found the first step of the staircase. Presently she could stand upright, and soon she was out on the barbican, with a fierce sun beating on her head, and the world at her feet, hot, intense, and coloured like blue steel.

The trouble was to get out of the pitiless sun. She could only find shelter by lying flat under the parapet, and moving as the sun moved. She had eaten not a morsel at luncheon, and now that her immediate terror was abated, she began to wish she had. She was safe here—she must be safe. She would stay till nightfall, and then slip down and meet Luis. Her confidence returned, and she felt herself almost free. But there were still dregs of fear in her mind, as she remembered the animal faces of the card-players, and the cold inhumanity of Romanes, to whom she was only a counter, to be protected until its usefulness was gone. . . . She looked every now and then over the parapet. She saw little figures cross and recross the avenue, but none had the slimness and the litheness of the Indians. Where were her deliverers? Luis had said that Archie would be there, but how in the name of all that was marvellous had Archie managed it? He must be somewhere within a mile or two, and she looked with a sudden friendliness at the circumference of forest. Yet the thought that Archie was near gave her a new nervousness. He too might be in danger. . . . She fixed her eyes on a distant blue mountain and told herself that she and Archie were not really far from home, for the other side of that peak must be visible to watchers from Pacheco.

She must have dozed, for she suddenly realised that the sun was behind the peaks, and that the swift tropical twilight had fallen. It was now time to nerve herself for action, for presently the Conquistadors would be sitting down to supper in their mess, and the Indians would come to block up the door. She wondered if, when they missed her from the mess, they would send her food, as they had done previously. She hoped so, for she was very hungry.

Down the staircase she groped her way, and crawled back into the tunnel. She only knew that she had reached the rotunda by seeing far off a slant of amber dusk. It showed her the way to her bed, and beside it, to her delight, she found that food had been placed. It was not an appetising meal, for the commissariat of the camp was running low, but she ate it ravenously, and emptied the tin pannikin of water.

Then she saw that the men had come to block the door. That gave her comfort, for they were Indians, Luis's people. She watched the oblong of pale amethyst slowly lessen, and as the blocks rose the remaining daylight seemed to take on a deeper tint, till it was almost crimson. When that had gone, she would light her candle and await her deliverers.

Suddenly there seemed to be a scuffle at the entrance. She heard a voice, a thick angry voice, and then the narrow gap above the blocks seemed to be filled—by a man's body. Someone was clambering over—she heard a thud as he fell on the inner side. . . . With a flash of dreadful illumination she knew who it was. The Bodyguard had cast lots for her, and this man had won. . . . She screamed for help to the Indians outside the door, but they took no notice. Instead, they went on with the last blocks, and the crimson segment disappeared in utter blackness.

Panic drove Janet's fainting limbs into motion. Her one hope was to reach the tunnel, but in the instant darkness she had lost her bearings and she fluttered blindly. The newcomer, too, seemed at a loss. She could hear his hard breathing. Suddenly he lit a match, and she saw the face of one of the card-players, a dreadful face, bestial and pitiless.

The sight was too much for her nerves, and once again her despairing cry for help rang out. The match flickered and died, but her voice had given him a clue, and she heard him moving nearer. He came slowly and cautiously, for there was no need of haste. He had the whole night in which to find her.

All power seemed to have gone from her body, her throat was dry so that she could not utter a word, her feet were like lead, she had lost all sense of direction. Hopeless now to find the tunnel; she could only struggle vainly like a fly till the spider reached her. Already she felt his clutch on her. And then from her palsied lips came one last gasp of terror, for she suddenly felt herself caught in a man's arms.

But it was not her pursuer. Even her confused senses could still hear him stumbling towards her. A voice spoke low in her ears: " Janet, darling, I'm here! Archie!"

Then many things seemed to happen at once. A circle of light sprang into being from an electric torch. She saw her pursuer stop in his tracks and blink. Then she saw his hand go to his side, and be pinioned there, and a pistol neatly snatched from it by someone behind him. And then between him and her a figure appeared, no Indian, but a stocky figure with bandy legs, a figure that whistled through its teeth like a groom and addressed her enemy in a tongue which fell like music on her ears.

" Sae it's you, my mannie? I'll learn ye to frichten a leddy."

There was a sound of a violent impact of fist on chin and then the rattle of a skull on hard stone.

" That'll keep him quiet till the morn," said the same voice. " I've gi'en that wheasel the same as he got on the *Corinna*."

For a little time and space disappeared for Janet. Overpowering relief and the sense of Archie beside her brought a happy stupor. She was conscious of kissing and fondling the hand which guided her, and murmuring idiotic endearments. They seemed to be descending stone steps, and then following long winding passages. Somewhere there was a light, and she realised that they were a party of four, but more often they moved in profound darkness. Then it seemed to her that they ascended, not by steps, but in a long slanting tunnel. The close air freshened, and at last with a scramble they came out into the night under a sky ablaze with stars. Luis held up his hand to enjoin silence, but Janet had no wish to speak. She was hugging Archie's arm as if to make sure that he was a bodily presence and not a dream.

They were in a little stone courtyard, on the edge of the forest, and at the far southern end of the Tronos del Rey. It was the frontier of the jungle and creepers had encroached upon the stone, completely hiding the tunnel's mouth, and making the courtyard look like a subsidence in the ruins. They were close to the camp, for voices sounded not a hundred yards away, and against the starlight they could see the pale flicker of fires.

Luis signed to them to follow, and they scrambled out of the hollow into the forest, which was thick as moss, except for an occasional trail. " We must go carefully," he whispered. " Carreras went out this evening to shoot for the pot. He may not have returned. It would not do to meet him."

Luis moved first with Archie at his heels, then Janet, and Hamilton brought up the rear. It was painful going, for chips and slivers of stone were everywhere embedded in the lush herbage and the stones were as unyielding as adamant. Janet felt her stockings and the fringes of her dress being slowly shredded. Then they reached an opening which she judged to be a trail. Luis took one look and then ducked his head, and the others crouched flat to conform.

Janet wondered what was coming next. There was still the glow of sunset in the sky, and it made the aisle through which the trail ran a slender cleft of opaque unrevealing light. What came next was a dog. To her horror she found Carreras's terrier breathing heavily at her shoulder. He had been trained not to bark, but he showed his recognition by shaking himself and sending the dew flying like a shower-bath.

She glared at him, she threatened him, but the beast stood wagging his imbecile tail. He had found a friend, and was determined to let his master come up and share in the discovery.

Luis did not wait for the meeting. He doubled back and clutched Archie's arm.

" The fellow will be here in a second," he whispered. " We must show ourselves. . . . You know the road. . . . Here, take the hatchet. . . . I will try to divert them. Once at Agua Secreta you are safe. Quick! "

The next five minutes were not for Janet a period of very clear consciousness. She was dragged to her feet, pulled through what seemed to be a fine-meshed sieve of creepers, and landed in a narrow avenue cut as if with a knife between two walls of forest. Then she seemed to be made to halt, and she had the feeling as if alone she was exposed to someone's gaze, while the rest were hidden. . . . She heard a cry, heard a shot fired, heard other pistol shots from the direction of the camp. . . . And then she found herself running faster than she had ever run before in her life.

Luis was last and he was urging them on. They were being pursued—she heard a distant crashing in the undergrowth—perhaps the trail twisted and someone was trying to take a short cut. Then Luis's clear whisper followed them. " I leave you. You know the road. . . . Do not for the love of God stop to fight. . . . I do not think you will be followed. . . . Say that I will be at Pacheco in thirty-six hours, no more. Adios! "

She had no time to look behind, for Archie's hand was dragging her, Archie whose game leg seemed to be performing miracles, but she had the sensation that Luis was no longer there. He had swerved to the right down a subsidiary path and was making mighty heavy going. His movements sounded like those of a bull rhinoceros; he was giving tongue, too, babbling loudly to himself. He will betray us all, she thought in a panic, and then she realised that this was his purpose. He was there to be followed. . . . Far back she heard a different kind of cry, the shouting of angry men on a scent which they have missed and recovered.

After that it seemed that for hours they struggled and plunged and slipped, always keeping to some sort of trail, but tripped up by creepers, or slithering on greasy earth, or edging painfully through acres of cruel thorn. She used to be famous for her good wind, and had been able to stride from Glenraden to the highest top of Carnmor without a halt. But that had been in clear hill air, with a bright world of salt and heather at her feet and no goad except her fancy. It was a different matter to run through this choking sodden forest, with life as the stake—Archie's life and her own—maybe, too, the fortunes of the campaign. The girl kept her mind savagely upon a single purpose—to keep up with Archie, and to give him as little trouble as possible, for she knew by his laboured breathing that the strain must be terrible for a lame man.

Hamilton, the leader, stopped. He was panting like a dog, but he had voice enough left to whisper hoarsely, " I hear nothing. Maister Lewis maun hae got the hale pack at his heels. They'll no catch him this side o' Martin-mas. We maun be better than half road. Tak your breath, mem."

But the merciful respite seemed only to last for a second. Again they were off, and now they seemed to be ascending. The ground was harder. They passed over banks of dry gravelly soil, and in places the roots of the trees showed as in a pinewood, instead of being buried deep in rank verdure. Once even there was a shelf of layered rock, and she had to give Archie a hand. But the gain in eleva-tion told them nothing of their position, for it was that murky mulberry dusk in which the foreground is just visible, but everything else an impenetrable blur.

They seemed to reach a summit, where curiously enough it was darker than below. After that it was flat for a little, with thinner vegetation but many thorns—Janet felt her hands ache from their attentions. She was feeling a little more at ease. They were on the right road—Hamilton seemed to have no doubt about that—they could not be very far from their goal, and there was no sign of pursuit. Luis must have lifted the enemy cleverly off the scent. She wondered if he were safe. . . .

It was Archie who stopped suddenly and put his hand to his head. "Hamilton!" he panted. "Listen! Do you hear anything?"

Janet pushed her hair away from her ears. Somewhere back in the forest there was a sound like a little wind. But the night was very still. . . . She listened again, and in the heart of it she heard the unmistakable note of human speech. . . . And then suddenly it sounded much nearer, not a hundred yards away: "Oh! Quick," she cried. "They're almost up on us."

She was not quite right, for the acoustics of the place were strange. Actually at the moment the nearest of the pursuers was at least a quarter of a mile off. But all three had felt the ominous proximity of the sound, and all in their different ways reacted to the spur of fear. Hamilton, being of a stocky build, could not quicken his pace, for he had come nearly to the end of his running resources; instead he slowed down, and his hand fiddled with his belt. He would have preferred to fight. Janet got her second wind, and felt an extraordinary lightness and vigour. It was she now who dragged Archie. Inevitably they passed Hamilton, so when they suddenly came to the brink of the gorge she was leading the party.

It was the kind of spectacle which cuts short the breath for the sheer marvel of its beauty. From her feet the ground broke into a cliff, but a cliff not of stone but of soil, for it was all forested. The trees were set on so steep a gradient that two yards from her she was looking into branches reached commonly only by high-flying birds. The angle was not less than sixty degrees, but some strange adhesive quality in the soil enabled it to cling to this difficult foundation and support life. But the miracle lay in the depth. In that luminous purple night it ran down from layer to layer of darkness, keeping an exact perspective, till it seemed that it had sunk for miles. The cleft must go to the centre of the globe, and yet a bottom could be detected, though not discerned. Somewhere at an infinite distance below there was water—the so-called Agua Secreta—strong water, too, for out of the deeps rose the murmur of a furious river.

From Janet's feet a bridge flung out into the void. It looked like a ship's bowsprit hanging over dark oceans, for the eye could not see its further abutment. And such a bridge! It was made of slats and twined osiers and lianas, solidly made, and its making was not of yesterday. But there was no planking to hide the abyss. Between the slats showed the naked void, and the slats were each a pace apart.

"On ye gang," a hoarse voice spoke behind. "It's the brig we maun cross. Haud fast by the side-ropes, mem, and ye'll no fa'. Sir Erchibald will keep haud o' ye."

But Janet had no fear for herself. This lath strung across immensity was a beautiful thing. . . . Suddenly one half of it seemed to become brightly gilt, and she realised that the rim of the moon had lifted above a corner of hill. . . . And it meant safety! It was Archie she feared for, Archie with his crippled leg. She stepped cheerfully out on the bridge. "Hold tight, Archie dear, and go very slow. Balance yourself by my shoulder."

The crossing of that bridge was a comment upon the character of each of the three. Janet was in a kind of ecstasy. To be islanded between sky and earth was an intoxication, and every step was nearer home. If only Archie . . . ! Archie, painfully groping his way, minded the vertigo of it not at all, but he realised, as she did not, how slowly they moved and how imperative was haste. As for Hamilton, the thing was to him pure torment, he was terrified half out of his senses, but he doggedly plugged along because there was nothing else to be done. He was praying fervently and blaspheming steadily, and prayer and blasphemy continued till the first shot was fired. After that he was more at his ease.

They were in the middle of the bridge when the pursuers reached the edge. A cry followed them, heard as clearly in that funnel as if it had been spoken in their ear, to halt and come back or someone would shoot. The warning was followed by a shot, fired wide.

The last part of the journey was a nightmare for all three. Speed was an urgent matter, yet a slip would send them whirling into unplumbed gulfs. For Janet all the exhilaration was gone, and her heart was fluttering wildly. She was terrified for Archie, who had had some ugly slips and was leaning heavily on her arm. Also the gulf was now lit with silver moonshine. Before it had merely been a sensation of dark space, felt but not realised; now she could see its shimmering infinity, and something of the old terror of the Abyss began to clutch at her.

Before she knew she was off the bridge and had pulled Archie beside her on to a tussock of dwarf arbutus. A deadly faintness was on her, and her head swam. Dimly she saw Hamilton busy with his hatchet. . . . What was he doing? . . . There were men on the bridge. She saw them clearly. They were getting nearer. . . .

Then she realised. The fear of the Abyss came back to her. It seemed an awful thing to sacrifice men to it, even enemies. "Stop!" she pleaded. "You can't. Let's go on. . . ."

"It's my orders, mem," said the other, stolidly cutting through the twisted lianas. "Maister Lewis says—at all costs ye maun destroy the brig ahint you."

The pursuit realised what was happening. They were more than half-way across, and the moonlight was so bright that the visibility was like day. Janet could see each of the four figures distinctly. They were all of the Bodyguard. One of them, the foremost, seemed to be the man who had pursued her in the rotunda.

A pistol shot struck the earth a yard from Hamilton.

"Ye'll maybe get hurt, mem," he observed between his strokes. "Get you and the Captain in ahint the buss. I'm near finished."

But apprehension and horror held both Archie and Janet motionless. There was one other pistol shot, which went wide. The men on the bridge had stopped shooting and were labouring grimly in the race with death. . . . Suppos-

ing they won, thought Janet. . . . But they did not win.
Very gently, without any sag or jerk, the bridge swung
out into the gulf like a silver pendulum, and several little
black things were shaken from it.

Two hours later four of Peters's troopers, patrolling up
the long moraine of shale in one of the tributary glens of
the Catalpas stream, came upon three very weary travellers,
who were staggering knee-deep in the shingle. To their
amazement they found that they were English—two men
and a woman, who asked to be taken to Pacheco. One of
the men was lame, and he and the woman were set on
horseback.
When after midnight they reached the camp in the valley
bottom their captain, Carlos Rivero, received the travellers
with excitement. He fed them, but they made only a hasty
meal, demanding at once to be taken to headquarters. At
the place which is called Maximoras, but in the old speech
Hatuelpec, Captain Rivero, who himself conducted them,
was again surprised to be met by a fresh troop from Pacheco,
which contained a woman. But it was the commander of
this troop who gave Rivero the third and most shattering
surprise of the night. For he recognised in him the
Gobernador of the Gran Seco.

BOOK III

OLIFA

I

GENERAL ALEXANDER LOSSBERG, the Commander-in-Chief of the Olifa Expeditionary Force, was in a good temper as he took the air one morning on his smart little blue roan on the long ridge to the east of his advanced headquarters. It was nearly four months since he had occupied the city of the Gran Seco, and he felt that the situation was now satisfactory to his orderly mind. At first it had been rather an anxious business, this groping in the dark for an enemy whom it seemed impossible to locate. With his superb force—his infantry divisions, his mechanised battalions, his cavalry brigade, his field batteries, and his light tanks—it had irked him to find nothing to spend his strength on. But he had been patient and very cautious. The enemy had an unpleasant number of aeroplanes and knew how to use them—he was a good soldier and could appreciate the merits of an antagonist—and his repeated demands to Olifa for more planes had brought a meagre response. But, in spite of the semi-blindness which this weakness in the air involved, he had groped his way steadily to the identification and the capture of the enemy bases.

There was Fort Castor—that had soon fallen. The name set him musing upon the fate of him who had once been Gobernador of the Gran Seco. He had never liked him; he remembered the insolent calm of his eyes, and his habit of asking unanswerable questions. The man had been an arrogant civilian, and his cleverness was futile in war. He had heard that he was an unwilling figurehead, a prisoner in the hands of the guerrillero whom the people called El Obro, and whom he understood to be a Scottish soldier-of-fortune. Well, this El Obro, he was not much of a soldier; only a flashy amateur. The General had heard a good deal of talk in his time about the importance of the psychological factor in war, and was a little sick of it. Why should he trouble himself to read the mind of this guerrillero; he knew by instinct the kind of mind he had—the ingenious schoolboy, treating war as a holiday game and banking on the unexpected. There was no such thing as the unexpected. War was an exact mathematical science. Cleverness and daring might delay for a week or two the advance of the great military machine, but in the end it crept forward, crushing opposition as a tank went through barbed wire and breastworks. Once again the professional had been justified, and the General flung out his chest and drew deep and pleasant draughts of the cool morning.

Fort Castor—and then Loa, and then the easy capture of the enemy's secret base up on that shelf between the mountains and the sea. What was the name of it? Los Patios de la Mañana. An amusing name, the kind of name that those play-acting folk would choose. He had not yet visited the place, but he promised himself that pleasure soon. It was said to be very beautiful. He could imagine worse fates than to be the Governor of this province, and Los Patios might be an eligible site for a country house. Soldiering in Olifa itself had been a little tedious for a man of his energy. But Gobernador of this rich province—that promised power, and amusement, and, of course, wealth. In these Latin republics he understood that there was a generous margin for those set in authority.

The Mines had been his great problem. Olifa had always been nervous lest the enemy should so destroy them that their restoration would be a labour of years. One part of the danger had been removed when he occupied the city and the smelting works; the other, the Mines, had been made his chief preoccupation, by direct instructions from his Government. It had not been his own wish. He did not believe in tying himself up with anything in the nature of a fortress. He had been taught that it was a general's duty to seek out the enemy and destroy him, and not to be entangled in the defence of property. His adversaries had guessed at this obligation, for they had made the Mines the scene of most of the fighting, and had managed by constant pin-pricking to tie up most of his troops on that long front. . . .

Yet, perhaps, in their blundering way the Olifa Government had been right. Against an enemy so light and elusive and with such a vast hinterland for retreat, their way had perhaps been the best. He remembered that he had not been very successful in his rounding-up expeditions. His cavalry nets had been drawn tight again and again without enclosing anything. The cavalry had indeed been a failure. It had been led a pretty dance by El Obro's commandos, had been split up and destroyed in patches, had lost itself, had fought against itself in fog and darkness. As a gunner, he had never been a cavalry enthusiast, and now he was more disillusioned than ever. Also the tanks had not been a success, since there had been nothing solid against which to use them. . . . No, perhaps Olifa by some fortunate accident had judged right. This long-drawn defence of the Mines had done its part. It must have depleted terribly the enemy's vanishing stock of munitions; he wished he could think that it had depleted his numbers. And now it was over. For three days the Mines front had been stagnant, and his patrols had reported no enemy force within twenty miles. The cause could only be that *débâcle* of munitionment which he had always foreseen and counted on.

There remained Pacheco—that robbers' nest in the angle of the hills. That, he believed, was the main enemy head-quarters, and he had been anxious for a long time to burn it out. This very morning he was advancing on Pacheco in strength. At last there was something to bite on. The result, of course, was a foregone conclusion, and after that——? Where would El Obro find his next refuge? It was on Pacheco, no doubt, that the attempts on the Mines front had been based. It was from Pacheco beyond question that the raids on the railway had been launched. These raids had for some time been happily abortive, and, now that he had his blockhouse system nearly complete, the only danger was from an occasional bombing aeroplane —if the enemy had any bombs left. . . . There was perhaps another base in the north-east—he had some evidence of that. But what were these bases? Mere twigs on which to perch, and always being moved nearer to the inhospitable hills. You could not call that a base which supplied nothing in the way of food or shells. His military soul repudiated the name. He ran his mental eye over the map of the Gran Seco. The city and the railway to Olifa securely held; the Mines now free from all danger; the enemy forced out of the whole western, southern, and northern parts, and holding only an unknown corner in the north-east with driblets southward towards the Tierra Caliente. The war was over. The country was conquered. All that remained was a little minor police work.

His reflections were so satisfactory that the General was compelled to ease his feelings by swift movement. He gave his horse its head against the slope, and, raising his cap, let the wind sing about him and ruffle his thinning hair. He drew rein at the crest and scanned the wide landscape. A fine soldierly figure he looked, his square tanned face flushed with exercise, his grey eyes with almost a boyish light in them, the slight heaviness and sullenness of mouth and jaw relaxed in good humour. He looked eastward where sixty or seventy miles away the great chain of the mountains stretched its white fingers into the unfathomable blue. He was no connoisseur in the picturesque, but suddenly those mountains gave him a feeling of pleasure. He felt a proprietary interest in this land, of which he might soon be Governor, and he was glad that his future satrapy included these magnificent creatures of God. They reminded him of his childhood, when from a Bavarian valley he had stared at the distant snows of the Wettersteingebirge.

He turned, and before him lay the grassy barrens that stretched to the city. On his right he could see the slim headgear of the Mines, and the defences of that now stagnant front. The sight initiated a new train of thought. He had always meant to have the Mines started as soon as possible. That would be proof positive of his victory. When he had broached the idea to Olifa it had been received with enthusiasm: those bovine ministers could not comprehend the meaning of his operations, but they could appreciate such a result as the resumption of their great industry. . . . That very afternoon he would send a dispatch, and he would begin to work out the first stages. . . . And then a reflection brought him up with a jerk. Where was he to find the experts to advise him? What had become of those strange gentlemen who called themselves the Conquistadors?

He had talked it all over with Romanes many weeks ago. He detested the type, the unwholesome pale faces, the low voices, the opaque eyes, which nevertheless in their blankness seemed to hold a perpetual sneer. But he had been instructed from Olifa to treat them with respect, and Romanes he found that he could get on with. The man had been a soldier—a good soldier, he believed, till he had fallen down —and he had not forgotten his earlier trade. The General had been impressed with the soundness of his military views. He had a contempt for anyone who fell out of his own hierarchy, but he did not show it, and Romanes had no doubt appreciated being treated as still one of the brotherhood. Romanes had been insistent on starting the Mines. Half-power, of course, at first; there would be a great lack of technical staffs and white foremen. But he was confident that all the labour needed could be got among the concentrados and prisoners, and that he and his colleagues could make up a skeleton staff.

But that was nearly a month ago. General Lossberg had owed his professional success to his remarkable power of absorption in the task of the moment. He had been busy conducting a war, and he had had no ear for gossip. But he seemed to remember something. There were queer stories about those people. They lived on drugs and got them somewhere—where was it? somewhere in the mountains? Yes. Olivarez had told him that they had gone to the mountains, they and the blackguard-looking fellows who had been Castor's Bodyguard. . . . Why had it been permitted? He would have something to say to Olivarez. . . .

The General cantered across the baked yard in front of his quarters, and, giving his horse to an orderly, marched into the office of his Chief of Staff. Olivarez was older by several years than Lossberg, and, along with General Bianca, was the military pride of Olifa. He was a slight man, with a long olive-tinted face, a fleshy nose, and grizzled hair cut *en brosse*. He jumped to his feet as the General entered, and was about to speak, when he was forestalled.

" What about that fellow Romanes, General? " Lossberg demanded. " I want to get hold of him at once—him and his friends. I propose to start the Mines."

The other looked puzzled for a moment. He had something of his chief's gift of absorption, and his mind had been much occupied of late by other matters.

" Romanes, sir? Yes, I remember." He turned the leaves of a big diary. " He left here on the 23rd of last month. Some private business. He was no use to us and we did not try to stop him. He was going into the mountains and was confident that he could get past General Peters's patrols. There was some talk of a sea-plane which D'Ingraville had got hold of in Olifa. D'Ingraville, you may remember, sir, was formerly of the French Air Service. He left a request that we should keep in touch with him—by air, of course —and he gave us certain bearings and directions by which we could find him. I do not know if anything has been done about it. Shall I send for Colonel Waldstein? "

Presently Waldstein appeared, a little man all wire and whipcord. He had something to tell, but not much.

" We had Señor Romanes's directions beyond doubt," he said, " but it is one thing, sir, to be given a line and quite another to be able to take it. That does not need saying. We twice tried to make contact with him, but you will remember, sir, that three weeks ago the enemy planes were very active between here and the mountains. There is reason to believe that both the fighting scouts that we sent out were shot down. At any rate, they have not returned."

" Have you done nothing since then? " Lossberg asked peremptorily.

" No, sir. Every machine we possess has been engaged in urgent business."

Lossberg tapped his teeth with a pencil; it was a habit he had when he was slightly ruffled.

"There is now no enemy activity in that area, Colonel Waldstein," he said at last. "You will please arrange that a machine is sent at once to the place indicated by Señor Romanes. No, send two, and send Hoffding carriers. I want Señor Romanes brought here at once, and as many of his colleagues as can be accommodated, and arrangements made for the transport here of the rest. Do you understand? The matter is urgent."

Waldstein saluted and went. Then Olivarez was given the chance of saying that which had been on his tongue.

"There is a message from Pacheco, sir. We occupied it an hour and twenty minutes ago."

Lossberg's face lit up. "But that is good business. Had we much trouble?"

"No, sir. We were not opposed. The place was abandoned."

Lossberg stared blankly. "Abandoned, you say?"

"Abandoned, sir. Not a shell was fired. No contact mines had been left. And apparently it had not been abandoned in a hurry, for every scrap of stores had been removed. The place had been deserted for several days."

The Commander-in-Chief, who was commonly a precisian in his speech, observed that he was damned. He stared with his eyes abstracted, thinking hard. He had always been contemptuous about psychology, but now he wished he could see a little into the mind of El Obro.

"Where have they gone?" he soliloquised. "Peters had five thousand men there a week ago. I wonder what diabolical game he is up to now? There's no way east or south. He has not come west, for we hold the land up to the southern scarp. He must have gone north. There's something preparing up in that north-east corner which we have got to discover. Tell Colonel Waldstein to arrange for an extensive air patrol of the eastern Tierra Caliente. Let him take a radius of 150 miles. Yes, telegraph the news about Pacheco to the War Ministry. It will make a good headline for the papers. But do not mention that we found it abandoned. I will give all the details in my dispatch."

" The wireless is working very badly, sir," said Olivarez. " We have been consistently jammed the last thirty-six hours."

" Atmospherics," the Colonel observed. He had moments of longing for the old days of war, when you stuck to the heliograph, and the dispatch rider, and the telegraph. Then, somewhat perturbed, he went to breakfast. The crystal-clear vision of the future which he had had that morning on the savannah was a little dulled.

Towards the late afternoon of the same day one of the Hoffding machines returned, and with it the pilot of the other, which had crashed in one of the glens. It reported a difficult and disastrous journey. It had followed Romanes's directions and made its way into the mountain range by an intricate series of valleys. It had found itself in a region where the wind came in baffling eddies, and where there was no possible landing-place. All the valleys were narrow and sheer and muffled with forest. It had discerned a shelf of flat ground, filled with the ruins of great stone towers. There, flying low, it had seen the remains of old camp-fires, but there were no human beings now in the place. After that came the disaster to its sister machine, the pilot of which had been saved by a miracle. Unless it attempted to fly over the main range, there was nothing more to be done, so it had come home to report.

Late that night one of Waldstein's patrols brought in a man who had been found in the tangled country under the lee of the mountains. He was half dead with fatigue and starvation, but had recovered sufficiently to ask to be taken to the General's Headquarters. The General had not had the pleasant dinner which he had anticipated. The meal, instead of being a cheerful celebration of the capture of Pacheco, had been an anxious confabulation with his staff. For something had gone wrong with his communications, and he could get no answer from Olifa. In place of the lyric congratulations on success which he had expected, his message had been followed by utter silence. The long-distance telephone had never been noted for its reliability, but hitherto the telegraph service had been perfect. Now, with the wireless out of gear for two days, it looked as if this too had failed. That, or some intense preoccupation at the Ministry of War. Consequently, when Olivarez brought in the rag of humanity which his patrol had picked up, it was with no friendly eye that Lossberg regarded him.

"We cannot find Señor Romanes," the Chief of Staff had said, "but this is one of those who were with him. One of the gentry whom Castor called his Bodyguard. He says he has something for your private ear. Jesucristo! Wherever he came from he has had a rough journey."

Mr Daniel Judson had not been improved in looks by his recent experiences. His clothes hung in rags, his skin was black with exposure, and short commons had sharpened his face so that his big head tapered to a jackal's mask. Normally his broken nose and rabbit teeth gave him a touch of comedy, ferocious comedy—but now these features seemed to be blended into one overwhelming impression of something snarling and ravening. The slouch of his thick-set shoulders gave him the air of crouching for a spring, like a mad dog. He had had food, of which he had eaten sparingly, being used to similar experiences and knowing the danger of a glut. Lossberg gave him permission to sit down, while his story dribbled out through the confusion of fatigue.

Most of it was startlingly new to the General and his staff. He spoke of a camp at Los Tronos del Rey. "Those guys had to have the dope, and the Indians fetched it. . . ." He told of the daily expeditions and of the discovery of a pass through the mountains which had excited Romanes. . . . "We were expecting you to send to us, but you never came, so Mr Romanes, he tried to get to you. The Indians must have double-crossed us, for nothing happened. We sent out Magee, and he never came back. Then the Indians turned nasty. There was a woman we had with us and she got away. The Indians must have helped her, and they cut the bridge behind her, and next morning the whole outfit did a bunk. After that we were between a rock and a hard place. There was a lot of unpleasantness with Mr Romanes, but by and by we see'd we couldn't do nothing by fighting each other, so we shared out the grub, and took what we each thought was the best road off that bloody mantelpiece. . . . I started out with two pals, and I don't know where in hell they've got to." Mr Judson appeared to be going to be sick at the recollection. He recounted haltingly something of his troubles, first in the forest and then in the glens of the foothills. Famine had been the worst. "A biscuit would ha' rattled in my stomach like a buckshot in a tin pan." He had several times decided that he was about to perish. "This world one time, then the fireworks," was the way he expressed his anticipation. By and by he had become so feeble that he could only crawl and weep, and in that condition the patrols had found him. Even now he had not the strength of a new-born cat. "If I slapped a fly this moment, I'd fall down."

Lossberg fastened upon one item in his story, the pass through the mountains. Judson strayed into vague profanity. He didn't rightly know how to describe it, but they had found it all right, and Mr Romanes had thought it as important as hell. That was why he had made his despairing effort to get in touch with the General. Judson's brains were too befogged to explain further, but he quoted a sentence of Romanes. "Mr Romanes, I heard him say to the long Frenchy, him that was the airman, 'By God!' he says, 'if we don't stop that bolt-hole the rebs one fine morning will be breakfasting in Olifa.'"

Judson was dismissed, and the General looked at his Chief of Staff.

"Romanes is not a fool," he said, "and he has been a soldier. He has found out something which he wanted badly to get to us. Remember he is on our side. Except by our victory he and his friends cannot get back to the life they enjoy. What is that something? A road through the mountains into Olifa? We have always understood that there was no road, no practicable road, except that which the railway follows. There may be a pass which we know nothing of. Romanes knows about it. The question is, does El Obro? If he does, it would explain Pacheco."

The two men talked long and gravely. One result of their conference was that Waldstein was given fresh orders. His air patrols must move a little farther south and explore the valleys east of Pacheco. At all costs they must find Señor Romanes and his companions, who must now be making their way down from the hills.

Lossberg had a disturbed night, but about ten next morning he had news which cheered him. There had been a sudden revival of enemy activity in the north part of the province. Mounted bands had been seen west of the line Fort Castor–Loa, and a motor convoy, bound for the latter place, had been captured. To Lossberg this was reassuring tidings. It seemed to explain the whereabouts of Peters and his Pacheco force. They had not gone south through any mysterious pass in the mountains, but north, to join the oddments up in that north-eastern corner. The General convinced himself that what he had always foreseen had now come to pass. The enemy was confined to the north-east of the Tierra Caliente, and all that remained was slowly and drastically to bring him to book. He would of course make sallies from his beleaguerment, but it would not be hard to cope with the desperate efforts of weak and ill-provided men.

Yet the whole of the following week was taken up with these sallies. The enemy had changed his tactics, and adopted a vigorous offensive. The Mines front was stagnant, and Lossberg was able to move one infantry division and all his cavalry to the threatened north.

The first thing that happened was that Loa fell to the guerrilleros, and the garrison in the Courts of the Morning had its land communications cut. This was interpreted by Lossberg as a feint, for Loa could be no value to the enemy. In this he was right, for after its stores had been removed, Loa was abandoned.

But the next move was startling, no less than a raid on the Gran Seco city. It happened about 1 a.m. on a night when there was no moon. The enemy cut up the pickets, and for nearly four hours held all the city west of the smelting works and north of the railway station. The thing had been beautifully arranged. The raiders, who seemed to know the place intimately, occupied the key-points, and used the machine guns they had taken at the northern approaches. They knew, too, where the stores were, and helped themselves to what they wanted, loading the loot into light motor-wagons which had only the day before arrived from Olifa. They destroyed a freight train in the railway yards and put no less than seven locomotives out of action. It was artful destruction, done by men who were skilful mechanics, and it would take weeks to repair. Then, after setting fire to the Gran Seco Club as a final *feu de joie,* they made off at their leisure, taking with them the light motor-wagons. It was well after daybreak before Lossberg's first reinforcements arrived, for the telephone and telegraph wires had been comprehensively cut. An attempt to follow was made with armed cars, but the pursuit struck the rear of the raiders about forty miles north-east of the city, was ambushed, and badly cut up. The enemy had vanished again into his north-eastern fastness.

All this was disquieting, but yet in its way consoling. Judson's story had deeply impressed the Commander-in-Chief, and he was relieved to have discovered the whereabouts of the Pacheco force. It must have joined the bands under Escrick, for hitherto Escrick had been far too weak to think of an offensive. So he set about with a will the task of hunting down the remnant. He established a cordon of posts in a line from the Mines to Loa, and, based on each extremity, he had a mobile force of cavalry and mechanised battalions. He believed that this cordon could not be pierced, and his plan was slowly to push it forward till he had driven the enemy into the mountain valleys. Of these he would then seal up the ends, and starve him out.

But the cordon was pierced, repeatedly pierced. There was no further raid on the Gran Seco, but there was a disastrous dash on the Mines, which ended in the explosion of a shell-dump and the shattering of two engine-houses.

Marvellous to relate, too, there was a raid on the railway, from what base no man knew, and the line was badly damaged in the crucial section between Tombequi and Villa Bar. Also there were perpetual pin-pricks. Not a convoy seemed to be able to move on any of the Gran Seco roads without some regrettable accident—a mined road, a broken culvert, a long-distance sniping of baneful accuracy. Lossberg, who had regarded the campaign as over, was forced to admit that it had miraculously entered upon a new phase.

In the thick of this guerrilla warfare the General forgot his other problems. He was kept so feverishly busy that he omitted to worry about the silence of the Olifa Ministry of War and the absence of a reply to his message about Pacheco. He was moving fast about the country and did not remember to inquire whether Waldstein's machines had picked up any news of the Conquistadors. Waldstein's machines were now on other duties. But there came a night when he was able to return to his advanced Headquarters, which had remained in the vicinity of the Mines. He dined alone with Olivarez, the first peaceful meal he had had for ten days. Both men were in better spirits.

"It is the last spasm of a dying animal," said Lossberg. "Now we know to a decimal the worst he could do, and we know that he cannot repeat it. In a week this activity will die down, and we shall turn to the question of starting the Mines. Even now it is police work we are engaged in, not war."

Olivarez nodded and smiled. "By the way, we have news of the Conquistadors. Señor Romanes is here, and the man they call Larbert, the Englishman."

"I will see them after dinner," was the answer. General Lossberg filled himself a glass of champagne—he had allowed himself champagne that evening—and looked complacently at its sparkle. He had had an annoying time, but he had come to the end of it.

The telephone bell rang, and Olivarez took the receiver. "It is from Olifa at last," he said over his shoulder. "A message forwarded from Base Headquarters."

The General continued to contemplate his glass, with a

smiling face. He awaited the congratulations which were his due. Suddenly he was startled to attention, for his Chief of Staff was speaking in an odd voice.

" Repeat," he said, and again, " Repeat! " He turned to Lossberg without hanging up the receiver and his hand trembled.

" I can't make it out. . . . It must be a mistake. . . . It is from Santa Ana, not Olifa. I don't know who sent it. . . . Good God, it can't be true! "

" What is it, man? " Lossberg asked.

" It says that Santa Ana was captured this morning by the enemy. Santa Ana! By the American Blenkiron, who was known here as Rosas! "

Lossberg's face whitened, but he retained his composure. He even laughed, a little harshly. " If that is true, El Obro is assuredly through the passes."

II

THE short spring had gone, and it was already early summer at Charcillo. The gnarled tamarisks which lined two sides of the great pebbled courtyard were hung with long lilac blooms, and the poplars and willows were green along the water-furrows. The estancia was of an older type than Veiro. There were no neat paddocks and English-looking stables; part of the house itself had stood for three hundred years, and the thick walls of the corrals were almost fortifications. The place stood on a low ridge between the main stream of the Vulpas and a tributary, commanding to the west and south long views over savannah which gradually dipped to the blueness of the coastal plain. Behind, to the east, was more rolling country, but from every ridge might be descried fifty miles off the dark loom of the mountains, and in clear weather the northernmost peaks of Los Doce Apóstoles.

For the past fortnight Janet had been a happy denizen of a fantastic world. She felt that she was now promoted to the rank of a combatant. Her adventure had by a marvellous chance been the turning-point in the campaign.

As she looked back upon the last month, the fear and horror were forgotten. Her week of captivity was only like a dark night between bright and bustling days. Far back in the corridors of memory she saw the Courts of the Morning, a platform lifted high above the world, whence with a divine detachment they had looked down upon the struggles of mortals. That life could not have lasted, but it had done its work, for it had wrought a miracle in the Gobernador.

What had become of the mysterious being with his inhuman composure and his secret thoughts? A new man had been born, a man who had forgotten his past and walked on a new earth with a curious innocence. He seemed to be happy, happy in companionship as well as in leadership. For beyond doubt he was a leader, and his post as generalissimo was no polite fiction. It was an unfamiliar world to him, but he had taken hold of it like a master. Modestly, simply, he had applied his mind to strange problems, and from the first day he had had an unquestioned authority. In the great movement through the passes, after Peters with the remnant of his command had gone north to Escrick, and Sandy had led his mounted three thousand into Olifa, it was the Gobernador who had spoken the ultimate word. By tacit consent he was always deferred to, and as he mastered the problems his authority became one of mind as well as of character. And he was happy—that was the immense change. He seemed to have rid himself of a burden both of years and cares.

Crowded days lay behind them. Charcillo was the base headquarters, but when the word to strike was given they would move to Veiro. Meanwhile the concentration was secret. The Olifa Government had no doubt news of trouble at the south-eastern edge of the Gran Seco, but they had no knowledge of what was happening in this wild corner of their own province. For the countryside was at their back and Luis's agents controlled all the communications with the capital. They had spent a feverish week over the coming concentration, and to Charcillo at all hours of the day and night had come Luis's lieutenants to consult. Some of them were young men whom Janet had met at the Polo

Club or danced with in Olifa; many were officers of the
Olifa reserve; some were grizzled haciendados from the
skirts of the hills or rich industrials from Alcorta and
Cardanio. . . . There was old Martinez and his five sons,
who owned hundreds of miles of ranching ground on the
skirts of the mountains. . . . And Ramirez and his clan,
who were the fruit kings of Olifa. . . . And the Zarranigas from Pecos, whose ancestors had come to the
country with Pizarro. . . . And young Miguel de Campanillo, whose kin had ridden with Toledo and whose family
had given a later Olifa three presidents. . . . She did not
quite understand them. These men were prosperous; they
had no grievance against the Gran Seco; they were not of
the rootless revolutionary type. Why should they want to
join in this quarrel? But the chief marvel was Don Alejandro Gedd. The little man had become a crusader. Why?
His patriotism in the past had chiefly shown itself in dislike
of all things American. He had disliked Castor, too, and
now he was his willing henchman.

There was a big map indoors, on which with coloured
pins the strength of the opposing sides was shown. Olifa
had three battalions in the city, in camp in the Plaza de
Toros, and she had a skeleton division at Pecos, and a
battalion at Santa Ana. There were detachments at Alcorta
and Cardanio, and on the latter place was based the small
Olifa navy. These points were marked with green pins, but it
was to be noted that sometimes close up to them was stuck a
red pin. That meant that in such places there was a strong
anti-Government element in the regulars. The red pins were
widely scattered, but there were certain spots marked with
black rings, which were the centres for concentration. One
was on the railway south of Santa Ana, another at the
junction south-east of Olifa, whence ran the line to Alcorta.
But the chief was at the railhead west of Veiro. To the
north the Gran Seco was unmarked. No news had come of
how Peters and Escrick were faring in their intensive
guerrilla campaign.

The thing fascinated the girl. She seemed to be herself
a player in a drama which was nearing its last act. Of the

ultimate purpose she scarcely thought. Victory was to her a concrete thing, a single culminating moment, beyond which her mind would not speculate.

Her one anxiety was Sandy. He had lost the briskness and the audacity with which he had begun the campaign. Perhaps he was tired; he must be, for he had worn himself to a shadow in the Gran Seco. A man has only a certain stock of vital energy, and he had squandered his lavishly. . . . But there was more in it than that, she thought. Sandy was a born adventurer, who must always be imperilling himself, working on the extreme edge of hazard, playing for an outside chance. But now the war was almost regularised. It was a revolution of the familiar type, where the rank and file took the risks. Sandy hated bloodshed. For war he had no use unless it was war on his special plan, an audacious assault upon the enemy's nerves. The other kind, the usual kind, he would only accept if it were in defence of his own country, and Olifa was not his fatherland.

Janet said as much to Castor, who had joined her where she sat on a low white wall, plucking at the long blooms of the tamarisks. He looked like a fighting admiral, who had strayed by accident into khaki.

He nodded his agreement.

" That is Lord Clanroyden's trouble. He is born out of due season. He does not quite like a game where the chances are not hopelessly against him. Now that the odds have been shortened he is uncomfortable. But let him console himself. We have still a long way to travel. General Lossberg and I are in the position of each facing his own capital, like the French and Germans before Sedan. That is not comfortable for him, but it is not altogether comfortable for us. We have to keep him shut up in the Gran Seco, for if his army got out it would destroy us in a week. Also we have to persuade the Olifa Government that it will be well to make peace, and that may not be easy. Let the señor be at ease. It is still a war not of brute force but of *moral*."

" I think you are happy," she said.

"I am happy because I have found something. I have found friends, and I have found a better philosophy. Also I have found what I never had before, a country. I am discovering the rudiments of life."

"You are ten years younger."

He laughed. "And yet I am destroying all the things I have given my life to make. I have jettisoned my old ambition. I hoped to be a Napoleon to change the shape of the world. Fool that I was! I should only have begun to yawn after it was done, and then somebody would have shot me. Now I am quite content if I can help to make an inconsiderable Latin republic a more wholesome State— and if I can prove myself not unworthy of my friends."

"That is the truth," she said. "This is not Sandy's country. . . . You have changed places, I think. You have come down into the homely world, and Sandy is beginning to wander in the cold uplands of his finical conscience. It is a side of him you have never seen, but I have. Unless he is tied to duties which need every atom of his powers, he will begin to torment himself with questions."

"That is perhaps the explanation of the adventurer," was his reply. "He is happiest when he need not stop to think. For myself, I have thought too much about large matters, and I now think only of little things, like Olifa."

That night Luis returned, bringing with him Miguel de Campanillo, Don Alejandro, and one of the young Zarranigas. At supper, which was eaten on tables in the veranda under a grape trellis, for the night was warm, there was the equivalent of a Council of War. It was the eve of raising the standard. The troops at Pecos had been elaborately tampered with, and at a signal the majority which favoured the revolution would occupy the barracks and the depot, much as the Mines Police had done in the Gran Seco. But before that it was necessary to make certain that Lossberg would be detained beyond the mountains, and for this purpose Santa Ana must be occupied. This task was entrusted to Blenkiron, who with two thousand mounted troops was to move next morning. Once his job was completed, he was to join hands with the Campanillos at Pecos, who hoped to add their local levies to the regulars who would by that time have seized the place. The railway beyond Santa Ana was to be destroyed and the telegraph wires cut. Lossberg's blockhouses did not come within eighty miles of Santa Ana, not farther south than the frontier station of Gabones, but, in case he attempted to break through, the narrow pass south of Gabones was to be held in strength, and the road which accompanied the railway was to be comprehensively mined. Meantime the concentrations at Veiro and Alcorta Junction were to be completed, and the dockyard at Cardanio was to be taken.

The talk at first was all of numbers and distances. Castor, who carried a multitude of figures in his head, satisfied himself that nothing had been omitted, and he was answered by Luis from a file of messages. Then, as the stars pricked out, and the wind from the hills began to temper the heat, the company relaxed. Soon the air was blue with cigarette smoke, and some, cramped by a long day in motor-cars on bad roads, strolled into the courtyard, where the scent of flowers from the great painted wine-vats was mingled with sharper smells of baked earth and miles of grasses. Presently Sandy went off with Blenkiron and Castor to verify some figures. Barbara and Archie walked with the young Zarraniga, and Janet found herself in a party of four with Campanillo, Luis, and Don Alejandro.

There was something in the tropic night which went to her head. Though she had no prospect beyond the courtyard shimmering under the stars, she seemed to be looking from a watch-tower over an immense country—steaming coast marshes, baked white cities, miles of waving green, cliffs red as blood falling into an angry blue sea, mountains that stretched cold fingers to the very courts of heaven. For months she had been breathing that air which only belongs to lands which man has not yet mastered, and its sharpness and strangeness had entered her blood. She was in love with space. For a moment she was a patriot of this huge child of a raw and half-made continent.

"Don Alejandro," she said, "do you remember the first night when we dined with you in the Olifa hotel? You told us about Olifa, how she had no problems—no discontents—because she was rich and secure. But you said that she had bartered her pride for prosperity."

Don Alejandro laughed. " True," he said. " I also said that she had no soul, but in saying that I lied. Olifa has always had a soul, but it has been sleeping. Now it looks as if Luis had awakened it."

" What puzzles me is why? " Janet said again. " You had no grievances—I mean the ordinary people. They had an orderly Government and light taxes and no conscription, and the reason was the golden eggs from the Gran Seco. What has made the ordinary Olifero angry with the golden goose? "

" He is not angry." It was Luis who answered. " He does not trouble. The ordinary man everywhere in the world only wishes to be left alone. Revolutions are not made by the many but by the few. Yet there are enough of the discontented, I think, to do our business."

" But why the discontent? "

" Because we have remembered our pride. We of the old houses have not been happy in a State which was no better than a big trading firm—with foreign brains to do the work which the Olifero should do himself."

" What work? "

" Governing us and defending us. Our army is mainly a force of skilled mercenaries. And our Government—well, the voice of the ministers was the voice of Olifa, but the wires which made them speak and act were pulled by the Commander-in-Chief, who is now having a final talk about Santa Ana with Lord Clanroyden and Señor Blenkiron. We have still an old-fashioned prejudice in favour of governing ourselves."

" How long have you been organising this discontent? "

" How long, Sandro? " Luis asked Gedd. " About three years come Christmas. The thing went fast, for the spirit was there waiting for it. Prosperity is not enough for us Oliferos. Our pride was outraged by our stout bourgeois ministers, who took their orders so obediently from another. . . . But we organised in the dark, blindly, for we knew that we needed some notable piece of good fortune to succeed. Then we found the Yanqui Wilbur, and through him Señor Blenkiron. And at the end came Lord Clanroyden. It is a simple tale of the mercies of God. Let us hope that these mercies are not exhausted."

"But if Olifa was under the thumb of Mr Castor, won't it be the same even if we win? He is our commander, isn't he? Can you have a nationalist revolution led to victory by the man whose domination of your country stirred up your nationalism? You have made your chief opponent your leader—a foreigner too, a man with no country."

"Not so. He is one of us."

"But he is an Austrian."

"On his father's side he is Austrian. But his grandmother was a Campanillo, a great-great-aunt of friend Miguel here."

"Does he know that? Does Sandy know it?" The girl was open-mouthed in amazement.

"He has always known it. I myself have known it this past year, and the fact was the basis of our plans. . . . It is a long story, Lady Roylance, too long to tell at this hour of the night. As you justly say, he had no country. That is a fashionable folly among certain clever people in Europe. To-day he has found one. . . . That was one reason why Lord Clanroyden and I planned to carry him off and maroon him up in the Patios de la Mañana—that he might find his country. There is no loosing the chains of blood. Once he got the bitter-sweet smell of our land into his nostrils and the clean air of our hills into his lungs, we believed that the cobwebs would fall from his eyes and very old ancestral things come to life. That has happened, I think. . . . More than that, of course. Between us—you, perhaps, especially —we have made him a human being. He will dream different dreams now, more wholesome dreams."

"What will you do with him? Can you fit him in—anything as big as he is?"

"We will of course make him our President," Don Alejandro interposed. "He is our great man, our show figure. We look to his brains to give us good government and to keep us prosperous."

"But can you harness him?" Janet persisted. "Can you turn Niagara into a useful stream which will irrigate gardens?"

"He will harness himself," said Luis, "for he is wise."

"And yet," she urged, "for years he has been hugging ambitions vast enough to set half the globe on fire—not silly whims, but closely-reasoned ambitions worked out to decimal fractions. He hated America—that was why Mr Blenkiron first decided to fight him. From what I remember of your table-talk, Don Alejandro, you also had no great love for America. Didn't you say that you regarded her patronage as an insult to your country? Why should you wish to put a spoke in the wheel of a man who has the same prejudice?"

"Because I am not a fool." Don Alejandro spoke with a brusqueness remarkable in one so suave. "Because I will not have Olifa made a pawn in a crazy game which means ruin. I do not love Yanquis, apart from Miss Dasent and Wilbur and Blenkiron and perhaps three others. But I want my country to be a rival to the United States in power and quality—not to be a blind mouse along with other blind mice in the hands of *déraciné* genius."

Luis laughed. "You have stirred up the gentle Sandro, Lady Roylance, by touching his sorest spot. I do not think you quite understand the meaning of Spanish blood. You ought to, for the British are nearest to us of any race. We are realists, you know, very calculating and prosaic and close to the earth. But we must have our glamour too, our touch of poetry. We make good monarchists—and good republicans, if we can hit on the right president. Castor will suit us admirably, for he will give us poetry, which the dingy camarilla now in Olifa never did. He will have ideas and imagination and colour, and the air of magnificence. With him we will advance so fast that we shall astonish mankind. But his brilliance will not be dangerous, for all around him will be Spaniards, we Oliferos, very appreciative of poetry, but quite resolved to keep our feet on the ground. Like your Scotch, who will quote the poets and weep over them, and the next moment make hard bargains."

A lamp had been put on the table by a servant, and round it white moths were fluttering. As Janet looked at the faces revealed in its light, she received a sudden clear impression of something she had not met before—an ardour which was not ashamed to reveal itself because it was in turn based on a revelation. Don Alejandro with his neat small features and high cheek-bones—Luis, fair, golden-brown of skin, with his glowing eyes—the young Zarraniga with his slender eyebrows and grave, rather sullen mouth—there was something innocently apostolic about them. They were in the grip of an idea. Their patriotism was an adventure, for their country was still to be made.

She smiled at the boy Miguel, and he smiled back at her. She had seen the same look, as a child, in the faces of young men starting for Flanders. Here was one to whom new horizons had suddenly appeared. Luis read her thoughts.

" We are going to make a country which will offer careers for youth," he said. " Our young men will no longer have to leave Olifa, or, if they stay at home, stagnate on their estates. Their future will be their country's future, for they will govern it, and thereby we shall have an advantage over that great people whom Sandro so much dislikes. We shall invent a new civilisation in this continent, which will be a bridge between the old world and the new."

Sandy's face suddenly appeared in the circle of light, and behind him Blenkiron and Castor. There was a hush, inevitable when serious talk is suddenly overheard. Blenkiron's jolly laugh broke it.

" Looks as if you folk had been picking on my poor little country," he said.

" No, indeed we haven't," said Janet. " We have only been deciding that Olifa is going to be neither a satellite nor an enemy of America, but an honourable rival."

" That's fine! They'll be mighty glad to hear it in Washington."

Archie and Barbara and the young Zarraniga

presently joined them, and the group reassorted itself. Janet sat very still, her eyes on two faces, Castor's and Sandy's. In the first she saw what she had not observed before, a certain kinship to the men with whom she had been talking. It was a subtle resemblance, a thing not of feature or manner, but of a look in the eyes, a tone in the voice. Castor belonged here after all. He could be captured by a dream. . . . She had once said that he had a short-range imagination, and it was true. He was the ready slave of an idea. . . . And he was young. He had never been anything else but young. She looked at Sandy, and suddenly felt that they were old—he and she and Archie and Blenkiron—even Barbara. They could not be happily rapt into a dream, because they dragged too great a weight of tradition behind them. They were children of an ancient world, and could not break from it. . . . She no longer felt herself a sharer in their enterprise, but a benevolent stranger. . . . And Sandy? The burden had left his shoulders and he looked a little bewildered. Perhaps a little homesick? These others had found a country. Might it not be that he was longing for his own?

She lay awake for some time after she went to bed, puzzling over this new direction of her thoughts. Might not something great come out of this venture, something of high moment for the world? And then she thought of a look she had caught on Barbara's face, and she fell asleep with her mind on a fresh trail. . . . She was awakened at three o'clock by the sound of departing motor-cars. That would be Blenkiron on his way to Santa Ana. Her friends might have no spiritual share in the fervours of the rebellion, but they had a very practical part to play in it.

III

THE succeeding days were full of bustle and excitement, for the train had been lit and the explosions were beginning. The road and railway to the Gran Seco were destroyed by Blenkiron with the completeness of a great engineer. The revolt of the troops at Pecos went like clockwork. Also the naval base at Cardanio was easily surprised, and the Olifa navy, except for two destroyers in Olifa harbour and a few patrol boats along the coast, was quietly put out of action.

But on the first news of success there followed less comforting messages. The concentration at Veiro was going slowly. The ordinary Olifero was nervous, and hesitated to declare himself till he was certain which was the winning side. At Alcorta, too, the industrial centre, there was a danger of Communist trouble, which would immobilise forces which should have been marching north.

"Whoever said ' *Il n'y a que le premier pas qui coûte,*' " Sandy told Janet, " was a fool. It is blindingly untrue of revolutions. The first step is easy. You can always start with a bang. It's the second step that is the devil. We haven't succeeded, or anything like it, for the country hasn't risen, and it isn't certain by a long chalk whether it is on our side. It is waiting to see how the cat jumps. We've got my Gran Seco troops, and about four thousand of the regulars. Add Luis's recruits and we may have a total of twelve thousand. Also we've temporarily bottled up Lossberg. But the Government has far more than three battalions in the city, as we believed. They've the better part of a division, and they've the pick of the artillery. Old Bianca is no fool, and they're fortifying like blazes. We haven't yet the strength for a *coup,* and it's a question whether we'll ever get it. It's all a question of *moral.* Unless we can bluff the Government into a surrender by cracking their *moral,* we can't force them. . . . Oh yes, once they surrendered it would be smooth going. The cat would have jumped and the whole country would be behind us. But you can't run a revolution, as Luis thinks you can, on a handful of grandees."

"What is the worst that could happen?" Janet asked anxiously.

" That Lossberg should break out. That would blow us sky-high. He would stiffen the Government, and put the fear of death on the Oliferos. They're not going to stand up against the first-class regular army they have bought and paid for. Down on these plains Lossberg would drive us like sheep, and we should all go to heaven in a whirl of aimless glory. . . . Janet, I'm sick with anxiety. I've brought you and Archie into this mess, and it's the kind of mess I don't understand."

He looked far more haggard than she had ever seen him in the Gran Seco.

" You're tired to death," she said, and knew that she was talking nonsense.

" I'm not tired," he replied wearily, " but I'm out of my element. I hate war, except my own sort, and any moment this may become the hopeless ordinary kind that I detest and am no good at. . . . You see, this isn't my country, and it isn't yours or Archie's. We can't feel about it like Luis and the others. I've done what I set out to do, and spiked Castor's guns. But the curse of life is that you can't stop short when you want, and I seem to have landed you all into the fire out of the frying-pan. . . . The worst of it is, I can do nothing. There's no job for me here. El Obro is dead and buried, and I'm only a foreign filibuster mixed up in a show for which he has no heart."

Yet he seemed busy enough. He was splitting up his command, and had already parted with most of the white mounted troops. Only his Indians remained, under their white officers; it had always been decided to reserve them to the last, because of their effect on the nerves of the Olifa population. Of them he had now a little over a thousand.

They were paraded one evening, tall, lean men on little wiry horses, who by now had almost the discipline of cavalry and were also trained marksmen. Janet and Barbara stood beside Sandy, as he watched them pass in the dusty sunlight.

" A fine lot," he said. " These fellows have something to fight for. Thank God, they'll never go back to the old slavery. If the worst happens, there'll be a new breed of bandit in the hills."

Behind them appeared Bobby Latimer. The aeroplanes had been left in the Gran Seco, all but one flight, which kept

Charcillo in touch with Luis and Blenkiron. Bobby himself
made long private patrols mostly in the direction of the
city. That day, however, he had shaped his course for
the north.

As he saluted, Janet saw that his face was solemn.

"There's hell loose in the passes, sir," he said. "I have
been up the road we came from the Gran Seco, and somebody's put Lossberg wise to it. There's a good-sized army
on its way down—ten troops of horse, and about four
thousand infantry, and an unholy lot of light batteries. They
were in the Thunderer Valley three hours ago, and should
make the place we called the Tennis Court before dark. To-
morrow evening they'll be on the Vulpas."

A slow smile spread over Sandy's face.

"I spoke too soon," he said to Janet, "when I complained
that I had nothing to do. I'm about to be the busiest man
in this continent. Bobby, when you've fed and washed,
you go off to Don Luis. I'll have a message written out
for you. Janet, dear, run and tell Rogerson to be in my
room in half an hour. I'll wait and have a word with
Ackroyd."

"It's pretty serious, isn't it, sir?" Latimer asked.

"It's so serious that if that column shows its nose on the
Vulpas we may chuck up the sponge. But thank God, it's
still in the narrows. I've got a thousand men—three times
what old Leonidas had—and I'm going to try the Thermopylæ stunt."

He found his arm clutched by Barbara.

"Is it worth it?" she cried, and even in his absorption he
noticed that her face had gone very pale. "Is it worth
it?" she repeated. "We can't spare you. . . . Nobody came
back from Thermopylæ."

Her eyes sobered him. He even flushed slightly.

"I'm coming back all right, Miss Dasent, and so are my
men. I might be spared, but we couldn't do without *them*.
We're not brave like the Spartans. Our Thermopylæ is
going to be a more cunning affair than the old one."

IV

HALF an hour later Blenkiron arrived by aeroplane. He had not been expected, and when he walked into the room where Sandy was giving his final instructions to Rogerson he was greeted with a shout of joy.

"Thank God!" Sandy cried. "You're the one man in the whole world I wanted. What providence has brought you here?"

"Why, I wanted to get some notion of the general proposition." His goggles had preserved his eyes from the fine dust which coated his face, so that he looked like a red owl with great staring eye-holes. "We've gotten our show pretty well advanced, and I could turn it over to Melville with an easy mind. There'll be no traffic south of Gabones for quite a while."

"You've closed that port?" Sandy demanded.

"Sure. Closed it and sealed it and put a heap of stones at the door. Things are going nicely at Pecos too. But I've heard nothing from the south, and I kind of hoped to be put wise about the general proposition——"

"Never mind the general proposition. There's a special one we've got to face. Lossberg is half through the passes."

"You don't say." Blenkiron's face ceased to be that of an owl, and contracted into something hard and vigilant. "Who brought word?"

"Bobby Latimer—less than an hour ago."

"Good boy! Say, this is getting central. We've certainly got to push him back."

"We certainly have. Do you realise that as yet we're nowhere near winning? Everything is still on a knife-edge. The country is waiting to see what happens before it makes up its mind—I mean the great bulk of the people, for Luis's lads are only a sprinkling. We've got to bluff the Government into surrender, and we haven't the foggiest chance if Lossberg shows his face in Olifa. If the passes are opened, we're absolutely done in. Have you got that?"

"Sure."

"Then in one hour's time we start out to stop that bolt-hole. You and I and a few others. Thank the Lord you've turned up, for this is more your kind of show than mine."

Blenkiron groaned, but his eyes were cheerful. "There's no rest for the weary, but it's mighty good for my figure. I've dropped thirty pounds since I went to the wars. Have you a map handy? I'd like to refresh my memory about that patch of country."

"We made a rough drawing coming down, and here's the result." Sandy spread out a big sheet on his desk. "The distances are more or less correct. . . . See, here's Charcillo. It's about ten miles to the main stream of the Vulpas, and about twenty more to its head. Then there's the pass—four more till you look into the Thunderer."

Blenkiron put on his horn spectacles and with a grubby forefinger traced the route from the Gran Seco, by which they had come and by which their enemy was now following. From Pacheco the trail ran to the valley under the hills which the Indians called the river of the Blue Wolf. It did not turn up the tributary water of the Catalpas, by which Janet and Archie had escaped, but continued up the main stream, which presently bent due eastward. When the valley narrowed to a glen the road turned south and crossed the southern containing wall to the upper waters of an east-ward-flowing river which the Indians called the Thunderer. Hitherto the road had been intricate and steep, but passable for men and animals and even for light motors, since it was reasonably broad and its floor was the shaly mountain gravel. But the glen of the Thunderer was ancient chaos, strewn with immense boulders and the debris of old land-slides, and in the middle was a torrent which amply earned its Indian name. Yet there was a road for those who knew it, and the stream could be forded at one place, where it spread into a broad shallow pool on a shelf of rock before hurling itself into its customary abyss. That ford was six miles down from the pass which led from the Blue Wolf, and after it the road climbed among the cliffs and screes of the southern containing wall, till it reached a broad flat

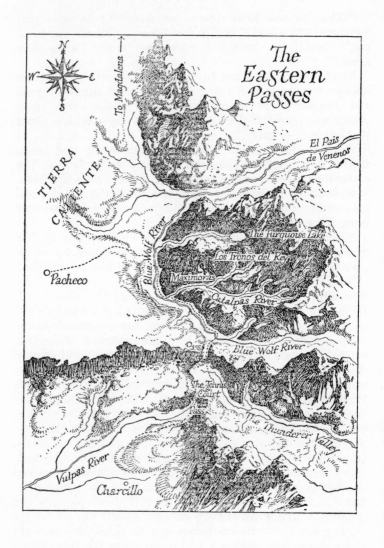

The Eastern Passes

To Magdalena

El Pais de Venenos

TIERRA CALIENTE

Pacheco

Blue Wolf River

The Turquoise Lake

Los Tronos del Rey

Maximoras

Catalpas River

Blue Wolf River

Pass

The Tennis Court

Pass

The Thunderer Valley

Vulpas River

Charcillo

mantelpiece which could have accommodated an army corps. This was the place to which Luis had given the name of the Tennis Court, and it was the key of the route. For from it a track led upward, a track which seemed to be driving aimlessly at a sheer precipice. But after running for a little southward in the moraine below the rocks, it turned a corner, and a cleft was revealed above it, a narrow saddle between two great fingers of mountain. The elevation was too low for ice, but the couloir, white with alkali, had the look of a long tongue of glacier running up to a snow saddle. . . . The saddle itself was a fearsome place, for above the pad of gravel the cliffs beetled in a dreadful overhang. Rockfalls were frequent, and on the journey down Luis had insisted on the troops making the passage in small detachments, very slowly, and in complete silence. . . . Beyond, the track corkscrewed down a long ravine until it reached the flowers and grass of the upper Vulpas.

Sandy put his finger on the Tennis Court.

" Bobby says they will be there this evening late, and they must camp. They will probably send on pickets to the Vulpas pass, . . . but they won't move till dawn, and the main body won't be in the pass till well on in the forenoon. I don't think they can be allowed to come so far. I've selected the Tennis Court as the *ne plus ultra*. What do you think? "

Blenkiron had screwed his forehead into a thousand wrinkles as he pored over the map. He now took off his spectacles.

" I guess they'd better stay there," he said blandly. " I get your notion."

" You see, when Providence made this country, He put it rather loosely together. We ought to be able to shake its bones a bit, and you understand that sort of thing better than I do."

" Maybe. How many men will you take? "

" I'll take Corbett—he knows the game. He was with Dick Hannay in Rhodesia. And I'll take a hundred troopers. Castor any moment may want every fighting man he can lay his hands on, and you don't need many in my kind of war. Only enough to put up a fight with Lossberg's pickets, if he has had the forethought to post them in the pass. . . . Now for food. We must be in the saddle by eight-thirty."

An hour later in the big paddock behind the corrals Sandy reviewed his men. Except for white troop-sergeants, they were all Indian, selected men of the foothills rather than of the Tierra Caliente. He spoke to them in their own tongue. "On the work of this night," he said, "the freedom of your people depends. The enemy is in the passes, but he will not leave them. We will move the mountains so as to close the way. But first it is necessary to get there. When the moon rises, we must be where the Vulpas is only a little stream. I trust you as I would trust my brother by blood."

Janet watched them go, but Barbara did not appear. As they swung out to the open downs, it might have been observed that certain of the horsemen had their saddles encumbered with mysterious packages.

The first part of the road was across open downs of which the starlight showed the contours but not the colours. One dark, opaque, velvet ridge succeeded another—a monotint world, though the sky above was so crowded with stars that part of it was like a phosphorescent belt, wherein there was more light than darkness. The going was good, for at this season of the year the coarse herbage of the savannah was short, and there were great spaces of grainy sand dotted with scrub scarcely taller than the grasses. It was like Sussex downland, since in most of the hollows there were no streams. Water was only crossed twice, till the troops found themselves on a long decline, and saw far below them the stars reflected in the pools of a river.

The Vulpas valley, before it runs out into the coastal plain, is some five miles broad and defined only by shallow ridges. But as the traveller goes eastward he finds that it narrows and deepens, until it makes a sharp-cut gulf among the foothills. The expedition struck the valley where it was on the edge of becoming a mountain-glen. Most of it was Luis's own land, and the only dwellers in it his vaqueros, but they were lower down, and in all its topmost course the stream flowed through lonely upland pastures, which would be heavily stocked later when the midsummer drought had parched the lower lands.

The scent of the place, drawn out by night, came to Sandy as a thing familiar. It was the scent of uplands all the world over, upspringing greenery and water and clean stone and shallow soil. The moon had not risen when they reached the meadows by the stream side, and rode eastward along a series of grassy steps, with the Vulpas water talking more loudly with every mile as it approached its mountain cradle. There was no sound, not even a wandering night-wind, except for the river and the beat of hoofs muffled in herbage and the occasional clash of buckle on rifle-butt. Even Blenkiron, short of sleep and rather weary, felt the intoxication of the hour and the place. Sandy beside him seemed to be happy, for just above his breath he was humming a tune.

Suddenly a wash of faint colour flooded the glen, a colour which deepened from a pale amber to the tint of ripe corn. The moon was beginning to climb the sky. Also the distances began to reveal themselves; the containing slopes, now the outflankers of the mountains, were clearly seen, and in front there was a dark loom into the mid-heavens. Sandy looked at his watch and nodded cheerfully to Blenkiron. They had made good time, and would be in the narrows of the pass before the moon was fairly up.

After another mile he halted his command. On each side the containing walls had drawn in till the valley was not half a mile wide, and the Vulpas had become a brawling torrent. The troops separated into detachments, and a patrol of five led the van at a distance of some hundred yards from the next group. Sandy and Blenkiron were with the second group. The course was now altered, and instead of keeping beside the stream they moved well up on the slopes to the right, which were of short grass and outcrops of rock set at an easy angle. They went more slowly now and more circumspectly, avoiding patches of shingle which might echo the sound of movement.

Quickly they climbed till they were in the throat of a ravine, a dark sword-cut where the moon gave only the faintest illumination. Far up its light could be seen golden on the cliffs and ridges, but they themselves rode in an umber dusk. The ravine twined and turned, so that the advance patrol was often completely lost to sight and hearing.

The word was passed back for extra care and quiet. " In two miles," Sandy whispered, " we shall be under the Saddle. There we leave the horses. There is a little amphitheatre where the Vulpas rises, with room enough to picket our beasts."

But at the next angle of the ravine Sandy reined in violently, so that Blenkiron cannoned into him. There was a shuffling and a drawing of breath as the men behind followed suit. Someone was coming towards them. . . . Sandy and Blenkiron lowered their pistols when they saw that it was the advance patrol. The riders forced their horses alongside till their leader could speak into Sandy's ear.

" There are men below the rocks," he whispered. " Many men—more than we have with us. They are camped beside the water, and they are confident, for they have made fires."

Sandy looked at Blenkiron and laughed. " They have done the right thing," he said. " Flung an advanced body across the Saddle to guard the descent while the others cross. I should have thought of that. . . . I've got into a bad habit of underrating old Lossberg."

He sat for a little whistling softly between his teeth. Then he began to think aloud, resuming between every sentence his low whistling. He seemed to be cheerful.

" Can we climb the rocks? That's the question. . . . If half a dozen of us can get to the Saddle, the trick is done. . . . We should be able to raise a few cragsmen. . . . Corbett would know. . . . Also we must make those beggars hands-up. How many did you say? Half as many again as ourselves. . . . Well, it's plain we can't do that job with our present strength. . . . Somebody has got to get back to Charcillo hell-for-leather and bring supports.

It's *force majeure* we want. No needless heroics and no needless casualties. . . . What do you say, John S.?"

"I guess that's correct. We'd better get our man off right away. If Lossberg has come this far, he'll aim to have the rest of his push over the Saddle pretty early in the morning."

Sandy tore a leaf from a pocket-book, and, using the cliff face as a desk, wrote a message. Then he folded it and looked round.

"Whom shall we send?" he asked Blenkiron. "Corbett would be able to find a man."

"Send me!" A voice spoke at his elbow, and it spoke in English. It could not be Corbett, for he was in charge of the rear, nor was it Corbett's voice. Sandy found himself staring at a slim figure in a trooper's kit, riding an animal which he recognised. It was Luis's favourite mare.

"Who are you?" he demanded. "Good God! It can't be! Barbara—Miss Dasent——"

There was not light enough to see the girl's face. It may have shown confusion and embarrassment, but there was nothing of the sort in her voice. The voice was cool, self-reliant, almost imperious.

"I'm glad I came, for now I can be useful. If I go, it will save a fighting man. I know the road—I'm accustomed to know how to get back any road I come—and I'm better mounted than any of you." She patted her mare's neck.

"You had no business to come. You did very wrong." Sandy's voice was hard and angry. "Good God, this is no place for a woman. I don't like you going back alone, but you're safer on the road than here. . . . Give this note to Colonel Ackroyd, and after that go straight to bed. You understand, Miss Dasent. These are my orders."

She took the note and sidled her mare round in the narrow space below the cliff.

"Send Corbett along as you pass," he added. "I needn't tell you that the business is urgent."

"You needn't," she said, and disappeared round the corner of rock.

The two men stared after her till the sound of her going was lost in the forward movement of the next detachment.

"I'd like to know," said Blenkiron reflectively, "just why Babs has gotten the bit in her teeth?"

"Can she do it? I mean, is it safe for her?" The tenseness in Sandy's voice was anxiety, not irritation.

"You bet she'll do it, and I don't worry about risks as long as she's on a horse. You can't puzzle her there."

Two hours later six men were perched high up among the rocks on the right side (what mountaineers would call the "true left") of the couloir which led from the springs of Vulpas to the Saddle. Five of them were Indians, hunters from the Blue Wolf valley, and the sixth was Sandy. It had been a precarious and intricate journey. First they had made their way up the cliffs from the point where the advance troop had halted. This had been easy enough, for the angle was not too steep and there was plenty of scrub. But even there they had been dismayed by the rottenness of the rock. Boulders would come loose in their hands, and be left delicately poised to descend in the first gale.

When the right elevation had been attained, the next step was to traverse the side of the amphitheatre where Lossberg's van was encamped. Here it was necessary to proceed with extreme caution. Happily that part of the ravine was in shadow, and no eyes from below could detect them, but it was essential that there should be no slipping or sending down of stones, lest the enemy should become alarmed and patrol the track that led to the Saddle. It was horribly difficult to move with speed and softness, and often it seemed impossible to move at all. For the whole hillside was loose, a gigantic scree with boulders instead of gravel, and each man of the six, beside his rifle, was encumbered with explosives. There were scaurs of crumbling earth, where the whole mountain seemed to shift at their tread. These were passed an inch at a time, holding hands, and in one place the last man swung into the void, while his foothold, with a sound like a great sigh, sunk into the depth beneath him. There were masses of friable rock, which had to be crossed with the body splayed out like a swimmer's. There was one point where, to circumvent the cliff, it became necessary to ascend a rotten chimney, and then traverse a ledge which looked like giving way any moment and precipitating the company on to the bivouac below. Sandy, to his disgust, found that he was the least efficient of the six. The Indians with their soft leather footgear had a certitude far beyond his, and more than once he had to depend on their aid. All the time the bivouac lights were plain eight hundred feet beneath them, and in the still night every sound of the camp rose as sharp and clear as if it were at their elbow.

But at last the circuit was finished, and the climbers stopped to rest in an eyrie well in the jaws of the ravine itself. There the rock was firmer, and they were able without much difficulty to traverse till they reached the track to the Saddle, a few hundred feet above the camp. Sandy's plan was to wait in the Saddle and lay his train of explosives, but not to fire the fuse till the signal had been given by Blenkiron that the reserves had arrived from Charcillo. This was to be two rifle shots in rapid succession, followed by a third at an interval of thirty seconds. The rockfall which he would engineer in the Saddle would bar escape in that direction. Blenkiron would hold the road down the Vulpas, and Lossberg's van would be summoned to surrender at the first light. He had also arranged that detachments of Indians should climb the rocks on both sides of the amphitheatre, so as to give point to Blenkiron's arguments. Now that he had made the traverse and had got between the enemy and the Saddle, the success of the enterprise seemed assured. There must be no mistake about the length of the time fuses. He and his men must be out of the couloir and round the angle of the mountain before the explosion started, for the couloir would be like the bore of a gun for the ammunition of the falling rocks. His cheerfulness was a little clouded by anxiety. He wished Blenkiron rather than himself had the job, for he was not an expert in explosives, but it would have been impossible to get Blenkiron's massive body across that treacherous hill-side.

The couloir was very dark. The walls rose precipitately to frame a narrow ribbon of moonlit sky. Far in front this ribbon descended to a V-shaped gap, which was the Saddle. All six moved with the utmost deliberation and care up the shaly track. There was no need to preach caution to the Indians. It was not the enemy beneath that made them step as lightly as dancers; there was in their blood the fear of the hair-trigger, unstable rocks. Besides, there was no hurry. It would be two hours—perhaps three—before Blenkiron could give the signal. Already the day's heat had gone from the air, and the chill of night was spreading from the far snowfields. It would be very cold waiting in the Saddle.

They were within two hundred yards of the top, when Sandy found his arm gripped. The Indian behind him had halted, poised like a runner, and had raised his head to listen.

" There are men in the pass," he whispered.

Sandy strained his ears but could catch nothing. He shook his head, but the Indian nodded violently. " Men," he repeated. " White men! "

The thing seemed to Sandy incredible. Lossberg was cautious, no doubt, but he would not picket the Saddle, as well as send an advance guard beyond the pass, when he had the bulk of his forces still at the Tennis Court. Could the whole army be advancing by night? Impossible. In another hour the moon would be down, and this was no road for a night march, with horses and batteries.

His reflections may have made him careless, for he stumbled, and in his fall clutched at a boulder. It gave, rolled out of its gravel bed, and plunged down the track. The others stepped aside to avoid it, and for a second there was a general slipping and clattering to break the stillness.

Suddenly the place was flooded with a blinding glare, which lit up every pebble and crinkle of rock. And then, almost in the same moment it seemed, there came a blast of machine-gun bullets fired a little too low. Sandy saw the white shale in front of him leap into living dust-devils.

He signalled his men to the cover of the right-hand rock, where there was a slight overhang. Again came a burst of machine-gun fire, and the searchlight maintained its unwinking stare.

Sandy thought hard and fast. There was a machine-gun post on the Saddle—a bold step considering its precarious environs. That post could not be large, probably not more than his own number. Before he could do his business and close the bolt-hole, that post must be destroyed. They must wait till the alarm had passed and then creep forward, trusting to the chance of surprise. Had they been seen? He hardly thought so, for at the first blink of the searchlight they had been on their faces. Probably it was only the nervousness of men perched by night in an eerie post.

But the nervousness did not seem to abate. There was no more shooting, but the glare continued for nearly an hour, while the six lay flat under the overhang, very cramped and cold. Sandy waited till the darkness had lasted for twenty minutes. They were not more than two hundred yards from the Saddle, and the intervening distance could surely be traversed so silently that it would be possible to rush the garrison.

But the last part of the couloir was the hardest, for it ceased to be a moraine of sand and boulders and came out on the loose and naked ribs of the hills. Keeping as far as possible in the shelter of the embracing walls, moving one at a time in line and flat on their faces like a stalker approaching a stag, they found it impossible to avoid making a noise, which to their ears echoed alarmingly in that funnel. Sandy was the chief offender. His belt seemed to catch on every jag, and his boots gritted harshly whenever they touched stone.

Again the searchlight leapt out. . . . There could be no question this time. They were seen. As they wriggled for the tiniest cover, a blast of machine-gun bullets swept by, this time over their heads.

" We'll have to rush 'em," Sandy whispered hoarsely.

He saw all his plans frustrated, and nothing left but a desperate venture. . . .

And then to his amazement, he found himself dragged to his feet by two of the Indians and whirled into a violent rush. But it was not towards the enemy. " The mountains fall," he heard in the throaty Indian speech, and the next instant he was leaping down the couloir.

Of what happened next he had only a dim recollection. A roar like the Day of Judgment was in his ears. " Those damned machine guns," he remembered repeating to himself. " They've brought the rocks down. . . ." Then from behind came a blast of wind which swept them off their feet. He seemed to drop for yards, and as he dropped he felt half the world rush past him. An eddy of wind seemed to plaster him against the rock wall. . . . He found himself on soft earth clutching an Indian by the hair. . . . A hand dragged him into a coign of rock and pressed him flat, while salvos of great shells seemed to be bursting all about him. . . . He must have lost part of his senses, for he was conscious of shouting the name of his platoon sergeant at Loos, and also babbling childishly " Those damned machine guns." . . . There seemed to be a perpetual rain of avalanches and in one of them he was half buried. He remembered the feeling of suffocation, and then of free air, which he could scarcely breathe because of spasms of nausea. . . . And then darkness came down on him, and he knew nothing till he woke on a shelf of rock far to the left of the couloir, with the early dawn bright around him.

He was a mass of bruises, and had a cut on his brow from which the blood trickled into his eyes, but he could find no broken bones. There were three Indians beside him, one with a smashed wrist and all intricately scarred and battered. When he asked about the other two, a hand was pointed downwards to where at the foot of the couloir a vast drift of rock and earth curled upwards like a sea-wave. It spread far into the little amphitheatre, and hid the springs of Vulpas. There was no sign of human life in the place.

Sandy's head was still too dazed to permit of thought. All he knew was that he was alive and very weary. He dropped back, and one of the Indians made a rest for him with the crook of his arm.

But presently his supporter moved. Sandy, hovering between sleep and waking, heard dimly a shouting which his companion answered. Then he felt himself being coaxed to rise. There were men below who were urging him to come down. He had never had vertigo in his life, but at the thought of descent his whole being revolted. A horror of space had come over him, and he knew that if he moved a step he would fall.

In the end he descended like a piece of baggage in the arms of Corbett and a squad of Indians. He looked up at the couloir, which at the top beetled in a new cliff. It would take a brigade laden with explosives a month to blast their way through that curtain of rock. At the sight his nausea returned. " Take me out of this hellish place," he groaned.

They carried him down the track, past the spot where the night before he had begun his escalade of the cliffs. The next thing he knew was that he was in a more open glen among grass, and that Blenkiron had him in his arms. There was a fire burning and Blenkiron, when he had laid him down, put a cup to his lips. " Black coffee and brandy," he said. " That's the dope for you. I've been singing hallelujahs ever since I got word you were safe. I oughtn't to have trusted you with that much lentonite. You must have been mighty rash in touching it off."

" I never used it." Sandy struggled against his weakness and his voice came with a croak. " There was a post on the Saddle with machine guns. They spotted us and loosed off. . . . We crawled nearer and were going to rush them when they loosed off again. . . . That last burst did the trick and brought down the mountain."

" Great Mike! And you? "

" I came down with the mountain. God knows how I got off with my life. Those Indians . . . gallant fellows . . . two of them gone . . . I'll tell you more later."

But presently the hot drink seemed to put life into

him, and he sat up. "What happened here? Did Ackroyd get my message?"

"Sure. We managed fine. I guess we could have done without reinforcements, for your avalanche put the fear of death into the pick of Lossberg's Pioneers. They reckoned the Last Day was come and they ran down the gully like mad folk. We shepherded them quietly, and waited till Rogerson turned up, when they hands-upped like lambs. We've gotten a nice little bag—fourteen hundred and seventy-three combatant soldiers, if you include your friend Mr Lariarty."

"Great Scott! Is he here? I want him brought to me at once. And Rogerson too."

The Lariarty who stood before him a quarter of an hour later was a different man from the dapper Gran Seco magnate. The sun and wind of the hills had put no colour into his pallid face, but that face was thin and peaked as if he had been through great bodily fatigue. The eyes, too, seemed less inhuman, for there was pain in their sombre depths. His clothes were little better than Sandy's and he had not shaved for days.

"Hullo, Timmy, you look as if you had been in the wars. Had breakfast? . . . Well, I don't know what you're doing here, but you're not a prisoner. I owe you a good turn for a certain evening in the Gran Seco. You can have a horse and go wherever you like. What's your fancy?"

The man seemed to have difficulty in finding words.

"Thank you, Arbuthnot," he said at last. "I should like to go to Olifa city."

"All right. But you'd better hurry, or there may be trouble in getting in. Have you plenty of money? Good. Well, there's nothing to keep you here. Colonel Rogerson will see about a horse. *Bon voyage!*"

Lariarty seemed to be about to say something, but changed his mind. He cast one curious look at Sandy, bowed gravely, and moved away.

Rogerson lingered.

"Miss Dasent specially asked me to give you a message, sir," he said. "It was that she would obey your orders and go straight to bed."

V

THERE was no communication between Castor's head-quarters and the Gran Seco. The revolt had captured early the main wireless station in Olifa, which was on the railway near Alcorta Junction; and since the installation at the Courts of the Morning had been destroyed, the only station in the Gran Seco was under Lossberg's control, and, so far as he was concerned, wholly useless. The telegraph and telephone lines followed the railway, and were now in a state of chaos. While Lossberg was cut off from his superiors, so were Peters and Escrick from their chief. They had their orders to worry the flanks of the enemy, and it would appear that they fulfilled them, for after the failure to break through the passes there was no activity for a week at the only outlet left to him, the railway to Santa Ana.

For the revolt it was a week of desperate busyness. Sandy had his hostages, captured at the Vulpas source, and he made ample use of them. They were, except for Lariarty, Olifa regulars, and mainly foreigners, but among them were representatives of well-known Olifa families. The latter, after Luis had had a private word with them, were given a courteous dismissal and returned to their homes. But the rank and file were used for a different purpose.

Throughout the country there were localities where the revolt was welcomed and the people were ready for its hazards. But in other districts the balance trembled. These were the richer parts, the great fruit-growing coastal regions, Alcorta, the environs of Cardanio, the corn and vine country towards Macheiro and Nimao and Jacinta. There both men and masters were prospering, and even those who favoured Luis preferred, if possible, to gamble on a certainty. It was to these districts that the prisoners went, in charge of Luis's young caballeros. Their internment was ostentatious, their progress a dignified parade. To the staring inhabitants this spectacle was proof that the dreaded professional army, which they respected as a costly luxury, was not invincible. Rumour spread and magnified the story of the affair in the passes, for, since the inland telegraph was in Castor's hands, rumour had no check. Lossberg, beaten in the Gran Seco, had made a desperate effort to break out, and had been utterly defeated. These prisoners were the advance-guard of a beaten army; the rest were shut in securely behind the bars of the Gran Seco hills.

The effect was instantaneous. The sitters dropped off the fence, and areas which had been lukewarm became the most fervent of all. Presently the sporadic fires met and mingled. Luis's small garrisons in districts which had been apathetic became speedily the nuclei of formidable risings. For a week there was no rest for the staff, for at last the concentration could begin. There were desperate problems of commissariat and transport to be solved, for most of the rolling stock of the railway was lying idle inside the defence lines of Olifa city. But every hour brought the armed levies of the south and east nearer to the city, and Castor's *poste de commandement* was moved from Charcillo to Veiro, where Don Mario found the peaceful routine of his life changed to a succession of excitements which made him younger by twenty years.

At the inception of the revolt Luis's first step had been to get possession of the telegraph. The lines were not destroyed, but the points of their debouchment from the city area were held, so that Olifa could not communicate beyond her area. At first the Government had been able to reach Cardanio through the foreign cables, but with the capture of the naval base that avenue was closed. But it was possible to send news into the city, and by various devices the fullest and most startling information about the advance and concentration was at the disposal of the President and his Cabinet. There were other ways. Olifa depended a good deal on country produce, and market carts passed daily through its outposts. Agents of the revolt had thus a chance for circulating rumours, and Veiro by the same means was kept informed of most things that befell in the city.

The reports varied.   At the start the Government had been confident.   The revolt was only a local and filibustering business, for there could be no fuel for any fire.   The State was prosperous, taxation was not oppressive, for years there had been no conscription. . . .   Then came a shade of anxiety, when it was discovered that Lossberg was silent. His last reports had been excellent, but he was singularly remiss in sending more.   It was impossible to stir him up, for they had no wireless at their disposal, the long-distance telephone seemed to have broken down, and their sheaves of telegrams were unanswered. . . .   Worse news followed. The Gran Seco railway had been cut by the rebels, there was trouble at Pecos, there was even a wild story that Lossberg had found an outlet in the eastern passes, but that his van had been cut to pieces and that bolt-hole stopped. . . .   Then came still wilder tales, of risings in the south, of Alcorta and Cardanio gone over to the enemy, of a great rebel force moving upon the city.   The hopes of the Government were still in Lossberg.   He and his expert army must soon arrive to save the State.   In his last report he had told them that the Gran Seco was conquered and the guerrilleros driven to the mountains.   He must be even now on his way down the railway, brushing aside the rebel screen. What if the line were cut and the road damaged!   He had his skilled engineers, and his mechanised battalions, his cavalry and his tanks, his unbeatable infantry.   As they looked from the Parliament House over the wide levels to the north they hourly expected to see the dust-cloud which would herald their deliverer.

One evening there was a council of war at Veiro.   It took place in Don Mario's dining-room, where the big table had become a council-board and maps covered the ancestral Murillo.   Sandy had come from the south, Blenkiron from Santa Ana, where he had left Melville in command, while Luis and Castor had returned from the concentration at Alcorta Junction, where they had received reports from the local leaders.   Archie, who with Bobby Latimer was responsible for the air reconnaissance, had just arrived from a long flight north of Santa Ana. He had dire forebodings about the petrol supply.

"There's a lamentable lack of juice in this land," he complained. "We've tapped all the supplies and are rationing jealously, but we're well within sight of a shortage. There was a big fire at Cardanio which wasted a lot, and of course there's none coming in at the ports just now. The Government seem to have skinned the country to provision Lossberg. I can't think how Peters is getting on. He must be very near his last gallon, unless he has raided some of Lossberg's stores, and even Lossberg can't go on for ever. It's about time that we were bringing things to a head."

Luis was optimistic. "We are very near the end," he said. "The people have risen at last. His Excellency will tell you what spirit we found to-day. Even the doubters are now convinced, and have become enthusiasts. Señor Sandy, your little affair in the passes has proved the conclusive argument. Now the Oliferos have no fear of Lossberg."

Sandy did not answer. For the past week he had been his old vigorous self, but now his vitality seemed to have ebbed again. He looked tired and preoccupied, and his eyes were always searching Castor's face.

It was the latter who spoke. "Luis is right," he said. "Things are very near a head, but this is the real moment of crisis. We cannot take the city of Olifa by force. We have no siege artillery, and General Bianca has made the defences very strong. The defence, I need not remind you, is in a privileged position with modern weapons. The policy of the Government is simple. They have sufficient troops to police the city and defend their lines against anything we can bring. They are waiting for Lossberg, and if Lossberg comes we are beaten."

"I do not agree," Luis interposed. "Lossberg cannot conquer a people in arms."

"I wonder," Sandy spoke at last. "You have a great levy of stout fellows, gallant fellows, but not one in ten knows anything about the business. We are infernally short of machine guns, and we are not too well armed. There's a variety of rifles in our ranks which would stock a museum, and our training is rudimentary. We are mostly third-line troops, and we have far too small a stiffening of first-line stuff. I don't want to croak, but Lossberg could go through us like a knife through blotting-paper. Our only hope is that he won't have the chance."

" Well, he is safely bottled up, isn't he? "

" For the present. But for how long? Peters and Escrick may keep him quiet for the moment, but he is bound to pull himself together and make for Santa Ana. And he is bound to succeed. Therefore——" He paused.

" Therefore? " Luis repeated.

" We must bring things to a head—now. The Government must surrender before he relieves them. How are we going to put on the screw? We are back at the old problem —of cracking their *moral*. . . . It's probably getting brittle. Bianca is a stiff old warrior, but the others are soft, sedentary fellows. They must be pretty jumpy by now. Is there anything fresh from Hamilton? "

" We had a report this morning," Castor answered. " Undoubtedly their Excellencies are nervous. Also their police. The lower classes are on our side, and there is a perpetual rounding-up of suspects, which makes bad feeling. I am a little anxious about the safety of our envoy."

" So am I," said Sandy. " It was a wild escapade, and I don't believe we should have allowed it. He's too good a man to lose. How on earth did he get through the lines, and how on earth is he concealing himself? "

Archie laughed. " I'm not worrying about that. He makes the best imitation you ever saw of a sulky drunken Olifero peasant, and he has picked up enough of the lingo to ask for what he wants and see that he gets it. Geordie is a very wise citizen. But I do worry about one thing. He has gone back to his old waterside and backstairs haunts, and what is to prevent him from being done in by one of the Bodyguard ruffians? They might recognise him, and for all we know some of them are in Olifa. More by token, has he seen Lariarty in the city? "

" He doesn't mention him."

" I would like to know where that sportsman has gone.
You were too easy with him, Sandy. Lariarty is the kind
of lad I would always keep under lock and key."

" May be. I don't know. . . . But to get back to the
main question—how can we put the screw on their Excellencies? I've been away for a week. What is the exact
position on the Santa Ana railway? "

Blenkiron put his spectacles on his nose and spread out a
map and certain papers. He expounded the strength in
Santa Ana and the reserves at Pecos—the exact destruction done to the railway—the present position of his posts
south of Gabones, and the results of Bobby Latimer's air
reconnaissance beyond that point. To the best of his belief,
he said, Lossberg was being so extensively worried in the
Gran Seco that he was not able yet to look southward. He
admitted that the look would come, but he was positive
that any advance would be a slow business. He drew a
sketch of several parts of the route, which he said could be
held for days by a small force against any army.

" That's good as far as it goes," Sandy said. " We have
probably a week at least in which to draw our people in
upon Olifa and rattle the Government. A week—but not
more."

An orderly summoned Blenkiron to the telephone. " Darn
those boys," he grumbled, " they're so mighty keen they
always want to be passing the time of day. I'm going to
call them down."

When he had gone, Luis spoke. He outlined the character
of the various ministers from the President downwards.
He was not complimentary, for he had the bitterness of
the old regime towards the mushroom commercialism of
Olifa, and especially towards the renegades of his own class.
But he was not unfair. He admitted quality—a coarse
toughness of fibre—the obstinacy of men who had been
successful beyond their dreams—above all shrewdness. " It
is on this last trait," he said, " that we must bank. They
will be a little awed by the Gobernador, whom they have
always looked upon as a wizard. They will be impressed

by the rising of the country, for they know that it is a difficult business to govern the unwilling. We have arguments, perhaps, to convince them, always provided they do not get back Lossberg and his army in time. They are not soldiers and will be afraid of us, but, being civilians, they will also exaggerate the power of Lossberg's professionals, and may be foolish enough to defy us. . . . A little while ago I spoke too confidently. We are still on the razor's edge."

Blenkiron re-entered the room, and without a word made for the table where lay the papers from which he had given his exposition. He picked up his sketch of the section of the Gran Seco railway, where he had located various points A, B, C, and D. Then, almost violently, he swung Sandy round so that he could see it.

"Lossberg has fooled me good and sure," he said in a voice which he tried to keep level. "It was Melville talking. There's been hell loose up the line. Our post at A was destroyed two hours ago. . . . Yes, cavalry and armoured cars and light field batteries. . . . There's a howling desolation on the railway between A and B, but Melville reckons that B is going to fall before night. He proposes to make a great effort at C and is pushing everything up. But God knows what strength Lossberg is in, and, though it's a darned bad fighting country, numbers are bound to tell. D isn't much in the way of a reserve position. It's my solemn opinion that, if C goes, in two days Lossberg will be in Santa Ana."

There was a moment of complete silence. Then Sandy observed casually, "I said we had a week. It appears we have only two days." Every man in the room knew that tone in his voice. Sandy could be explosive and vehement when things went well, but in a crisis he often seemed to be a detached spectator from another planet.

Castor's face did not alter, except for a slight knitting of the brows. Blenkiron was on his feet. "I'd better get back to Santa Ana," he said.

"I don't think so," Sandy drawled, and looked at

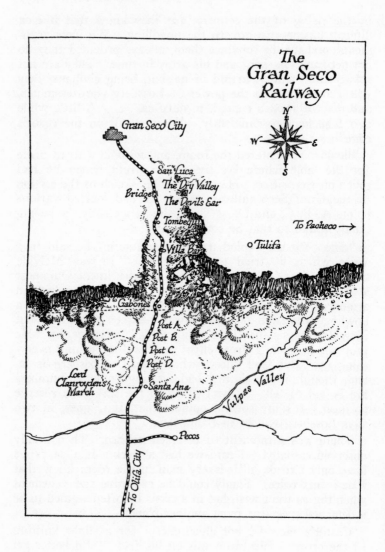

The
Gran Seco
Railway

N
W   E
S

Gran Seco City

San Vuca
The Dry Valley
The Devil's Ear

Bridge

Tombequi

To Pacheco →

Villa Bar

Tulifa

Gabones   Frontier

Post A.
Post B.
Post C.
Post D.

Lord
Clanroyden's
March

Santa Ana

Vulpas Valley

Pecos

To Olifa City ←

Castor. " I suggest, sir, that I go instead. I will take my Indians, every man of them. There's going to be a pretty rough-and-tumble on the railway, and that suits me better than Blenkiron. I'll push off at once, by car, and Rogerson can bring on the troops. I hope to be able to send you good news within forty-eight hours. If not—well, the game's with you. I shall be out of it."

"The game is with me," said Castor. " I propose to-morrow to have a talk with the Excelentisimo and his Cabinet."

"No, no," Sandy exclaimed. "I beg your pardon, sir, but not you. You are too valuable. We must send ambassadors. You would be a hostage."

Castor allowed his head to sink on his breast.

" I must go," he said after a pause. " The responsibility is mine. We are playing for high stakes, and I should cast the dice."

"And be a loser from the start! You are our reserve, sir. You must stay here in Veiro, while your plenipotentiaries speak in your name. It is not a question of taking risks. We know you're a glutton for them. It is a question of playing the right hand. Send Luis and Blenkiron. The one can speak for the republic of Olifa and the other can talk business. And meantime get your levies up to the edge of the Olifa lines. The Government have got to yield before Lossberg reaches Santa Ana. If he ever gets there, he must find that the whole country is in our hands. If we head him back, I'll send you word, and that will be a clinching argument. But even if we're scuppered, you may still win. . . . Let 'em know you're coming. No, no! No flag of truce business. Get Archie to fly you to the Plaza de Toros. They'll be hungry to see you. We're gambling on the outer edge of sanity, and the wildest course is the safest. You must impress them—it's their nerves we're gunning for. Good-bye, sir. Good-bye, all of you. If I see Veiro again, we'll be smoking the peace-pipe."

VI

A LITTLE before noon Archie brought his plane to a smooth
landing in the great dusty amphitheatre which had been
the bull-ring of an older Olifa, and was now sports ground
and polo ground. The journey had been uneventful, and
they had crossed the lines saluted only by a few rifle shots.
It appeared that they were not unexpected. The place was
empty, but there were pickets at the different entrances.
As the travellers climbed out of the plane a squad of soldiers
came forward at the double, and they completed their dis-
embarkation in the presence of a substantial military guard.
The officer in charge saluted.

" We have come to keep an appointment with their
Excellencies," said Luis.

" Their Excellencies await you," was the reply. A big
closed car had drawn up beside them, and he motioned them
to enter. A minute later they were moving swiftly from
the Plaza into the road which led to the Ciudad Nueva.
Archie pulled up the blind of the back window and laughed.

" They've got the needle, for they are putting the plane
out of action. They must think we're devils of fellows.
Well, our boats are burned right enough."

The Avenida de la Paz slept in the noonday sun. On
its broad sidewalk there were few of the well-dressed
Oliferos whom Archie had seen on his first visit, but many
of the riff-raff from the old city. There seemed to be little
life in the splendid offices. The headquarters of the Gran
Seco administration had no longer sentries at its doors.
Olifa had lost its comfortable bustle and its confidence,
and had acquired the air of a city in a crisis. At the street
corners there were not police, but soldiers, and as the car
swung up the hill towards the great copper dome of the
Parliament House, there were frequent halts and the inter-
change of passwords. Archie reported that a car was
following them containing an armed guard. " I feel as if
I were in Black Maria," he said. " Have either of you
fellows ever been in quod before? "

Their reception in the Grand Court was one of high ceremony. The sentries presented arms at the gate, and they were met at the main door by an aide-de-camp. There were soldiers everywhere, in the great entrance-hall, and at every turn of the broad marble staircase. First they were taken to an ante-room, where on a table light refreshments were laid out. "The señores may be thirsty after their flight," said the aide-de-camp, as he bowed and left them.

"Very handsome," Archie observed.

"Very politic," said Luis. "The Cabinet believe that we have come to treat. No doubt they have their terms ready. It will be a shock to them to learn that our minimum demand is complete surrender."

Blenkiron's eyes had been slowly taking in the magnificence of his surroundings. "We've gotten into the wrong atmosphere," he explained. "The folks that live in a shack like this are bound to think that nothing can go wrong with them. It'll stiffen their backs, for it looks as if it were built for eternity. We should have aimed to shift them somewhere where they could get a sight of Sandy's braves or Melville's roughnecks. You can't scare kings sitting in their palace."

"Dwellers in palaces," said Luis oracularly, "have weaker nerves than dwellers in tents."

The aide-de-camp appeared again. "Their Excellencies are ready to receive you," he announced, and, holding himself very stiff and straight, he opened a door which led to the Council Chamber.

It was a vast room, copied, like all the Olifa buildings, from an Old World model—in this case from a room in a Venetian palazzo. The ceiling was painted with nymphs and goddesses, and statues stood in the alcoves of the panelled marble walls. The light was dim, for the sun-shutters were partially closed. At a table near the window sat, not the full Cabinet which Archie had expected, but five men. One was the heavy bull-necked President, with on each side of him Vicente Sanfuentes, the Minister of External Affairs, and Aribia, the Minister of Finance.

Next to Aribia was General Bianca, and on the Foreign Minister's other side a figure which made Archie stare, for it was Romanes, whom he had last seen in the Tronos del Rey. The President and his colleagues were in their customary black frock-coats and stiff linen, the old General was in uniform, but the Conquistador wore a suit of white drill. There was much bowing, and the three took their seats opposite the five, like witnesses before an official inquiry. A big silver box of cigars stood before the President, which he pushed towards Blenkiron, who shook his head. Archie alone helped himself; he wanted something to occupy his hands.

The five showed no sign of embarrassment or strain. The President had still his air of massive composure, though the pouches under his eyes seemed a little heavier. The two ministers, Sanfuentes with his round shrewd face and Aribia with his well-trimmed beard, looked as if they were at an ordinary board meeting. The old General's thin knotted fingers drummed on the table, but that had always been his habit. Romanes's neat light-cavalry figure seemed more dapper than ever in its cool clothing, and his lean sallow face was as expressionless as the marble at his back.

"Don Luis de Marzaniga we know well," said the President, "and we have the honour of Señor Roylance's acquaintance. You, sir," and he looked towards Blenkiron, "I take to be the late Vice-President of the Gran Seco Administration."

Blenkiron did his best to bow. He seemed to find amusement in the scene before him, for his face wore a broad grin.

"You have come, gentlemen," the President continued, "to ask for terms."

"No, Excellency," said Luis, "we have come to offer them."

The President frowned slightly, and General Bianca threw up his head.

"It is a trifling change of a word," Luis continued, "but it is well to understand each other clearly from the start. We desire to make peace—on the basis of facts. The republic of Olifa is in our hands, and therefore we are in a position to dictate the terms of peace."

The General laughed angrily. He had a long face with finely cut features and very large black eyes. His skin was like ancient yellow parchment. That day he wore all his many orders, and they trembled as he squared his old shoulders.

"You are insolent," he said, "insolent dreamers. You have been driven out of the Gran Seco, and as a last gambler's throw you have stirred up trouble in Olifa. Pouf! It signifies nothing. Our army, having finished with the Gran Seco, will presently arrive, and where will your rabble be then?"

His voice was becoming shrill and he was embarking on a fierce tirade when the President checked him.

"Have patience, General," he said. "Let the señores state their case. We can be patient, for we are confident!"

Luis laid a map on the table.

"General Lossberg is not happy in the Gran Seco," he said. "We have still an army there—an army in being, and it is occupying all his attention. I will be candid with your Excellencies. Your General holds the Gran Seco city and the Mines and much of the country, but for the rest we are masters. He is immobilised, for he cannot come to your aid. Already he has tried it. Sixteen days ago he attempted to break out through the passes of the south-east, which he had just discovered. He was beaten back, the door is closed, and some of his troops are our prisoners. As for the railway to Santa Ana, that route has been destroyed, and, as you know well, it is a route which is easily blocked. I do not think that he can come to you by that way."

"These are lies," the General shouted. "We have the most expert army of its size on the globe. What can a handful of bandits and guerrilleros do against it? General Lossberg can burst his way through your barrier whenever he pleases. He has the latest guns and tanks——"

"I know, I know," said Luis soothingly. "But it is too

expert an army. It cannot compete with our rude simple ways."

Aribia laid a hand on the General's arm.

"You have a map, Señor de Marzaniga? You have perhaps something to say about Olifa."

Luis had much to say. He was dealing with men who knew their own country well, and he spoke as to experts. He took his hearers up and down the land, and explained how far the revolution had prospered in each district. He expounded in detail the revolt of the regular battalions, at Santa Ana, at Pecos, at Alcorta and Cardanio, and what accession of strength they represented. He showed them the position of each railway and railway junction. He gave the names of leaders, and at some of these names the ministers started. He was constantly interrupted with questions, which he patiently answered. He had an air of extreme candour, the air of a man who has nothing to conceal, and who is anxious to give the last tittle of information in his power. . . . Then he expounded the nature of the different concentrations, and the strategy of the advance on the city. "I take you into our innermost confidence," he said. "That is proof in itself that we believe we are victorious. If we had any doubt, we should not be disclosing our plans."

The exposition lasted till two o'clock, when there was an adjournment for luncheon. They did not lunch together, for the three ambassadors ate in the ante-room to which they had been taken on their arrival. They talked little at the meal, for a heavy sense of futility had come upon all the three. "You can't make that bunch understand facts," said Blenkiron. "That is what comes of living coddled up in this palace. They're still hanging on to Lossberg's coat-tails."

Luis rather wearily agreed. "If Lossberg gets to Santa Ana, and their Excellencies get wind of it in time, our game is up. We won't be having meals like this. It will be the Old Prison for us, and a very nasty corner of it, and the Gobernador will have to do without our services. I pray God that Sandy can hold the line a little longer."

Luncheon was followed by a short siesta, and they did not meet again till after four o'clock. The glare of the sun was no longer on the windows, and the green shutters were clamped back, so that the great chamber swam in the mellow light of afternoon. To Archie's surprise the ministers were notably less rigid than in the morning. The President took the lead in the conversation. He did not deny Luis's statements, as Aribia had done, but asked for some means of confirmation.

"We offer you whatever you ask," Luis answered. "This morning our nearest concentration was at Alcorta Junction within ten miles of this city. Appoint your emissaries, Excellency, men whose word you trust. They can go there under a flag of truce, and there they will find Manuel Martinez, and see for themselves. Or is there any other whose word you will take? The telephone service is working well."

"Is there no loyalist?" the President began.

"I am afraid that what you call a loyalist may be hard to find. We have been too successful, you see. But . . . there is Don Mario at Veiro—your cousin, Señor," and he bowed to Sanfuentes. "Don Mario is no politician, and he has never in his life been able to lie. I will give you the password, so that you can telephone to him at Veiro. He knows little of the campaign, but he has eyes in his head, and he will tell you of the forces moving from the east and south."

"That is good sense," said the minister, and he left the room. He returned after an absence of half an hour. "I have spoken to Don Mario," he said shortly. "He is an old man and an innocent." But it was clear that he had had news which discomposed him.

To Archie the situation was like some preposterous stage play in a dream. He had suddenly an overpowering sense of detachment, so that he seemed to look at the scene before him as at a picture small and far away down an inverted telescope. . . . What on earth was he doing helping to deliver an ultimatum in a theatrical chamber in a hot white city many thousands of miles from home? . . . He sat a little away from the table, and saw only the back of Luis's head and half Blenkiron's profile, but he had the others in full view. The paradox of the scene nearly made him laugh out loud. He was a revolutionary, trying to upset a Government to which his own had accredited a Minister. These solemn five, what did he know about them? They were creatures of a world infinitely remote from his. He studied the President's large swarthy face, heavy with the gravity of one accustomed to be obeyed and flattered—stupid and dull, but not without traces of quality. In Sanfuentes he saw the family likeness to Don Mario, as far as an overfed sedentary man can resemble a hard-bitten country squire. He looked a little cunning and self-indulgent, but there was humour somewhere. Aribia was the ordinary business man, with cold shrewd eyes, but he had a pleasant smile. . . . Romanes! It was on him that his eyes chiefly rested. A wash of sunlight seemed to bring every feature into startling prominence. Archie saw the leanness of his head, the odd skull beneath the smooth hair, the curious hollows in his brow, the skin opaque as if no blood ran beneath it. This was Castor's doing; the man had once been Castor's creature, and Castor was their leader! . . . For a moment he felt some sympathy with the perplexed Cabinet of Olifa.

It was Castor's name which roused Archie to attention. Romanes spoke in his toneless voice for almost the first time.

"It would have been well if the Gobernador had accompanied these gentlemen. No doubt they have full power to treat, but it would have been more satisfactory to meet the Commander-in-Chief himself."

"The Commander-in-Chief cannot leave his command," was Luis's answer.

"Naturally. Still . . . there have been rumours, you know. We do not know if he is indeed in command. We do not know if he is in Olifa at all."

"You can be assured that he is. He is at Veiro."

Archie thought that he saw a flicker of sharp intelligence in Romanes's eyes, but the next second it was gone.

"I think their Excellencies would have welcomed a meeting. For after all, whatever is the destiny of this country, Señor Castor must mean much to it."

"He owes us an explanation," the President growled. "He was our trusted colleague. Whatever he advised was done. Señor Sanfuentes will bear me witness when I say that he had a large share in the external policy of this State. The Administration of the Gran Seco was granted to him as if it was his private domain. . . . Suddenly, with no warning, he becomes our enemy. He must be mad."

"He is not mad, Excellency, but it is permissible for a man to change his mind. The Gobernador has to-day a policy for the Gran Seco and for Olifa itself which conflicts with that of your Excellency. Some of us, independently of the Gobernador, had the same notions. We have been endeavouring for months to persuade you and your colleagues that our views must be accepted. That is why we are here to-day—to apply, if your Excellency will permit the metaphor, the last little weight to the inclining balance."

After that the five consulted in private, and it was dark before Aribia returned with an announcement.

"We have decided to send representatives to Alcorta Junction to meet Señor Martinez and see for themselves. Do not be offended, please, for, as you yourself have admitted, confirmation is desirable. Will you arrange with Martinez for the reception of our envoys? The party will consist of two of General Bianca's staff-officers and Señor Romanes. They leave to-morrow at daybreak."

So Luis had a busy hour on the telephone and then joined his two companions at dinner. They spent a dismal evening, before they sought their beds in the cheerless state apartments. "This is going to be worse than a League of Nations meeting at Geneva," Blenkiron moaned. "I hoped they'd treat the thing as a business proposition, and I was ready to explain to them just how the Gran Seco should be run, and how it is going to be mighty advantageous to Olifa. They've all got fat bank accounts, and could understand my arguments. But we never got near business. A blind kitten could see that they're not going to let go till they're choked off. There's more sand than I reckoned in that big President."

" They are waiting on Lossberg," said Luis. " They will not give up hope till they are compelled. How in the name of God can we compel them, unless Sandy brings off some colossal stroke?—and that is as likely as snow in summer. Jesucristo! At this moment he is perhaps making a desperate stand in the skirts of Santa Ana! "

The conference was resumed next morning with the half-closed sun-shutters again making a green twilight. It was now Blenkiron's turn. Pending the arrival of the envoys from Alcorta Junction, he was permitted to state the views of the Gobernador on the future of the Gran Seco. The discussion was long, and necessitated many calculations, in which Aribia shared. The profits of the State of Olifa from the business need not decline; nay, there was every chance of their increasing, if the organisation were put upon more stable and permanent lines. The arrangements about Indian labour must of course be altered—in any case they would have presently altered themselves. The extreme high-pressure production must be given up; also the Gran Seco must be put outside Olifa politics, except for its scale of contribution to the Olifa exchequer. It must be regarded as a special territory, to be governed under a special charter. The discussion was amicable. The ministers were all share-holders in the company, and, as an academic proposition, were prepared to consider it on business lines.

In the afternoon the envoys returned, and, when after the long midday siesta the conference reassembled, Archie tried hopelessly to detect some change in the air of the ministers. He was disappointed. Romanes for some reason was absent, but the other four seemed in good spirits. Their placidity was unshaken. The President himself touched on the matter.

" Your veracity has been vindicated, Señor de Marzaniga," and he bowed politely, " but not, I fear, your judgment. You have undoubtedly recruited many men, but they are not an army. Our officers report that it is no better than a rabble, ill-armed, ill-disciplined, and led by amateurs."

" It is the people of Olifa," said Luis hotly. " And you have seen only the spear-head—one of the spear-heads. There is a weighty shaft behind it." He spoke of the extent and variousness of the rising. . . . Every class was in it, every condition of life. . . . Among its leaders were representatives of every family that had been great in Olifa's history. . . . Also the chiefs of every calling, the ranchers, the fruit-growers, the wine-growers, the industrial magnates of Alcorta. He was a little carried out of himself, and it was clear that his eloquence had some effect on his hearers. " We have all Olifa with us," he concluded, " all Olifa that is worthy of the name."

The President laughed, but his laughter did not seem to come easily. " I know my countrymen, Señor de Marzaniga," he said. " They have returned for an hour to the traditional habits which we hoped they had forgotten for ever. But they will not fight—they cannot fight—they have nothing to fight for. The ranches of Señor Martinez could not be more prosperous under a different regime. Ramirez has no complaints from his fruit farms. The Zarranigas breed their fine horses without Government requisitions, unlike the old days. These men are not fools. Presently they will learn wisdom."

" Or be taught it," put in old General Bianca.

Luis had recovered his balance.

" There is one thing you forget, Excellency. We are patriots and love our country. Olifa is prosperous, no doubt —but it has no soul. You and your colleagues have made it the appanage of a commercial corporation. We want to be a nation again."

Sanfuentes spoke impatiently. " A nation! What would you have? When your crazy war broke out we were on the eve of taking the leadership of this continent. We would have made Latin America a power in the world."

" I guess I know all about that, sir," said Blenkiron. " You were going to make bad trouble in this continent, but it wasn't for the sake of Olifa. The Gobernador was using

you as a pawn in his own game. Well, Mr Castor has
thought better of it, and I can't see why in thunder you want
to go on alone. Our slogan is ' Olifa all the time and for
its own sake.' I advise you gentlemen to listen to reason,
for you can't fight against the whole people."

"The whole people," said Aribia sweetly. "But that is
precisely the point on which you have failed to convince us."

Presently lamps were brought, and the discussion
wandered into a morass of futility. The ministers were
waiting, not very confidently perhaps, a little shaken, but
determined still to wait. It was the habit of their race,
for the Oliferos are not a hasty breed. With a sinking of
the heart Archie realised that there would be another day
of indecision, while Sandy might be struggling hard to win
an extra hour for their inconclusive diplomacy. Any
moment the crash might come.

It came about six o'clock when General Bianca was
summoned by an aide-de-camp to the telephone. He returned in five minutes, almost at a run.

"News," he cried, "glorious news! Lossberg is in Pecos.
I have spoken to his Chief of Staff."

The ministers were on their feet, and the exuberance
of their relief showed the depth of their anxiety. They
clamoured for details, but the General could give them little.

"I spoke to Olivarez. . . . I recognised his voice at
once. . . . He gave his name. . . . What did he say?
Only that he was in Pecos, and was coming here without
delay. . . . He is evidently pressed—Lossberg's orders no
doubt. . . . Where he is, the General must be, and the
Chief of Staff is naturally sent on in advance. . . . We
have conquered, my brothers. To-morrow the city will be
relieved, and the rebels scattered to the points of the
compass. . . . It is the moment for toasts, for much
talking has made my throat dry."

The ministers did not forget their manners in their hour
of triumph. The three envoys were not asked to witness
the toast-drinking, but were conducted ceremoniously to
another apartment, where they too were supplied with sweet

champagne. Only Archie tasted it, for the two others sat
back in their chairs with the faces of broken men. It
was at least an hour before they were ready to speak of
fresh plans—futile plans, it seemed, for they must now
regard themselves as prisoners. As for Archie, he still
felt himself living in a crazy world of illusion, but he was
so tired by the strain of the day that he fell asleep.

About nine o'clock an aide-de-camp appeared.

"General Olivarez is arriving," he said, and his air was
noticeably less civil. "Your presence is required in the
Council Chamber."

Once more the three envoys seated themselves at the
table. It was obvious that the ministers had dined and
dined well. Even Bianca's parchment skin had a colour.
Romanes was still absent.

The door opened and General Olivarez was announced.
Two men entered. One to Archie's amazement was Alejandro Gedd, a figure like a scarecrow, dusty, dishevelled,
grey with fatigue, his ancient dapperness utterly gone. The
other was a slight man in the service uniform of Olifa, with
a long olive-tinted face, a fleshy nose, and grizzled hair
cut *en brosse*. He too seemed the worse for wear, and
he had his left arm in a sling.

It was Gedd who spoke.

"Your Excellencies," he said, "I have been sent to bring
General Olivarez to your presence. This morning General
Lossberg was decisively defeated in the passes north of
Santa Ana. His main army has fallen back, and his
advance forces were cut off and taken prisoner. Of this
advance General Olivarez was in command. I was ordered
by Lord Clanroyden to bring him to you that you might
learn from his own lips the position of affairs."

The ministers were silent. Then old Bianca found his
voice.

"Is that true, sir?" he rapped out.

"It is unfortunately true." Olivarez spoke in a voice
in which weariness left no room for bitterness. "Of the
rest of General Lossberg's army I cannot speak. I myself

and over nine thousand of my men are prisoners in the enemy's hands."

The President behaved well, for he showed no emotion of any kind. His face was like a stone, and his voice level and toneless. He turned to Luis and bowed.

" We accept your terms, Señor," he said. " General Bianca will issue the necessary orders to the city defence force."

VII

THE long-drawn fight on the Santa Ana railway was begun in the Gran Seco itself by Peters and Escrick. There was no communication between them and Castor by wireless or telegraph, but there might have been a telepathic understanding, so exactly did they time their operations to meet the crisis in the south. Their aeroplanes were now terribly hampered in their reconnaissance work by shortage of petrol, but one of Grayne's economical flights brought news of Lossberg's movement down the railway with the larger part of his field force. At that moment Escrick was north of the city on the road to Fort Castor, and Peters's bands were south of the Mines in the neighbourhood of Tulifa. Escrick's first notion was another raid on the city in quest of stores, but Peters, in whose old field of operations the Santa Ana railway had been, urged that it was their business to hang on to Lossberg's skirts. The blockhouse system had made raiding difficult, but he argued that their first duty was to hamper Lossberg's communications with the city which was still his base. Escrick was convinced, the more because he was still completely in the dark as to what was going on at the other end of the railway. It might be that Lossberg would have an easy road to the plains of Olifa, in which case their task must be to delay him by fastening on his rear.

Under the new blockhouse system they could not hope to cut up any great length of line, so they must make their effort at a single vital point. There was only one such till Gabones was reached, the bridge of San Luca. But it was likely to be the best guarded, for since the first raid

Lossberg had supplemented the posts at each end of the abutment with two companies in the valley bottom. The garrisons at the ends, it will be remembered, were at San Luca itself and at the Devil's Ear, the valley was more than half a mile wide, and the bridge had sixteen arches. Two of the central arches had been blown up by Sandy, and the line now ran across the gap on an improvised platform of steel girders.

It was clear that a midnight dash in the old manner would effect nothing, so Escrick decided to make an effort not to destroy a part of the bridge but to capture the whole of it, and hold it long enough to alarm Lossberg about his communications. There was now no Pacheco to serve as a base, and all the northern slopes of the southern frontier of the Gran Seco were strongly patrolled; for this was the critical flank of Lossberg's new advance. Roger Grayne reported that the eastern side of the railway up to the frontier was watched like a trench line.

Thereupon Escrick made a bold decision. He resolved to attack from the west side, where a hideous country of scrub and sand and rocky kopjes stretched from the railway to the sea. This area had never been part of the battle-ground, chiefly because of its immense natural difficulties, and because it led to nowhere. So he ordered Peters to slip north by night from Tulifa, between the Mines and the city, and to join him on the road to Fort Castor.

The concentration was effected on a Monday morning. That day Lossberg was at Gabones, and his advance force under Olivarez was feeling its way south along the devastated line. That night Escrick's whole command, nearly four thousand mounted men with every machine gun it possessed, had made a wide circuit and was in the hills some fifteen miles south-west of San Luca. There they lay during the following day, while with immense care smaller detachments made their way eastward to the ridge of kopjes on each side of the dry valley where stood the bridge. Lossberg's aeroplanes were busy down the railway, and to the garrisons at San Luca and the Devil's Ear no warning sight or sound came from the baking red cliffs over which they were accustomed to see the sun set. That day, Tuesday, saw Olivarez's great thrust southward. Before night fell he had taken Blenkiron's Post A, where once Toledo's chivalry had been cut up by the Indians, had forced the difficult narrows at Post B, and was threatening Post C, where Melville had brought up every man for a last stand.

During the night of Tuesday Escrick made his attack on the San Luca bridge from the west. It was a far easier task than he had anticipated. Lossberg's advance had switched the attention of the garrisons from defence to transport. Peters's right wing took the Devil's Ear with scarcely a shot, and his left, creeping up the boulder-strewn valley, surprised the post in the hollow with few casualties. San Luca put up a better fight, but by midnight it was overpowered, and an ammunition train, standing in its siding, was captured. Before the dawn broke there was another huge rent in the bridge, and both abutments were held in force, with a wicked chain of machine-gun nests commanding their approaches from north and south. A big breach had been made, and, what was more, the breach was held, and might be held for days against a considerable army.

The news found Lossberg on the Wednesday morning about to push forward troops to support Olivarez in his last thrust. Already he saw himself in the Olifa plains approaching the capital. He had had no news except Indian rumours, but he had by this time realised that the rebels in the Gran Seco were only a vanguard and that El Obro was now in Olifa. He had beaten the enemy in the Gran Seco, and his place was now in the lowlands. But the news from San Luca made him pause. Part of a mechanised battalion which he had sent back hastily was checked and beaten by Peters at the Devil's Ear. Lossberg halted in deep perplexity. He must explore the situation behind him, before he could support Olivarez with an easy mind. So instead of concentrating in an immediate assault on Post C, which would have given him Santa Ana, he pushed more troops back towards San Luca and ordered Olivarez to postpone his main attack for twelve hours.

It was at this point that Sandy entered the game. He

had arrived at Santa Ana during the course of the Tuesday night, and had had his Indians there before ten o'clock on the Wednesday morning. The reports from Melville at Post C were not reassuring. Olivarez was in great force, and once he had his field guns up not all the natural advantages of the place could keep it from destruction. The defence had already tried a night sally, which had been driven back without effecting much. Melville asked for nothing in the way of reinforcements, for he knew that there was nothing to send, since Pecos and Santa Ana were already bare. Feverish efforts were being made to strengthen Post D, the ultimate position, but everyone realised that, if C fell, D would follow.

When Sandy arrived he asked for the last air reports. It was believed that Lossberg was at a point thirty-seven miles south of Gabones, and that a gap of at least fifteen miles separated him from Olivarez and his van. Sandy shrugged his shoulders and turned to Rogerson.

"We're getting implicated in a field action," he said in the mild voice which he reserved for extreme emergencies. "It won't do. If I join Melville, we shall still be outnumbered and outgunned. Latimer had better keep his planes in touch with Melville. I'm going to get to that fifteen-mile gap. Please God, Lossberg is in no hurry this morning. He must be cocksure of success after yesterday, so if I know my man he'll take his time."

Lossberg, as we know, was compelled to delay, but of this Sandy was not aware, and as soon as the Indians had broken bread he had them in the saddle. The eastern side of the railway valley was not practicable for horses, scarcely even for cragsmen, but he had some hopes of the western side. His expectations were all but doomed to defeat. The total distance of the circuit proposed was some thirty miles, but, after the first twenty, horses became impossible. The local guides were useless, for they led him into a network of barren ravines too far to the west—a route no doubt to Gabones, but separated from the crucial part of the line by an increasing width of rocky mountains. Presently the horses had to be left behind, and under the heat of a tropical sun the way had to be pursued on foot up and down moraines of shale and crumbling precipices and sand-choked hollows. Not all the Indians lasted the course, for many were horsemen by habit and no mountaineers. Of the white men only Sandy and five others found themselves that afternoon looking down upon the railway, with aching limbs, and eyes filmed with weariness, and heads that throbbed and swam in incipient heatstroke. But that part of the railway valley which they saw was empty except for a small body of pioneers repairing the road. They were in time. Lossberg had not yet closed the gap which separated him from his Chief of Staff.

The time was now about four o'clock on the Wednesday afternoon. San Luca was in the hands of Peters and Escrick, Lossberg's first attempt to oust them had failed, and that general, much perplexed, was beginning to move troops northward again. Melville, to his surprise, was managing to hold his own at Post C, since Olivarez, under Lossberg's orders, was not pressing too hard. Blenkiron, Luis, and Archie were sitting in Olifa in their futile conference.

The events which followed have become famous in Olifa history, and they are told fully in the work which young Campanillo has published. Staggering with weariness but goaded on by a sense of the shortness of their time and the magnitude of their chance, Sandy's blear-eyed following descended from the rocks and took possession of the segment of valley. He had dragged explosives with him across the hills, and with him were men from the Mines who understood their use. Before the hot night descended they had contrived a great destruction, and the early darkness was lit with flame and loud with earthquakes. Between the cliffs which rimmed the place they achieved a desolation which for days no troops could traverse, except painfully, in single file, on foot. Presently the remainder of his men straggled in, and after a short rest Sandy led his force southward, to where Olivarez's guns could be heard at their noisy bombardment.

The charge of that wild commando at dawn is a tale not

for dull prose but for some swinging ballad. The surprise was complete, and most of the batteries were taken in the rear. Olivarez was a stout soldier, and he rallied gallantly, but he was caught between two fires, whose magnitude he could not guess. Melville had heard the explosions of the night and knew what had happened, and he flung every ounce he possessed into the struggle. The defence became an attack, and C was no longer a beleaguered post but the base of a furious offensive. A little after midday Lossberg's van was huddled into a rocky gut, with its own batteries turned on it, and the enemy secure on the circumference. Then came one of those moments of sudden quiet which mean the realisation of defeat on one side and incontestable victory on the other.

Olivarez, like a wise and humane man, surrendered. But to his surprise his surrender was received not by Melville, of whom his Intelligence scouts had fully informed him, but by a slight figure with a begrimed face and clothes in rags, who addressed him in perfect Spanish and seemed more embarrassed than himself. He learned with amazement that this was the notorious El Obro. When the guerrillero recalled a former meeting in a Moroccan town, Olivarez stared in bewilderment. " I was called Arbuthnot then," the other said pleasantly. Then recollection awoke in the general, and his face lightened. He had heard too much about this man to feel any shame in accepting defeat at his hands.

VIII

THAT night, as we know, Sandy dispatched Olivarez in company with Don Alejandro Gedd to Olifa city. The following day was spent by the ambassadors in Olifa, and by Sandy at Pecos, in adjusting their plans to the new situation. There was an immense amount of work to be accomplished in the minimum of time. The great concentration at Alcorta Junction, which was now pushed up to the defence lines of the city, had to be regulated, and throughout the republic a stop-gap military Govern-

ment had to be extemporised. Between the revolution and
the ultimate settlement a difficult interregnum must intervene. Manuel Martinez came into the city to consult with
Luis, but Castor remained at Veiro, whence he issued orders
to the different provinces. So far as possible the work
was left in the hands of the Olifero leaders themselves.
Luis was the chief executive officer, and it was Martinez
who became temporary governor of Olifa city, and old
Ramirez of Cardanio and one of the Zarranigas of Alcorta
who were his lieutenants, while young Miguel de Campanillo carried to Lossberg the instructions of General
Bianca. It was wise to keep the foreign element in the
background, that Olifa might believe that her redemption
had come from herself.

It was a torrid day with thunderstorms grumbling on the
horizon, and Sandy, having received reports from the city
which announced that all was quiet and orderly, and from
Gabones, which told of young Campanillo's arrival on his
way to Lossberg's headquarters, flung himself on a bed in
the Pecos hotel, and tried to sleep. But sleep he could not,
though every bone and muscle cried out for it. It may have
been the weather, or it may have been the strain of the past
days, but his mind refused to be composed and his thoughts
beat a weary treadmill. He had none of the exultation of
a victor, none even of the comfort which comes from a
task accomplished. He laboured under a heavy sense of
oppression, out of which anxiety stood like jags of rock
in a stream. He could not believe that the end had been
reached, not even when his reason approved that conclusion. Therefore he could not sleep.

An aide-de-camp made a timid appearance, for he was
afraid to break in on the siesta of his chief. But it appeared
that the occasion was urgent. A man wanted to speak with
the General. He had given his name. Sandy looked at the
card proffered him, and read " Mr T. S. Lariarty."

" Bring him here," he said, " and see that we are not
interrupted. Wait . . . don't be far away, in case I want
you." He smoothed his ruffled hair, and sat on the bed
awaiting his visitor, and as he waited a ridiculous memory

kept recurring—the Eton Beagles in the fields beyond
Slough, and himself and Lariarty, both newly become uppers,
struggling desperately to keep up with the field, each determined not to be outdone by the other. Much water had
passed over Cuckoo Weir since then.

The man who presently stood before him would have
made no figure in running over English ploughfields.
Lariarty was no more the dapper and inscrutable Conquistador, armoured against a world which he despised.
Some spring had broken within him, for he looked like one
mortally sick in mind and body. But his eyes were no longer
opaque. There was light in them, broken lights, like the
eyes of a sick dog.

" You're looking ill, Tim," said Sandy gently.

" I think I am dying. . . . But that does not matter.
. . . I must speak to you, Arbuthnot. You have behaved
to me like a gentleman, and I pay my debts. . . . You
think you have won, but you are wrong . . . unless . . ."
The man seemed to gulp. " Veiro," he croaked. " The
women are at Veiro—and the Gobernador. . . . They will
be dead before midnight unless you can save them."

Sandy was on his feet, his lethargy gone. He shouted
for his aide-de-camp. " Get through to Veiro," he told
the boy, " and to Olifa—to the Ministry of War. Ask for
General de Marzaniga. . . . Get a whisky and soda, too—
a stiff one."

The drink was brought by an orderly. " Swallow that,
Timmy," he said. " You're all out, and it will buck you up."

But the other refused it. " It would kill me," he said.
" Never mind my health, Arbuthnot. You won't get
through to Veiro . . . nor to Olifa. . . . My colleagues
have made their plans. Veiro will be isolated. . . . Why
in the name of God did you leave your friends in that
lonely place? They should have been in the midst of an
army. When men are desperate, they think only of
revenge."

" Who are ' they '? The Conquistadors? "

Lariarty nodded.

" D'Ingraville is there, and Pasquali, and Suvorin, and

Romanes—Romanes above all. Larbert is dead, and I have not heard of Calvo. But Romanes——" He choked again. "And there are some of the others too. . . . Judson and Radin and Martel, and, I think, Laschallas. . . . They have all death before them, the rope for some and for others a slower torture. Therefore they are mad. . . . Oh, what in God's name are you waiting for? I tell you . . ."

The aide-de-camp returned. "We cannot get through to Veiro, sir," he said. "There seems to be some break-down on the line. And there is no answer from Olifa."

"So," said Sandy. The grimness had gone out of his face, and he was smiling again. "I want the Rolls, Truslove," he said, "at once. Captain Zarraniga will come with me. Tell him to pick four troopers, with a hundred rounds apiece. . . . I want the two big Daimlers to follow, with eight troopers in each. At once. There is not a moment to lose. Let General Melville know."

Lariarty had drawn himself erect.

"Can I come with you, Arbuthnot?" he stammered.

Sandy looked in his eyes, and he seemed to see behind the sickness and fever and the wreckage of the tragic years a shadow of the boy he remembered.

"Most certainly you are coming with me, Tim." He glanced at his wrist-watch. "It is now a quarter to nine. We shall be at Veiro by ten. God grant we are in time!"

The night was warm and still, for the thunder had now gone out of the air, though it still grumbled on the horizon. It was a slow business clearing the environs of Pecos, for the roads were congested with transport, owing to the moving of troops from Alcorta Junction. But once the Vulpas valley was left behind, the car swung briskly along the hard, broad roads of the plateau called the Marpas, which is one of Olifa's chief horse-breeding areas. There was only a finger-nail of moon, but the stars were like harbour-lights. Far behind could be seen the broad glow of the head-lamps of the following Daimlers. Sandy at the wheel did not slacken speed at the patches where the road had been ruffled by the winter rains. He drove like a man possessed, looking every now and then at his wrist-watch.

"Half-way," he announced to the young Zarraniga as they passed a farm in a clump of chestnuts. Then the road climbed to a greater elevation and the light of the Daimlers behind seemed to come out of a trough. "Ten miles more," he whispered, and Lariarty, who was jammed among the troopers behind, muttered something that sounded like a prayer. Still the road rose, and then came a long downward incline, and far away on the left a light twinkled. "Veiro," said young Zarraniga. "Presently the good road will end, and we shall have Don Mario's cart-track. We must be near the ravine of St Paul and the iron bridge."

Three minutes later there was a jarring of brakes and the car came to a stop. A deep narrow cleft lay before them, and where had once been a bridge there hung only a drunken girder.

"They have planned it well," said Lariarty.

The men tumbled out of the car, for the great Rolls was as useless as a child's go-cart.

"There are yet four miles," said Zarraniga, as he followed Sandy down the side of the ravine and up the steep overhang of the far bank. "Four miles, and my men are not long-distance runners."

Sandy had squared his shoulders for the race, when Zarraniga halted him. "Half a mile on the right is the farm of Pedro Aguilar. He has young horses."

Pedro, who was a tenant of Don Mario's, was roused from his sleep by the sight of seven armed men demanding mounts. Zarraniga he knew, and he trotted obediently towards his stables.

"I have not saddles for so many, señor," he explained.

"Saddles be hanged! Give us bridles. Rope halters if you have nothing better." Sandy was already delving furiously among the debris of Pedro's harness-room.

"Two are young beasts and scarcely broken," said the man.

"So much the better," said Sandy. "I will take one and Señor Zarraniga the other."

Within five minutes two scared and angry colts were
being hustled out of the corrals by the help of two pairs of
Pedro's long-rowelled spurs. Once in the open they found
their heads turned firmly to the east, and fled like scared
deer they knew not whither. They led by at least a hundred
yards, flying the deep sandy scaurs, spurning the ant-heaps,
slipping, stumbling, recovering, while the troopers on their
more manageable mounts pounded heavily behind. When
after the first mile Sandy had his animal under control, he
found to his surprise that Lariarty was beside him.

Now they were on the edge of the alfalfa fields and the
water-furrows, and before them was the dark loom of trees.
They swung to the left, avoiding the road which ran from
the railway-station, and making for the line of poplars
which hedged the garden. A light twinkled beyond the
trees, a light which suddenly went out.

And then, with a cry, Lariarty swung round his horse's
head and set the beast capering and plunging. He had
all but ridden down a woman—a tall girl in black, wearing
pink roses at her breast.

The same evening about half past seven Don Alejandro
Gedd was taking the air in that part of the Avenida de la
Paz which adjoined the Parliament House. He had had
a busy day. For hours he had sat in consultation in the
great Council Chamber, for he had two kinds of knowledge
invaluable at the moment—a wide acquaintance with the
organisation of the revolution in the provinces, and considerable insight into the psychology of the capital city.
He had been of great value to Luis and Blenkiron and
Martinez, while they worked out the next moves—the
proclamation to the people of Olifa, the demobilisation of
the levies, and the preparations for a presidential election.
He had also been constantly on the telephone with Castor
at Veiro, who was busy with the draft of the new con-
stitution, which was to be embodied in the proclamation.
Don Alejandro was contented, exhilarated, but also very
weary. He decided that he owed himself a short spell of
leisure, and resolved to dine alone at the club.

But his hopes of a little rest were frustrated. He found himself accosted by a villainous-looking peasant, whose left wrist was bound up in a dirty handkerchief, and whose mahogany face showed a long shallow scar from right temple to chin, which must have been done recently, for the blood was scarcely dry on it. Also the man appeared to be drunk, for as he clutched his arm he swayed.

"Maister Gedd," came a hoarse whisper, "Maister Gedd! Haud on, for God's sake! Ye ken me? Ye saw me at Charcillo? Hamilton's my name. I was wi' Sir Erchibald. Ye ken Sir Erchibald? . . ." The scarecrow tottered, and would have fallen had he not leaned heavily against the wall.

Recognition broke in on Don Alejandro's mind. He remembered the square Scots soldier who had been with Lady Roylance in her escape from the Tronos del Rey and who had been Archie's special henchman at Charcillo. He had heard that he had been in Olifa before the city surrendered. Don Alejandro was a man of action. There was a small café at hand in a retired side-street, and thither he led him. He compelled him to drink a claret glass of liqueur brandy. Obviously there was some story worth hearing. He was just about to begin a leisurely cross-examination, when the soldier seemed to recover his dazed wits and forestalled him.

"What am I sittin' here for?" he exclaimed. "Come on, sir," and he struggled to rise. "We maun get haud o' Sir Erchibald or Maister Lewis. There's awfu' things gaun to happen afore the nicht's oot. It's Veiro . . . the twa leddies . . . and him they ca' the Gobernador. . . . Oh, sir, let's oot o' this and awa' up to Heidquarters. They'll let me in if you're wi' me. I've been tryin' to win in my lane for the last hour, and the sentries just shoo'd me awa'."

His earnestness and alarm communicated themselves to Don Alejandro. Then the man seemed to recover his balance, and, leaning forward, clutched Don Alejandro's knee.

"I've been in this toun a' week. The folks think I'm

a native frae some landward bit. . . . I've been bidin' doun near the harbour—it's an auld haunt o' mine. . . . Some o' thae Bodyguard blagyirds is there, and I got chief wi' ane o' them. . . . Syne Judson appeared—ye mind him? and he kenned me, and there was a wee bit o' a turn-up. I had to rin for my life, but I had fund oot what they were ettlin', and I've been jinkin' about the closes and tryin' to see Sir Erchibald. . . . This verra nicht. . . . Man, they're clever. When we're a' crackin' about the grand victory and thinkin' that there's nae mair fecht left in the ither side, they're plannin' a bloody revenge. . . . Wha's in it? Judson, for ane, an' yon lang, black-avised lad they ca' Laschallas, and some o' the white-faced gentry that used to manage the Gran Seco. . . . What do they ettle? It canna be ransom, for there's nae hidy-hole they could carry their prisoners to. It maun be murder—black murder. Oh, haste ye, sir. The blagyirds or now will be well on the road to Veiro. They've gotten cars, and they'll no be easy stoppit. . . . What's the time? Gettin' on for eight?" The man staggered to his feet with wild eyes.

" Is there no an aeroplane?" he cried. " We maun gang by air, for they'll beat us by the road."

But when a quarter of an hour later Archie and Blenkiron were roused by the news into violent activity, it was found that there were no aeroplanes to be had in or near the city of Olifa. Also it was discovered that the wires between Olifa and Veiro had been tampered with. It was impossible to communicate even with Alcorta Junction.

IX

THAT day the life at Veiro had returned to something of its ancient serenity. Castor, indeed, was kept busy with constant telephone calls from the city, and on four occasions messengers came to him by car. But otherwise there was no sign that the place was any kind of headquarters. No garrison was in the house, and no sentries were at the gates, for considerable armies lay between it and the city on one side, and Pecos and the road to the Gran Seco on the other.

Don Mario pottered about the stables and the garden and had a long siesta in the darkened library. Janet also slept, for the strain of the past weeks had fatigued her more than she knew. Barbara wrote letters and went riding in the first cool of the evening. In the dim, musty-smelling rooms, in the sunny courtyard, in the garden where the lawns were beginning to brown under the summer heats, there was an air of calm after storm, of a general relaxing. The feeling was in the atmosphere, but with Janet it was less a positive satisfaction than a mere rest from anxiety. She understood now that she and Barbara had been living for a long time on the extreme edge of their nerves. The news that victory had been won brought relief rather than triumph. She had not yet adjusted her world to meet it; she was simply aware that her mind could leave the weary treadmill and be still.

But at dinner she realised that a change was coming over her mood. She felt light-hearted again, and had begun to look into the future. Barbara seemed to have suffered the same change, for she had been singing as she dressed. Don Mario was in his usual placid humour, but Castor was in tune with her new temper. His work for the day was finished; he had bathed and got himself into dress-clothes, for some of his kit had been sent out that morning from the city; and now he relaxed into something very like high spirits. Janet had never witnessed this new mood of his, and she found it delightful. Before he had always retained the manner of one in command, one a little apart, for whom friendliness involved a slight descent and unbending. But now he had dropped without effort to the level of ordinary folk, he laughed without constraint, his eyes had a frank companionship.

At dinner he talked to Don Mario of past days in Olifa. He even spoke of his Campanillo grandmother. The old man presently passed from his stilted English into Spanish, which Janet could not easily follow, but it was clear that he was pleased by Castor's questions and was expanding happily on some matter very dear to his heart. Once again Janet saw in the two faces that which she had noted weeks before at Charcillo in the faces of Luis and his young caballeros—something innocently apostolic, the ardour of men in the grip of an idea. She looked across the table at Barbara, who wore pale pink roses on the breast of her black gown. Barbara had spoken little, but there was a pleasant content in her dark eyes—and now, as she caught Janet's glance and followed it to Castor's ardent face, there was also a flicker of amusement.

They drank their coffee in Don Mario's own room, among the spurs and whips and sporting pictures. The French windows were open wide, for the night was warm, but a fine-meshed curtain of gauze hung over them to keep out moths and flying ants. Without the stars burned fiercely, and in their light an ancient baroque group, which adorned the terrace, had the appearance of a knot of eavesdroppers. Barbara had started at her first sight of the statuary.

Castor stood before the empty fireplace which had been filled with a tapestry screen. There were three lamps in the room set on little tables, which illumined the heads of the two women and of Don Mario in his high-backed chair. The face of the Gobernador, being only partially lit, revealed none of the lesser details of age. The fine lines on the forehead, the streaks of grey in beard and hair were unseen; only the trim figure and the noble contour of the head stood out, and these had an air of vital youth. The impression was strengthened by the new note in his voice.

"You are twenty years younger to-night, Excellency," said Don Mario.

"I am beginning life again," was the answer. "I have been middle-aged—I have been old—and now I am young."

"Can one begin life anew?" the old man asked in his precise English. "It is the fashion for people to talk so, but I wonder. It has never been my fate, for I have carried into each new stage of my life heavy burdens from the last stages. But perhaps I was always lazy—lazy and a little timid."

"I have been fortunate," said Castor gravely, "for Fate

itself has shut the door on that which I would leave behind."

" But is the door fast? Will nothing creep through? "

" It can be kept fast and well guarded. I do not mean that I must not atone for my blunders. God knows I have made many and I have much folly to expiate. Yet that too is part of my good fortune. I am in a position to mend what I have done wrongly."

The old man shook his head.

" You are luckier than I. The blunders I have made were such as did not permit themselves to be atoned for. Witness my error in crossing the Vidas and the Cintra blood. I was warned by my father about the Cintra stock, which he said meant speed but no heart, and in the mares a lamentable barrenness. But I would not listen, and all my life I have paid the penalty."

" I am not a fatalist," was the answer. " That is the blindest of superstitions. The spirit and mind of man are free to shape life if they are resolute enough and wise enough. A man is not the slave of his father's actions, or of his own. Any error can be redeemed on this side of the grave."

Don Mario laughed. " I will not discourage your optimism, Excellency. It is a pleasant gift of youth. I who am old practise humility."

" I too would practise humility," said Castor. " That is what I have learned in the Courts of the Morning. Before, I was arrogant and self-centred and friendless and inhuman. But up in that mountain eyrie I found a juster perspective. . . . Call it a revelation. I was granted a view of life from a great height, and many things, including myself, took different proportions. That I owe to you, Lady Roylance, and to your friends. If I were to die now, I should die happy, for I have become young again. You opened a door for me, and I have passed through it."

" You are certain that it is closed behind you? " Janet did not know what made her ask the question. The words seemed to come mechanically to her lips.

" Closed and bolted and guarded." There was both solemnity and exhilaration in his tone. Janet never forgot the picture he made in that moment, his head flung back, his eyes looking down under their heavy lids with a glow of something more than friendliness, his voice grave and vibrant and masterful. It challenged Fate, but in the challenge there was no vanity. She felt a sudden kindling of enthusiasm, a longing to follow this man who was born to lead his fellows. The cold Olympian had disappeared, and Prometheus was in his place, Prometheus the pioneer of humanity, the bringer of gifts to men.

In the pause which followed Janet alone caught Barbara's whisper. "Turn your head slowly round . . . to the window. . . . Watch the group of statues. I saw them move . . . there are people there."

She obeyed. She saw the edge of the group, where Hercules was engaged with the Hydra, move ever so slightly. She saw, too, a dark blur close to the right of the window, which had not been there before. In an instant she divined the truth. This was Fate's answer to the challenge. The Gobernador had shut the door on his past, but something had forced it ajar and slipped through.

She heard Barbara speaking low and composedly. "They cannot see me. I am behind the light. . . . I will slip out. . . . Go on talking."

Janet's heart seemed to stop, and then resumed its beating, so loudly that she felt that it must drown the ticking of the silver clock behind Castor's head. In a voice so steady that it surprised her, she began to question Don Mario about the coloured print of Eclipse beside his chair. She was aware of a slight stirring in the shadows and knew that Barbara had left the room.

Barbara found herself in a long corridor which had suddenly become very dark, and realised that the lamp in the hall beyond had been put out. Why? It was too early for the servants to have gone to bed. Someone must have entered the house, someone different from the group outside the window.

It required all her courage to traverse the corridor and reach the hall. It was in black darkness, and she began to grope her way to the passage beyond, which led to the court-yard. . . . She stopped to listen. There seemed to be a sound coming from the courtyard—servants, perhaps—there were four men indoors, a butler, two footmen, and Don Mario's valet. Outside by the corrals there were the grooms and the cattle-men, hardy peons who might be trusted to defend their master. She must get to them—at any cost she must get to them. She stilled every other thought by clenching her teeth on that purpose.

Presently she was at the foot of the main staircase, a broad shallow thing which led direct to the galleries of the upper floor. Here there was a faint glimmer of light, for the stars were shining through the staircase window. Her eyes were on it when she stumbled over something which lay sprawled across the bottom step.

She bit hard into her lips and stood shivering. It was a man's body. She bent, and even in the dim light she saw by the uniform that it was one of the house-servants. He was dead. Her hands, as they touched his shoulder, felt something warm and sticky.

At the same moment sounds, stealthy sounds, reached her ear from the direction of the courtyard. The murderers were there, and that way there was no escape. Scarcely knowing what she did, she stepped over the body and ran up the staircase. She had a blind idea of getting to her own room, as if there she would find sanctuary.

She sped like a hare along the top gallery, and reached her room. At the door she stopped to listen. All seemed quiet on the upper floor. Inside the door there was the same faint sheen of starlight. Barbara sat down on her bed, and struggled against the terrible lassitude which weakened her limbs and dulled her brain.

She forced herself to think. She did not trouble to guess who the enemies were—it was enough for her that they had come for murder. The little party in the room below were unarmed, and one was a girl and another an old man. She must act—at once—rouse the peons—destroy the ruffians

outside on the lawn before they had time to shoot. It was
the only way, and she tottered to the window.

The room was at the other side of the house from the
garden, and the window looked down on some outhouses
and part of a little enclosed court. The peons lived beyond
the big orchard where the corrals began. She must get to
them, and almost before she knew she found herself on the
veranda. There was a drop of a few feet to a roof whence
she might reach the courtyard. . . . But the courtyard might
be a *cul-de-sac*. It must be, for the enemy would guard all
the approaches.

She dropped on to the roof of a shed. The courtyard was
empty, but she thought she heard a sound from the gate
which led to the stableyard. That was on her left; on her
right were other roofs and then a grove of trees; in front a
wall ran straight to the edge of the orchard. This last
must be her road, and she started climbing along the top of
the adobe wall, which was plentifully studded with sharp
tiles.

The pain of the traverse seemed to restore her balance.
She felt her gown tearing, and her stockings in shreds, and
her knees and wrists ached. In her haste she had no
time to pick her way, but when the wall suddenly
broadened she scrambled to her feet, and the last stage she
almost ran.

Now she was at the transverse wall which bounded the
orchard. She remembered that the place was walled all
round, and that once inside it might be hard to get out. So
she still kept to the wall, which continued to be of a fair
breadth, and endeavoured to circuit the orchard so as to
reach the corrals. But this took her at right angles to her
former course, and brought her back again to the edge of
the first courtyard.

Suddenly she flung herself flat. There were men in the
courtyard. Two men came at a run from the direction of
the house. There must be a back-door there which she had
forgotten. The door into the stableyard opened, but they
did not pass through. They seemed to be listening. Had
they caught sight of her? She lay in a cold terror for

several minutes, till she dared to raise her head again. They were gone, and the door into the stableyard was shut.

Barbara did not venture to rise again, but crawled for the rest of the road. . . . Presently she was looking into open ground, the ribbon of rough pasture between the orchard and the alfalfa fields. . . . Her sense of direction had become a little confused, but she thought that the peons' quarters were to her right beyond the orchard.

She dropped off the wall. It was higher than she had thought, and she felt her ankle wrenched. Then she began to run, keeping in the shadow of the orchard wall. The need for haste was urgent, but her legs seemed to have no power and the pain of her ankle sickened her. Also her heart kept hammering so fast that it choked her breathing.

Now she was at the angle of the orchard wall, but there were no peons' quarters before her—only the savannah, with the alfalfa lands on the left, and the rails of a paddock on her right. . . . She turned blindly to the right . . . ran a few steps . . . changed her mind . . . and suddenly found herself almost ridden down by a mounted man.

The face she saw had the pallor of a Conquistador. She had blundered into the enemy. The man had just avoided her, and was now in difficulties with his beast. A second horseman had leaped to the ground at the sight of her, and it was into his arms that she staggered. To her amazement she heard her name spoken, and looked up into Sandy's face.

She clung to him, while she stammered her story.

"Murder," he said quietly. "And they are desperate men with no care for their own lives. . . . Timmy, it's the mercy of God that sent you with us. You're our only hope. You've got to get into the house."

Janet realised that the great crisis of her life had come. . . . Don Mario expounded in his hoarse old voice the merits of the Eclipse print—it was from the Sartorius picture which he preferred to the better known Stubbs—he had picked it up in St. James's Street in '98—no, it must have been '96, when he was in England for the Fitzgibbon sale. . . . And all the time her eyes were on Castor, who still stood before the fireplace. He lit a cigarette and the match made a spurt of light before his face.

Janet did not dare to look towards the window. . . . The only hope was to keep still. Perhaps the cat would linger over the watching of the mouse. Barbara would now be alarming the house-servants; they would get at the arms, which were all in the gun-room; probably they would first get in touch with the outdoor peons. That would all take time, and meantime they must let the murderers savour their revenge at ease. For she had no doubt of the meaning of it all. The Conquistadors and the Bodyguard could have no thought but vengeance; ruin and death lay before them, and they had nothing more to hope or fear. . . . She wished the clock did not tick so loudly.

Suddenly Castor turned towards the window. Her eyes were on him, and she saw his face go grim. At the same moment there came a sound, which she knew was the rending of the gauze curtain. Now at last she turned her head, and Don Mario craned his from the depth of his chair. Outside in the starlight, close up to the sill, were half a dozen men, each with a pistol held to cover the inmates of the room. She saw what she had expected—the rabbit teeth and the weasel face of Judson, Radin with his high cheekbones and his scar, Suvorin's parched skin and albino hair, Laschallas's thick eyebrows. It was as if a wave of corruption had flowed out of the night, and hung, ready to break, at the window.

One man had entered the room and stood beside Don Mario's chair. She recognised Romanes. But it was a different figure from the trim cavalryman whom she had last seen in the Tronos del Rey. The lamp on the table at his left showed him clearly, and it seemed as if some screw had been removed which had dislocated the whole fabric of his being. He was unshaven and dirty, his clothes were ragged, and there was a long blue weal on his forehead. She saw the lean, knotted neck, the oddly-shaped skull, the pale, sneering face, as if the soul had wholly mastered the body, and transformed it to an exact reflex. But the eyes, which had once been dull and expressionless, now danced and glowed with a crazy brilliance.

"Good evening, sir," he said, and his voice, once so passionless, had an odd lilt in it, like a parson who intones a litany. "Ah, it is the old horse-breeder, Sanfuentes! . . . And you, madame! I have been longing to meet you again, for the last time you left in rather a hurry." But he looked not at Janet or Don Mario, but steadily, devouringly, at the Gobernador.

Janet sat very still in her chair, a yard from each. Castor had moved his head and she saw the clock. It must be ten minutes since Barbara had slipped out. She kept her gaze rigidly on its minute-hand, as if by some mental concentration she could hasten its circuit, for she had a notion that if the end did not come for another ten minutes there was hope.

"Good evening," she heard Castor say. "You've an odd way of announcing yourself. You look a little off-colour. Would you like some food?"

The other did not reply. He was smiling, but so close were his lips to his teeth that it looked like a snarl.

"A cigarette anyhow." Castor was about to feel for his case in his pocket, when a pistol barrel confronted him.

"Stay still," said Romanes. "Not a movement. You will stand quite rigid, please, while I say what I have to say."

"Right!" was the answer. "You used to have better manners, Romanes. Let me hear what you want to say. You have come, I suppose, to ask for terms."

The coolness of the Gobernador's tone seemed to move the other to fresh mirth.

"Terms!" he cried. "Oh, yes, we ask for terms. A free pardon, of course, and our passage paid to Europe, and five hundred apiece on which to begin a new life. Terms!" and his voice rose almost to a shriek. "Do you not know that there are no terms on God's earth you could offer us?"

"There is nothing I intend to offer you," was the answer.

"No. You are wise. I never underestimated your brains. . . . You have used us, and I think we have given

you good service. . . . Now you have changed your plans,
and would fling us on the scrap-heap. You have different
ambitions now, and your old tools are no longer required.
But the tools may have something to say to that."

"True. I am inclined to agree with you. I am not the
man to shirk my responsibility." Castor's eyes had made
the circuit of the room. He saw the ravening faces at the
window, old Don Mario huddled in his chair, Janet below
him white-lipped and tense. He saw something else—a new
figure which had slipped in by the door, and which he
recognised as Lariarty. He saw him before Romanes did,
and it was the almost imperceptible start which he gave
that caused the other to cast a swift glance to his left.

Romanes smiled as he observed the newcomer. "Just
in time," he said. "I wondered if you would bring it off.
We are going to be offered terms after all. Our old chief
says he admits his responsibility."

Lariarty's sick, drawn face made no response, but he
moved nearer Romanes, till their elbows almost touched.
His hands were empty, but there was a bulge in his side
pocket.

"Terms!" Romanes cried again. "You have broken our
world in bits, and you speak of recognising your responsibility! You have played with souls, and you are going to
find that it is an awkward game. We are dying—dying.
Morituri te salutamus. And the way we salute you is to
take you with us. There will be no Castor, the regenerator
of Olifa, for little boys to read about in their history
books. For in about two minutes Castor will be dead."

The man on the hearthrug flung back his head.

"When we worked together, Romanes," he said, "you
did not make full use of your opportunities. You cannot
know much about me if you think that I can be frightened
by threats of death. I am afraid of many things, but not
of that. . . . You seem to hold a strong hand. Take me
away with you—anywhere—away from this house. Then,
if you are determined on it, put a pistol bullet through my
head, or put me against a wall for the rest of your gang to
have a share in the pleasure of killing me. I accept what

Fate sends—I have always accepted it. But why should you
bring an old man and a girl into this unpleasant business?"

Romanes thrust his face close to the other's, and to Janet
it seemed that it was now the mask of madness. She had
forgotten about the slow minute-hand of the clock, for
with Lariarty's coming—and coming through the door—
she had realised that all hope was gone. But in that
moment she did not think of her own danger. What held
her gaze was Castor, who seemed to have risen to a strange
nobility. There was not a tremor in his face, not a shadow
of hesitation in his grave eyes. It was man towering above
the beast, humanity triumphing even in its overthrow. . . .
These broken things before him were in part his handiwork. They were the world he had left—but he had left
it. Yes, whatever happened, he had left it. . . .

"Not so," Romanes was saying. "We are not civilised
executioners. We are damned and dying, and our vengeance is the vengeance of the damned. The women go
with you—there was another here who must be found.
And the old horse-coping fool. . . . After that we will
find Rosas . . . and Clanroyden, curse him . . . and . . ."

It was then that Don Mario struck. He had been quietly
reaching with his right hand for a loaded riding-whip
which was on the rack on the wall beside his chair. Its
handle had a heavy metal knob, and, without rising in his
seat, he swung it with surprising agility at Romanes's head.
But the eyes of age are not those of youth and he missed
his aim. The handle only grazed Romanes's shoulder,
glanced off, hit the lamp on the table behind him, and sent
it crashing to the ground.

Romanes half turned to his assailant, and as he moved
Lariarty leaped on him. As he leaped he cried in a strange,
stifled voice the single word "Pecos," the signal which he
had agreed upon with Sandy. If he could deal with the
tiger within, it was for Sandy to frustrate the wolves
without.

But Don Mario's unexpected attack had deranged the
plan. Lariarty should have trusted to his pistol; instead,
he yielded to that ancient instinct which urges a man to

grapple with an enemy who is suddenly unbalanced. The signal which he should have shouted was muffled by his haste, and the watchers at the window were given a moment to act before Sandy could strike. When " Pecos " rang out a second time with a desperate shrillness it was too late.

For Romanes, even in his madness, had judged the situation right. He could make certain of at least part of his vengeance. Castor, too, was upon him, but his right hand was free, and he shot him at close quarters in the neck. The Gobernador fell forward on the sitting Janet, and in the same instant shots were fired from the window. They may have been meant for Castor, but they found other quarries. Lariarty dropped with a bullet in his brain, and Romanes clutched at space, gasped, and fell beside him.

Janet, struggling to rise, with the shots still like whip-lashes in her ear, heard a second burst of fire. It came from outside the window, and she knew it for rifles. Then there seemed to be a great quiet, and the world disappeared for her—everything except a dying man whom she had laid in her chair. . . .

He was beyond speech, and his eyes were vacant and innocent like a child's. She pressed her face to his and kissed him on the lips. . . . A fresh lamp seemed to have been lit behind her, and by its aid she saw the glazing eyes wake for a second, and through them the soul struggle to send a last message. There was peace in the face. . . .

When Archie arrived ten minutes later his first demand was for Janet. Sandy drew him gently up to the ragged gauze curtain.

" She is safe—by a miracle," he said. " But Castor is dead—he died in her arms. Don't disturb her yet, Archie. A woman can only love one man truly, but many men may love her. . . . Janet was the only love of Castor's life. He died happy with her kiss on his cheek. . . . Let her stay a little longer beside him."

EPILOGUE

EPILOGUE

THE Courts of the Morning had recovered the peace which till a year ago had been theirs since the beginning of time. Where had once been the busy depot was now only shaggy downland, and a few blackened timbers, over which Nature had begun to spin her web. Choharua looked down again upon meadow and forest as free from human turmoil as the blue spaces of ocean beyond. Only at the head of the seaward gully were there signs of life. A small group of tents had been set up, almost on the spot where Barbara and the Gobernador had first looked down the four thousand feet of green dusk to the land-locked bay. The ruins of the power-house and the chute were already masked with creepers and tall grasses, and only certain scars on the hillside, not made by the winter rains, told that there man had once wrought and striven.

The day was passing from the steady glare of afternoon to the light airs which precede twilight. The sun was nearing a broad belt of amethyst haze which lay on the western horizon, and the face of Choharua was beginning to break up into shadows. The party who occupied the tents had come there by sea, and made their way up the rugged steps of the ravine to the plateau. The reason of their journey was apparent, for between the ravine and the mountain, on a mound which rose like a sentinel above the meadows, could be seen a tall wooden cross. Presently that would be replaced by a stone memorial, to mark the resting-place of him who had been the Gobernador of the Gran Seco.

There was the smoke of a destroyer far below in the gulf. That very day it had brought to this eyrie the new President-elect of the Republic of Olifa. The said President-elect was sitting beside Sandy on the very edge of the ravine, so that he looked down fifty feet of red rock to the tops of tall trees. He was amusing himself with dropping his cigarette ash into the gulf.

"If I slipped off this perch I should certainly break my neck," he observed. "That has been the position of all of us for so long that we have got used to it. I wonder when I shall feel accustomed to being secure?"

Sandy asked about the condition of Olifa.

"It is a marvel. We are a stable people after all, and, having gone a little off the lines, we have now jolted back to the track and are quite content with it. . . . The elections went as pleasantly as a festa. . . . Lossberg is content, for he has Bianca's place, and the army reductions will be made slowly and discreetly. There is a vast amount to be done, but bit by bit we shall re-make the machine. I shall have Blenkiron to assist me, praise be to God. Him I have left wallowing in business, while I made the trip here to see you. *You*, my dear Sandy. For some months the destiny of Olifa has depended on you. I want that to continue."

Sandy did not speak. His eyes were on the downs which ran southward along the scarp, where far off he thought he saw two figures.

"I have come to offer you the post of Gobernador of the Gran Seco," Luis continued briskly. "In effect, as you know well, it will be an independent province. Its problems are not those of Olifa. It cannot be an integral part of the republic. It is tributary, yes—but not dependent. He who governs it must be a strong man and a wise man. And it is of the first importance, for on it rest the wealth and peace of Olifa."

"It is a great charge," said Sandy, but his eyes were still on the distant figures.

"You are already a king among the Indian pueblas. You are a king among the mine-workers. You will have Blenkiron as your lieutenant to direct the industry. We will build you a palace, and up here in the Courts of the Morning you will have your country estate. It is a good watch-tower, señor. Here you will be able to think high thoughts."

He laid his hand on the other's arm.

"Consider! Are you the man to go home to Europe and sit down in cities? Will you dabble in your politics, like Sir Archie? I do not think so. You would be restless in an old country where things move slowly and everything is done by long speeches. . . . You are a landowner, are you not? Will you settle down upon your acres, and shoot little birds, and entertain your friends, and in time grow fat? I know the life a little, for I have seen it, and it is pleasant —oh yes. But is it the life for you?"

Luis's air suddenly became very grave.

"You are my friend, and I love you more than a brother. Therefore I want you to stay with me. But you are also a great man, and I am jealous that your greatness shall not be wasted. You are a creator, and you cannot escape your destiny. The era of the Old World is over, and it is the turn of the New World to-day. I have often heard you say that the difficulties even of Europe must be settled in the West. Listen to me, señor. The time will come when the problems of the West will be settled between the United States and Olifa. Yes, Olifa. We have wealth, we have won stability, presently we shall have leadership. I cannot do the leading. I can only, as you say, 'carry on.' Castor would have done it if he had lived. Now his mantle awaits you. You will have work worthy of a man, work which will need all your powers of mind and will and body. You will make a name that will live for ever. Will you choose to be a sleepy squire when you might be a king? You are not a provincial, you are not a native of any land. Your country is that which you can make for yourself. . . ."

Sandy shook his head. "I don't think you understand."

"But indeed I understand. I understand *you*. I have studied you with admiration, and, what is more, with love. I know you better than you know yourself." He smiled. "I said that you could be a king, and I did not speak altogether in metaphor. Forms of government are not eternal things. Olifa is a republic, because republics were in fashion when she began. But some day she may well be a kingdom. . . . Do not laugh. I do not mean any foolish dictatorship. We are a free people. But Olifa demands a leader, and whoever the leader is whom she follows he will be her king."

Luis rose. "Think well over what I have said. I now go to stretch my legs before dinner. Within a day or two I must have your answer."

Sandy remained alone on the pinnacle of rock. The sun was now close to the horizon and the west was like a great flower in blossom. The face of Choharua was rose-red, and the levels below were all purple, a deeper tint than the amethyst of the sea.

Out of the circumambient glory Janet appeared, hatless, her hair like an aureole.

"I left Barbara a mile behind," she said. "She wanted to see Geordie Hamilton about one of the vaqueros who is sick. You look pensive, Sandy. A penny for your thoughts."

"I have been talking to Luis. . . . He has just offered me the governorship of the Gran Seco, with apparently the reversion of a kingdom."

"Well?" she asked. She was picking a flower to pieces to hide trembling hands.

"What do you think, Janet? You are the wisest woman in the world. Shall Ulysses settle down in Phæacia and forget all about Ithaca?"

"That is for Ulysses to say."

"But Ulysses has no ambition left. He never had much, and what little he had is buried up there."

The eyes of both turned eastward to the slim cross on the high ground above the meadows, now dyed blood-red by the setting sun. Against the background of the mountain it stood out like a great calvary.

"I think we saved his soul," he said gravely, "but we also brought him to his death. The glory of the world does not seem to amount to much when it all ends in six feet of earth. And the things that matter more than glory! I can't feel up to them, Janet. I am a very ordinary sort of fellow who shirks responsibility. I am no Castor. I can take a hand in king-making, but a king-maker is never a king."

" Other people think differently, Sandy dear," Janet said softly. " I have had one great moment in my life that I can never forget—when the Army of the Revolution entered Olifa. You remember, Olifa had got back her old assurance. The Avenida was like a river of white light between two banks of roses. . . . People in masses on both sides, and at all the windows, and on all the house-tops, and everywhere flowers. . . . The Olifa regulars as smart as Aldershot, and the new President in his carriage, and the new ministers. . . . And then, after all the splendour, the lean, dusty fighting men! I cried like a baby when I saw Archie —horribly embarrassed he was, poor darling, not knowing what to do with the flowers that fell on his head and his saddle—rather like a schoolboy being kissed by his mother after a famous innings. . . . But when you came, I stopped crying and my heart stood still. You remember? All the shouting and the flower-scattering seemed to stop when you appeared at the head of your battered commandos. There was a great hush, and for a moment that vast multitude seemed to catch its breath. It was because they saw the man who might be their king. . . . You never moved your head, Sandy, and you stared straight before you as if you were asleep. What were you thinking of ? "

" I was thinking of Castor, and longing for him to be alive."

" Only that? Had Ulysses no thought of the vacant throne of Phæacia—of carrying on a dead man's work? "

" No, by Heaven, he cannot. . . . He couldn't if he wanted to, but he doesn't want to, for his heart isn't in it. . . . I'm an alien here and I'm sick of being an alien. . . . I'm not Castor. I haven't his ambition, I haven't his brains, I don't want to be on a pedestal. Perhaps I'm tired, perhaps I'm getting old, but I want my own people. I've seen Luis and his gallant lads on fire about this country and planning what a great land it is going to be, and it made me sick for my own. . . . Castor too. . . . He had never known a fatherland before, but he found one here. . . . I've got the best in the world, and I'm homesick for it. These last months I've been living with half my mind on my work and half on all kinds of small, ridiculous, homely things. You would laugh if you knew the kind of picture I've had in my head whenever I wasn't engaged on some urgent job. . . . How good the beer at Tap used to taste in a pewter mug . . . the scent of the hay in the Oxford meadows . . . bacon and eggs for tea after hunting . . . the moorburn and the peat reek in April . . . the beloved old musty smell of the library at Laverlaw and logs crackling on a December evening. . . . I'm sick with longing for my own Border hills. . . . It's no good, Janet. You can't cut adrift from the bands that God has tied. I've had enough of Abana and Pharpar, rivers of Damascus. I'm for the modest little clear streams of Israel."

Janet dropped her flower and looked up smiling.

"You are lonely, Sandy."

"I am lonely. That is why I want to get back to companionable things."

A sudden happiness came into the girl's face. She looked away from him and spoke rapidly.

"Barbara once went over to Laverlaw with the Manorwaters. Do you remember? You pretended that she annoyed you. . . . I wonder. . . . Less than a year ago we spoke of her in the Regina Hotel. You pretended you couldn't remember her name. . . . I wonder again. . . . Oh, Sandy, you are an old fool. . . ."

He scrambled off his perch and stood above her. He was flushed under his deep sunburn.

"Janet, you witch! How did you guess?"

"It wasn't very hard. When a man like you grows tired of wandering and has a sudden longing for home, it is because he is in love with a woman and wants to take her to the place where he belongs."

"You've guessed right. I suppose it has been coming on for a long time, but I didn't know it—not till that awful night at Veiro. When we rode up and I found her in the midst of plunging horses—with her shoes all cut to bits and her ankle twisted, and dropping with fatigue, and yet as brave as a lion—and when I saw the roses on her breast all crushed and torn with her wild scramble—I think I knew.   And later, when Archie arrived and his first cry was for you, I remembered that I had nobody to feel like that about . . . and I wanted someone—her . . ."

He stopped, for he felt that words were needless in view of a depth of comprehension in Janet's crooked smile.

" I haven't a chance, I know," he stammered.

" Not a ghost of a chance," she said briskly, " but you can always ask her.   She'll be here in about five minutes. I'm going for a walk to look for Luis and the others.   We shan't be back for hours and hours."

THE END